# KARMA BUTTERFLIES

# KARMA BUTTERFLIES

*Jeremy Fulmore*

© 2024 by Jeremy Fulmore

All rights reserved. This book or any portion thereof may not be reproduced or used in any manner whatsoever without the express written permission of the publisher except for the use of brief quotations in a book review.

ISBN: 9798309039463

# PART ONE

# CHAPTER 1

Joseph Silver III stood on the front porch of his grandfather's home near the beach. His nostrils flared as he took in the sharp saltwater air while scanning the sky, reminiscing. He jingled the keys in the palm of his hand, then got emotional, pressing his teeth against his bottom lip in an effort to fight off the tears.

He turned away from the sky toward his wife Sara. She was standing next to him. Sara, with her shiny, long black hair and bright, cheery smile, gazed at him. Her eyes sparkled. Her hand rubbed the center of his back. A calming influence. She had a happy-go-lucky disposition protected by a solid layer of toughness. If anyone was strong enough to support Joe in his time of need, it was Sara. She often bragged about the time she'd spent in the Israeli Army beating the men at sharpshooting and hand-to-hand combat. At their wedding, she'd been spotted by guests smoking a cigar with the groomsmen. It had embarrassed her mother to no end.

Behind Sara was Jasmine, their youngest at age twelve. Jasmine preferred her light-brown hair, long and combed to glossiness. She had faint freckles scattered about her nose and cheeks. Jasmine was thin and petite and didn't seem to be taking after her mother in any way other than her developing attitude. She always kept a handbag over her shoulder or nearby, filled with nail polish, hair clips, and lip gloss—everything a young girl might need. She was sighing because her parents had made her dress in old, ratty hand-me-downs for the day. She seemed embarrassed that someone she knew might see her wearing it.

Adonis Silver was on the stairs. He was the oldest at seventeen. After examining his family, he took a deep breath, not liking what the day had in store. After ninety-eight years on earth, Joseph Silver, his great-grandfather, had passed on. They'd come here to clean out his belongings, collect mementos, and divvy out what possessions other family members might like to keep.

Don, as he preferred to be called, used to visit the place regularly before his great-grandfather Zadie became sick. Zadie loved the water and always wanted to be close to it, so he'd built his home by the beach. The rickety deck was worn and grayish and needed a new paint job, but its bones were solid. Although the ocean wasn't visible from the house, the salty-pungent scent of the sea was ever present. In the distance, Don could faintly hear the crash of the ocean and the squawks of hungry seagulls.

They'd visited Zadie's home in Montauk, New York, many times when Don was younger. Don loved it best during the summer months, when the island came alive with tourists. Long ago, the founders of Montauk had envisioned their little piece of Long Island as the Miami Beach of the North. A place where the people of Manhattan could enjoy a bit of sand between their toes. Zadie bought into that dream and purchased the house to stake his claim. Even though the place had remained a small tourist town known for fishing and summer homes, that was fine with Zadie. He'd learned to live with the bustling summer season and enjoy his peace in the offseason.

Joe put his hands on his back, stretched, and exhaled. He was ready. He steadied the keys and opened the front door of the modest house. One by one, they walked inside, with Don the last to enter. It was a shell of what he remembered. The house smelled like old people, which was strange when Don thought about it. How would one describe it? Skin cells dying off at an accelerated rate? Internal organs not working properly? Was it the smell of adult diapers mixed with Efferdent?

Perhaps it was the smell of death.

"It smells funny in here," said Jasmine, saying what he was thinking.

"Shut your mouth," chided Sara. "Show a little respect. Ninety-eight years on this earth, survived World War Two, and without his sacrifice, you wouldn't be here!"

Being scolded and forced to wear rags was too much for Jasmine. She hemmed, hawed, and slammed her butt down on an old wooden chair at the dining table, about twenty feet from the rest of the family. The table was covered with magazines piled three feet high. Mainly tabloids purchased at the checkout aisle of the supermarket. Zadie had been obsessed with the absurd stories contained in them. Alien abductions and prophecies about the end of the world. Zadie never missed an edition in nearly forty years.

As for the rest of the house, it was a mess. Very little wall space had escaped a proliferation of junk. Piles of old newspapers hoarded since the 1940s were stacked in a corner next to the twenty-one-inch console television. Old shoeboxes filled with bills and letters, at least two hundred of them, gathered dust on top of each other and stretched along the walls. Don had never thought much of it when he was a regular visitor years ago. Now that he was older, he could see Zadie needed help long before he was diagnosed with Alzheimer's.

An old brown couch and chair, worn so thin their material was see-through, claimed a space on the hardwood floor, as well as a matted and stained tan rug. A lamp with a torn lampshade stood bent and forlorn next to a lone window with curtains so old they looked like they'd turn to dust if touched.

Sara pulled up the shades to let some light into the living room. The shades rolled up on a spring that she had to tug to unlock, and then it was tricky to get them to stay in place. Just when she thought she'd managed it at last, they snapped and unfurled, making quite a racket. Dust particles floated in the air as light greeted the room, undeterred by the accumulated grime of many decades.

Joe drifted off in a daze at the sight of the disaster before him. He told the family there was no point in keeping the place as a summer home. Yet renting it out as an Airbnb was also out of the question. He no longer wanted the responsibility of maintaining it. The stained ceiling and cracks in the walls signaled it would take a pretty penny to make the house presentable. Everything else that needed to be fixed would be assessed after the place was cleaned out.

Don started by pushing aside the television to get to a stack of old newspapers behind it. The heavy wooden console looked more like a piece of furniture than a television. The screen was tiny, no bigger than his computer monitor back home. It was busted before Don was born, yet Zadie had refused to get rid of it.

"Remember how Zadie felt about that thing?" asked Joe. His classic Jewish New York accent got thicker when he grew nostalgic. "He'd throw a fit if anyone went near that television. I mean, he would get livid. I went through the newspapers, looking for the comics, one time as a kid, and when he caught me, he tore me a new asshole."

Sentimental value, he guessed. Don didn't see it. It seemed like nothing but junk. Funny how things of value to one person are considered trash to another. People value their possessions, only to have someone sell them or throw them away when they die.

Joe shook his head, possibly thinking about the beating he took that day. He went over to the shoeboxes, reached up to grab one near the top, and the whole stack collapsed. A family of mice jumped from the box in midair and scattered in all directions. Joe yelped and brushed mouse feces from his T-shirt.

Sara laughed.

"You're a wuss," said Jasmine, barely flinching at the sight of the scattering mice.

Don cradled the old newspapers in his arms, carrying as many as he could at one time over to the window. From there he could toss them directly into a dumpster at the side of the house. He made three trips. After he nabbed the fourth stack, a small box fell from inside the pile. The box had the word *Timex* embossed on its lid. It was black and worn and dusty like everything else. He picked it up and flinched. Something inside it moved. He shook the box. It had some weight to it.

"I found an old watch," said Don to his father, who was collecting shoeboxes from the wall and tossing them.

"A Timex," said Joe. "I would like to think that that would be worth something, but I doubt it. Unless it's new. Is it?"

Don took the cover off the box. Inside was a gold charm with two hearts joined side by side and overlapping. Cute. But it was the other object that carried weight: an eye. A complete eyeball with an amber iris rolling around in a Timex box. Don touched it and withdrew his hand quickly. Not only was it real, but it was also fresh. Impossible.

"Let me see it," said Joe. His father held out his hand. "Let me take a look."

Don flipped it shut and handed it to his father. He opened it. "It's empty," said Joe. "By the way you were looking at it, I thought that there was something incredible inside."

"Uh, no, Dad. It was just a box."

"OK. Well, get back to throwing out those papers. It's been nothing but a fire hazard for fifty years."

Don turned and slipped the eye and charm into his front pocket. No need for Dad or anyone else to be alarmed by something so morbid. The eye might not be real anyway. It was best he take care of it, discreetly.

# CHAPTER 2

The next morning Don took a shower and got dressed. He could hear his mother downstairs in the kitchen getting breakfast ready but didn't want to hang out with the rest of the family yet. He had a situation to think over, so he lay back down on his made bed and cradled his hands behind his head. The ceiling fan spun slowly along with his thoughts.

He could understand Zadie saving a charm for safekeeping. It was a pair of hearts. Something sentimental. Having an eyeball bordered on the demented. Was his great-grandfather some sort of serial killer? The last ten years that Don could remember, he'd been too old and frail for that. There were no other souvenirs of kills scattered throughout the cupboards and cabinets, not behind walls or under loose floorboards—he knew because he'd checked.

He peered along the light-blue walls of his room, thinking about where else a person could hide things they didn't want anyone else to find. As for furniture, Don was satisfied his search had been thorough. Zadie had left nothing stuffed in his bed or inside any hidden compartment in his armoire. Nothing in the refrigerator or freezer. Not behind the bookshelf or in the back of the television console…

there was tons of room to hide stuff there. Thinking of the TV show *Dexter*, Don had even checked the window air-conditioning unit.

He had performed a complete inspection.

The furniture had been loaded into the moving truck and taken straight to the dump. The silverware and plates and cups had been packed up in boxes headed to the local Goodwill. Everything else had been loaded into the dumpster parked off to the side of the house. Then they swept and wiped clean everything. The last thing removed was an old oriental rug from the living room, rolled up and tossed on top of the rest of the junk.

Afterward, Don had done the once-over, checking everything: tapping walls and exploring crawl spaces. He went under the house through a floor opening in the utility room and crawled on his hands and knees. With the cold earth underneath him, Don spied the floor joists and support beams. He pulled down insulation and peeked behind plumbing lines. He saw all kinds of strange insects that looked straight from alien movies. But he found no more body parts.

Only a single eye.

His eyes shot open wide with alarm. He'd realized something. Now that the eye was in his possession, *he* was one who was culpable. If anyone were to find it, the label of psycho or serial killer would be placed on him, not Zadie.

He scanned every crevice and dark corner of his room and couldn't think of a single hiding place he was willing to risk. In that case, it was best to keep changing locations. It was currently in a sock in the bottom of the dresser. He considered where he should move it next.

The inviting aroma of fried salami drifted up the stairs. His olfactory senses triggered his stomach into a growling fit. He hopped off the bed, nabbed his notebook, and went downstairs to the breakfast table. It was alive with hungry mouths. His mother, father, and sister had already started eating the Jewish breakfast she'd prepared: fried salami and eggs, latkes, toast, fried mushrooms and tomatoes, and milky tea. Don sat down, scarfed down the first helping, and finished off another helping of latkes before pushing his plate aside.

He glanced at his mother, whose mind appeared to be elsewhere. Her long black hair was hanging off to one side of her shoulder, revealing the short patch of hair she kept on the left side of her head. It was her style. Part of her rebellious youth. With a flip of her hair, she could change from a tough punk-rock mom to traditional and elegant. It was kind of cool.

She spied him looking. Her eyes sparkled as they normally did when she smiled. They were close. A special bond between mother and son. She looked at his empty plate. "You need to stop eating like that, or you will start to gain weight," she said. "A perfect body like yours won't last forever."

"Aw..." said his little sister Jasmine mockingly. She seemed much happier with her normal clothes on. Pink T-shirt with rainbows, jeans, and the pink fuzzy slippers she wore around the house. "Don is just the perfect son with the perfect light-brown hair and perfect light-brown eyes all the girls dream about." She propped her hands under her chin and batted her eyelashes several times.

"Yeah," said his father Joe before taking a sip of his tea. He was wearing a yellow dress shirt and black pants as if he were going into the office, even though it was his day off. "Don's not only better looking, he's also taller than me. Sara, whoever you cheated on me with to get this kid I can't be upset about."

"Tone it down," said Sara, giggling. "You will embarrass Adonis."

*Embarrass? Why would those comments make me uncomfortable?* he thought. People said those things about him all the time. Why would he be ashamed?

Don's mother examined him suspiciously. She seemed like she wanted to say something but didn't know where to begin. "Adonis," she said while collecting a bit of yolk from her plate with toast. "What's with the sudden interest in Zadie? Last night, you asked a bunch of questions about his upbringing and his time in the old country, Poland. Are you writing about his life in that journal?"

Don peeked down at the binder. It was beside him as always. Black cover, glued binder, about a hundred pages. He took it everywhere. He had already started a section on the eyeball he'd found in the house and his thoughts about to whom it might belong. He didn't have to worry about people finding the binder and reading it. It was encrypted. His own scrambled means of interpretation.

Don placed his hand on top of the journal. "Just wanted a peek into his past."

"Why are you harassing the boy, Sara?" said Joe from across the table. "I think it's good he's asking about Zadie."

"I'm not harassing him. It was just sudden," said Sara. "I'm trying to figure out what is going on in that brilliant little mind of his."

"Maybe he thinks Zadie had a secret treasure or something," said Jasmine. "I caught him yesterday tapping walls and going into the crawl space, like he was searching for something."

Don shot his sister a look.

"What was that for, Adonis?" said Jasmine, snapping her head back from his cold, contentious glare.

"It's to mind your own business," he said. He took another piece of toast from the bowl at the center of the table. "And it's Don to you! Only Mom can get away with calling me Adonis."

A clang of the plate recaptured his attention when his mother set her fork down. "Is that what you were doing?" she asked, her eyes searching his for clues. "He didn't have much, you know. He could barely pay the taxes on the house."

"Not barely," said Joe. "He couldn't pay! I had to pay them! If you found anything, Don, it's mine. I prefer cash." Dad was always trying to play the comedian. In this case, Don welcomed it. It deflected his true intentions. Joe was about to take a sip of tea when he lowered the cup back down. "You didn't find any cash, did you?"

Don shook his head.

"If you found money, I have first dibs," said his father. He held his hand across the table, palm up.

Sara clicked her teeth and pushed it away. "He was making sure we got everything," she said, rolling her eyes. "Finish your breakfast."

"I love you too, pumpkin," said Joe.

Jasmine was still picking at the eggs and salami on her plate. Don's dad was shoveling in eggs and latkes between checking how his stocks were doing on his phone. His mom stood up from the breakfast table and gathered her plate along with Don's. Don stood to help, scraping the legs of his chair across the floor. He took the empty cups to the sink and placed them inside. His mom was grinning while she rinsed the dishes, like she was proud of something. Entertaining a pleasant thought in her head.

"You know, Adonis," said Sara, over the sound of running water. "Zadie was a war hero, and he liked to meet with those he served with at the VFW in Brooklyn. A group of them used to meet once a year from 1978 to 2004. By then there was a handful left. Now there is only one person I know of who is still alive. He and Zadie were very close. I remember talking to him last year in Brooklyn to tell him Zadie wasn't doing too well. He hangs out at the VFW just about every day. I have the number there. I can call and see if he would like to talk to you about Zadie. Tell you some stuff from that time. Since you were asking so many questions about it."

A person who'd known Joseph Silver for decades. Surely, he would have some type of insight into whether Don's grandfather was a serial killer or something worse—and why on earth he would have an eyeball.

"I would appreciate if you could set it up, Mom," said Don.

"I most certainly can," she said. She was touched by it. He could tell she was getting emotional. Like with Don, his mom and Zadie had been close. "I like that you are taking such an interest."

"That's what I said earlier," said Joe. "Now you're trying to take all the credit for complimenting the boy. You love stealing my glory."

"Be quiet, Joe," said Sara. It was weird between the two of them. Like his dad knew when she was about to become too emotional and injected his dry humor to lighten the mood. It was enough to distract her mind from delving into the hard emotions of the past. "I will make the phone call when I'm done here."

# CHAPTER 3

Don went back upstairs to his bedroom. It was small, but the bonus was it was the corner of the house so he had two windows. One at the front of the house toward the main road, one facing the neighbor. The adjacent wall had his desk with his laptop and computer chair. Next to it was a small bookshelf and a six-drawer dresser. The other wall had the bed and door to the closet. He put the journal on the desk, next to his laptop, and opened the drawer to nab a pen. He updated the section about Zadie, adding the tidbit about him being in the war. The trauma of being in combat could have triggered the lust for collecting body parts. Would Zadie's friend be coherent enough to remember details? He had to be well into his nineties.

Don thought of the questions he might ask. Clever ones to spark memories. He wrote them in the journal in preparation for the trip to the VFW in Brooklyn and estimated he would be gone for up to six hours. Too much time to leave the eye unattended. Besides, he wanted to take the double heart charm with him. It might jar a memory with Zadie's war buddy, and pulling the charm from an old sock would be strange.

Don had received a necklace from a girl in his class at the beginning of the school year. It was a thin gold herringbone chain on which hung a small gold rectangle with an *A* engraved on it for Adonis. He never wore the charm because he didn't want to give the girl the wrong impression. Besides, he preferred to be called Don. She'd picked the wrong initial.

The gift was in a black box in his dresser. He opened the top drawer, retrieved it, and dumped out the contents. He knelt to pull out the bottom drawer and took it off the rails, setting the drawer off to the side. At the base was the black sock with the eye and double heart charm inside. Carefully, he guided the eye and charm through the sock and into the gift box. He placed the charm on top of the cotton and put the eye underneath. It barely fit with the lid closed. The bulging eye had the lid teetering like a seesaw. It was the best he could do. Don placed it into his backpack and zipped it shut.

Startled by a knock on the bedroom door, he fumbled with the drawer to get it back on the rails. He lined it up and pushed it past the stops all the way shut.

"Don," said his mother. She jiggled the doorknob.

"I'm changing. Sorry, Mom." A quick check to make sure everything was in place, and he went to the door and unlocked it. He opened the door fully and stepped back, knowing he was in trouble.

The household rule was no one opened a door without knocking and getting consent first. She'd drilled that into them all from the time they were born. But after ten seconds with no answer, she was free to enter. No exceptions. Those were her rules.

"Why was the door locked?" she asked. "You know I don't like it when the door is locked, Adonis."

"Sorry. Sometimes I need a little privacy, Mom."

Don had imagined that in her past some terrible tragedy had happened behind a locked door. A trauma that led to her viewing locks inside the house as a bad omen. He'd tried to ask her about her aversion to locks, but she always seemed to sidestep the question.

"I will remove the doorknob and the lock next time," she said sternly. Something she threatened to do often.

"It won't happen again, Mom," said Don.

She swallowed hard and took a step inside the room to look around. Don went back to his computer chair and sat down. He pretended to be searching for something on the laptop.

"I came to tell you I called the VFW in Brooklyn, and Zadie's friend is going to be there today," said his mom. "If you want, I can take you down there after lunch."

"I got it, Mom," said Don quickly, working the touchpad. "I can take the train there myself."

"Are you sure?" she asked. "It's no problem for me. Gives me a chance to get out of the house, and I know right where it is, so…" She paused and gave Don time to change his mind.

"I can take the train, Mom, thanks."

"I wanna go!" said Jasmine, dashing into the room. The walls were thin, and her room butted up against his. She had braided her brown hair into pigtails. They hung past her shoulders in front of the rainbows on her pink T-shirt. "Can I, please, Mom?" she said with big eyes.

"Mom isn't driving me," said Don. "I'm taking the train there."

"That is why I want to go!" She moved closer to their mom, pleading. Fingers intertwined. "All yesterday I was cleaning that god-awful house, and you promised if I worked hard, I would be rewarded. This is what I want. I want to go into the city with Don."

Don watched uncomfortably as his mother considered it.

"Remember?" said Jasmine. "I wanted to get a shirt at the Pretty Girl store in the Atlantic Terminal Mall. It's right there at the last stop. It's right there!"

Sara looked at Don. "It's not out of the way, Adonis. Please take her."

Don sighed and ground his teeth. What would be worse? Having his mother tag along or Jasmine? He conceded with a nod, and Jasmine jumped in the air, rejoicing.

Don shut his laptop and opened the backpack. He shoved the laptop into one of the pockets and was surprised by his mother coming close to give him a peck on the forehead.

"You are such a good brother," she said. "And an even better son."

"Oh boy," said Jasmine, rolling her eyes. "Here we go again with you fawning all over him."

"And you are the bestest daughter," she said, giving Jasmine a bear hug.

Mom left, and Don continued loading his backpack with his journal and jacket. Jasmine was grinning from ear to ear. Don stopped to scold her. "Make sure you bring a jacket and hat with you just in case."

April in New York that year was unseasonably warm, but the temperature was known to plummet after the sun went down. He loved his sister, just not enough to give her his jacket if it got too cold.

"Yes, Master Don," she said in her best British accent and skipped off to her room to get ready.

They left their house in North New Hyde Park, Long Island, and walked to the bus stop. They took the bus to the Long Island Rail Road station; from there, they would take the train into Brooklyn. They arrived at the station, bought tickets, and waited on the platform. The train arrived on schedule, pulling to a stop with a screech. The car was less than half-full, and they had plenty of room to pick their seats. They sat in the middle side by side. It would take about half an hour to get there provided they didn't have to wait too long for the transfer heading into Brooklyn.

As the train moved, Don tried to get his head focused on the questions he would ask. It would prove to be tricky bouncing around the subject of how his great-grandfather could have possibly taken an eye as a memento. *How do you even dance around a subject like that?*

Don picked his head up from his notebook to acknowledge Jasmine, who had been staring at him for several seconds. He sighed. "What is it?"

"You notice everything," she said. "Mom said you could spot a broken hair on the leg of a fly. She says it's kind of scary, and I believe her."

"And your point?" asked Don.

"You didn't notice those girls over there staring at you."

Don looked over at the three young women at the end of the car. High schoolers. They were plotting and whispering, looking right at him.

"I noticed," he said. "Not interested. But now, thanks to you, they know I noticed."

"I don't get you, Don," said Jasmine, elbowing him in the ribs. "What kind of high school boy are you? You think girls and sports are boring."

"Sports *are* boring," he said. "Others are crazy about them. To me, they lack any real purpose."

"That's what people who suck at sports would say," she said. "Last year you had the football coach calling Mom so she could convince you to join the team. You raced the fastest kid on the high school track team and beat him by nearly a foot. And I heard you beat the best basketball player in high school in a one-on-one matchup."

"I almost beat him," said Don. "He won."

She tossed her hands in the air in frustration. "Why do you bother competing if you think it's boring?"

"Because athletes can be so full of themselves," said Don. "It's the arrogance that pisses me off. The last guy was in gym class showboating, dribbling between the legs of other people and trying to belittle them with his skill. He was being an asshole. A basketball bully, if there is such a thing."

Don replayed the moment in his mind when he put down his journal and walked out on the court and challenged him to a one-on-one match. The six-foot-four-inch guard recruited by Duke under a full scholarship looked at Don and shrugged, an "it's your funeral" type of thing. But Don gave him everything he could handle, despite him being four inches taller. It was a game of twenty-one points. They were tied at twenty when the guy elevated and scored the bucket, followed by a free throw at the top of the arc to finish it.

Don lost and was prepared to receive his fair share of crow. He thought the brazen athlete would badger him and grandstand, but to Don's surprise, he did no such thing. He was excited. He immediately wanted to play Don again. He begged Don for another round. Don refused.

He walked around for weeks holding Don in high regard. He told everyone on the team Don was a baller and he would be a star if he played with them.

However, Don felt no gratitude for his praise.

The basketball browbeater taught Don something. His motives became crystal clear. The guy was being a jerk not to throw his skill in anyone's face but because he was bored. He needed a challenge. When Don took him to the brink of defeat, it energized him. It was fuel to the fire. He wanted to play Don again and again not because he knew he could beat Don but because Don was a worthy opponent.

What fun was a game you knew you could never lose?

"Hey!" said one of the girls loud enough to get Don's attention.

He turned to them, and one in particular returned the gaze. She was a blonde wearing a jean jacket and tan capris. Don's age. Sassy. Staring at him purposely with a hand on her hip. Daring him to speak. Don turned away to look straight ahead, and from the sound of her reaction, she was not too pleased.

He felt nothing there either. Neither embarrassed nor intimidated. Don knew he was not gay and he was not asexual either. There was no passion. Especially for that girl.

He went into his backpack, opened up his journal, and began writing.

# CHAPTER 4

Don was confident when he and Jasmine emerged from the train station at the last stop, the Atlantic Terminal exit. They were pressed for time. He convinced Jasmine it would be better if they went to the mall afterward and promised her he would throw in a bonus of ice cream if she was patient. She seemed content.

They walked seven blocks to the VFW station. It was in the middle of the block with an aluminum sign above the door and a window unit air conditioner hanging out of the brick front façade. Zadie's war buddy was named Harold Karwoski.

Don pushed down on the door handle and pulled it open. Sunlight invaded the dark space, grabbing the attention of the bartender, who was wiping down her station. She was a slim redhead in a black Metallica T-shirt with a gaggle of keys jingling around her waist. She folded her rag and draped it across her left shoulder as they entered.

"Are you the ones Harold's been expecting?" she said.

Don nodded. "He is a friend of my great-grandfather. *Was* a friend."

She shook her head as if the news was something that happened all too often around the VFW. "I'm sorry for your loss. I'm going to miss old Joseph."

"Thank you," said Don.

It was sincere. She appeared to be in her midforties, maybe early fifties. Had to have been working there for at least ten years if she knew Zadie.

Don looked around the space, with its light-gray tiled floors, wood paneling, pool tables, and dartboards. There were pictures, placards, and displays of hundreds of military members and patches on the walls, covering the outdated dark wood paneling all the way to the corner and on the adjacent wall. A person could spend hours looking at each picture and each patch, and Don imagined someone would probably be around to tell the story behind each one, as they drank beers into the late evening.

The bartender stepped out from behind the bar and motioned for them to follow her. "Harold is in the next room," she said. "I'll take you to him."

They walked between the empty stools at the bar and the pool tables all the way to the back of the building. They went through a hallway where a couple of old uniforms encased in glass were hanging on the wall. They entered another room at the end. Sunlight through the windows illuminated the space, with its white walls and the same light-gray tile floors. There was a slight chill in the air.

A man in a wheelchair was sitting hunched over with a blanket covering his legs. He was next to a brown table, which had a coffee machine sitting on top with foam cups beside it. A full cup of black coffee was within arm's reach of him.

"Young lady," said the bartender. "Would you like to come back with me into the bar? This kind of talk might not be fit for a sweet girl like you. How about we gals hang out together? There is a pool table, a pinball machine in the corner, and darts if you promise not to put too many holes in the wall."

Jasmine asked with her eyes if it would be OK, and Don nodded his approval. She and the bartender walked back down the hallway to the bar. Don stepped inside the room. There were no other chairs. He walked up to Harold and extended his hand. Harold had a kind old face, with overgrown white eyebrows and a jiggling patch of skin under his chin.

The jacket he wore was old and worn. The brown leather was covered with patches and an insignia. Don imagined that at one point, Harold had filled the jacket quite nicely, but now it looked as if he were a child wearing his father's coat. Harold reached forward with a trembling hand to shake Don's, then took the foam cup from the table. The skin on his hand looked paper-thin as he held the cup and slowly brought it to his lips.

"I feel honored a fine young man like you came all the way down here to see me," said Harold, sounding much like an old man. "You are Joseph's great-grandson, but you are much better looking than Joseph ever was." He laughed a bit. "How old are you?"

"I just turned seventeen," said Don.

"Great age," said Harold. "I was seventeen when the Japanese bombed Pearl Harbor. I had never been so scared in my life."

"Did you and Zadie fight together?" asked Don.

"We did. We met up in France, where our two companies merged out of necessity."

"Perhaps we should start there." Don pulled out his phone and began recording to make it look official. He would ease into the sensitive questions later. "What was he like?" He rested the phone on the table next to the coffee maker.

Harold looked down at the phone. The frequency meter moved like waves of water as he spoke. "Joseph would give you the shirt off his back," Harold started. "Quiet guy, until he got to know you—then you couldn't get him to shut up. Anna would often tell us, 'Please, get him drunk so he will stop talking and pass out.'"

He chuckled a bit, straining to breathe in the process. Then it was as if he suddenly remembered. "You never met your great-grandmother, Anna, did you? She died before you were born. They were married for over forty years, I believe. They met…oh, well, that's another story. There I go running my mouth again. I am as guilty as Joseph when it comes to running my mouth. It was amazing how we could be such good friends with both of us talking up a storm… It's a wonder we heard what the other had to say."

"I wonder if you could tell me who this belonged to," said Don. He went into his backpack to retrieve the small black box. He slipped his fingers inside and pulled out the dual heart charm. He closed the box, placed it in his pocket, and held out the charm for Harold to see.

"Have you seen this before?" asked Don.

Harold stared at it for a long time. His eyes narrowed in curiosity and opened wide with shock. Don was certain the sight of it triggered a memory. And it wasn't a good one. "The first time I saw that was in the hospital," said Harold. "Your great-grandfather was clutching it."

"Anna, my great-grandmother, was a nurse, my father mentioned. Was this hers?"

Harold shook his head. "Enough about the charm. Some things are best left alone."

"What was he in the hospital for? Was it a war injury?"

Harold raised his head as if to signal he was thinking, then wrinkled his nose and said, "Not my place, I guess. Maybe you should ask your father."

Don could see he would get nowhere without giving Harold a push.

"I found something else besides this charm," said Don. "Something disturbing. I am hiding it from my family until I can get a better understanding of what it means. I was hoping someone who knew Zadie for years might be able to help me. I found the other item along with this charm."

Harold placed the cup of coffee back onto the table. "What did you find?"

"I'll tell you after you tell me the significance of the charm," said Don.

Harold shook his head while wrinkling his nose. "Mmmm…I don't think it is my place. You don't want to hear about things like that. Everyone has a past. Not everything is rosy in life. You come against your bumps and bruises."

"The thorns of life are what make us who we are," said Don. He reached for his phone and turned off the recorder. "This is off the record. It's between us."

The loose skin under Harold's chin retracted as his Adam's apple slid up and down. His index finger trembled on the arm of the wheelchair. He looked up at the ceiling, took a deep breath, and spoke. "Anna, your great-grandmother, was a nurse in a mental hospital. Joseph was there because he was suffering a great deal. Anna was there for him. When he needed someone the most."

Harold stopped there. He appeared to be deep in thought. Apprehensive about continuing.

"I can see where a lifelong bond could be formed with someone in that situation," said Don. "I imagine the PTSD after the war must have been a terrible experience."

"PTSD?" said Harold. "There was not a name for it then. In those days we all suffered in silence, afraid to say anything. Scared of being called something less than a man. If they knew then what we know now, many of us would not have suffered so dearly afterward. The ignorance about the mental aspects of war is probably what created VFWs. It was our form of support for one another, since we were the only ones who knew the type of suffering we'd experienced."

"I commend you for your sacrifice," said Don. "Without your friendship, Zadie may not have been the person we knew. But the charm." He held it up in front of Harold. It swung on its chain like a pendulum. "What is the significance of this object?"

Harold was visibly struggling with letting go. Fighting to keep the secret sacred. He took another sip of his coffee, then blurted it out: "It was another woman." He looked up at Don, embarrassed. "I don't mean while he was with your great-grandmother, Anna. He would never do that to her. I mean, this woman was there before he met Anna. Anna changed his life for the good. His other girlfriend, before Anna, she was the thing that crushed him."

"What happened to her?" asked Don.

"She died," said Harold.

Don wasn't certain he wanted to continue this conversation. Yet he had come all this way to hear it. "What happened to her? How did she die?"

"She was hit by a car."

A part of Don was relieved. It wasn't an act of heartbroken rage.

"She died in his arms," said Harold. "He blamed himself for not being able to save her."

"Were there witnesses?" Don had to be sure.

"Of course. It was on the street."

"Guilt caused him so much pain he was committed."

"It wasn't guilt," said Harold. "It was an obsession." His lips poked in and out several times. Like sucking through a straw. A sort of nervous response. "This love was cancerous. Joseph always believed he and...Rebecca...were destined to be together. I witnessed it personally. Joseph told me one day he had a vision of a girl with black hair and bright blue eyes. She would often wear a hairpin, one with a flower, and he said he dreamed about this girl for many days. One day, we went to this little pub down on Port Street, near the docks, and lo and behold, there she was. Just as he had described her. It was eerie.

"She was a beautiful creature. Petite, black hair, blue eyes. Gorgeous. She was sitting by the billiard table with friends. Joseph went over to her and immediately started talking to her, but some big brute came by and chased him away. I thought that was the end of that. I was wrong. A week later, Joseph ran into the same girl at the movie theater. I mean, we were sitting in a seat when she and her boyfriend came and sat right in front of us. What a coincidence. I began to think Joseph was right. They were destined to be together. The boyfriend went for popcorn, and Joseph swooped in and started talking. He told her he saw her in his future and he was not about to let anyone get in the way. He said her boyfriend would come back and kick the crap out of him, but that still wasn't going to stop him."

"Did he?" asked Don.

"Of course he did. He dropped the popcorn and walloped Joe real good. I thought he was going to kill Joe. I jumped on the big oaf's back, and he threw me off like he was flicking a bug. The police came to break it up, but by then Joe was black and purple, with one eye swollen shut."

Was killing the boyfriend how Zadie developed the thirst for keeping body parts? Don was an instant away from asking what color the boyfriend's eyes were before deciding against it. "I imagine he had another opportunity to finally win over Rebecca," he said.

Harold nodded slowly while his cloudy eyes drifted off somewhere else, trying to catch the details in his mind. "We went to the fair. She was with friends when we turned the corner by the booth with the ring toss. Joseph walked up behind her while her friends were trying their luck. He asked her what stuffed animal she would like. She pointed out the big panda bear hanging up in the middle. Everyone wanted that one, but it was almost impossible to win.

Three rings on the same bottleneck. No one could do it. Joseph said if he won her the panda, she would have to go out with him. It was a deal, she said. Joseph gave the fella a dime and took his three rings. To this day, I have never seen anything like it. It was magical. Like a movie. Three tosses, right over the same bottleneck. It was incredible. People were cheering. Hell, I was screaming at the top of my lungs, it was so amazing. He won a date with his dream girl, and later he won her heart."

It sounded exactly like a fairy tale to Don. He imagined the passion Zadie must have felt in achieving his deepest desires. Then it all came to an end. "How long were Zadie and Rebecca together?"

"A little over four months. He bought her that charm. He told me the details of how he planned to propose to her in the following weeks. However, before he could give her the charm, she was struck by the car and killed. Joseph was holding her hand when it happened. The car was actually heading toward Joseph. Rebecca saw it first and pushed him out of the way to safety. After her death, he was a broken man."

Don imagined how tragedy affected people differently. How it could push a person over the edge. "Is this when he went to the hospital?"

"He was delusional. He kept saying that was not how it was supposed to happen. They were supposed to have kids and a family. This was not supposed to be his future. Rebecca was supposed to be by his side. When he refused to eat, he was institutionalized. Fortunately, that was where he met Anna. In the end, everything turned out for the best."

Don was not about to call it the fairy-tale ending of a tragic tale. There were gaps. Holes to be filled. Explanations about this eye inside the jewelry box he was holding in his hand. "What was his mental state afterward?" said Don, pushing the issue.

"What do you mean?" said Harold.

Don was forceful. Direct. "I believe something happened to him during the war that affected his well-being. He came to the VFW all the time, right? Don't you guys share your problems here? Did he tell you anything disturbing?"

"What are you getting at?" Harold's eyes narrowed.

"War changes you, sometimes not for the good."

With his hand shaking, Harold placed his coffee cup on the table. "When your mother called me, I was under the impression you wanted to know more about Joe as a person. But you just want to know the details of his secret."

Don nodded. "So you know about it, then."

Harold placed his frail hands on the armrests of his wheelchair. For a moment, it appeared he was going to stand. But he was just propping himself upright. Adjusting the weight from sitting in a chair too long. "I have been on this earth a long time, and I can tell you no one is going to live up to who you think they are. Everyone has secrets. Most are shocking. That is why they are secrets. Is what you found going to hurt your family if anyone else finds out?"

Don lowered his head before nodding a single nod.

"Then bury it!" said Harold, barking the order. "It is best that this thing die along with Joe's body so the good memories of him continue to live on. He is no longer here to explain whatever it is you found, and I certainly don't have the answers you're seeking."

Harold pressed a button on the end of the armrest. He pressed it several times impatiently. A few seconds later, a woman Don had not seen before came into the room. She stood at attention, dressed in green hospital scrubs and black shoes with rubbery soles.

"Are you ready to go?" she asked.

"Yes," said Harold, looking up at Don. "I would like to stroll through the park one last time in memory of my best friend."

# CHAPTER 5

The abrupt ending of the interview put Don in an uncomfortable position. He thanked Harold for his time and headed to the bar to retrieve Jasmine. The bartender proceeded to tell Don funny stories about how Zadie would come into the VFW and try to hustle people in darts, along with his inability to hold his liquor. But Don's mind was elsewhere. Letting go of where the eye had come from was difficult. Would he be able to do as Harold suggested? Jasmine poked his shin with her foot, which snapped Don out of his trance. She gave him a look that said *It's time to go to the mall and be done with this boring bar.* Don took the hint and thanked the bartender for her time. They left out the front door, stepping into the bright sunlight.

He could feel Jasmine's excitement as she walked next to him. If only he could be as carefree. He was trying, but it was hard to let it go. Across the street was the park, and Don quickly located Harold puttering along in his motorized wheelchair. The caretaker, in scrubs, was walking beside him, while bikers and joggers strolled past at their own pace. Harold did not seem troubled at all. He laughed at something the caretaker said and kept smiling until he was gone from Don's sight.

Perhaps it would've been different if he had shown Harold the eye instead of the charm. He would then know how serious this problem was. Then again, Harold was not even the slightest bit curious as to what Don had found. Perhaps he really did know something he was not letting on. Or maybe, Harold had a point in not asking. What good would it do to be weighed down by this burden? Zadie was dead, and Don's questions could never be answered. The quest for answers had the potential to haunt Don for the rest of his life. Is that what he really wanted?

Don was embarrassed, not from wanting to know the truth but because he was expecting the worst. What kind of great-grandson was he, not giving Zadie the benefit of the doubt? Harold was right to scold him. He understood now. They turned the corner and entered the subway station attached to the Atlantic Mall. It was crowded. Enthusiastic shoppers bustled all around them. Jasmine rushed to the Pretty Girl store and used the gift card her mother had given her to buy several items of clothing while Don sat on a stool near the fitting rooms.

When she was finished, she asked if they could stop for the ice cream he'd promised. Don had nearly forgotten and nodded in agreement. A deal was a deal. He treated her to a cup of chocolate gelato while Don went for the pizza a few stores down. They sat down and relaxed in the busy mall, finishing their treats, then heading to the bathroom before going back to the station for the long trip home. He didn't say much. He was mostly lost in thought. But Harold's words kept ringing in his ears, so he decided to do something about it. Bury the evidence, as Harold suggested.

While standing on the platform, Don slipped the black jewelry box into his pocket and slid his hand inside the box where his sister couldn't see. He scooped the eye in his palm and held it tight. By now he was no longer squeamish about holding it. He twirled it between his fingers, waiting for the right time to dispose of it when his sister was distracted.

His focus was inside the tunnel. If he tossed it into the darkness, no one would be able to tell what he had thrown. He was close enough that it wouldn't have to travel far, and with a firm flick of the wrist, there was zero chance of it bouncing into the light. If his sister asked, he would tell her it was an old piece of gum or trash from his pocket. Don was ready. His sister turned to look down the other side of the tracks.

He flexed his wrist and was poised to throw it when a vision swept over his eyes.

He was walking down the stairs. He was wearing black oxfords with gray slacks. Looked like business attire. He began to notice the landmarks, the scenery. It looked like the same platform he'd walked down a few minutes earlier. Just seeing it was strange enough, but even more puzzling, Don got the impression that it was not him seeing it. It was as if he was looking through the eyes of another person. This person checked his watch, silver with big numbers. He was approaching the bottom of the stairs when he looked up and he saw himself. Don was standing near the edge of the platform by the stairs with Jasmine to his left. He was wearing the same clothes. Don's right hand was in his pocket.

"Whoa!" said Don.

"Are you OK?" asked Jasmine. "You were standing there frozen. Like you zoned out for a moment."

Don was looking down the tunnel. He could see the signal lights deep inside. "Yeah, I'm OK." He shook the cobwebs from his head. "Just got dizzy for a moment. I saw the strangest…"

He was distracted by the sight of a man coming down the stairs. Gray slacks. Black oxfords. When the rest of his body came into view, Don saw the man was looking at his watch. Then he looked at Don.

He was a middle-aged man, probably around forty years old. He had light-brown hair and a full beard. His suit was gray. He had a black scarf over his shoulders. Thin build and about Don's height, six feet. He nodded after noticing Don looking at him. Then he walked past him and took up a position on the other side of the platform.

Don was speechless. "What the hell?"

"You spaced out," said Jasmine. "It was freaky."

"You are never going to believe this, Jasmine." Don wasn't sure he believed it. "I was standing here and…"

Another vision flooded his senses. He heard his sister calling out to him in the background. The sound of her voice was beside him, but he could see her in front of him. She was not on the platform; she was somewhere else. A room of some sort. Dark and private. Jasmine was terrified while looking at him, pleading. Crying. He could see her mouth moving, but there was no sound. Her cheeks were rosy, with darkened splotches all over her pale face. Tears ran from her eyes, snot dripped from her nose, and spit flew from her mouth as she begged him. Hands began grabbing at her, choking her, holding her down. Touching things he should not be touching. To Don, it appeared as if it was him, but it was not him. It was a vision. One of the future.

"Don, you're scaring me!" said Jasmine.

She shook his arm fiercely, which loosened his grip on the eye in his pocket and jolted him back to the present.

"What is going on with you?" she said. "You were just standing there frozen, and you began making all these crazy faces, like you were about to scream or something. What was that?"

Don looked down at his sister's worried face. It was clean, with slight freckles on the skin. Nothing like the splotchy, red, swollen mess he'd witnessed seconds ago. "Sorry," said Don. "I must be losing my mind."

"Who does that?" she said. "You're scaring me."

Nervously, Don looked around to see if his episode had attracted attention from others in the station. His eye caught one person in particular. It was a glance. Among the dense crowd of people, this man turned away when Don looked in his direction, but it was not Don he was staring at. It was Jasmine. The man was somewhere in his mid-to-late twenties, dark hair and glasses. He slipped back into the shadows of people around him, but it was too late. Don was onto him. It was one sole pair of eyes on a crowded platform, but for Don, it was like a spotlight shining. A beacon. Don had locked onto him. The connection was clear.

Don had been looking through the eyes of this man, somewhere in the near future.

# CHAPTER 6

The conversation Don had with Harold turned out to be most useful indeed. He quickly pieced together information and weaved it to form a roadmap to the eye.

Harold had told Don that Zadie insisted he and his first love, Rebecca, were meant to be together. Harold believed the times when he and Zadie had run into Rebecca were random. Lucky coincidences. They were all public places, so at a glance it would seem so. However, Zadie had known she would be there. The eye had shown him. He'd won Rebecca's heart. The eye had shown him that too. Then she'd lost her life. The eye had not shown him that one.

The eye gave the ability to see into the future, but it was not perfect. Nearly perfect, Don guessed. There had to be something Zadie had missed about determining its accuracy, which was why he spent time in the mental hospital. His mind could not wrap itself around the fact that the eye had failed him when he needed it most.

Be that as it may, changing the future was not out of the question. Don had seen through the eyes of the man coming down the stairs. He'd seen himself throw the eye into the tunnel, which was what he'd planned on doing. He was so shocked that he'd forgotten to do it.

There was a knock on his bedroom door. Don looked around the room to see if everything was in order. He was sitting at his desk with a laptop in front of him. The eye was in his pocket. "Come in," he said.

His mother peeked her head through the door. Her long hair was tied up haphazardly, and she was wearing jeans and a long T-shirt with pink house slippers on her feet. She stepped inside cautiously, looking him straight in the eyes. "Are you OK? Jasmine told me about what happened on the train platform. You've been pretty quiet since you got back. Do you remember any of it?"

A child molester was in his sister's future. He remembered everything. He gritted his teeth at the thought of that asshole assaulting his sister. "I'm OK, Mom. No big deal. I was thinking about something. Lost in thought."

"Jasmine is worried about you. She said you barely said a word to her afterward. Like you were avoiding her."

How was he supposed to behave after seeing someone fondling his little sister? He was angry. Embarrassed and humiliated. But how could he explain everything he knew without seeming crazy? "No. I'm not avoiding Jasmine. It's good. Everything is fine, Mom."

She nodded. Her face made it seem like she wasn't accepting his explanation, more like she'd made up her mind about something else. "I am going to make an appointment with the doctor."

Don rolled his eyes. "I'm perfectly fine."

"From what Jasmine explained, you might have had a seizure," she said. "It's very dangerous, Adonis." She reached forward with the back of her hand and caressed the side of his cheek. "I don't know what I would do if anything happened to you."

She turned and left, as if convinced she was doing the right thing. The motherly thing. The door remained partially open, and Don heard her sweeping steps down the stairs. He stood and went to the door to close it but saw Jasmine standing there, next to her room. She had been eavesdropping. She was wearing one of the pretty pink shirts she'd bought the day before in Brooklyn. Her face apologetic as if waiting for big brother Don to tell her she did the right thing. That he forgave her for telling their mom about the apparent seizure on the platform.

Don closed the door without a word. He needed to be isolated from her for a while. It was better that way. She would have to understand.

Don had learned several things about the eye in the last twenty-four hours. One, he had to be holding it, or it had to touch some part of his skin for at least five seconds or more to become active. Possibly to give it time to connect with the optic nerve or however it worked to transfer the images. If there were other people close by, he would begin to see parts of their future. Flashes of it. He didn't care to see any more from Jasmine. Not until he figured out how to change it.

The second thing Don had figured out was if he focused on a person while holding the eye, he could see through their eyes in the present. This turned out to be very confusing if he was out in public. Walking and moving in ways your brain cannot control is not like watching a movie. It is more like the virtual reality headsets you see people wearing while playing a game, where to the outside world, the user is looking around and feeling for things that are not there. Don quickly gathered he would look awkward and silly trying to move while looking through someone else's eyes because his own vision was cut off completely. For that reason, he limited his views to when he was seated.

The third thing he'd noted was there was no sound. He could spy by seeing, but he could not hear what was being said, which made sense since it was just an eye. Yet it also robbed him of the story behind the act. If people were doing nothing but talking, it made it difficult to make out what was going on. Don was observant, well enough to where he could make out key words by reading lips, but not everyone would be looking at who they were talking to. Still, the greatest flaw came when witnessing conversations with the person whose eyes he was looking through. He had no idea what they were saying.

Don looked over to the corner of his room, where a small digital clock rested on top of the nightstand. It was nearly 9:00 p.m. Mandatory lights out for Jasmine. He would give it another hour before trying the eye. For some reason, the eye avoided those in REM sleep. Possibly because the alpha and delta brain waves disrupted it somehow. But Jasmine often sat in bed playing on her phone for about an hour. He took all of that into consideration. He was patient.

---

His eyes sprang open. He was lying on his back in bed. He looked over at the clock. It was after midnight. He pulled the eye from his front pocket and held it firmly between his fingers. He fixed the image of the man from the subway firmly into his mind. Brown hair, glasses, height and weight, and the features of his face. Then he waited. Was there a limit to its range? If so, was it two meters or two miles?

After several seconds, the eye made the connection, and Don found himself under the bright lights of a computer monitor in a darkened room. A study perhaps.

He turned his head abruptly from the monitor to look around the darkened room. Don could see bookshelves and a door. Not much else was in the small space. Was this live, or was this something in the future? His focus returned to the monitor, and Don could see the time and the date in the bottom right corner. This was live. He was seeing through someone's eyes in the present. A click of the mouse, and the screen changed. It was an email. Looked official. Carlo's Furniture Warehouse was at the top of the letterhead. The email was addressed to Connor Richardson, Regional Manager.

Was he the one? Was Don looking through the eyes of the man who would assault his sister?

Don read along with Connor. He was scheduled to meet one of the store managers in Long Island about inventory. Something about making sure all items were accounted for because records indicated some level of inconsistencies within that store. The meeting date was today, late afternoon. Carlo's Furniture Warehouse sounded familiar to Don. He believed it was no more than three miles from where he lived.

Strange coincidence? Possibly. With Jasmine being only twelve and not being into any activities outside of YouTube, the only way Connor could take Jasmine was if she was somehow separated from the family.

Perhaps his mom and Jasmine would go to the furniture store to buy something for her room. *They get separated. He hides her away in one of the storage spaces. That's it.* The place his sister was kept did not seem like a space in the nice room he was looking at. Instead, it seemed dark and damp. Like a basement of sorts. But grungy. Old.

Connor glanced across his desk. He spied a picture of a woman and a small child. A petite woman with brown hair and a big smile. The girl seemed to be no older than three, with bangs and a ponytail, sitting on her mom's lap wearing a yellow dress. Don was disgusted even further. *He has a little girl of his own.*

His hands began sorting through papers on the desk. Looking for something. There were letters addressed to him. Don spotted the address. Manhattan. It was locked into his photographic memory. He would google the exact location later. For now, he kept his attention on finding clues as Connor searched.

He stopped to look up from the desk. Distracted by something. At the door, Don saw the woman in the photo. She was leaning against it, sleepy, talking to Connor. Pleading. He leaned back in his chair and looked at the ceiling. Then returned his gaze to the woman at the door, his wife. She seemed to be listening to him. Then she closed the door.

In that moment, Don wondered what he was doing. Sure, he'd seen the vision of his sister being assaulted, but he could not clearly see who her attacker was. He'd latched onto Connor, who was watching his sister on the platform. But it could be anyone. Perhaps he should focus on keeping a closer eye on Jasmine. Make sure whoever was after her would never get the chance. The thought of looking into his sister's future was too frightening for Don to endure. That was out of the question.

Connor shut down his computer, and the room went dark. Don was about to release the eye. Placing protections around Jasmine should be paramount. The bright light of the cell phone got Don's attention. Connor went into his photo app and began viewing pictures he had stored in an unnamed folder. Don's heart dropped as if it had tumbled off the bed.

He was looking at pictures of Jasmine.

There was one of her in front of the school. Then another with her walking with friends. How long had he been watching? There was a picture of the two of them when they were at the train station in New Hyde Park on the way to Brooklyn. That was before Don saw him on the platform. Had he been following them all day?

Of all the things Don had noticed that day, he had not picked up on Connor Richardson following them until the eye showed him.

Not noticing this man stalking his precious little sister was incendiary. A fire grew within his heart. Dangerous. Malevolent. He was angry because people like Connor were free to do perverse things to the innocent, but beyond that, he was fuming with himself for not seeing it.

Don dropped the eye on the bed and found himself staring at the ceiling. The sound of the locomotive he was hearing was his heart beating. He was sweating. Shaking.

Flashes of the assault to come entered his mind. He pushed away the main focus, his sister, and concentrated on the periphery. There were cinder block walls and a dusty concrete floor. In the left corner, sitting on the floor, was an old red fire extinguisher. To his immediate left was a galvanized pipe sticking out of the ground, probably an old gas line. If he wanted to change what was going to happen, finding this place was his best bet to stop it and punish Connor Richardson for thinking of his sister as prey.

# CHAPTER 7

Don woke up early that morning, showered, and got dressed. He turned on his computer and did recon on Connor's address. He lived in a brownstone in Manhattan. Purchased four years ago. Hefty price. Information about the sale was still on the realtor's website along with pictures. He checked over the layout—in particular, the basement. It had tile floors. Finished. Modern. It was a long shot that he would take her there, especially with his wife and child at the house. But Don had to be prudent and cover every angle.

His heart jolted when he looked up the address of Carlo's Furniture Warehouse. It was three blocks from Jasmine's middle school. He was now convinced. The room he was searching for had to be in the warehouse.

He shut down the computer, cleared the search history, and went downstairs to the kitchen, where his mother, father, and sister were seated for breakfast. They held hands, gave their blessings, and ate.

Don could feel his sister's eyes upon him, searching for any signs of forgiveness. She was still stuck on the idea of him being mad at her for telling their mom about the incident on the platform. No one except Don knew how close she had been to becoming a victim.

If he thought about Jasmine while holding the eye, images of her would flood his vision. He had to push her as far away as he could. Focus on Connor.

*He's the one you want to see,* he said to himself.

"Adonis," said his mom, "how are you feeling today?"

"Excellent," said Don, keeping his eyes focused on the eggs on his plate.

"Good," said his mother. "I have an appointment set up with you for next week. It's just a precaution." She placed a hand on his thigh for comfort. "You will be going away to college in five months. I don't want there to be anything I have to worry about."

Don raised his head from the plate of eggs. He remembered something.

"Are you excited to visit Yale this weekend?" she asked.

"Oh, it's this weekend?" said Don, as if he hadn't just remembered. "Honestly, Mom, it slipped my mind."

"How can you forget something like that, Adonis?" She frowned. "You got accepted to Yale University at seventeen years old. Of course, you finished all your requirements for high school in only three years, but that's beside the point. Only six percent of the people are accepted there. It's a hell of an achievement, and I am so proud of you. How can you be so casual about it?"

"I think I speak for us all when I say that you, Sara, have enough excitement for the whole family," said Don's father. He rolled his eyes playfully. "Don showed plenty of emotion when he first got the letter. Here, let me show you." Joe picked up a magazine from the middle of the table and looked at it without one twitch of a facial expression. "Hey, Mom. I got accepted to Yale," he said with an aloofness. Joe put the magazine back on top of the stack. "Trust me, Sara, he knows how important it is…to you."

"Important to me?" she asked. Her jaw opened as if she were in shock. She looked around the room, stunned. "Adonis, please don't tell me you are doing this for me. It's not for me—it's for you. I am excited for you, Adonis. I don't want you to feel like I am forcing this on you."

Don smiled. "You're not, Mom. I am going to Yale because that is where I want to go. Not because you went there."

"Good speech, son. Good speech," said Joe. "Notice how she threw in the six-percent-of-applicants fact? Dear old Dad could only manage to get into Cal. I guess anybody can get into Cal. Well, not anybody, but more than six percent can go there, so it's no great achievement. Don't dream of going to Cal, son. You might only end up making $175K a year as a finance manager." He slapped the side of his head as if he'd remembered something. "What am I saying? The money isn't important, son. What is important is you graduate as a six percenter!"

Sara's mouth widened farther than the last time. "There is nothing wrong with Cal. I never said anything was wrong with going to Cal. Why would you think that? It's just too far away. I want Don to be closer. If we lived out West, then Cal would be perfectly acceptable."

She sighed, used her fork to pick at her breakfast, and pouted like a six-year-old who had been told she couldn't have any more cookies "But…come on. It's Yale we're talking about here!"

Joe busted out in laughter as Sara could not contain her smile any longer.

"Yes," said Joe. He raised his glass of orange juice in the air. "Here is to Yale! And the good-looking schmuck who is probably Don's real father. Mister, wherever you are, you do good work."

"If he went to Yale, then he couldn't be a schmuck," said Sara. "Because it's Yale!"

"Oh really, honey," said Joe. "Well, I have the last laugh because Don has *my* last name!"

Don smiled as his father drank his orange juice and his mother threw a hunk of scrambled egg in his direction. The humor took Don's mind off his worries momentarily. They were all going to visit Yale this weekend.

Don's smile disappeared.

All of them except Jasmine! She was staying at a friend's house a few blocks away.

"Are you OK, Adonis?" asked his mother.

He looked around the table to find everyone observing him. Concerned expressions on their faces. He smiled. "Yes," he said. "I will be ready for our trip this weekend. No worries."

"No," said his mom. "I am worried. You seem to be more distant than usual. Different. Is there something you are not telling me?"

He was getting everyone's attention. He needed to be cognizant of that. Perhaps he should deflect his troubles. Throw them off his scent. "It was Zadie's death, I believe. Ever since then, I haven't been feeling myself."

He observed their reactions. Dad seemed to slump his shoulders ever so slightly. Relaxing a bit. His eyes dropped to his lap. Remorseful. Understanding. Jasmine turned away. Somber. But his mother's deep brown eyes were ever so piercing. Her brow furrowed from inspection. They were much the same. Observant. Her senses must be telling her there was more to it.

"Are you taking anything, Adonis?" she said softly. "Putting things into your body?"

He found that amusing. Drugs? He had a perfect mind and had no inclination to escape from it. Not even curiosity about smoking or drinking alcohol had ever crossed his mind. "No, Mom. It's nothing like that."

It was like a silent interrogation. Focused on his energy. Searching his mannerisms for clues to validate or refute her assumptions.

"I miss Zadie too," said his father. "He was a special human being. Sara…Sara…"

She blinked out of her trance and leaned back ever so slightly. "We can set you up with counseling if you like, Don. Would you like to speak to someone about it?"

"Stop interrogating the boy," said his father. "For years, we wondered if Don was even human, he was so perfect. Now we know. He is a normal human teenager. Let him grieve in his own way. Don… if you need help, please come to us, OK?"

# CHAPTER 8

Don went to school while devising a timeline in which he would execute his plan. It was Monday. On Saturday, the family would leave Jasmine to head up to Connecticut. He would leave nothing to chance. Too risky. He needed verification at the warehouse, and it had to be done today. Then he could use the rest of the week to get to Connor somehow. Confront him. Let the police know about the photos of his sister on Connor's phone. Anything to disrupt the timeline.

He sat through science and history with an elbow on his desk and his fist pressed against his cheek like a kickstand. It didn't matter if he paid attention or not. He would coast through with As, as usual. Absorbing all high school had to offer was a breeze, and he never understood the concept of teaching. Don learned by opening books and reading. A teacher standing there going over what was already in print was counterproductive to his time. His high school had boosted its rankings when he received a perfect SAT score, as if his success were attributed to the faculty's teaching methods. How absurd. He would have achieved the same score if he'd stayed home and watched television all day.

However, his detachment in class would serve him well. Unlike his ultraobservant mother, his classmates were too consumed with their own problems to notice any change. He would appear as he did every day. His normal aloofness would serve as his alibi should things go south. The bell rang, and most students bolted for the hallway, on to socialize before the next class. Don had lunch period. He navigated through the crowded hallway to the lunchroom.

In the lunch line, Don stared down the assortment of schoolhouse classics, like Salisbury steak and sweet corn, mashed potatoes, and string beans. He picked out what he could stomach and took his tray of food to a table by himself. That didn't last long. A group of seniors saw Don sitting at the table and decided to join him. Six of them. Don knew them but didn't really associate with them. It was not that he gave anyone the cold shoulder; it was just that Don was not into the social media scene, which tended to kill their inquisitive requests to get to know him.

There was Brad King, a tall kid with curly black hair. Verbose with a confrontational personality. His sister Paula King was tall for a girl, also with curly black hair. Brad was a year older, but Don was unclear if Paula had skipped a grade or if Brad had been held back. There was Ronnie Blankenship, the reader in the group. He was an average kid with brown hair who had a thirst for knowledge, but his deductions were askew. Then there was Charlie Proctor, a big and scary high school kid who looked as if he were twenty-five years old. Rumor had it he was growing facial hair by thirteen. He was a gentle giant who was really into his studies. Fifth in the group was Carlos Martinez. He had the classic New York Hispanic accent. Very good student, with a crush on Paula, although it was uncertain if Paula noticed. Lastly, there was Jackie Patrick. She was the quiet one. Blonde hair, retainer, and slightly out of place with the rest of the group. Don was not quite sure how she fit in, but wherever they were, she was, too, so she was clearly accepted by them.

They sat down at Don's table, three of them staring at their cell phones and swiping, Paula taking selfies and sending them to whomever. Don could feel Jackie's eyes on him. He ignored the glances as usual, hoping they would all finish their lunch and leave him in peace. This group was much too close for him to grasp the eye and spy on what Connor was doing. The eye would most likely lock onto Jackie, who was clearly thinking about Don. That was another thing he noticed when using the eye: he would see the future of anyone thinking about him who was nearby. Perhaps it was some sort of defense mechanism.

"I read AIDS was created in a lab," said Carlos, after raising his head from his phone.

"Not AIDS—that's the condition," said Ronnie. "You mean HIV. And that's not what I heard. I heard HIV came from fucking monkeys. Some sick shit right there."

"Monkeys?" said Brad. "They can't bang sheep like other perverts?"

They laughed and dapped fists.

"You know what I always wondered?" said Paula. "Why do they still have babies when there is no food? I mean, you see these pictures of famine, bellies full of air, thin as a rail, and then you see pregnant women. Why would you bring a baby into conditions like that? It's so stupid."

Jackie looked over at Don. "What do you think, Don?" she asked. "Is Paula right?"

Don was now drawn into the conversation. Perhaps it was useful. It would take his mind off Connor. Don replied, "The way I see it, there are two natural pleasures of the body, food and sex. They are already denied one in a lack of food. Who are you to deny them the other?"

Brad and Ronnie high-fived each other. "Got that, Paula?" said Brad. "Always trying to take away somebody's fun."

"It's irresponsible," said Paula. "Bringing another life into the world under those conditions."

"So you are in favor of genocide?" asked Don. "Let all the starving Black people die off because there is not enough food? Do you think the same about Jews?"

Paula was struggling for words. She stuttered and tried to put together something coherent before Don smiled. It was how he entertained himself.

"Damn," said Brad. "Don knows how to fuck with people mentally. That's why I love talking with this guy. Yo, Don, back to the HIV thing. I hear people saying it was a government conspiracy. They sought to wipe out gays, so they released it into the gay community. Was it cooked up in a lab or what?"

"Not," said Don. "Viruses are alive, and like all living things, they evolve. They change all on their own. You don't have to engineer a killer virus. They've been killing millions of species since long before there was biological warfare. Also, a virus that kills its host is an evolutionary mistake. Killing the host is like killing themselves. No virus wants to kill. It happens unintentionally."

"So there's a chance it was cooked up by the government," said Brad. "You said no virus intends to kill its host, so the ones that do must have been tampered with."

"I also said it's an evolutionary mistake," said Don.

"But the government can do that stuff, right? Create a virus as a weapon. You can't rule out that the government was behind it. That's the kind of shit the government does."

Don sighed. "More like a plot in a comic book or a movie. There is no benefit for the government to kill for the sake of killing."

"They were targeting the gays," said Brad.

"No…that's not right either," said Don. "The reason gay men spread the disease like wildfire is because they typically have sex with multiple partners several times a day."

"Several?" asked Jackie. "Like how many?"

"I've heard as much as five times a day," said Don.

"What the fuck?" said Paula. "That's got to be a lie. Nobody does it that much. Insane!"

"Men reach their sexual peak at eighteen," said Don. "That means when young men proposition other young men, the chances of there being a consensual act increases dramatically. For men, there is no greater aphrodisiac than novelty. Women reach their peaks somewhere around their forties and yet are still persnickety about who they have sex with. If men and women reached their sexual peaks at the same time, and women were as openly promiscuous, I guarantee five times a day would not be ridiculous."

"Hell, yeah," said Brad. "One…two…three…four…and five." He pointed to several of the hot girls around the lunchroom. "Then I wouldn't need so much porn."

Brad and Charlie high-fived each other this time.

"So there is no conspiracy about how it spread to gays first," Ronnie said to clarify.

"The government isn't that organized," said Don. "And what benefit would that serve? There has to be a reason for the kill. It must serve a purpose. Just to see the world burn is not good enough. Especially with a virus that kills indiscriminately."

"I disagree," said Carlos. "What about serial killers?" Don figured Carlos was secretly upset about what he did to Paula. "They don't need a reason. Serial killers kill people just to watch them die."

"Not true," said Don. He watched Carlos's expression to see if he would get hot under the collar. He wondered if any of the others knew he was only speaking because he wanted to impress Paula. "The term *evil* is something that satisfies the minds of those who do not understand we all function from the same desires."

"What? Sorry, Don," said Carlos. "There are plenty of sick fuckers in the world who kill to be killing. That's evil. A government can be evil. They smile while people suffer because they like it."

"Serial killers receive personal gratification from taking another life," said Don. "It's about empowerment and pleasure, not evil. If the head of the government were behind releasing a virus to watch people die, there would be a lack of connection there. It would satisfy your sense of evil; however, a serial killer would get no pleasure from that. If the purpose were to watch people die, they could hang out in a hospice with the elderly and see all the death they wanted."

"But governments are evil," said Ronnie. "Look at the news and take your pick."

"Evil is not real," said Don. "When people don't understand motive and culture, they call it evil."

"What about Hitler?" said Carlos. "He killed the Jews because he was evil."

Don was a bit surprised. Carlos was actually trying to trip him up with a sound point, throwing the race card back in his face. *Touché.* It showed balls. It was commendable, and he could see Paula was impressed somewhat as well. But all for naught.

Don could not let their apparent declaration of victory go unanswered.

"Hitler had good reason to kill Jews, and it wasn't just to watch them die," said Don.

"I never heard of any reason," said a new voice not sitting at the table. "No one ever gave a reason." The voice was from behind Don. It was older, more mature. It was one of the teachers. Mr. Humphries was his name. Don turned around to see him standing there. Mr. Humphries was in his fifties. Brown hair mixed in with gray here and there. He wore big glasses and was always known to joke around with the students. But he was very serious this time.

"I deduced a reason," said Don, not backing down an inch. "Because people don't kill without one."

"Six million people," said Mr. Humphries. "Seventy years later, and no one really understands why. I'm curious what you think the reason was. Keep in mind there were millions of others in those camps—gypsies, gay men, Jehovah's Witnesses. They were murdered too."

"Fair enough," said Don. He turned around in his chair to face the teacher. "I will start with the Jews. The Third Reich was a religion. They seldom teach that. Most texts leave that part out. Never mention it. Note how the statement of the thousand years of the Third Reich mirrors the thousand years of the messiah's rule over the world from Israel."

"I'm following," said Mr. Humphries.

"The Reich believed the Aryan race was God's chosen people. Not the Jews. But over time, the Aryans had mixed with other races, like the Romani, and were no longer pure. This is what caused them to lose favor with God, and he stripped them of their supernatural power. In order to reestablish their connection and their place, they had to purify the blood, and then God would then reward them once more. That is why they sought out the purest of Aryan blood to mate with. The Lebensborn Policy. The origins of the master race."

"I heard something along those lines. What's the point?" said Mr. Humphries.

"For the last four thousand years, the world had known only the Jews as God's people. It would be easier for the new pure-blooded Aryans to replace them in the world's idea of God's people if God's original people no longer existed. That was his reason. As far as the Roma, the gays, Jehovah's Witnesses, and such, it was easier to kill the defiant than to try and reform them. The Catholic Church didn't stand up to him. The pope folded under Hitler's thumb. That's why regular Christians were not persecuted. But make no mistake, if they fought his dream of God's people being the Lebensborn, they would have been wiped out too."

"What proof do you have of this, Don?" said Mr. Humphries.

"About as much proof as you have to believe that my synopsis is wrong," said Don. "People are not monsters. They have good reason for doing what they do, even though they look like monsters to everyone else. A reason for Hitler's actions would humanize him. Something historians were not willing to do. Especially American historians, who have their own history of racial bias."

Mr. Humphries was always cheerful. Jovial. Now, he was visibly agitated. He was fighting with something internally, something deep in his core.

"No. I disagree," said Mr. Humphries with a frog in his throat. "You're wrong, Don. Some people are sick, twisted monsters who enjoy watching others suffer in misery. That is what evil is. There is no humanizing that, Don. There is no explaining it. I'm shocked at you, Don. Especially as a Jew."

He walked off without another word, and Don let him go. He recognized something. Out of all the staff, Mr. Humphries was perhaps the most student-friendly teacher. Kids at the school felt they could approach him about anything. He would help any student no matter what the problem was. Yet, as he walked away, a student said something to him jokingly and he brushed them off. His cheery armor had been penetrated, and he was visibly wounded. This had to be something personal.

"See, Don," said Carlos. "I told you."

It was his last jab, and Don was content with letting it go. His interest had shifted elsewhere. This talk of evil had punctured a hole in someone's armor, and Don was curious to find out why.

With the others returning to their food and their cell phones, Don took hold of the eye in his pocket. He wanted to try something different. Could he look into someone's past? Mr. Humphries was the perfect candidate. Don was hoping all the other people around him would not cause interference. He decided to try it. He focused hard on the teacher and then through his current view. Then Don turned the dial back with the focus of a person's view of evil. The view moved fast as if years were passing by in a blink of an eye, then it stopped.

Don could see an adult male with no shirt standing over Mr. Humphries. Overweight, hairy chest, scraggly beard, big forearms, and thick fingers. Mr. Humphries held up his arms in defense, and Don could see his limbs were small and frail. He was a child. The man was screaming profusely into his face. Phlegm and rage came spewing out of his mouth. Then the first slap hit the side of his head, sending the young Mr. Humphries straight to the ground. There were more screams in his face, then he waited. The young Mr. Humphries outstretched his left arm and placed his hand palm-side down onto the floor. Don could see the man raise his leg and stomp his heel down on the back of young Mr. Humphries's outstretched hand.

A scream caused Don to release the eye and return to the present.

"What happened?" said Jackie.

"Over there," said Brad.

Don looked at where he was motioning, and he saw Mr. Humphries. He was sweating and breathing heavily, holding the back of his left hand. As others approached him, he waved them off, indicating he was all right, but he was visibly shaken. The side of his face was red, as if he had been struck. Mr. Humphries stormed out of the lunchroom, looking frightened and confused.

*Interesting*, Don thought.

# CHAPTER 9

A simple mention of a doctor's appointment got Don past security and out the door of the school. He was the top student; why would they not believe him? He took a bus from his high school in Hempstead to North New Hyde Park and got off at the stop a few blocks away from Carlo's Furniture Warehouse. There was a park nearby. He decided to wait there until it was time for Connor's meeting. There was no specific time in the email. It had only said he would be coming to visit the manager in the afternoon. It was a waiting game. Don would intercept Connor on his way there. After that, he had no idea what he was going to do.

He had the eye, which was a strategic advantage. He didn't have to stand by the furniture store, giving others a chance to remember the strange kid hanging out on the corner should there be violence. Learning from what Harold had said about Zadie, he could pop up at the same time, making everything seem like a coincidence. He saw a park bench off the concrete path and decided to sit down. The air still had a chill, but the sun was shining directly on him to provide some warmth. The grass was brown with small patches of green coming through. A couple of female joggers came by the path pushing their jogging strollers. They gave him a suspicious look as they ran by.

He thought it was best to keep himself occupied or at least give the appearance of being so. He pulled out his journal and began writing about looking into one's past. He hadn't known it was possible. He'd simply thought about it, and the eye had provided the images all on its own. He wondered how it worked and thought about Mr. Humphries's reaction. Mr. Humphries saw and experienced the past as Don was looking.

The past was things that had happened. The present was what was happening at that moment. How would the future be explained? Where were those images coming from, and how reliable were they? Zadie was not shown the future with his first love's death, which meant what Don was shown could not be guaranteed one hundred percent true.

Don reached into this backpack compartment and pulled out a pack of Skittles. He tore it open, poured out a handful, and tossed them into this mouth. He crunched down on the hard shells and into the sweet and tart, chewy center. The gel released an explosion of fruity flavors all over his tongue. He looked across the field to the trees in the background, their flowers beginning to bloom, and quickly grew impatient.

He placed his hand in his pocket to touch the eye and thought about Connor Richardson. He was connected with his present view. Again, he was right where he was the last time, glued to the monitor of his office computer and working on spreadsheets. Connor's main office was in Manhattan. Even if he left at that moment, it would still take him over an hour to get to the warehouse.

Bored Don, with nothing but time on his hands, thought of ways to entertain himself without looking conspicuous. The joggers and walkers in the park kept glancing at him when they passed by. He was the thing that stood out from their normal routine. If he pulled out his smartphone, he could at least keep his head fixated on it, to make himself look more like a harmless teen skipping school, but Don thought of something better. He opened his journal.

If he kept his head down in his journal and saw something he was not prepared for, it might not appear alarming to others like when he was on the platform. Besides, he had been practicing. Don decided to look for something in the surrounding neighborhood. He did not want anything random; he wanted to direct it like he had with Mr. Humphries in the lunchroom. Don sought out anyone who was suffering great pain and grief. Even more precisely, he wanted someone who was suffering right now.

He found himself inside something that looked like a dog kennel. He could see that his skin was slightly brown. Whoever it was had small limbs. He got the impression it was a female. He was in a basement, from what he could see. The windows up near the ceiling were blacked out. Painted over with a few cracks of light leaking through here and there. Dark wood paneling on the walls. The room had an old couch, boxes, a bathroom, a staircase, and tan tiled floors.

Whoever she was, she was not alone. Someone else was on the other side of the room, in a kennel, curled up in a fetal position. A small Asian woman with pale skin. Possibly in her midtwenties to early thirties. There was a large combination dial lock on the latch mechanism, similar to the one he used on his locker at school.

Don wondered who these women were. The woman across the room was moving her mouth. Whether she was singing or saying a prayer he couldn't tell. But she was not in conversation because her mouth did not stop moving. She was reciting in a loop, whatever she was saying. Maybe in her native language because he could not make out any words by the way her lips moved.

It reminded him of what he saw in store for his sister. So there were other monsters out there. It strengthened his resolve.

Don returned his attention to Connor Richardson. He found himself in the office checking his wristwatch. It was 12:12 p.m. Connor used his left hand to click the mouse and pull up his calendar on the desktop computer. From 1:00 p.m. to 3:00 p.m., he had a meeting with a man named Cameron Bolton. It did not say where this meeting was. Connor began going through emails. Clicking and typing and sending. He seemed rather busy.

He spied an email in the chain below. It looked like Connor had canceled the meeting at the warehouse today and changed it to Wednesday.

*Shit.*

How many times could he skip school without arousing suspicion?

He had to do something. The weekend was four days away, and he could not risk it. He needed the location of the room he'd seen in the vision. If he knew where it was and Connor knew that he knew, Connor could no longer take her there, ensuring that future would never come to pass.

Don released the eye to see with his own eyes. The park was quiet with the exception of a few moms talking as they pushed their strollers. Don packed up his journal and bag of Skittles and took off for the warehouse. He walked down the concrete path of the park all the way to the street and beyond. He walked two more blocks of the main street, lined with small businesses, and turned a corner. About a hundred meters ahead was a chain-link fence entwined with green plastic privacy slats. The gate for deliveries was open. A forklift on the elevated platform sat unattended.

Don walked across the street to get a better view. He reached a spot where he could see straight inside the warehouse to the main office. A middle-aged woman with glasses and brown hair was sitting behind a computer. Next to her was the main door to the warehouse. It was wide open. The steel roll-up door was three-quarters of the way up. Security was also there by the entrance. Fat chance of slipping in and wandering around unnoticed.

The guard was a large man who appeared to be a few years older than Don. He also appeared to eat, sleep, and dream barbells and protein. He was tanned and shredded and probably would not take too kindly to Don trying to slip past him. No telling how his mind would react to trickery. Don stuck with his best bet, which was the receptionist in the office. But how would he get her to let him in there? He had the eye. It was the best way to gain some kind of dirt on someone in order to bribe his way past.

He touched it with her in mind. A few seconds later, he was in. Now for his latest skill: dialing back time. When he did it with Mr. Humphries, his past flew by in a flash and then stopped on what Don was interested in. It passed by everything else so fast he could not even see it. So Don thought about something salacious, something embarrassing, something that was shameful he could use to gain entry.

The eye went straight to text messages on a phone. Why they were embarrassing or salacious he did not know. But the texts were racy, for sure. They were pictures the receptionist had sent of herself. Sexually suggestive but none of them exposing anything sensitive. The pictures could be deemed harmless, so who they were sent to was probably the embarrassing part. It was some guy named Tim H. The rest he would have to put together.

But that was not good enough. He needed something that would get him inside the building to snoop around. Suggestive photos were not a big enough bargaining chip. Again, he thought hard about something embarrassing but related to work.

A vision solidified in his mind of a couch being hauled into her house. He could see it came from the warehouse, but there was something off about the accounts on it. She had not paid for it. The eye flashed and showed him the couch was delivered to the warehouse by accident. He could see her going through the invoice and wondering where this extra couch came from. And then penciling it in on the sheet as if it were supposed to be there, even though it was not.

Then he saw another vision of her pulling up to the warehouse door after hours; she and another man loaded the couch into her van and left. Since he saw images of that other man in a house with her, Don assumed he must be her husband. Helping herself to a couch that showed up without being accounted for in the inventory was something he could work with.

So she was the source of the inventory inconsistencies. Convenient.

Don released the eye and crossed the street, went through the open chain-link gated fence, and walked right into the office. It was a tiny room with a desk in front. The desk had a placard with the woman's name on it. Charlene Camp. Behind her was a big glass window with a clear view of the warehouse. Furniture. Mostly in boxes except for the couches, which were wrapped in plastic. He could see an area over to the left where they assembled things like desks and tables. To the right stood the door leading to the warehouse. It was slightly open, and he could see the big arm of the guard on the other side.

Charlene had glasses over her green eyes. She was average as far as body, height, and weight, and she had fair skin with a healthy bit of freckles all over. "Can I help you?" she asked. Her voice was soft and pleasant.

"Sure," said Don. "I am from Carriage Sofas. About four months ago, we shipped an order here. Fifteen couches in all as indicated on the invoice, but I believe there was an extra one shipped here. My supervisor sent me to check the received bill of lading to see if it was delivered here."

She blinked several times. "Carriage? When was the delivery… exactly?"

"I don't have the paperwork on me, but it was four months ago," said Don.

"Without the shipping documents, I can't be sure. We get trucks delivering things daily. You work for Carriage, you say?"

"Yes, just started," said Don.

She smiled politely and shook her head slowly, like she was scolding him, as if he should know better. "Yes, I thought so. Without the proper shipping documents, there will be no way to accurately account for what was delivered here. Furthermore, the bill of lading is what I use to verify each and every delivery that comes in. I assure you it was gone over several times to check for accuracy, and my supervisor signs the documents once all items are accounted for. So, you see, if there was something lost on your end, it was on your end and not here. But if Carriage wants to play this game, then I can pull out the paperwork for you to show you. I guess I will have to do that to satisfy you. And by the way, let your boss know my paperwork does not cover a screwup on your end."

"If the sixteen couches are on the bill of lading, then that means the extra couch came here," said Don.

She spun around her chair and rolled her seat over to the file cabinets against the wall. Then she flipped through the folders using her fingers, peering down through the bottom of her glasses. The files were all neat and orderly, and she was able to find the delivery in a few seconds.

"There were fifteen. Only fifteen. It was checked and verified and even delivered to the main store. We keep digital records of each one after it arrives, and I could probably tell you if the couches were sold in our regional stores if you wanted."

Don leaned over to whisper to her. "Blue couch, reclined on both ends, center console with cup holders in between. Perfect for a movie room or good enough to watch TV in comfort. Great for a standard living room. Do you know what I mean? Now, Orville told his supervisor he was sure he loaded that couch on the truck bound for this warehouse that day. That's why I am here to check. Did you know the regional manager, Connor Richardson, was due to come here today for a surprise inventory check?"

"What?" she said with a slight frog in her throat.

"I was asked to take a look around and check to see if his property was here," Don said calmly. He popped some Skittles into his mouth and chewed. "A quick look is all I need, and I will be satisfied. Or I could go back and tell him you would not let me do my job. Connor will be down here later, and then he will be the one asking questions. Light-blue couch with the cup holders." Don looked around the warehouse. "Who knows, maybe someone here took it home with them?" Then he looked straight down into Charlene's green eyes. "I really don't care. I was asked to take a look around the warehouse. That's all. Then I'm gone."

"Well," she said, clearing her throat and placing a hand on her chest. "That was a mouthful. When you put it that way, I fully understand." She giggled coyly. "You need to take a look in our warehouse. No problem."

She did something with her computer and put the paperwork back in the file cabinet. Then she stood up and offered for Don to go into the warehouse through the door on his right. He did as directed and led the way. He walked out onto the polished concrete floor of the warehouse where several guys were busy moving things. Three forklifts were toting boxes here and there. Others with floor jacks drove around taking things to little squares on the floor outlined with caution tape. Shelves upon shelves of items and boxes were stacked on top of each other with little number and letter designations separating sections.

Charlene took Don down one aisle and then turned left at the intersection. Halfway down the aisle, she stopped and showed him where they kept the couches. Don scanned over the area, but his eyes quickly wandered around the entire space. From what he could see, at the end of that aisle was another section, elevated.

"What about up there?" said Don.

"More office spaces," she said.

"I would like to check there, please."

It appeared she was about to object, but Don gave her a stern look to discourage refusal. She bit her lip and said, "Let's go."

Don knew he was pushing it, but nothing in this warehouse looked like the space he'd seen his sister crammed into. It was smaller, darker, brick walls, dusty, old looking, moldy looking. This was a new warehouse with slick concrete floors and rugged shelves. Cinder block walls and corrugated aluminum rooftops. This was not the place.

He was about to thank Charlene for her time and assure her his boss would be satisfied when he spotted another area on the warehouse floor near the corner. Cellar doors that led to a structure beneath the warehouse floor. Black diamond plate steel doors, level with the floor. They were padlocked.

"What's down there?" asked Don.

"An old section of the warehouse from before we upgraded the facilities," said Charlene. "We used to use it to store chemicals and paint. No one is brave enough to go down there now. Could be rats the size of cats for all we know. It's locked, and I don't have the combination."

Don grabbed the eye and thought about Connor and the combination. The answer came to him quickly—7-3-7-1—as he saw Connor typing it in. "Let's go take a look. There would be no reason to keep it locked if there were nothing down there. I just want to see if it's open, and then I will report back to my boss."

They went back down the stairs and over to the corner of the warehouse, past the rows of boxes on warehouse shelving and to the corner where the cellar doors were located.

"Locked, see!" said Charlene.

Don reached down to the padlock and gave it a tug. Then he punched in the number and released the latch. "Flimsy lock. I guess it was open all along."

Don pulled open one door and then the other. It was pitch black, and he could barely make out the crumbling concrete stairs; he could only see the first couple of steps before they vanished into blackness. He pulled out his cell phone and pressed the flashlight feature. He shined it down into the space far enough to see a light switch at the base of the stairwell.

"It was not open," said Charlene. "You knew the combination somehow. Who are you?"

"I'm checking it out," said Don.

He went down the stairs and felt the grit of worn concrete under his feet. When he reached the bottom, he found the light switch and turned it on. A small yellow light bulb on the ceiling lit up the space. There was headroom for a six-foot-tall person but no more. Brick walls, grime, grit, all the components of what he saw in his vision but not everything.

"Come out of there right now!" said Charlene. "The stairwell is so narrow you couldn't even get a couch down there. I'm calling your supervisor."

Don heard her heels tap away as she hurried off. He didn't care. He continued to pan his phone. The space was small with empty shelves that went all the way to the ceiling. He could see rust spots on the shelving and spills on the concrete floor. Then he saw a door to a room on his left. It was an old wooden door painted brown, and it had a latch and a padlock. This one was unlocked. Don pushed open the door. He flipped the light switch on his left and inside he saw a bed.

He looked over at the wall on the side of the bed and froze. He was speechless. The outline of paint on the wall was from a box that had been removed. Below it was an eighteen-inch section of galvanized pipe that had been cut, held on by a C clamp. It was the pipe used to assault his sister in his vision. In the corner was the old red fire extinguisher. Don went over to the pipe and grabbed it with both hands, elongating the C clamp wide enough so he could slip it through. He opened his bag and put the pipe inside.

"He's down there now, Tim." Charlene's voice floated down to him. "The Carriage furniture supervisor said they did not send over anyone to check on a delivery. He's some imposter."

Don left the room in time to see the big security guard ease his way down the stairs. He was tanned and fit and had muscles bulging out of his neck, a buzz haircut, and a gold chain around his neck.

*Oh, that's Tim*, Don thought.

Charlene had sent the racy pictures to the muscle-bound freak who stood right outside the door of her office. Seemed fitting since they spent the workday close to each other. In any case, Don prepared himself. He was not going to let Tim or anyone else throw him out of there. He was not going to give them the pleasure.

"Who the fuck are you, buddy?" Tim asked.

Don felt the anger rising. More so than before. He placed his hand in his pocket and decided to look for a way out of this. One where he would not be touched because he did not want anyone in this place to touch him. But Tim moved toward him quickly. He was licking his chops. Guy like him was probably bored with the lack of action here. Probably moonlighted in the clubs of New York and was well acquainted with forcibly removing someone.

Don, with his hand on the eye, concentrated on something new. He wanted to know the future, specifically what this guy planned on doing. In an instant, Don could see the guy grabbing him by the arm, then Don resisting, and Tim pivoting on his heels to swoop around him and apply a chokehold. Don changed his thought process, and the sequence played back again from the beginning with Don pivoting on his left heel then circling around Tim until he could bolt up the stairs, but Tim would grab him by both legs and lift his legs from underneath him violently and Don would come crashing down the stairs face first.

Then the scene rewound to the beginning again, and Don scrambled to think of something else he could do. While he was thinking through all his movements, he thought about something else. Why was he not being hit? Tim was less than a yard away from him when the eye started showing him images of his future, and it had to be thirty seconds or more that had passed by. In any case, not being pummeled while he worked things out was good enough for him. So he kept at it.

Don kept going through all the moves he could make to get away from Tim untouched, and when he had it down, he released the eye. To his surprise, it was like when he kept rewinding the thoughts in his mind; Tim started right from where his visions would start, and he was moving fast.

Don went through his sequence; he made a motion as if he were going to throw a punch, and Tim tried to close the gap even faster, leaving Don open to pivot on his heels and shift his body weight. As Tim was lunging forward, he went to grab Don but missed. Using his momentum against him, Don grabbed his arm and used his hips to topple Tim's center of gravity. Before Tim could blink, he was airborne. Don held on to his arm so Tim couldn't brace himself, and he came crashing down on his head. There was cracking and crashing as his legs hit the empty storage shelves against the wall and they tumbled down onto his body.

Don ran up the stairs after adjusting his backpack. He walked past the small crowd of onlookers, including Charlene, at the top of the stairs.

"Investigation concluded," he said to her. "The couch is in your living room anyway. Good day!"

Don walked out of the warehouse with no one else trying to stop him.

# CHAPTER 10

Blood was racing through Don's veins. He could not go home. He could not eat. He could not even sit down. He was pumped. Excited. He rode the adrenaline high all the way on the train to Manhattan. Around five in the afternoon, he called home to his mother and told her he was going to the library to study.

"Will you make it home for dinner?" she asked.

Monday evening was family dinner. The one day of the week when everyone put their hectic schedules and extracurricular activities aside and sat down together for a meal. Every Monday at 7:30 p.m., like clockwork, they sat at the table, held hands, and gave thanks as a family.

"I will be there," said Don, knowing he wouldn't make it.

He pressed the screen to end the call and left the subway, entering the streets of Manhattan. A vendor was standing outside his store selling various T-shirts and other items. Don spied a baseball cap. The Mets. He bought it with cash and pulled it down tight over his head. He looked up between the skyscrapers as the sun was beginning to set, then checked the GPS on his phone for the exact location. He circled around several blocks, trying not to get too close to the house.

He surveyed the neighborhood. He wanted to know all he could about the layout. Where he could run or hide if he needed to. He looked for watchful eyes, and most of all, he looked for cameras.

Holding the eye as he walked, he could think about who was watching him and the eye would show him. He could then move his head or lower his hat as needed to conceal himself. He plotted his next move as he walked. If he was seen inside the house, it would not be good. Don did not want to drag Connor's wife and child into this fight. This was between Connor and Don. Nor did he want the police to show up before he was finished.

Connor lived in a group of brownstones. Nice neighborhood. Several people on the block had open blinds and open windows—a confrontation on the street would surely be noticed. He needed somewhere private. Not in the house and not somewhere on the street. But somewhere in between. He'd wanted to catch Connor leaving the subway station, but it was too late. Connor was home.

He was eating dinner and then talking with his wife and playing with his child. That sense of normalcy was not going to deter Don from doing what he'd come here to do. He knew it was just a façade. He knew the real Connor Richardson. The perverted monster who needed to be dealt with. The laughing and living a seemingly innocent family life was like a show. A performance. Don was not about to let those peaceful images soften his heart.

He circled a few more blocks, making his range as wide as possible, hoping no one would see him repeat any type of pattern and grow suspicious toward him. It was getting later and darker. Fewer people on the streets. A repeating pattern would cause attention. He thought it best that he head back to the trains and return home. He had four days to make a plan and execute it. Maybe he could sneak back out of the house after everyone was asleep and wait for Connor in the darkness.

It had been a long day, and he was exhausted. Too many emotions. It was draining. He checked the time. He was going to be late for dinner and was preparing himself for a sound scolding. Don walked back to the subway and headed down the stairs. He checked with the eye one more time and saw Connor was preparing to leave. He could see Connor's wife saying something and showing him an empty jar of mayonnaise. He had to be heading to the store.

Don doubled back, up the stairs and out onto the sidewalk. He was about three blocks away from where Connor lived, so he hurried to get there by the time Connor left the house, but he was too far away. He could see Connor walking down the street to the corner and around it. Down the block halfway and into a small convenience store.

Don stopped to go over his plan. He would go in there, confront Connor, and bash his face in. There were a few people inside the store. Then there was the guy behind the counter. What would he do about an attack in his store? Don pulled a T-shirt he had worn in gym that day out of his bag. It was black with no distinguishing writing or patterns on it. Great. He would tie the shirt around his nose and mouth, partially concealing his face before he pulled out the pipe and did his thing. If he covered his face beforehand, the guy might think he was being robbed and react accordingly. For this plan to work, Don had to avoid the cameras in the store. He used the eye to check the angles with the guy behind the counter. With his blue ballcap pulled down toward his eyes as low as possible, he quickly entered the store.

It was set up like most convenience stores. Just a quick place to stop to grab the items you would normally get at a real grocery store but didn't have time for. No great choices or variety. One of each, two if you were lucky. Bread, milk, eggs, cheese, ketchup, mustard, mayonnaise, paper cups, canned goods, drinks, hot dogs, lunch meat, and plenty of junk food. Four aisles of stuff, with the beer, soda, and energy drinks behind the glass refrigerator door at the rear.

Don held his T-shirt balled up in his left hand. His backpack on his back, right hand in his pocket. He knew where the cameras were, so he twisted and turned to avoid a clear image of his face. He gave them nothing that could identify him. Once past the main cameras, he kept his head down toward his target. Connor was leaning down looking at stuff on the bottom shelf, some sort of canned milk, possibly baby formula. Don walked up to him and stopped. He said nothing. Just stood over Connor as he was searching for what he wanted. The pair of sneakers close by caused Connor to look up in aggravation. His slightly peeved look quickly turned to shock as he saw who was standing over him.

"You're a fucking sicko," said Don.

Connor stood. He was a little taller than Don. Maybe six foot, two inches. He had a slight athletic build, something Don did not pick up on the first time he saw him.

"Do I know you?" said Connor.

Don didn't mean to laugh. It escaped before he knew it. This guy was cool under pressure. Didn't flinch. Didn't even bat an eye. "Twelve-year-old girls. That's what you're into, isn't it?"

"I would watch my mouth if I were you," said Connor. "I am not going to stand here and take crap like that from a punk kid. You have the wrong guy. Whoever you think I am, you're wrong."

Connor tried to walk away, but Don stepped in front of him. Connor stopped and backed away, visibly frustrated. "Let's not do this, OK? You want some money? Are you trying to rob me, is that it? Extortion? I don't know you, and I don't know what you're talking about, so if you don't leave me alone, I am going to call the cops."

"Call them," said Don. "Take out your phone and call them. While you're at it, why not pull up the picture of my little sister and explain how someone in Manhattan has a picture of a twelve-year-old girl who lives in Long Island?"

"What?" said Connor. "You are taking this too far. What kind of shit is this? Kid, I am going to scream for help and have the store owner call the cops for me. Then you can explain your behavior to them."

*Did the eye get it wrong?* The conviction with which Connor spoke was overwhelming. Don had envisioned Connor cowering in fear after being confronted, stuttering and stammering while begging for mercy, but he got none of that. Don saw the vision, saw the room, the pipe, everything. He was so sure about what he was going to do before, but now he was having doubts.

"Pull out your phone," said Don. "Show me you don't have pictures of my sister on there, and I will let you go." He touched the eye one more time to see what it said about Connor's future.

"Let me go?" said Connor. He saw Don's hand slowly sliding into his pocket. "OK, kid, I'll show you my phone."

Connor went into his back pocket. Don was instantly given a vision. It was his immediate future. Don could see Connor thrusting a knife into his chest. Don would fall back, clutching at his wound. Connor would escape. Don would see him run around the end of the aisle and out of sight as he clutched his chest. The blood. There was so much blood. It was hard to think he would survive it. Then the vision ended abruptly.

In the present, Connor's hand came forward and Don could only get a glimpse at what looked like a knife. He saw it even before his mind registered the click of the switchblade. He instinctively pulled his backpack into his body as Connor tried to thrust the blade into his midsection. The blade stabbed clothing and schoolbooks and did not get anywhere near Don's chest. With his other hand, Connor pushed Don into the shelves and tried to run for the door.

Little did he know Don was already holding the pipe concealed in his backpack. As Connor tried to slip past, Don smashed Connor on top of the head. Connor fell into the middle of the aisle.

Everything happened so fast. Wait, Don thought. Sure, when he envisioned the plan, he pictured punching Connor in the face a few times. Maybe stomping his guts as he lay on the floor, but that was it. This was getting out of hand. His heart was racing in a panic. Where was all this leading? He hit Connor over the head with a pipe! The only reason he took the pipe from the storage area was because Connor would later use it to…

Don could see the guy behind the counter duck and grab the phone. The knife had slid across the floor. In Connor's back pocket, he saw the phone. Don grabbed it. He took Connor's finger and used it for the fingerprint ID. He went to the photo icon and into the folders. Everything was right there. Pictures of his sister. He was right. This was justified. He could escape knowing he had saved his sister, however, he kept swiping at images.

There were other girls on that phone, some as young as seven or eight years of age. At the beach in bathing suits and at shopping malls. At parks and playgrounds and everywhere a family would take their little girls to have a good time, this son of a bitch would be there snapping photos for his collection.

What about them? Were they safe? Don posed the question in his mind, and the eye showed him. Don stopped him from targeting Jasmine, but that would only make his hunger worse. The eye displayed the faces of other victims spanning decades. Eight young girls in his future before he would get caught again. All raped, most of them murdered and disposed of.

Don didn't just see their suffering, he felt it. Each one. And in every frightened face he saw his sister, pleading for someone to help. Connor would go to jail for the rest of his life, but those lives would still be destroyed. Families pleading with Connor to show them where the bodies were buried while Connor continued to profess his innocence.

Don slipped the phone into his pocket. His soul gripped by the images of terrified young girls screaming for help. He picked up the black tee and tied it around his face. Connor was on the ground crawling, begging for aid. After securing the shirt on his face, Don kicked the knife away from Connor's reach. Another person in the store came around the corner as if he were going to help Connor. The man was about three feet from Don. With his face covered, Don held the pipe straight out toward the man, warning him not to get involved.

"Help me, help me," said Connor, pleading to the man.

"This is none of your concern," said Don to the man.

He held his hand up in a gesture. Open palms toward Don. Then he slowly backed away.

The rest was easier than he thought it would be. Don raised the pipe and brought it down on Connor's head, again and again. He lost count. With each blow the image of another young face was affixed in his mind. He kept striking until he could see parts of Connor's skull cavity. Then he stood over him. His skin was speckled in blood. So were his pants, shirt, and shoes. After calming himself, he picked up Connor's phone and dropped it into his backpack along with the pipe. By that time, the man looking to play Good Samaritan was long gone; he'd run out the door while Don was in a bludgeoning frenzy.

Don looked for the guy behind the counter. He was gone too. Probably made it to the back room to safety. Don touched the eye and told it to look for anyone watching the store. There was one guy, the one who was inside the store and he'd warned to stay out of it, and a young woman who was about to enter who he'd probably stopped at the door. Don asked the eye to look through their pasts, and he found their names. He made sure the hat was down and the makeshift mask was still in place. He hit the sidewalk and looked directly at them.

"Don't play the hero. Put the phone down, April Gardener, who lives two blocks from here and has a son named Christopher. Stay out of it like Barnaby Wilson, standing next to you. This has nothing to do with you."

She dropped her phone on the concrete, and Don took off in the other direction. His study of the landscape served him well. At this point, he knew these streets like the back of his hand. He ran with the eye clenched in his palm, asking it who was watching him, who was around the corner, and where the cops were located, while navigating his way through the dark, hidden areas of the street. The images came in flashes, like warnings, when he was being watched.

Don found a hidden area and ducked inside when he was sure no one was looking. It was an alley behind a group of businesses. He saw no cameras nearby. It was a dead zone. He pulled a pair of shorts out of his bag and put them on. Took the T-shirt off his face and put it on his body. Put his pants, hat, and hoodie in the backpack and went back out of the alley as if he were jogging. He kept a steady pace, checking with the eye here and there to make sure no one was following him. After a good mile or two, he looked for the subway and got on a train back to Long Island.

# CHAPTER 11

She barely heard the click of the door closing, but it was enough to awaken her. Sara Silver looked at the clock on the nightstand of Don's room. It was after 1:00 a.m. Across the darkened space, she could see him looking at her. He was sitting at his desk and didn't seem startled to see her. He was calm and assured, in no way ashamed or defiant. But why? It was not like him to be out so late. This was his first time ever exceeding curfew. He was seventeen, and she remembered what she was like when she was that age. She was rebellious to the point it made her mother sick. She understood what it was like to want so desperately to be treated like an adult.

Yet, she had to let him know it was not OK.

"Where were you?" she asked firmly. She could feel her jaw tightening in anticipation of his excuse.

"There was something I had to take care of, Mom," he said plainly. "Please understand."

"You could have sent a text or called. I sent you"—she looked at her phone—"twelve texts and called three times. You could have responded just once…and you missed family dinner."

His eyes dropped in regret. Good. It was nice to see he was still penitent. Family dinner was important to her. Especially since she knew that in a year, he would no longer be sitting at the table with her. This was her baby boy. He wouldn't remain her baby forever. She knew that. But this defiance was not like him. No response by text or call. She worried something could have happened to him. Didn't he understand?

"Sorry about that, Mom," he said. "As I told you, there was something I had to take care of that could not wait."

"What?" she asked. "There are no secrets here. Not in this house." Had he been with a girl? Was that it?

He pressed his lips together tightly and forced air through his nose in frustration. "You will have to trust me."

Flabbergasted, she asked, "How can I?"

He sighed again. "Someone was planning on hurting Jasmine, and I put a stop to it."

Her body straightened. Got taller. "What do you mean? Who? What did you do?"

"I told you I took care of it."

She struggled to find words, looking around the room as if that would help her. "You can't just drop a bomb like that and tell me you took care of it. What is going on, Adonis? Do we need to get the police involved?"

"No police," he said. "They would have only made it worse."

Her head was spinning as she tried to process the vague bits of information he was feeding her. Was this serious? Was it a verbal threat made against Jasmine? A bully at school? Had he stumbled upon some kind of plot among students? In her lack of understanding, her eyes were beginning to adjust to the darkness. She noticed the black T-shirt he was wearing because there was something off about it. Shining.

"Is that blood?" she said.

Adonis said nothing. He just looked into her eyes. It was not a cold look. Not distant or defiant. Not scared or apprehensive. It was the stare of someone in complete control. No uneasiness. No nervousness. Even in the face of the interrogation, with blood on his shirt, he had no fear of what came next.

"Did you get into trouble, Adonis?"

"I'm not in any trouble. Things could not have gone any better."

Adonis was always obedient. He never raised his voice to her in anger or even gave her an intimidating look. He was the most responsible person she knew, even though he was only seventeen years old. He was dependable to a fault. He was also a genius. Much smarter than she ever was at his age. He had to understand the blood on his shirt and his cryptic words were not going to put her mind at ease.

"You know we have the meeting at the college this weekend," she said to him with her voice cracking slightly. It was a test. If he'd done something to jeopardize his career and his future, he would probably look at his visit to Yale differently.

"I'll be ready," he said calmly. "If you don't mind, I would like to get some sleep. I have school in the morning."

"OK." She held out her hand. It was shaking. "Give me the shirt. I will wash it in the morning."

Don took off the shirt and then fished out his hoodie, pants, and hat from his backpack. "Here, you should wash these too." He lay down on his bed and fluffed the pillow under his head.

Sara looked at the clothes he pulled out of the bag, and her heart dropped. There was so much blood. She looked at him, and her vision grew blurry from her tears. "Did anybody see you, Adonis? Were you seen?"

"No, Mom. No worries."

His calmness kept her from screaming hysterically. She stuffed everything back into the backpack, quickly. "I will wash the backpack and get rid of the clothes."

He may have been too immature to understand the implications, but she was fully aware of what could happen. Washing was not good enough. She needed to burn the evidence. She went to take a step and felt uneasy on her knees. She walked slowly. Her mind went through all sorts of hideous scenarios where Don would be taken away, dragged out of the house on his knees, and prosecuted like a common thug. Did he beat this person up? Was it someone from Jasmine's school? Anything like this on his record, and he could kiss all his scholarships goodbye. His bright future thrown away.

All he would say was he was protecting his little sister. Over what she did not know. But she trusted him. That was the strange thing. It made no sense for a mother to trust a seventeen-year-old boy because she remembered what it was like to be at that age. *They think they have things figured out but really have no clue. So sure of themselves, yet so ignorant.*

Sara had the backpack in hand when she stopped at the door. She was going to plead with him to tell her exactly what had happened, where he was, what he did, and who he did it to. But after she turned around, she could see he was sound asleep. Peacefully. On his side with both hands under his pillow, like the very image of an innocent child resting.

She gasped in horror. His future was in jeopardy. And here he was, without a care in the world.

## CHAPTER 12

Detective Kevin Duval had a great record clearing cases. His partner Carrol was older and had been a cop longer, but Carrol was new to the department. Arrived there about six months ago from Boston, where he'd worked in narcotics. Undercover. He needed a change, both from the career and the city, so he'd come to New York and pulled a few favors to get into homicide. But Duval was the rising star. The hotshot of the duo. It was no surprise when Duval got the call in the middle of the night to investigate a brutal murder inside a bodega. Especially after the chief informed him the victim was the oldest son of a man running for governor.

He ran his hands over his face, rubbing the sleep from his eyes as he sat on the bed. His beautiful wife of nine years was sound asleep. Out cold after a passionate night of lovemaking. He didn't get the opportunity often in his line of work. Dinner uninterrupted, no emergency calls from the babysitter, a walk through the park under moonlight, and then…it was a perfect evening. Yet, just before midnight, here he was, back on the grind.

Through the bedroom blinds, he could see the flashing strobes of police lights. Carrol may have been divorced for the fourth time, borderline drunk, not the most observant or worthy of promotion any further than he already was, but he was dedicated to the job. And he was always ready to roll.

Duval rubbed some lotion over his brown skin and got dressed. He kissed his wife on the cheek; she grunted and smacked her lips together several times. Then he went downstairs and out the door. From wake-up to the car in less than five minutes.

He sat down in the passenger's seat of the Cadillac CTS. Detective Arnold Carrol's personal vehicle. That was his style from back in the narc days. Black with black interior. Comfortable leather seats. He buckled in and looked down into the cup holders in the center console. There were two cups.

"One for me?" he asked.

"Check to see which one is warm," said Carrol. "The other is my spit cup."

"Fucking gross," said Duval, turning away with a frown.

Carrol laughed. "You know I don't do that shit. I smoke…The cold cup has my ashes in it."

"Oh, much better," said Duval. He felt for the warm cup and took the lid off to check before taking a sip. Black coffee. The best.

Carrol had dark-brown hair that was graying at the sides. Thick guy with a little extra girth in the midsection. Everything on him was big. He had a big, bushy mustache that covered his upper lip. He had big forearms and long hair on the back of his palms. Everything he wore was from Goodwill. Blue shirt, brown tie, brown slacks…anything he could find that fit. He claimed that after the fourth divorce, it was all he could afford.

Duval was not exactly the epitome of style, but at least his jacket and pants matched as a suit. He kept them dry-cleaned and pressed to make them look more expensive than they actually were. He pulled down the visor and slid open the cosmetic mirror to check himself. Important people were bound to be at the scene. Reporters and brass from the force. His hair was brushed and wavy. Eyebrows tamed and not a wrinkle on his clothes. Charcoal-gray jacket and pants, light-gray shirt, black tie.

Duval lived in Whitestone, Queens, not too far from the bridge. They would be in Manhattan in less than twenty minutes with lights blazing.

"Who is the guy running for governor again?" asked Duval.

"Barney Richardson," said Carrol. "An ex-prosecutor from upstate. He made a lot of friends during his time. His platform is tough on crime."

"His son…didn't he get protection?"

"Claimed no one knew who he was so he didn't need it. If his father won the election, he would change his mind." His big blue eyes turned from the road to Duval. "Too late for protection now!"

"With the internet, how could he be so naïve?" Duval took a sip of coffee. Colombian Roast. It smelled as good as it tasted. "Do you think this is politically motivated?"

"Absolutely. With all the whack jobs running the streets, this could be a sick message. We need to play this one by the books. All eyes will be on us."

Duval was thinking the same thing.

West 88th Street and West End Avenue: the Upper West Side of New York City. At the other end of the block was a tourist attraction: the apartment building in *Will & Grace*. The streets were blocked off by police cruisers. Uniformed officers controlled who got inside the blockade.

They parked and made their way to the first officer they saw. Duval and Carrol flashed credentials and walked between the cruisers. Captain Reynolds was there in a red windbreaker and blue sweatpants with sneakers. He was known to work out at odd hours in one of those twenty-four-hour gyms. He was in his late fifties, but besides the spider-leg-type wrinkles in the corner of his eyes, you never would have guessed.

"The chief is on his way," he said to them. "Get in there and give me something."

*They woke up the chief,* he thought. This was bigger than he expected. Well after midnight, and residents were out of their homes trying to get a glimpse. Reporters were gathering as well. Setting up cameras down the street in view of the crime scene. He counted twenty officers and estimated nearly sixty residents along with three vans belonging to the press.

He snapped on his vinyl gloves after Carrol handed him a pair. A sea of blue uniforms parted when they got close to the entrance of the bodega. On the floor was a body in an awful bloody mess, face down, arms spread out. The victim's head was bashed in to the point some of his brains were visible. Speckles of blood dotted the white ceiling tiles above.

"Murder weapon?" asked Duval, still looking upward.

"Witness said it was a pipe," said one of the officers. "The clerk saw the perp hit him over the head as the vic tried to escape."

"Then he went to town on the back of his skull," said Carrol, bending down at the knees. "It's a message. A political message. Antifa!"

"Now is not the time for this shit, Detective," said the captain. "The chief is…"

Captain Reynolds was interrupted by a commotion outside. Duval stood and peered through the window of the bodega. Camera crews were chasing after someone who'd crossed the police boundary. A man, early sixties, white shirt, red tie. Important looking. He was wrestling with officers, trying to get inside. The bright lights of the cameras were on him. He was screaming. Wailing. He wanted to see his son. Carrol stepped in front of Duval, blocking his view.

"Gubernatorial Candidate Barney Richardson," said Carrol. He was smirking. He often did when his theories were proven to be true.

But Duval was more concerned with the scene outside. The cameras, they were eating it up. The future governor's son had been murdered on the Upper West Side of Manhattan, and the future governor was hysterical. Officers fought to gain control while being respectful. Reporters were chatting away, describing the scene as it was happening. Through the open door, a pair of eyes locked onto Duval. He stood tall with very little expression on his face. Chief Jonathan McGlinchey.

Duval stared back and thought it was good he and his wife had had a great night out. It might be their last one in a while.

# CHAPTER 13

On Saturday, Don was in the city of New Haven, Connecticut, touring the campus of Yale University. The sky was cloudy, but rain was not in the forecast. People were scattered all about the campus. It was difficult to tell who were the students and who was roaming around admiring the architecture. It was a beautiful campus. Green and luscious with Gothic buildings that gave parts of the campus the look of a medieval city. The clock tower and cathedral were something straight out of *The Hunchback of Notre Dame*. It was a place that felt good to him. The atmosphere was everything he thought an institution of higher learning should be. With a guidebook in his left hand, Don walked through the courtyards, taking it all in.

In front of him, leading the way, were his parents. His mom was wearing a sweater over a brown blouse, with a black skirt and flat shoes because she knew there would be plenty of walking. There was a chill in the air, and Don noticed her pulling the sleeves down over her wrists past the palms. His father was wearing a hoodie and jeans. Don wondered if it was because he was trying to look young and not like a dad sending his oldest off to college. Mom was talking, explaining this and that about what Don could expect come the fall.

Yet, her voice lacked the usual energy she exuded.

She held on to her husband's hand firmly. Her steps were not as carefree. Don knew the reason, but it couldn't be helped. She was worried about the bloody clothes she'd taken from him. The ones she'd burned in a trash can in the yard. She was worried someone would be coming to get him. That he would have to explain himself and his actions. But she had nothing to worry about. Don had thought about explaining it to her many times but decided against it. It was best she did not know. So she talked about the various parts of the campus she'd roamed more than twenty years ago with a twinge of anxiety ever present. Wondering if the future would become a nightmare.

And it would have been if Don had not taken action. Imagine if she'd returned home to find Jasmine was missing.

"Let's get something to eat," said Joe. "I'm starving." He turned around to look at Don following behind them. "What do you say? Hungry?"

"I'm famished," said Don.

They ventured off campus, down the streets of New Haven, where there were businesses and restaurants. A burger joint caught Don's eye, and he suggested they eat there. It was on Temple Street. It felt woodsy and cozy. A popular spot for students according to Don's guidebook. They sat down in a booth on the left side of the restaurant. Menus lay on the table. They had all kinds of choices—gourmet burgers, sandwiches, and for Joe there were plenty of draft beers on tap.

Don watched his mother as her eyes drifted down; she was looking at the menu but not seeing it.

"Mediterranean burger," said Joe, snapping his head up from his menu. "It's perfect. What are you getting, Don?"

Don wiggled his lips left and right. "The quinoa crunch burger sounds good."

"Quinoa patty?" said Joe. "Don, are you going to be some kind of yuppie when you grow up? You probably already speak the coffee-house lingo, don't you? Double shot, whip, foam, latte yatte batte. And what the hell is with the sizes? In every language that uses the word, *grande* is the big one!"

"I don't drink coffee…and Dad, it's called eating healthy. You should try it sometime. Might shrink that beer gut of yours."

"Do you hear this smart-mouth kid, Sara? Just for that, I am getting two grande glasses of beer with my meal. And when I say grande, I bet they will bring me the biggest glass they have! I already know what your mom is getting. It's the kale falafel pita, am I right? I could call her a yuppie, too, but she is just Jewish."

Sara barely smiled. She stared at Don, a look of concern welling in her eyes.

"Your boy will be fine, Sara," said Joe, cognizant of her anxiety. He placed his hand on top of hers. "He can handle this place. He's grown to be a fine young man."

"He sure has," said Sara, nodding. She looked into Joe's eyes. She wanted to tell him something.

"I need to use the men's room," said Don. "I'll be right back."

Her nerves seemed so fragile that she might break down in tears any moment, so he had to get away. Don slid out of the booth and walked toward the back of the restaurant where the bathrooms were. He entered the small bathroom with one stall and one urinal, looked into the mirror above the sink, hit the soap dispenser, and began washing his hands. He snapped off a couple of paper towels to dry his hands and then exited.

Between the men's and women's restrooms was a corkboard where people hung various business cards, notices for roommates, and flyers for rooms for rent. But one thing in particular caught his attention. There was a sign up asking if anyone had seen a young woman who was a student at Yale. She had been missing for three weeks now. There was a picture of her above the description.

Charisma Starlette, brown hair, blue eyes, bright big smile. Five-foot-seven, 118 pounds. *Tall enough to be noticed and small enough to be easily overpowered by someone a hundred pounds heavier,* Don thought. Sad story, and his concern would have ended right there under normal circumstances, but he began thinking. *Maybe she's hiding and doesn't want to be found.* She was twenty years old. Perhaps she could have decided school was not the thing for her and taken off to explore the world. Find her better self. Could be camping out somewhere in California with a new man she met online. Who knew?

He could find out very easily. Don decided to take a look. He touched the eye in his pocket and thought about the girl. It was much easier if he had a face; all he had to do was picture it, and the eye would do the rest.

She was alive. But in serious trouble.

The men's room door opened, and a young man walked out. He looked to be about Don's age, probably a future classmate. He had sandy-blond hair and glasses. His head was down, but he glanced up at Don as he walked past.

"Excuse me," said Don. "I wonder if I could ask you something?"

He stopped and turned to Don, saying nothing. Waiting. He looked somewhat sheepish. Like the whole experience of being there was overwhelming.

"Can I borrow your phone for a minute?" said Don. "My battery has gone dead, and I need to find my parents. We got separated on campus somewhere. It's huge, isn't it?"

"Ginormous," said the teen. He pulled out his phone and handed it to Don after putting in his passcode.

Don turned his head with the phone and dialed the number on the flyer. He then said what he had to say and handed the phone back to the teen.

"Weird," said the teen. "Is that some sort of code for where to find you?"

"You mean what I told my parents?" asked Don. "Yeah. It is a code. Turns out they were here in the restaurant all along. Thanks."

Don walked away as the teen was preparing to speak. It was possible he wanted to introduce himself, but Don was not feeling the same sort of sentiment or comradery. He needed to get back to the table. His mother's mental well-being was on his mind. When Don slid into his side of the booth, drinks were already on the table. He tried to read the mood of his parents, but their attention turned to the teenager standing beside Don. He'd followed Don back to the table.

He stuck out his hand awkwardly and said, "I'm Tim Dusseldorf."

Don looked at his parents and then took Tim's hand. "I'm Don Silver. Pleasure."

Tim turned to Don's parents. "Sir…ma'am." And with a nod of his head, he left the restaurant.

"What was that?" asked Joe.

"I met him in the restroom. He's a future classmate."

Still, it was troubling. Don did not want Tim to know his name, which was why he'd tried to be as distant as possible while borrowing his phone, but Tim had not let it end there. Tim's forcefulness was something Don had not anticipated. Don wondered if there would be repercussions for being careless. He touched the eye to use its gifts. He looked into the future of the missing girl, then into the past of Tim Dusseldorf.

There was something strange about it. He went from Charisma's future to Tim's and saw one thing in particular. A shadow. A void shaped like a man. It was tall and thin. White gloves on its hands. Large, pearly teeth fixed in a smile. The rest of the body was not really there. As if a body should've been there but had been stripped away, leaving only an outline. Inside was a black nothingness.

It spoke to him. It was the first time his dealings with the eye had produced any sound at all.

"Your aplomb overshadows most men like a darkened abyss," said the being. "It will lead to your downfall."

Don was not sure how to respond. He was sitting at the table with his parents. If he spoke aloud, it would be bad. He talked with his mind. "Come again?" said Don.

"You are not in the least bit shocked by my presence, are you?" the being asked.

"How could I be?" said Don. "I have used the eye and I know of its power, so meeting another powerful being outside this world should not be shocking at all. Are you the reason Zadie hid the eye away?"

"Very perceptive as well," said the being. He moved closer, moving slow and smooth. His fingers danced like the legs of a spider walking on a web. "Most who stumble upon the eye have big dreams of what is possible, until they actually change something to their benefit. From that moment on, they are able to see me. The more I appear, the more it haunts them. Especially after the first time I speak to them. Yet, you are taking this encounter completely different. As if you expected something like this."

"It would be foolish to possess such a thing without it being coveted. By beings of this world and the next. However, I will not let it go unattended. I am going to keep using it. And I get the impression you can do little about that. If you had the power to take it, it would not have been sitting behind a pile of old newspapers in my great-grandfather's house."

"You abuse its power, Adonis Silver."

"The pervert was after my sister, and so I dealt with it!"

"And the other man who had the women trapped in cages?" the being asked, its smile and large teeth glistening. "You didn't know them. They were not family. Yet you set up a timely accident for the captor, and now he is dead. You saved the two women, yes, but did he really deserve to die as well?"

That was two days ago. It was the women he'd seen trapped in a basement when he was sitting in the park Monday afternoon. He'd thought about how they could use his help. He hadn't wanted to confront the man personally, as his mother might suffer a nervous breakdown if she found out, so he'd thought of something clever instead.

"You disapprove of my sense of judgment?" asked Don.

"Taking justice into your own hands might seem like something noble, but it is a double-edged sword. Always has been and always will be."

"No one else is doing anything about it. I thought I would fill the void."

"Watch what you say," said the being. One of its long, gloved fingers pointed at him. "You could have thrown a hint to the cops by telling them everything you've seen. If you were smart, you would be able to connect them with hard evidence that lands these people in jail. Those are the laws of your people. The laws of your land, which you should adhere to."

"Sorry, but I believe otherwise."

"People will take notice if you continue, Adonis. What happens when those same humans whose job it is to seek justice begin to view you as the threat?"

"I can handle them."

"You astound me, Adonis Silver. Can that confidence hold up in the face of an opponent like me? Especially since I am letting you know I am here for the eye?"

"I guess we will find out," said Don, smitten by the challenge. "Who are you?"

"I am Tartarus, the angel who presides over hell. In a way, my name is indistinguishable as a term for hell itself."

"So hell is going to come after me," said Don. "Thanks for the warning. I have to go now."

"Adonis…Adonis!" said Sara.

Don could see his mother. Her hand was on his hand as it was stretched across the table; she was shaking it.

"Sorry," he said. "I zoned out there for a few seconds."

"It was more like ten seconds," said his father, looking deeply concerned. "I see what Jasmine was talking about…and why your mother was so concerned. You need to get checked out. When is the appointment, honey, Wednesday?"

She didn't speak. Her lips pressed together tightly, and she shook her head as if she were refusing to let her grief take hold.

"You are going to make sure you make that appointment, Don," said Joe. "Do you hear me, or do I have to drag you there myself?"

"No, Father. I will be there," said Don.

# CHAPTER 14

She had faith. Siobhan Starlette listened to the messages on her phone on a regular basis. When she first put up the flyers for her missing sister, she used to answer them directly. That was when she got a quick lesson on the sick side of humanity. You would think people would have a general concern and respect for the safety of another human being, but no. From people telling her they had her sister in a freezer, to others claiming she was a whore, a slut, and a degenerate, to men claiming Charisma's mouth was full and she couldn't talk right now, to others asking Siobhan for a date after hearing her voice—it was extremely disheartening. The average number of calls was about forty-five per day. Siobhan would relentlessly answer with the hope this was the one serious and genuine call regarding the whereabouts of her sister. She had faith, but it was surely tested.

The search was entering its third week. She called the police station and asked the detective working the case for daily updates so much that the detective began ducking her calls. Every single day, she went to church and prayed with the priest, asking God to return her sister to her. She checked her messages, posted flyers, and asked people on the street, as exhausting and frustrating as it was, until that fateful call came through and it appeared her resolve had been rewarded.

The message began by saying her sister had a scar on her right knee that came from a stingray barb. Siobhan was five years older than Charisma so she remembered it well. When Charisma was six years old, she was playing in the waters at a beach in Florida and stepped on a small stingray that was slightly buried in the sand. As a reflex, the ray whipped his tail, inserting the sharp edge of the barb into her knee and breaking it off there as it sped away. Who would know that unless it was someone who was close enough to see the scar and ask questions about it?

This was someone with physical knowledge of Charisma, so she listened further. The next words provided an address. It was on the edge of the city. Afterward, the instructions were very clear, and they ended by saying she should take the Arab-looking guy with the beard with her. That was very important.

That was it. She played the message repeatedly to make sure she got it right. The problem for Siobhan was she did not know any Arab with a beard, or an *Arab-looking guy*, as the message stated. Who was he talking about? Everything else was specific. "Do not notify the police, or your sister will be shot in the head," it said. "Follow these instructions, and she will be returned safely." The address was specific, the date to go there was specific, the time was specific, the direction she should travel to get to the address, specific. But the Arab-looking guy? It could be anybody.

She had to figure it out. The date was tomorrow evening, and she was supposed to be at the address at 8:47 p.m. That was over thirty-five hours from when she first heard the message. It was the longest thirty-five hours of her life. She could not sleep. She could not eat. Her mind swam endlessly from the joys of being able to hug her sister again to the pain of identifying her lifeless, abused body at the morgue. She had no idea what to expect or if she should even trust the message. But she had to. Outside of messages from people who thought they'd seen Charisma here and there, this was the only solid bit of information she had.

By 8:15 p.m., she was on the verge of collapse. Siobhan got in her tiny Chevy Volt and loaded the address into the GPS. By this time, she knew the directions by heart but chose to load the address into her phone anyway. The synthetic female voice was somewhat soothing and reassuring. She could trust it to guide her on her way into the dark unknown where her highest hopes could be crushed like they had been so many times in the past three weeks. But she held on to that final sliver of hope and drove on.

It was a townhouse on the corner. A neighborhood she knew about but had never visited before. Cars were in a line all down the block on both sides of the street. Siobhan circled the same block twice looking for a space to slip into. She decided to go two blocks down and try those streets. She was early, so she would still make the 8:47 p.m. time frame. But there was no Arab or Arab-looking guy with her. It was too vague of a description, and she'd run herself ragged calling friends, trying to find someone who looked like that with a beard.

She found a space, parked her car, and checked the time, then placed her phone into her pocket and got out of the car. Her legs were wobbly, her hands visibly shaking. But this was it. It was time to push the doorbell and retrieve her sister.

Siobhan turned the corner and decided to walk down the main street because it was well lit and other people were about. She felt safer. She passed by local businesses, most of which were closed for the evening. On the corner, about a block away, she saw a group of young men hanging out on the corner. They were speaking Spanish. She took a deep breath and crossed the street. She was now on the same block as the townhouse, but it was on the opposite end.

Instinctively, she pulled the flyer out of her pocket because she wanted to hold it up so that whoever opened the door could see her sister's face. She was about fifty feet from the corner when someone called out to her.

"Hey, you! Hold up!"

It was one of the men hanging out on the corner. Normally, she would not pay any attention to the catcalls. She was attractive and knew that wherever she walked late at night, there was bound to be someone trying to get her attention. But she was tired and frustrated and frankly, she did not give a damn, so she turned all the way around to face him. The man was walking toward her with his hand raised. Waving. He was a big guy. Hispanic. And he had a beard.

*Arab-looking guy with a beard.*

"I see you holding that flyer of Charisma," said the young man.

"You know her?" said Siobhan.

"Hell, yeah. She was in one of my classes. She helped me out a ton."

Siobhan looked at him strangely.

"What?" said the man. "Some big, tough-looking Hispanic guy could not possibly go to Yale, right? Never mind, then. I was just trying to help put up flyers and shit, if that's what you were doing. Fuck it. I'm out."

"That's not why I was looking at you," said Siobhan. "Someone said…" She looked at her watch: 8:45 p.m. on the nose. "I need you to come with me to the house on the corner there."

He looked down the street. "On this corner right here? It should be vacant. People left about a month ago. Moved to Miami. My uncle owns that joint. He rents it out. But no one is there now. Trust me."

A warm feeling came over Siobhan. "No…that's the place, and I need you to come with me to check it out."

Just the sound of it, as she bounced around the details in her head, was crazy. It was reckless and foolish, and now she had some stranger with her and she was not sure if it was even the right guy or if he could help, but she had this feeling that would not let go. It was going to work. Tonight, she was going to get her sister back, just as the message had said.

He walked with her down the street to the last townhouse on the block. It was well maintained despite the news there had been no one occupying the property for at least a month. There were no lights on, no windows open, no blinds open, all curtains drawn. It looked the part of no one being inside.

Siobhan walked up to the front door and banged on it with a clenched fist. She tried the doorknob. It was locked. She peered into the window, hoping to catch a glimpse through the blinds. She took out her phone and activated the light to direct it inside the small cracks of the blinds. Then she banged on the door once more.

"I told you no one was here," said the man. "Who gave you this address? Why are you here?"

"Let's go around to the back," said Siobhan.

He led the way. They went around the corner to the small alley between the row of homes and through the back gate. The big guy went through first, looking around the small yard with tall grass. There was no sign of anything strange or unusual. They walked up the small row of stairs to the sliding glass door. He went to pull it open, but as expected, it was locked.

"Hey, what do you guys want?" said a voice.

Siobhan looked up at the house next door. A man leaned his head out of the window, looking down at them from the second floor. He was skinny, wearing a dingy white T-shirt. Ratty looking. Shaking like an addict in need of a fix. Behind him was a woman. She was bigger than he was, Hispanic, broad shoulders.

"What are you doing over there? I'm going to call the cops."

"Call them," said Siobhan.

"Wait…wo…what are you doing?" the Hispanic with the beard asked her. "My uncle owns the place. I told you that. He doesn't want any trouble." He looked up at the guy in the window. "No worries. My uncle owns the place. I was showing her the layout, that's all."

"Your uncle owns it?" the man asked. "Bullshit. The previous owners just left. Ramirez."

"Sorry, dude, they were renting from my uncle."

"Is that right?"

There was a brief moment of silence. The skinny guy turned to look at the woman standing behind him.

"OK," said the Hispanic with the beard. "We are leaving now."

"No, we are not!" said Siobhan. "My sister is missing, and I was told she was in this house."

"What? Are you serious? Why didn't you tell me before?"

"I needed you to come with me," said Siobhan.

"I don't know jack about your missing sister," said the guy in the window. "I've been keeping an eye on this place. Nobody has been here since the Ramirezes left. Go look somewhere else. You are disturbing the neighborhood."

The big Hispanic guy grabbed Siobhan by the arm. "Let's go."

She pulled free from his grip. "My sister is in there," she said, pointing to the sliding glass door.

The big guy jumped in between her and the door. "How do you know? Who did you get this address from? Was it someone who called the number? How many calls have you gotten with credible information? Twenty? A hundred? Listen, I feel for you. I want Charisma found as much as you do. But there is no one here. The neighbor would have seen them, and this place is locked up tight."

"What about the people who lived here? Did they take off suddenly? Could they have done something to my sister and then taken off to avoid getting caught? Who are they? Where are they now?"

"I will find out for you. I promise. But for now, let's get out of here. I don't want to attract too much attention. My uncle is…never mind. We need to go."

"My sister is missing, and I desperately want to bring her home. I don't give a fuck about attracting attention if it means she is coming home."

It struck her that she had bet everything, all of her emotions, hopes, and fears, on that one message she received two days ago. It was sobering. All of the tension left her body as she instantly grew numb. She looked up at the couple in the window next door and wanted to apologize but felt it did not matter, so she said nothing. As Siobhan walked away, tears glistened in her eyes. She was so sure this place was the one. Even though she felt stupid believing it.

The big guy jumped in front of her and turned to face her. "I promise you. I will ask my uncle about the people who lived there. He will be able to get some answers."

There was no reason for her to believe him. Desperation, she thought, because she felt somehow his words provided hope. It was pathetic. She got back to her car and cried with her head on the steering wheel for ten minutes. Then she started up the car and went home. She sat on the couch and tried to drink a beer, but after about half a bottle, she stopped. Not even that could hide the pain she felt. Sitting on the couch motionless was the only thing she could manage to do properly.

It was well after one in the morning when she received a phone call. Was she sleeping with her eyes open sitting on the couch? She could not remember. The time flew by, and it felt like an instant. She picked up her phone and looked at the caller ID. It said *Hartford County Services*, so she decided to answer it.

"Is this Siobhan Starlette?" said a voice.

"Yeah," she said. Her voice cracked and dry from weeping.

"This is the sheriff's department. We just picked up a young woman wandering on the side of the highway. She says her name is Charisma Starlette. We need you to come down to the station because…well, she was reported as a missing person and she has no identification. Right now she is with investigators telling her story."

The phone slipped from Siobhan's hand.

# CHAPTER 15

At the breakfast table the following morning, Jasmine was wide-eyed and staring right at Don. It took him a moment to notice he had been staring at her first. And his mood toward seeing her was pleasant. The disturbing images of Jasmine's suffering were no more. Subconsciously, he was happy. Ecstatic, actually. A smile grew slowly across her face as she realized everything between them was OK. How could it not be? She was there with the family, none the wiser about what could have been.

He dug into his scrambled eggs and brisket, his favorite. Fried potatoes and leeks sat in a bowl at the center of the table. He scooped up another helping and shoveled it into his mouth. He was the same old Don again. Aloof but happy.

His joyous mood was contagious, invigorating Jasmine to the point she began to open up and be her normal self. Bright-eyed and smiling. Her glances toward him were no longer reserved and sheepish. She spoke to him directly for the first time in a week. "Did you hear about what happened not too far from here? It's all over Facebook."

"No, Jasmine," said Don, playing along with eyes even wider. "What happened?"

"You know about the man who died because his car fell on him while he was changing the brakes? There was more to it than that. Turns out the story was more like a horror movie."

"How so?" asked Don, pretending he did not know.

"The man who died had two women locked in his basement. He tricked them into coming here from Thailand, making them think they were coming to work at his company. Then he locked them up and made them his sex slaves!"

"What do you know about sex slaves?" said Joe, popping his head up from his plate. "And what are you doing reading that stuff anyway?"

"Sophia told me about it. The guy lived not too far away from the school."

"You shouldn't be reading garbage anyway, Jasmine," said Joe. "You're too young." He looked over at his wife. Her long black hair was down over her shoulders. Her head lost in the clouds, picking at her food.

"Crazy!" said Don. "Something like that going on so close to Jasmine's school." He hoped his mother would pick up on the parallels. Lighten the bearing on her shoulders. "Too many innocent people are being taken advantage of."

She did not budge. She barely acknowledged they were talking.

"He was the deacon of a church!" Jasmine added. "Sophia said her mom claimed it was a sign of the end of days."

"We don't believe in the end of days, sweetheart," said Joe.

And Don agreed. There was plenty of time left in this world, especially with the trafficker no longer among the living. His only wish was his mother would pick up on his hints and realize there was no need for worry. The world was becoming a better place. But she sulked, looking down at her plate of food, absent from the conversation.

"He got what he deserved," said Jasmine.

Don was euphoric about that as well. His plan had worked to perfection. It took nothing but a loose screw on a floor jack and a well-placed bolt wedged into the brake pad to bring the car crashing down on the man while he worked in the garage. His legs were pinned, and he was still very much alive after the jack collapsed. He had the opportunity to dial 911 as his cell phone was within reach, but he hesitated, knowing the paramedics would choose to bust down the front door as a means of entry. On their way to the garage, they would pass right by the door leading down to the basement.

There was a good chance the women would hear what was going on and call out to the paramedics. He had left them with a meal so they were not gagged, as they usually were when people came to the front door. Instead of taking the chance, he decided to work himself free and in the process ruptured an artery in his leg and bled out. It was the perfect form of judgment. Let the man's own fear of getting caught be his downfall.

The butterfly effect: the notion that a butterfly flapping its wings thirty years ago in Kyoto, Japan, was the impetus for a tornado in Oklahoma today. The problem with determining its relevance was trying to calculate the endless and infinite variables that went into the butterfly cause with the resultant effect. It could be tricky to prove. You could argue any number of factors, any number of points and references to throw off or skew the results, but the bottom line was for every cause, there was an effect. Some were intangible, while others were direct and precise. How would one surmise any number of seemingly random events and link them to a definitive cause if the effect was driven by multiple variables that all had to fall perfectly into place?

It would seem to be impossible to deduce, especially when considering what course of action a person might take. However, human beings are not as impulsive as they imagine.

It called to Don's mind a spiritual dilemma, one people seldom considered. If people are given free will and God knows the beginning and the end, then the actions people take are really predetermined. Meaning, free will is an illusion.

If you walk into your home and see a pencil on the floor, what do you do? If it is your pencil, you might think nothing of it and pick it up. But what if it is a pencil you have not seen before? Maybe there are no pencils in your house or you don't use pencils, then what? When you are caught off guard, another part of the brain takes over, an otherworldly subconscious portion, and that part works the same way every time. It's consistent. The eye had shown him time and time again.

"Adonis," said his mother.

The disruption to his thoughts startled him. He turned to her. Her dark-brown eyes still absent of their usual sparkle.

"For missing dinner the other night, you will go to the synagogue and perform confessional prayers before God. You will do this every day for two weeks."

Don could see the confusion on his father's face. A sign she had not told him about the incident that night. "Prayers for missing dinner?" said Joe.

She raised a single finger in the air. Her way of telling him to stay out of it. It was a family code. When one of them was delivering punishment, the other should never disagree in front of the children. It was their way of showing a unified front. It didn't have to be explained. It was easy to figure out. Don devised the meaning of the finger in the air by the time he was seven.

Joe said nothing more.

"Do you understand me, Adonis?" she asked.

If this was going to help her feel better, he would gladly go to the synagogue for two months. "Yes, Mom. I understand."

"You start today," she said.

Jasmine looked alarmed and confused. She blinked hard, trying to comprehend what had happened, before gingerly placing a forkful of eggs in her mouth.

"Yes, Mom," said Don. He picked up his plate and stood up to leave for school. The mood was awkward. Half of the family knew nothing about what was going on. The other half knew the punishment was worthy of the crime. Still, Don wasn't complaining.

In his daily search with the eye, he'd found someone else who deserved to be punished. A woman had done something horrible, and she was going to get away with it scot-free. His time alone in the synagogue would help him sort out the best way he could handle it. Two weeks was plenty of time to come up with something fitting.

# CHAPTER 16

It took less than a week to map out a course of action. The wheels were in motion. Don was at the mall sipping a milkshake. People were busy doing their shopping, but the mall was by no means busy. It was a weekday. The crowd was average at best. He was in the food court, sitting alone at a table, waiting. He looked over the details he had written in his journal. The precise path to get his desired outcome. Then he saw her. She was riding down the escalator heading toward him.

The woman was in her early thirties. She wore her hair in a tight bun. She was neither fit nor out of shape. She was taller than the average woman and dressed nicely in a tan blouse, black skirt, and black heels. Don had seen her many times through the eye. She had a pleasant demeanor. Her cheeks would swell with deep dimples when she smiled. She seemed happy. Cheery-eyed and amiable. But she had a dark side. This mask with the big smile and playful personality was so false it made his skin crawl.

The last two times Don bent the future to his will, it was distant and impersonal. He had to admit, he missed the adrenaline rush of the first time he'd changed someone's fate. He wanted to witness this one firsthand. See the fruits of his labor.

The fight he had with the guard in the basement of the furniture warehouse taught him how to use the eye properly. It was perfection. He could indirectly control the outcome of someone's life, moving items like chess pieces so precisely that their very existence rested in his hands.

She stepped off at the bottom of the escalator. Her bags ruffled as they brushed against her legs. Her heels made that distinct click-clack sound when she walked past where Don was sitting. Don set the timer on his watch to three minutes, and it began counting down. Then he closed his journal and let her get a few feet away before he stood up to follow. He walked behind her, keeping her in clear view.

How far in advance could he control events in the future? That was the question now. It was introduced when he made the call to Siobhan Starlette about her missing sister just under two weeks ago. He thought about her. He figured she was happy. She'd gotten her sister back safely. Charisma may have been a little malnourished and her muscles atrophied, but other than that, she was fine. Siobhan had no idea that the specific reference to the Arab-looking guy was the only way she would bring the right person. The eye could not provide sound; it was when Don was thinking of describing Edwardo that it came to him. Arab-looking guy. It was the only thing that worked.

Getting Edwardo to follow her had been the key to getting her sister back safely. After Siobhan got back to the car, Edwardo called his uncle and told him about Siobhan and why she was there.

Edwardo's uncle, Manny Pinero, did not take the news well.

Manny was connected. Cartel connected. Mexico to Colombia, some of his friends were on the highest levels of various organizations. A missing White girl from Yale University said to be on a property he owned was not the kind of notoriety he could afford. He wanted to make sure, a thousand percent, that his property had nothing to do with this girl's disappearance. Manny Pinero not only sent his men to check it out; he went with them.

They went around back where they would not be seen and pulled on the sliding glass door. It was open. The three men eased themselves inside. They heard sounds coming from the basement. People in a discussion about what to do. Manny and his men eased down the creaky wooden stairs to find a skinny White man and a large Hispanic woman crouched over one another. A young woman who was chained up and blindfolded.

With guns drawn, they quickly got the story. The girl had been coming from a party somewhere close by, and she'd wandered off drunk and gotten lost. They'd found her passed out in the alley and taken her inside. The couple thought the girl was from a wealthy family and tried to get her to clean out her bank account. It didn't work.

They tried working her for several days but then had no idea what to do after. They did not have a backup plan or the nerve to kill her. That was what they were discussing…how to get rid of her. They pleaded with Manny to handle the situation, and he did.

Don could have called the police and told them about the couple. He could have planted information on a hotline or given their descriptions, saying he saw Charisma outside their home. Don could have gone down there with a bolt cutter and set her free. He saw all of those futures, each resulting in Charisma being with her sister. But to hell with that.

The future in which Manny had his men escort the couple back to their home before putting two bullets in each of their skulls and then setting Charisma loose on the side of the highway was the one he chose. The phone call was the butterfly that set Hurricane Manny in motion.

But the plan was spur of the moment, and there were many ways in which it would have ended badly for the couple. This was different.

The woman in front of him would die in two minutes and nine seconds. She would fall down the steps at the mall entrance and break her neck. He checked his watch. The sun shone through the skylight of the mall as she took each step. This was it. Not much time left on this earth for Cynthia Kavanagh.

She stopped walking and turned to face him.

"Are you following me?" she asked. Her voice was sweet and subtle.

Don was caught off guard. This was not supposed to happen. He took hold of the eye and looked into her future beyond the next five minutes.

She would not die today.

*This cannot be happening.*

# CHAPTER 17

Cynthia was supposed to walk straight out of the mall exit with Don following fifteen feet behind her. On her way down the steps, she would slip and fall, breaking her neck. She was not supposed to stop. She was not supposed to turn her head and talk to Don. She should have never known he was there. The two of them were never supposed to meet or have any type of conversation.

*Now what?* he thought, his heart hammering. The timing of everything was critical. He paid attention to every detail as he had seen it. All of his actions today had mimicked what he did in her prescribed future. So what had changed?

"What's wrong?" she said. "Cat got your tongue? Are you following me?"

*Cat?*

There was a slight smirk on her face as if she were a cat who'd trapped a mouse to play with. Yes, he was caught; however, his surprise was not aimed at her discovery but at the sudden change in her future. The smug look on her face made him incensed. She was staring at him as if he had been outsmarted. Unknown to her, her life was supposed to end in less than three minutes, yet she was acting all haughty about discovering him. Her future had most certainly been changed, but it was that look on her face, as if she were the one in control, that annoyed Don to the point he was determined to steer her previous future back on course.

He had less than two minutes.

She had asked if he was following her.

"I was," he said. "I smelled your perfume and got lost in the scent." Don dropped his eyes to the ground in shame. "Great…now I bet you think I'm a stalker."

"Yeah, something like that," she said. She was smiling. "Does my stalker have a name?"

"Oh yes, Adonis Silver," he said, making eye contact. "Everyone just calls me Don."

"You must be kidding, right? Your name is Adonis?"

"Yes. What's wrong with that?"

"I mean…look at you."

He pretended not to know what she meant, but he did. Adonis, the mortal man in Greek mythology who was so handsome that Aphrodite, the goddess of beauty and love, fought over him. Any parent who named their child Adonis would certainly appear pretentious and vainglorious. But at seventeen years old, Don was worthy of the name. Dark-brown hair, brown eyes, fair skin, and a face the gods would consider perfect. His height was a shade under six feet. His body toned and athletic. There was not a genetic blemish on his skin.

"And you are?" Don asked.

"Cynthia," she said.

This small talk was boring him. He knew who she was, what she did, where she ate, and whom she slept with. He did not care about hearing the information from her firsthand. He wanted to see her future realized, one in which she slipped on the stairs and broke her neck. How could he make that happen? Was it too late for him to manipulate things so they all fell in line? Probably, but he refused to give up so easily.

He could push her, but that would be problematic. Too many witnesses. Too many cameras. Besides, those days were over. Too much work, and the risks were astronomical. Running from the cops after beating the pervert who wanted to defile his sister had been exhausting. One mistake would land him in jail. That sort of cause and effect was boring. It lacked depth and imagination. True power was created. True talent was admired. A man with a knife or a gun killing another was just a common thug. Don was trying to create something. With intelligence, the eye could be used to change the world. Which was exactly what he was doing. *Stick to the plan.* If he could make her fall and break her neck now, the next stage in his mastery of the eye would be achieved.

He put his hand in his left pocket. Just touching the eye sent impulses of its vision through his body. But those impulses had to be directed and focused. Now came the tricky part. He had to try to see what was going to happen and synchronize it with the current course, make sure the two parts didn't overshoot, and make the correction.

"Pleasure to meet you officially," said Don, extending his right hand. "I was just leaving the mall. I have to get home and do some homework."

She took his hand. Her skin was soft and delicate. "College?" she asked.

"No. Still in high school."

"What a shame," she said.

"Can I walk next to you this time? I promise I won't follow you afterward."

"Yeah, I need to keep track of your eyes. Make sure you're not staring at things you're not supposed to."

Don blushed. He had been practicing the move. It was meant

to put people at ease. Manipulate his emotions to let blood rush to his face. It produced the desired effect. She tried to fight back a smile, which made her cheeks look full. Her dimples were deep. Then they began walking side by side toward the exit of the mall.

With his first few steps, the visions flooding his mind were dizzying. He felt like he was going to puke. Cynthia noticed his unsteadiness and reached out to grab his arm, which made it worse. Each time he looked at her future and thought about the actions he would take, it changed. It was so rapid he could barely make sense of what he was seeing. The range of futures for the next ten minutes covered everything from her puking after drinking too much to her having sex with Don in the back seat of her car and everything in between. It felt like too much for him to control, which was why he avoided direct interaction to begin with.

There had to be another way around it.

Cynthia's demise was supposed to begin with the cleaning crew working the stairs outside the mall. A guy was supposed to look up toward the exit just as she was expected to come through the door. He would ultimately be responsible for Cynthia falling down the stairs, but it would appear to be a case of bad timing. He had already gotten the phone call he was supposed to receive. He seemed to be in place and waiting. He was looking for the kid who was the likely culprit causing him a bunch of work outside. Someone had been throwing food—peanuts, in particular—into the bushes beside the stairs. Cleaning pigeon shit off the stairs was no fun. His friend at the food court had told him it was probably the kid he saw every day who ate peanuts and left his milkshake cup on the table. That spoiled kid had left another milkshake cup for the custodian to throw away, and he was about to leave the mall. When he did, the man would see if he tossed some peanuts into the bushes. He often walked with his hand in his pocket. It had to be him.

The alarm on Don's cell phone began to play a tune. Three minutes had expired.

"Are you going to get that?" asked Cynthia.

Don turned off the alarm. The man outside was still waiting. With the right timing, the sequence could still come to fruition. It would all transpire between Cynthia opening the door and the man looking at the exit. The timing had to be perfect. If anything was off by even a fraction of a second, Cynthia would regain her balance. Each and every time Don ran through the sequence of him interacting with Cynthia, it produced a different result.

Changes had to be made to inanimate objects in order to get a consistent result. He knew that. But what inanimate object could he get her to react to on short notice? Don took his phone out of his pocket and typed in Cynthia's phone number. Then he put the phone back into his pocket. A few seconds later, he pressed send.

Cynthia peeked at her phone and canceled the call without answering. It was a number she did not recognize, and she did as he expected. They reached the first set of doors leading to the exit and Don opened it, walking through first. He put his hand on the second door, but before he opened it, he pressed send on his phone once more. Cynthia looked at her phone and then answered it.

"Hello?" she said while standing in the doorway.

Don pressed cancel on his phone. Cynthia waited for a response, sneered at her phone, ended the call, and walked through the door.

The cleaning man by the bushes looked up at the top of the stairs on cue. Don held a bag of peanuts in his hand, and then he tossed it to the side. The cleaning man made a face to declare he had identified the culprit who was causing him all that extra work. He looked over to where the peanuts landed and saw the pigeons. He hated pigeons and the dirty, nasty shit they left all over the place for him to clean up.

He swatted at the bush with his broom, causing a flurry of fifteen pigeons to take to the air. They flew low and up the flight of the stairs, swooping upward to rest on the overhang above the door. Cynthia was so enamored by Don's gesture of holding the door open for her that she saw them too late. She was startled and moved without reaching for the handrail. She began to fall. Her heel hit the first step at an angle and broke off. She reached out with her free hand to grasp the closest thing to her—Don. Her hand was extended; all he had to do was take it. But he did not. He did nothing except smile and keep his hands in his pockets. He let her fleeting grasp slip down his arm. She tumbled head over heels to the bottom.

Don heard screams and gasps and other sounds as Cynthia tumbled to her death. It was different seeing it all again in reality. There was no sound with the eye. He had to guess what was happening based on the gestures and expressions of the onlookers. The sounds seemed to fill in the blanks and make it all real. Sound produced a decisive end. Like the final words of a great novel.

The fall to her death was nothing like the first one. This tumble was much more violent. Messy. Here she broke a few more bones than in her other future. Her hip was contorted, and she ended up looking like a rag doll filled with stuffing that a child had thrown out of a moving car. Parts of her limbs were twisted this way and that, not the way arms and legs were supposed to turn. There was blood, pooled and splattered, beginning halfway down the stairs to the bottom. Cynthia's neck appeared to be broken. She was looking up toward the top of the stairs at Don, trying to speak. The nerves to her heart and lungs were severed, so there was no way for her to breathe. Perhaps she knew death was near, even though she could not feel it.

But what had caused this change? He put his hand on the eye to look into her past before her life ended. He was only interested in the last four minutes.

He triggered the time when he was standing behind her in the mall. Cynthia was walking with her head straight ahead. Don could see everything she saw. The mother with the little girl in front of her talking and smiling. He could see a group of teens farther ahead roughhousing. Beyond them was the entrance, and coming in through one of the glass doors was a woman with a shawl and dark sunglasses. There were other people scattered about; nothing Don had not already seen through Cynthia's eyes in the past.

Then she looked over to her right at a tall Black man standing in front of a store selling Perfect Sleeper mattresses. He was hard to miss. He was staring intently. He began talking as if there were someone next to him. Like he was asking a question and waiting for an answer, but there was no one beside him.

She glanced at him out of the corner of her eye. Then she noticed he was not looking at her. He was looking at someone behind her. The reflection off the glass of the storefront showed who the tall man was focused on. It was Don. He could see her focus on the image through the mirror. She looked at the tall man again, then returned to Don. That was when she stopped to turn around and speak to him.

"You seem very confused," said a voice. It echoed inside of the vision of Cynthia's past, which Don was trying to sort out. It could only be one creature. Tartarus.

He appeared from the inside of the mattress store. A black void of a body with a big white smile and white gloves on his hands. He slunk his way toward Don and stood before him, moving his fingers like the legs of a spider. He was some sort of demon, from what Adonis could determine. Very cryptic. And annoying.

"I am not in the mood right now," said Adonis, frustrated by Tartarus's appearance while he was searching for clues. He was focused on the tall Black guy. Specifically, why the man was watching him. Where had he come from? Why hadn't he shown up in the previous visions? The Black man had on a black T-shirt with blue jeans, tight around the legs. He wore ankle socks and blue shoes with a soft sole. He was really tall. He loomed above everyone else, except for the demon Tartarus, smiling at Don's frustration. He was hard to miss. Why didn't the eye show him this before?

"I think you're in shock," said a voice.

Don remembered where he was and released the eye to return his vision to the present. On the top stair of the mall exit, a young man was standing next to him with a look of concern. He was Indian. Silky black mane on his head. Slim with a windbreaker unzipped. He was leaning toward Don with a drink in his hand.

"I saw you were not quick enough to save that woman," said the young man. "You had a chance to grab her arm but froze. Don't beat yourself up about it. It happened so fast you couldn't think. It's not your fault."

"But it is my fault," said Don. "So fuck off."

The young man pulled his head back in disbelief and stared wide-eyed.

"Beat it," said Don. "I have bigger problems."

The Indian man flipped Don the bird and went back inside the mall, pissed off and mumbling under his breath. Don scanned the growing crowd at the bottom of the stairs, looking for the tall Black man who wasn't supposed to be there. He found him near the body, fighting through the crowd to get a closer look at poor Cynthia.

*She murdered her children, don't you know,* Don wanted to tell him. A little boy and a little girl. Seven and four years of age, respectively. She claimed the father had taken them and they all ran away together. She said they were living in California. But she was a liar. They were sitting in the family car at the bottom of a lake upstate.

The father and both children. She'd drugged them all and driven the car into the lake herself, escaping out the open window. Then she'd come back to the city and pretended she had been abandoned by her family. By the time the car was recovered from the lake, six years from now, all remains and evidence would be gone. Fish food. The investigation would lead nowhere. She would get away with it.

Well…not anymore.

The tall Black man was talking to himself again. Weird habit, but he didn't seem crazy. Was he her friend? Perhaps a private investigator looking into the disappearance of her family?

Don took hold of the eye and thought about the tall Black man and got nothing. Visions of others in the crowd tried to enter the space of the eye, and Don pushed all of those images aside. He wanted the tall Black man. The one standing at the bottom of the stairs. But there was nothing. No past and no future.

"What will you do now?" said a voice. The sound was like a freight train through the night.

"Tartarus," said Don. "Come to torment me again? Seems petty of you. Invade my use of the eye until I put it back in the box and hide it behind a stack of newspapers. Perhaps I will throw it into the ocean. Maybe even bury it in the ground."

"Not likely," said Tartarus. "You don't seem like the type." Tartarus walked up beside him. Black void of a man. Tall, lanky, white-gloved hands, big, glowing, evil smile. "Actually, I am just an observer. I want to see what you will do. You are most clever, Adonis Silver. Getting people to kill themselves by their own sins and shortcomings is genius. But what will you do about this man?"

"Nothing, I guess," said Don. "I have bigger fish to fry."

"That is what is most puzzling, Adonis. Out of all the things you could be using the eye for—fame and fortune, sexual desires, other earthly pleasures—you are using it for this." He waved his white-gloved finger toward Cynthia Kavanagh's twisted body at the bottom of the stairs.

"Why would I use the eye for possessions I am perfectly capable of obtaining on my own?" said Don. "Satisfaction comes from achieving things you are not certain you can do. The mundane achievements others pursue seem so elementary. As easy for me as breathing."

Don thought about graduating with honors in a few months. His life at Yale and afterward. When it came time to choose a course of study, he could not think of anything that would be satisfying. So he would choose law. It seemed to be what the career-smart people with no love for science picked. But it was not something that spoke to his heart. "I wish for more," said Don.

He looked down at the crowd, which increased in number as people became aware of the accident. There was a man who seemed to be acting as crowd control, trying to move others back out of the way. A paramedic ran past Don from inside the mall. He had bushy hair and was wearing a blue uniform with a medical patch on the sleeve. Funny, Don never thought there were emergency people on hand at the mall, but it made sense. The paramedic looked at the trail of blood as he ran down the stairs toward poor Cynthia.

"So confident," said Tartarus. "You remind me of someone else I knew long ago."

"Is that a compliment?" asked Don.

"A warning…It didn't end well for him either."

Don quickly grew tired of the scene and of Tartarus, so he released the eye.

There was a man in Missouri. A serial killer. Nineteen women to date. He hunted on the highways of the United States. Perfect place to travel great distances, across state lines, where it took a while for authorities to put things together. It was his turn to die. With a phone call, he would have the most horrific accident on the side of the highway as he changed a flat tire. Plastered to mush by a semi. Don had less than an hour to make the call. It was time he be on his way.

As for the strange Black man, he was coming up the stairs. He seemed flustered by the death of Cynthia. He was by no means accustomed to death. He wasn't a threat at all. It did not matter that Don could not see him with the eye. Whatever this guy was, he could easily be handled.

Don began walking down the stairs to leave. The handrail was between them. Don on one side. Tall man on the other. When they were right next to each other, Don locked eyes with him. A kind of glance to say, *You stay in your lane, and I will stay in mine.*

# CHAPTER 18

Cardigan Paige could not wait to leave school that day. Her employer, Jericho Black, had told her he had a gift for her. Access to the program created by Jake Coltrane, an app that allowed the user to find anyone anywhere at any time. When she asked Jericho how he was able to obtain access, he said he did a sleight of hand with its creator. Jericho had pretended to throw Jake's phone out the window of a moving car after the phone was unlocked. What Jake saw shatter into a million pieces was another phone, and while he was distracted, Jericho pocketed the original.

The final bell rang, and Cardigan rushed out through the main door of her high school, Sister Mary Catherine Spalding, toting her backpack, wearing her blue jacket with the crest above the breast pocket, a white shirt, and a matching blue plaid skirt. Behind the row of school buses out front was a limousine sent by her employer. A black Lincoln Navigator, executive coach build, twenty-seven-foot stretch, with captain's chairs that fully reclined, three televisions, an iPad, and a Maybach-style LED panel with mood lighting on the roof.

Everyone at school thought she was rich as fuck. Truth was it was just her and her mother, struggling to get by in a regular two-bedroom apartment in Brooklyn. Their life had changed when she met Jericho Black. He was the one who paid for her school and the occasional electric bill when needed. Still, she loved the glares of the haters as she drove off, straining to get a peek inside through the dark-tinted windows.

"Did you bring it?" she asked the driver, slamming the door shut after sitting in a captain's chair. She could feel the blood rush to her cheeks and imagined that with her glasses, she looked like the kid who wanted the Red Ryder carbine action two-hundred-shot range model air rifle with a compass for Christmas.

Arnie, the driver, shifted his eyes to look at her in the rearview mirror. He was an orange-haired gorilla. A massive man with a neck so thick he could barely turn his head to the side. He was assigned to look after her. Take her where she needed to be whenever Jericho summoned her.

"There," he said, pointing his chin upward. "By the cupholder."

She looked down, and there it was, resting on top of the polished wood at the end of the armrest. Jake Coltrane's personal phone. An ordinary late-model iPhone. She pushed the button on the side, and the phone came to life. A picture of Jake smiling with some Hispanic hussy cheek to cheek was on the screen. She swiped a finger over the woman's face to get to the apps. The phone was unlocked. Jericho thought of everything.

Cardigan felt her palms sweating. She was eager to run the program through a test. The third page had the blue square with a cursive *C* in white. She was going to use the program to find the app's creator. Jake Coltrane. She had not been able to get her mind off him ever since meeting him a few days earlier. Yeah, he'd gotten in trouble with Jericho and the Russian mob, but that was all sorted out for the moment. Now she just wanted to chat. Make a connection. So what if he was in his thirties and she was still in high school? They had something in common. They were both computer geniuses.

The limousine pulled out into traffic and coasted to a stop at the light. Cardigan copied a picture of Jake from his phone. She pasted his image—brown skin, magnetic smile, dark eyes, long eyelashes, baby-smooth face—into the search portion of the app.

"What is so special about that thing anyway?" asked Arnie. He glanced at her through the rearview mirror. "Everyone is in such a tizzy about it."

"It uses hacking techniques to access thousands of public and private cameras," said Cardigan. "Anything that transmits data wirelessly. Home computers, doorbell security, office computers, bank and street cameras, you name it."

She raised the phone with one hand to take a couple of selfies. She reversed the camera so she could see herself. Her tanned skin, bangs, black-rimmed glasses, and girlish charms all on display. She snapped a few pics, pivoting her head left and right, trying to turn on that schoolgirl sexy. If Jake's phone ever did make it back to him, she would give him something to look at. Let him see what a great couple they would make.

"Isn't that illegal?" said Arnie. He made a left turn and accelerated through traffic. "Hacking into private stuff?"

"Of course," said Cardigan, as if it were elementary. "That's what makes it fun."

The small icon on the app started spinning, indicating it was accessing the server. She had no idea how long it would take since it had to comb through millions of processes. Jake Coltrane had written the program in desperation, all to find a mysterious man who was rumored to have the power to heal his brain tumor. He'd pitched the idea of his tracking program to his employer because he needed the computing main framing power and resources he could not afford on his own. And when he successfully completed the program, he hid it from his employer and made them believe it was still a work in progress. All so he could use it in private.

"But how can it track your location from a picture?" asked Arnie. He pressed his palm on the steering wheel and spun it, whipping the limo around another corner. "I find that ridiculous."

"It's EXIF data," Cardigan said.

Arnie made a face that signaled he'd never heard that before. "What is EXIF data?"

"Exchangeable image file. When digital pictures are created, they leave a footprint containing information. It's encoded in the photo. It tells you what kind of camera was used and the location where the photo was taken. GPS information when taken from a cell phone." She looked back at the phone, checking to see if the search was complete. It was still searching.

"The program also scans Google Maps street by street to look for similarities in backgrounds of photos," Cardigan continued. "Buildings, street signs, trees, et cetera in order to get location information when EXIF data is not available."

"Amazing," said Arnie.

And it was. But for now, she was only interested in seeing where Jake was and what he was doing. Eavesdropping. The spinning icon stopped, and she was shown a live image. It looked like the food court at the mall. There he was, Jake Coltrane. He was standing outside a mattress store, just chillin'.

She smiled.

She had a thing for older men that she couldn't get past. And didn't want to. She loved them. Mature men. It was torture for her going over to her friends' homes and seeing all those strong fathers about. Beautiful, strong men who loved to help out if anything needed help. And those hands. Big, strong hands. Not butch hands that looked like they ate their fingers as snacks; they had to be well kept. Clean. Those hands had to touch you, for goodness' sake.

Plus, Jake was really tall. Someone she could look up to. She batted her eyes playfully to no one in particular. It was between her and her thoughts of Jake Coltrane.

The camera switched angles every ten seconds or so, trying to capture the perfect image of Jake's face. There were enough cameras around the mall that she could see his features and what he was doing. He appeared to be following a couple. A man and a woman. The camera changes allowed her to catch a glimpse of the male Jake was following. Cute but not her type. He was in his late teens or early twenties, she guessed.

Cardigan's front teeth dug into her bottom lip as she thought about it. Jericho had said to make sure Jake stayed out of trouble until the heat with the Russian mob cooled down. This looked like trouble. A second later, her hunch was confirmed. Jake sprinted toward the exit after the couple he was following left the mall. The camera outside caught the image of him running down the stairs. There seemed to be a person at the bottom in need of help. Her body was contorted. There was blood.

Images began flashing in an instant. It must have been the program's way of going through various camera feeds to try and pick out his location. There were too many people around to get a good image, but the software knew he was still in the area, so it kept searching. Someone began streaming the accident with a cell phone, and the camera came alive again with Jake in the background.

This allowed Cardigan to see the woman on the ground at the bottom of the stairs. She remembered this woman was one of the people Jake was following. Cardigan's job was to keep an eye on him. Looked like he was in trouble once again. She had better find out what he was doing.

"You got quiet back there all of a sudden," said Arnie. She looked up as the limo veered through downtown Manhattan traffic.

"Yeah," said Cardigan. "Working the program. That's all."

The first step was to find out who these people Jake was following were. She had command of Jake's master program at her fingertips. She went right to work. She played back the images of the last minute to capture images of the woman. She let the program do a historical search. There was a webpage with her image. Someone had created a GoFundMe campaign to help find a man who was missing. Her picture was next to it. She was the wife of the missing man. Cynthia Kavanagh. The person she was with at the mall was certainly not her missing husband. Her husband was blond and had a beard. Much heavier.

She focused in on the male, captured his image, and waited. He was a high school kid from Long Island. A couple of pictures of web articles showed up. He was some kind of child prodigy. Accolades out the wazoo. Then a video popped up on the search. A violent one. A man swinging a pipe inside a bodega, intent on making the person's face he was smashing unrecognizable.

But the person in the video had his face obscured. A hat pulled down tight and some sort of cover over his face. Looked like a T-shirt tied around the mouth and nose. Her eyes got big as she remembered. This was big news. The son of some guy running for governor got killed with a pipe in a store. This must be it. What didn't make sense was how the program identified the assailant with the male Jake was following.

She took a closer look at the pictures, and then she saw it. Her heart dropped. Was that what Jake was doing? Trying to play detective?

Yes. Jericho had said to make sure Jake didn't get into any trouble, and this seemed like trouble.

Cardigan decided to take the initiative and forwarded the information to the proper authorities.

# CHAPTER 19

It was after midnight. Duval sat in front of the monitor at the police station, rubbing his eyes. The soft glow of the screen lit up his cubicle. He took a peek to his left at the cubicle beside him and saw Carrol dozing off, then springing his eyes open as if he had been awake the whole time. This was the less glamorous side of police work. Investigations going nowhere. And the pressure was on.

The captain was breathing down his neck. The chief was perhaps a day or two from pulling him off the case and destroying any future chances for his advancement within the ranks. High-profile cases were the double-edged sword of the department. Work them flawlessly and people remember when it comes time to advance. Fail and people remember when it comes time to advance.

The gubernatorial candidate was furious. He called the station daily for progress. And he wasn't talking to the board operator when he called. He had a direct line to the brass. Hard on crime was his platform, and he was using the delays in his son's murder investigation to push for sweeping changes. He directed those threats at the chief, who in turn passed them on to the captain. Since shit rolled downhill, Duval was feeling the weight of stench bearing down on him.

Then a ping came through his computer. He had a new message. It was piled up with all the old messages he received throughout the day when he was pounding the pavement. Eighty-seven of them. He decided to go through them all and clear them out before morning. By this time tomorrow, he would have eighty-seven more. He clicked the mouse through to the latest one. He planned to delete as many as he could. All the irrelevant nonsense.

After the thirty-first email he deleted, he came upon a message from someone he did not recognize. It had an attachment. The subject of the email was *This is who you are looking for.*

It was apparent this was junk, and he was about to delete the message when something deep inside told him not to. Perhaps it was desperation. Why else would he be entertaining the thought of opening a strange email? Duval clicked the file, and a message popped up from the IT folks at the precinct. It asked if he was sure this was from a trusted source and said to never open an attachment if he was not sure where it came from.

He paused momentarily, thinking of the implications of possibly spreading a harmful virus throughout the system. What the hell. He clicked on it anyway. The video was from a mall. It was of a young man in a red T-shirt and blue jeans, with a backpack, sitting at a table at the food court sipping on a drink of some sort. He was looking around and writing in a journal. He certainly looked the part. Same type of build. But there was no ball cap pulled over his head; you could see his face clearly. He looked like a teenager. Then he stood and began heading toward the exit.

That was when Duval saw it.

A chill ran down his spine. The kid was walking behind a woman, and the woman saw him and they began conversing. When he was talking, he slung the backpack over his shoulder. The same type of backpack. Duval had watched the video of the assault until he could recite exactly what happened at each time stamp down to the second. He remembered when the assailant shoved the pipe and phone into the backpack. The color, style, and shape were all identical.

Below the attachment was a name. Adonis Silver.

# CHAPTER 20

"Adonis," said his mother.

He opened his eyes and stared at the ceiling. The sun peeked through the blinds with beams of sunlight strewn across the comforter. He looked over at the time on the nightstand. It was half past seven in the morning. He was usually an early riser. Up, showered, and dressed by now, no matter if it was a school day or not.

"Time to get up," she said. "Breakfast is ready."

Her voice was calm and soothing. She waited with one hand on the door, watching him, wearing her favorite blue pajamas with white unicorns under her housecoat. He was still a bit groggy but was pleased to see the sparkle was returning to his mother's eyes. She was like a different person after Don showed her the bloody clothes. And not just psychologically. Perhaps this was what guilt did to a person. Weighed them down to the point of physical change.

"I'll be ready in ten minutes," said Don.

He got up and went into the bathroom, showered, and got dressed. Ten minutes on the nose. Then he went downstairs to join the rest of his family at the breakfast table. Jasmine was there already. His mother was seated, and so was his father.

"Nice to see you graced us with your presence, Lord Adonis," said Joe. "Late night?"

"Studying." Don smiled. Actually it had been a late night, but that was beside the point. Family time at the table seemed to be returning to normal.

"Sure," said Jasmine. "Studying for Don is like this." She mocked cracking open a book, turning a few pages, then closing it. "Done. And I get another one hundred percent on another test. How disgusting!"

"Adonis has his own way of doing things," said Sara. She placed a hand on top of his. "Let's give thanks."

They said their prayers and began eating. His mom had made a dish of scrambled eggs and cheese mixed with tabbouleh, one of Don's favorites.

"I have an idea for today," said Sara. "How about we all pick you up in Manhattan and we eat in the city tonight?"

"Seriously?" asked Jasmine, wide-eyed.

"Who came up with this plan?" asked Joe. "My work-from-home day, and I still have to drive into Manhattan…thanks, my love."

"Don't mention it," said Sara with a wink.

"And who do you suppose is going to pay for dinner?" said Joe.

"Don't be silly," said Sara. "You are the only one around here who has a job. You are my big hero." She buttered a piece of toast and put it on Don's plate.

"I make the bread around here, but you put the butter on his toast," said Joe, motioning to Don. "It's nothing new. I've had seventeen years to come to grips with the fact that I'm no longer number one around here."

"You're one and a half, sweetie."

"I'm one and a half," said Jasmine. "You're number two, Dad."

"Wow, number two. I feel like a big stinking pile of number two right now, I can tell you!"

Don looked around the table. He was happy. This was his final day of confessional prayers at the synagogue, and his family was going to join him for dinner on the town. "How about cheesecake at Junior's?" asked Don.

They all sat up a bit taller.

"I guess I have to pay for that too?" said Joe. "And Sara, you are going to pay for it because you are the one who has to look at my diminishing six-pack."

"Oh, you've had a keg for years, baby," she said.

# CHAPTER 21

Duval got out of bed that morning and kissed his lovely wife on the cheek. There were still about ten minutes before she needed to get up and do those motherly things like wake up their daughter, get her dressed, get herself dressed, and rush her off to the babysitter so she could get to work. He wished he had the type of job that would allow him to lend her a hand, something with a set schedule. But there was nothing scripted for homicide. The case dictated his work hours, and today he would be out the door before she got out of the shower.

Duval stood and went to the closet. He tore the thin clear plastic off his clothes from the dry cleaners and bunched it up in a ball to throw it in the trash. He got dressed in a charcoal-gray suit with a light-gray shirt, slipped on his shoes, and headed out the door. The sky was clear. The sun, ready to peek over the horizon. He could see the Whitestone Bridge off in the distance to his right, over the sea of homes in the neighborhood. The Cadillac was out front. Sometimes Duval wondered if Carrol slept in the car. After he opened the door, the state of Carrol's clothes in the morning sure made it look like he did. White shirt, brown tie tied too short, brown slacks lightly wrinkled, with a brown jacket flung on the back seat.

The smell of fresh coffee in the cupholder was a bright spot.

"Good morning, partner," said Carrol.

"Top of the morning," Duval answered.

Pleasantries upon greeting for the day. It was one of those things Carrol insisted on before canvassing information from the streets. Police saw the very worst in people. It was a constant bombardment of misery and pain mixed with a heap of vile and disgust. The least they could do with each other was give themselves a friendly and pleasant greeting. Especially when the day was going to be filled with interviewing people whose first reaction was to bicker and curse upon seeing them.

The car rolled smoothly through the streets. The radio played the kind of music heard in a spa. Instrumentals. Relaxing and soothing. It didn't fit Carrol's personality one bit.

"Do you remember the video I sent you a few months ago?" asked Carrol.

Duval took a sip of coffee. He knew where this was going. Off course. To the right. "Which one?"

"The video of the nanotechnology."

"How they are planting it in vaccines? Yeah, I remember."

"I came across another video in which Judge Joe Brown is explaining how Obama and George Bush are related. Crazy shit. But they took it down before I could forward the link."

"They took it down," said Duval. "Why do you think they took it down?"

Carrol paused. His lips tightened to a frown. "I know…I know. You think they took it down because it is completely false, and I think they took it down because they don't want you to know the truth."

"All I am saying with this is you are not looking at human motives," said Duval.

"What? Like I don't know people? I am a homicide detective in Manhattan. How could I not know about motives?"

"I'm not talking about murder motives. What I am saying is you are not applying the same logic of a motive to everyday life. No one does anything without a motive. What time you get up in the morning, the clothes you choose, how fast you drive, the coffee you drink—all done with a motive. When I apply a motive to the validity of those stories, I think, what would that information be worth? Millions? Fame? Endorsements? Interviews? Book deals? The fact that it is posted on random YouTube channels, covertly, until it's taken down tells you that what they have on the story is nothing. No proof whatsoever. Because if they had proof, it would make them rich."

"What if the motive is to reveal the truth?"

"The motive for posting on the internet is to be seen and heard. With proof, you would be seen and heard for decades. You can't even remember the name of the person who posted it. Hell, who is the person who made the original recording? The motive of a person who makes a recording and then shows the recording is they want you to see the recording."

"That's the dumbest thing I ever heard," said Carrol. "Of course they want you to see the recording. That's why they posted it!"

"But their motive is to stir you up. Get you spreading the word and asking questions. Their intention is to have people like you spread falsehoods through word of mouth because they want as many people as they can get to believe it…without providing any real proof."

"So you are saying I took the bait."

"Bingo! If they had proof, they wouldn't need you to spread the word. They could do it all on their own and get rich doing it."

"Look. All I am saying is we have to think differently about this case. Expand the scope of the investigation from petty criminals to an intentional coordinated attack." The Cadillac roared up the ramp and onto the highway headed toward Manhattan. "This is political." Carrol slapped his large palm down on top of the steering wheel with a thud. "We need to start looking at political activists in the city. Specifically, those who support the radical left agenda. And I mean those who want to do away with policing."

Duval scratched an itch on his sideburn. He wondered if his emotions drove a nervous tic of some sort. "Why would eliminating policing be a reason to kill Connor Richardson?"

"His platform is being tough on criminals. How can you protect the state when you can't even protect your own son? You think it is a coincidence no one saw this guy's face clearly? They saw it. But they also know there will be serious repercussions if they talk."

"Gangs and the mob operate the same way," said Duval. "It's a stretch to say the reason people aren't talking is anything other than fear of the common thug." He was about to take another sip of his coffee when a thought interrupted him. "What does this have to do with those videos you sent me, anyway?"

"Someone sent me a link to a video. It might blow this case wide open."

Duval felt a pang of guilt. He hadn't shared the mall video with his partner. He'd kept it to himself while investigating it covertly. Connor Richardson was a manager of a chain of furniture stores. It so happened that on the day he was murdered, there was a disturbance at one of his stores reported to the authorities. A kid, impersonating some kind of insurance inspector, assaulted a guard at a warehouse Connor was scheduled to visit that day. The warehouse was less than a couple of miles from the home of Adonis Silver. Duval had been up all night thinking about it.

How could he tell the chief that his major lead into the murder of Connor Richardson came by anonymous email of a recording of a teenager in the mall...simply because the backpack was the same type as the one of assailant in the video? It wasn't like the backpack hadn't been investigated; it was part of the protocol. The backpack was a State Kane Double Pocket retailing for $115. It featured a padded laptop compartment, side pockets for a water bottle, and tons of pockets for everything else.

State estimated it had sold about ninety thousand of the backpacks. The one in the video was black, which narrowed it down to half as black was a popular color. About ten thousand people had purchased the black backpack in Manhattan. So what was the likelihood of identifying a person by the backpack? Little to none, until Duval saw the video. It was the way the kid hoisted the pack onto his shoulder that caught his eye. The mannerisms. The way he hooked the top loop with the back of his thumb, curled his open palm through the shoulder strap, then brought it over to his other arm and put it through the strap like one would slide an arm through the sleeve of a jacket.

Both the bodega video and the mall video showed the same backpack maneuver. It was worth questioning. Worth checking out. But how could he convince the chief it was worth pursuing? Adonis Silver lived all the way in Long Island. He was an honor student. Hell, by all accounts, he was the smartest kid in New York. Nothing but perfect scores. He was a model student and citizen. Not a hint of trouble from him. His future was brighter than that of any other high school kid he'd ever looked into.

Just the notion of focusing on Adonis Silver because of the backpack would be laughable. However, if he could connect the assault at the warehouse with Adonis, he might have the ammunition he needed to approach the chief about questioning the boy. He wanted to be sure before he sprang it on his partner. Save them both the embarrassment of looking foolish.

"When were you going to tell me about this link you got on the case?" asked Duval.

"When I was sure it wasn't going to make me look ridiculous."

"What do you have?" asked Duval.

"The woman in the video died shortly after the recording was taken. I looked at the date and time stamp on the video. It was taken from a mall camera. She fell down a bunch of stairs and broke her neck. No one saw it, but it was possible the male she was with pushed her. Same backpack as our perp in Manhattan."

"What makes you think this is the same guy we're after?"

"Because someone sent this clip to both of us."

Duval nodded. "Motive of the sender?"

"They want this guy off the street, same as us."

"Let's roll, then," he said.

Carrol whipped the car around at the next exit and headed back the other way to Long Island.

# CHAPTER 22

Duval and Carrol arrived in New Hyde Park, Long Island. Duval stopped to look at himself in the window of the car. He checked to see if everything was snug and straight with all of his lines in order. His hair was in place. His eyebrows arched and smooth. His teeth free of bits of food. His nose free of obscenities. It was important no one was distracted or offended by him when opening the door. Well, important to Duval. Carrol put on his wrinkled brown jacket and headed for the property.

Single-family home, white with green shutters, two stories with a basement, small driveway, and garage. Typical for an upper-middle-class family home outside the city. Duval walked up the three brick stairs and rang the doorbell. He stood straight and tall with his head slightly turned as if he were not eager to see who opened the door but ever aware of when it did open.

The front door was green. It looked old and might have been there when the house was built. Hardwood and solid with a big brass knocker below the peephole. The crack of the door opening was like releasing a vacuum. A woman stood behind it. She had shiny black hair, long, but it was tied up clumsily, as if she were getting it out of her way while she was working. She appeared to be in her forties, wearing an oversize light-blue T-shirt with black leggings. She had bright, caring brown eyes that did not seem particularly pleased to see them.

"Sara Silver?" asked Duval. "I am Detective Duval, and this is Detective Carrol." They held up their credentials so she could see them.

She touched the closest badge, Duval's, as if she had to see if it was real. No eye contact, no real pressure applied, just a touch. "What is this about?" she asked.

"It's actually about your son," said Duval. "May we come in?"

Sara shook her head. "I'd rather not. Do I need a lawyer?"

Duval and Carrol exchanged glances. People often asked if they needed a lawyer before questioning. It was a common thing. However, people who asked before they were told the details of the police visit were usually guilty of something.

She stood at the door waiting for an answer, turning her attention from Duval to Carrol and back. Then Duval heard the sound of rubber wheels rolling slowly and the crunching of fine gravel in the driveway. A car was backing out.

Sara suddenly looked relieved. "Joe," she called out. "This is my husband. You can talk to him."

A black Tesla came into view after it cleared the side of the house. A man was driving, and a young girl sat in the passenger's seat with a backpack on her lap. It was multicolored. Pink and aqua with designs Duval could not make out at that distance. The car stopped, and a man in jeans and a white polo shirt got out. He made a face, clearly wondering who they were and why they were at his front door. Carrol took a few steps toward him, extending his arm with his identification.

"Detective?" asked the husband. "What is this about?"

"Joe, is it?" asked Carrol. "I thought we could all talk inside. It would be better." He looked over Joe's shoulder at the girl in the car. "Probably better if she stayed there. The car is running, right? Never can tell with those electric doodads."

"Sara?" asked Joe, looking at his wife, uncertain. She didn't answer. She didn't move. "Sure…come on inside," said Joe. He walked up the stairs to the door and had to pry the door from her hand. He opened it wide and walked past her. Then he turned around. "Come inside, detectives."

Sara didn't hide her apprehension and moved away from the door so the detectives could enter. Duval walked in first and heard the light creaking of the wood floor under his weight. The foyer was filled with potted plants on the floor and hanging from hooks in the ceiling near the windows. He spotted a spider plant, with green and yellow leaves, hanging in the corner. It was his mother's favorite plant. There was an antique phonograph against the wall, and there were stacks of vinyl records inside a wooden bookshelf.

"What is this all about?" asked Joe. His head was angled slightly upward as he turned his attention to Carrol, then Duval.

Carrol began to explain, but Duval cut him off. "We are inquiring about an accident at the mall the other day." Change of plan, and Carrol quickly got on the same page. The mother asking for a lawyer meant they had to put her mind at ease. A direct accusation would get them thrown out immediately. This would take some massaging if it was going to work.

"What kind of accident was this?" asked Joe. He folded his arms across his chest. Skeptical.

"A woman fell down the stairs and broke her neck," said Duval. "It was tragic. Video surveillance at the mall has your son there, talking to her, minutes before it happened."

His eyes narrowed and shifted suspiciously. "Why are two detectives investigating an accident?" asked Joe.

Duval hesitated. He was unprepared for the question.

"The woman's children are missing," said Carrol. "No one knows what happened to them. With her dead, the family is worried. We desperately need to find these kids. Any information we can gather from your son in regards to what they may have talked about could provide valuable clues as to where these kids might be."

"No," said Sara. Her arms stiffened at her side. The only thing missing was a heel stomp to the ground as she said it. "You need to leave and come back with a warrant."

"It's OK, Mom…Dad," said a voice. He walked in from the living room. He was almost six feet tall. Athletic build. Handsome. All of the attributes Duval had seen in the footage from the mall, but up close, there was something more to him. He had a presence. "I have no problem talking to them about Cynthia."

She blew air, confounded. "You'll be late for school!" said Sara.

"No worries, Mom. Biology review first period. I'm good. We can talk in the living room," said Adonis. "Can I get you anything to drink?"

"No, I'll be fine," said Duval.

"I have coffee in the car," said Carrol.

Duval stepped past Sara, feeling her objection like heat radiating from an oven. They followed Don through the foyer into the living room. There was a couch on one side and a chair and ottoman on the other. Brown, soft, and comfortable. Duval picked the chair to sit down in. He felt the family would be more comfortable sitting together on the couch. Carrol stood with his back to the window. Adonis slid the ottoman over toward the middle of the room and sat on that instead of next to his parents.

"There are missing kids?" asked Adonis. "What are the chances they are still alive? Not good, I would say."

Duval was shocked by his candor. Also by his temperament. He was completely calm. No worries. His parents were visibly nervous, and rightfully so, but Adonis was the complete opposite. The simple assumption was his overconfidence came from arrogance. But Duval did not get that feeling at all. Arrogant? Yes. However, his confidence was more like a certainty.

"Did you know Cynthia had kids?" asked Carrol.

"We didn't talk about kids," Adonis answered.

"What did you talk about?"

"Nothing in particular. She came on to me. I told her I was a high school student, and it stopped right there."

"Then how is it that you called her?" asked Carrol. "Phone records indicate you called her at the mall."

There was a pause. Don smirked. "She gave me her number. I called her so she could have mine. Easiest way to do it."

"But you are a high school student," said Carrol. "Thought you said it stopped after that?"

"I don't see how this is helping to find these missing—"

"Did you know Harold Sheki?" asked Carrol. He unwrapped a piece of candy and tossed it into his mouth. He rolled it around the inside of his cheek before saying, "He lived not too far from here."

"The guy who kept those women in his basement?" said Adonis. "My sister mentioned it at the breakfast table one morning." He turned to Duval. "Never met him."

"How about Ajani Adebayo?" asked Carrol.

"Nope," said Adonis.

"Excuse me," said Sara, holding her hand in front of her as to pause. "Who is this man, and why are you asking my son about him?"

"Ajani lived about half a mile from here. He was from Kenya. Turned out he fled his country escaping prosecution. He was one of the gangsters who specialized in forcing young girls into prostitution. Anywhere from nine to sixteen years old. He was particularly brutal when he broke them in. Nobody knew where he was until he turned up dead, a few days ago."

"I don't understand how this pertains to my son," said Joe.

"Ajani was murdered," said Carrol. "Police arrested the man who did it. An ex-soldier from Kenya confessed and told authorities why he killed him. He lived in Delaware before he got wind of where Ajani was hiding."

"You're not doing a very good job of explaining what that has to do with my son," said Joe. "Why did you ask him if he knew a pimp from Kenya?"

Carrol rolled the piece of candy around his mouth before answering. "The man in custody said he received a letter telling him exactly where Ajani was. When police asked where the letter came from and who wrote it, all he would say was it came from someone who'd spotted Ajani in the area. Then he went silent. Said Ajani deserved to die a horrible death. He poured gasoline on Ajani and set him on fire. Said it was a fitting way to enter hell."

"You want to know if I sent the letter," said Adonis.

"You caught that," said Carrol. "You are as bright as they say."

"Sounds like you are trying to connect the dots," said Adonis. "But is connecting the dots worth it? Ajani sounds like he got what he deserved. Are you really wasting tax dollars trying to figure out who is sending these people to their graves?"

Duval was confused. This exchange between his partner and Adonis was nothing like what he expected. Carrol must have been up all night. Looking into what? Random deaths in the area? Why was he doing that? But even more frightening, this kid was returning the serve. He knew exactly what Carrol was talking about. They'd come here to ask about the backpack and the murder of Connor Richardson. What had Duval missed?

"Vigilante…" said Carrol. "The belief of taking justice into your own hands—a child's fantasy, you know. Those of us who have lived long enough know you can't eliminate violence. That's a dream. A make-believe world. No matter how many weeds you pluck out, new ones sprout up in bunches."

"Childish, huh? I thought your main concern was for those missing children. Seems as if you have an ulterior motive. Isn't your time more precious than that?"

"Safety is my utmost concern. The safety of those kids. The safety of the innocent, the accused, and the guilty. Our system of justice—"

"Is flawed!" said Adonis. He glared. Hand in his pocket, staring intently at Carrol, almost in frustration. He was rattled. Losing composure for the first time. "How about you focus on protecting the innocent? Using tax dollars trying to figure out how guilty people are dying by accident seems like a complete waste of resources. I am sure the would-be governor would be interested in hearing how you are wasting time with me instead of finding his son's killer."

"What?" Duval's mouth opened wide out of reflex. "What the fuck did you just say?"

"Are you cursing at my son?" asked Sara, with clear aggression in her voice.

Carrol smiled. He shook his head in disbelief. "You are something, Adonis Silver." He moved from the window a bit closer to Adonis. "Before I got here, I was about thirty percent sure you had something to do with all four deaths."

"Deaths?" asked Joe, his eyebrows furrowing in anger. "Are you insane?"

"And now?" asked Adonis.

"I'm up to fifty percent," said Carrol.

"Whoa!" said Duval, pumping his hands in front of him. "Let's all slow down here." He shifted in his chair to look back at Carrol. "Nobody is accusing anybody of anything."

Carrol and Adonis were more than eight feet away from each other, but it was as if they were preparing for a heavyweight fight. Both of their egos were in the ring, chest to chest, nose to nose, eye to eye with each other, waiting to see who would make the first move.

Joe stood up in anger and pointed toward the door. "That's it. Time for you to go! And you two will be hearing from my lawyer."

"We are just in search of the truth," said Carrol.

Sara shook her head. "No. You are not. These questions you are asking. This is an interrogation of someone you think is guilty. You said it yourself."

"I'm sorry we offended you, Mrs. Silver," said Duval, standing with his hand on his chest. "That was not my intent."

"No. Your intent was to rattle Adonis." She glared over at Carrol, who seemed to be in fight mode with Adonis. "I see what you are doing. This is how people who are innocent find themselves in prison. Police investigators have a hunch. That's all they have. That CSI nonsense of 'follow the science' is bullshit. That is not how you guys work. The police believe someone is guilty, and they throw out all other facts and information."

"Mrs. Silver," said Duval, pleading his case, inching closer to her. Trying to calm her down. "I promise you we are not here for that."

"Bullshit," she said. Tears were beginning to form in her eyes. "Don't you think it is contradictory, or shall I say hypocritical, that a person can say they did not do something for hours upon hours of interrogation and you don't believe it, but the instant they say they did do it, just one time out of a thousand, you choose to believe it? You convict people by saying, Hey look, he confessed…after three days and fourteen hours of interrogation, yeah, he said he did it so he could be left alone…but you take the confession and run to get a conviction, and when the guy says he was lying about the confession, do you believe that he was lying about it? No. You only believe what benefits you in closing a case."

"Mrs. Silver," said Duval. "We don't act without evidence. It's true we respond to hunches." He looked over at Carrol, who was in a zone: a staring contest with Adonis. "But the two have to match up before we can get a conviction."

"And if the evidence was false, then what? I've read that even after DNA evidence exonerates a convicted felon, that person still sits in jail for years while the paperwork is being processed. There are other cases where people who were locked up confessed to murders someone else was convicted of, giving intricate details only the murderer would know, and still, that evidence is ignored. So forgive me if I fly off the handle here in defense of my son. I don't trust you! And I don't trust your fucking evidence."

"You sound like a defense lawyer," said Carrol, finally breaking his gaze from Adonis.

"I have a law degree from Yale!" she said.

Duval sighed. This thing had been blown way out of proportion. Off track. They may have screwed themselves, even if the evidence showed Adonis Silver's backpack had Connor's DNA on it. Duval looked at Joe Silver, standing angrily, pointing to the door. He looked at Sara Silver, in tears. Then he looked at Adonis, staring indiscriminately, eyes moving at small intervals but not really looking at anyone, fiddling with something in his pocket.

"Thank you for your time," said Duval. He reached into his jacket pocket to retrieve his sunglasses. He didn't know why he put them on. Just seemed like something to do before walking out the door. He passed by Carrol, who didn't seem ready to leave. After standing shoulder to shoulder with his partner, Carrol regained his composure and followed Duval out the door. They went down the three brick stairs and out the front gate. He went to yank the car door open, but the door was locked and his hand slipped off the handle. Duval erupted.

"What the fuck was that about, Carrol?"

"I was up all night. I told you. I didn't want to look ridiculous."

"What the hell was that about accidents? I thought we were going to check out the backpack. Obtain it somehow. See if there were traces of blood inside. Maybe he still had Connor Richardson's phone." He placed his hands on his hips and looked around at nothing in particular, miffed about the questions his partner had asked. Even more upset he did not know as much as Carrol about the woman in the video or its relevance to the case. He was narrowly focused on one thing. "Is the story about missing kids true?"

"Yeah," said Carrol. He crunched down on the hard piece of candy, bulging the muscles in his jaw as he chewed. "Cynthia Kavanagh was being investigated. Husband and kids are missing. She said they ran away, but the husband's family isn't buying it."

"What about that other shit?" said Duval, tossing his hands in the air. "The guy from Kenya and the other one?"

"Strange fatal accidents. All within a five-mile radius of this house. I typed in a search of any violent crimes being investigated in the area, and the guy who had the car fall on him came up. But the investigation started after he died. Then I saw the man from Kenya was arrested and read his story."

"How is that even remotely the same thing?" Duval asked, feeling the wrinkles in his forehead tighten.

Carrol could only shake his head. "I don't know. The story kind of fits together in my head. It unfolded right before my eyes. You saw his reaction to it, didn't you? He knew all about it."

Hell. Somehow, he knew they were investigating the murder of the would-be governor's son.

Duval was even more frustrated after his hand slipped off the door handle a second time while trying to pull it open. It was still

## Karma Butterflies

locked. He glared at his partner sideways over the top of the car. Carrol clicked the fob to unlock it, and Duval opened the door. He sat down in the car, which smelled like warm leather and coffee. Carrol sat down beside him and pushed the button to start the car. He gripped the steering wheel tight.

"Did you hear what the mom thought about us?" said Carrol, putting the car in drive. "Told you it was someone who wanted to defund the police!"

Duval turned away in disbelief. As the car pulled away from the curb, he spotted a young woman approaching the house. She was talking to the young girl in the car in the driveway and turned to wave when they began moving. Seemed like the Silvers had visitors lined up today.

## CHAPTER 23

Don knew his first attempt at using the eye would eventually come back to bite him. He'd acted impulsively without taking enough precautions to protect himself. Just like he'd figured would happen, here she was. Siobhan Starlette had on a thin blue jacket, jeans, and an olive-green T-shirt with white Japanese symbols written on it. She was standing outside his front door waiting for someone to answer. Don peeked at her through the blinds as his parents bombarded him with questions about the police visit. Her deep blue eyes were glowing in contrast to her dark-brown hair, which was in a single braid down to the middle of her back. She stood straight, head bent slightly to the ground, with her hands crossed in front of her. Almost penitent. Willing to accept her punishment for intruding but nonetheless determined to intrude.

"Who is that?" asked his mother.

"I know her" was all Don said, still peeking through the blinds.

"Why were the police here?" said Joe frantically. "What were those crazy questions and accusations?" Joe was looking at Sara more than at Don. He realized there was something he had been excluded from. The two weeks of teshuva Sara had insisted Don perform at the synagogue without explaining the offense certainly had something to do with the visit. "I'm going to take Jasmine to school, and then we are going to sit down and have a long conversation...all of us." His expression was stern and powerful.

He went to the door and was surprised by Siobhan, as if he had forgotten she had just rung the bell seconds ago. "Excuse me. Who are you?"

"Siobhan Starlette. I've come to see Adonis Silver."

Joe scoffed. "I have to take my daughter to school."

He walked by her, leaving Don and Siobhan face to face.

She had a striking beauty to her, something Don had not thought about previously. But her intrusion came at a bad time. "What do you want?" said Don.

She took a moment as her eyes looked up at him in awe. "You are exactly as I imagined."

Yet, Don was a bit more troubled by her visit. None of these interruptions were things he could see. It was his future after all. A future that would change the instant he tried to look upon it. He could only look into the future of others with any consistency. And this visit was not in Siobhan's future. It must have been an anomaly, caused by the tall man with no future. Just like the visit by those detectives. An anomaly.

"Are you going to invite me in?" asked Siobhan.

"Why should I?" said Don. "I don't know you."

"Send her away," said his mother, standing at the edge of the foyer. "We need to talk!"

And he would have told Siobhan to get lost, but as he looked into her eyes, he could see she would not go away. There was a sense of determination about her. She'd hunted him down for a reason. He sighed and stepped aside, allowing her to enter. "This is a private matter, Mom. This won't take long."

"Private?" she screeched in disbelief. "Adonis."

"Please, Mom. This will only take a minute."

He escorted Siobhan through the living room and up the stairs to his room. He took hold of the doorknob and closed the door. At the top of the stairs was his mother. She was looking at him, desperate for answers as the door shut. He'd promised her there would be nothing to worry about, and he'd failed. She was worried. Beyond worried. Her worst nightmare was the police would barge through the door to take him away for whatever he'd done to get that blood all over his clothes. She'd been carrying that worry around in her gut for weeks. He'd seen how she nearly broke down in tears when Detective Dimwit began asking about the missing children. Her mind was putting the wrong scenarios together. He had to do something to remedy that. Talk her off the ledge. Before his father returned.

Don turned around to face Siobhan. He needed to make this quick. She stood there in front of him, quiet and apologetic. He took a deep breath and exhaled hard so she could hear his frustration. What was he going to do with her?

"Why did you come here?" he asked.

"Do you know how many people go missing in the United States each year?" she asked.

"Tell me," said Don.

"Nearly six hundred thousand. Half of that number turn up again on their own. Another two hundred thousand are people who run off and don't want to be found. That leaves nearly one hundred thousand who are abducted and never found."

Don was gone for a moment. In another place. His thoughts on the countless number of missing people he had seen through the eyes of others who were no longer walking among the living. When he was experimenting with the eye, testing his limits, the majority of the time, he witnessed the pain of loss.

Her blue eyes shifted to look up at him. "I didn't tell anyone. Not the police. Just as you instructed. Even after Charisma was returned home." She held her right hand in the air as if she were on the stand swearing under oath. "I told no one I was coming here or what you could do. I found you through your phone number, from when you called me."

Noble of her. But he couldn't have her poking around. "I never gave you my phone number," said Don plainly.

"I understand if you don't want anyone else to know you are a powerful psychic. That's why you instructed me not to go to the police. I'm sure they would never have believed the word of a psychic, but you are the real deal. The instant the Hispanic, or should I say 'Arab-looking,' guy walked up to me and said his uncle owned the place on the corner, I knew you were special."

"Cute, but I never called you. I hardly use my phone to call anyone. You can check it." Don pulled the phone from his pocket. He held it out for Siobhan. "Look through it. You have the wrong guy. Better look somewhere else."

She frowned. "Timothy Dusseldorf's phone is the one you used to make the call. Any amateur could track that down. Why are you pretending it's not you? I spoke to Timothy. He said you borrowed his phone to make the call. You were giving instructions. Then he said you handed him back the phone and said your parents were already at the restaurant. Don Silver is your name, and you are going to be attending Yale in the fall."

Don walked around the bed to the window and skirted open the blinds. He looked out into the neighbor's yard. It had a white privacy fence around the property. A mulberry tree near the back fence was beginning to bloom, and a blue bicycle was leaning against the trunk. His thoughts were on how to get rid of her, and make sure she wouldn't return, without using the eye.

"Think about it for a second," said Don, indulging the first thing that came to mind. "Suppose I just walked out of the bathroom at the restaurant and saw your sister's picture on the wall. Suppose I was one giant asshole and wanted to play a prank using your sister as bait. I borrow the phone of some guy going into the bathroom and tell him some tale to get him to give me his phone. Then I call you and rattle off the first thing that comes to my mind, sending you on a wild goose chase because I am that kind of person. By chance, it turns out your sister comes home safely. It doesn't make me some powerful psychic. It makes me an asshole."

"Are you suggesting what you did was a prank?"

"Yes," said Don as it occurred to him. "It was an elaborate prank."

"You knew about my sister's scar," she said.

"I was just guessing."

She walked over to him by the window. She tried to get his attention by staring, but Don ignored her gaze and continued to look out the window. "There were specifics in your orders that were uncanny," she said. "I can't explain it exactly, but I would have brought one of my Hispanic friends along, which would have been the wrong person. By telling me the person was Arab, it forced me to do some searching. I actually gave up until I ran into the actual person I was supposed to bring."

He turned to her with an expression of absurdity written on his face. "When people want to believe something, all random, unconnected events suddenly become connected. I was an asshole who played a prank on you, and by chance, your sister was freed. That's it, Siobhan."

Don stood there in silence, hoping she would believe him. She could scream, cry, slap him in the face…anything so long as she left. Instead, she stepped back and sat on his bed. Her shoulders slouched slightly, and she crossed her legs down at the ankles.

"I hate to admit this," she said, sounding slightly dejected. "I don't really believe in psychics, tarot cards, or horoscopes, but desperate times call for desperate measures. I went to a psychic during the second week Charisma was missing. A tiny place off the main road with a purple neon sign that said *Psychic*. A gypsy woman with a weird eye held my hands and stared into my eyes. She started out by saying I had lost something very precious to me, which got me all excited. I said, 'Yes, my sister is missing,' like a dumbass, feeding her all the information she needed. Yada yada, with all the crap that followed. She said I had a powerful aura and would attract the elements that would eventually bring my sister back to me." She rubbed her hands over her thighs as if she was warming them. "I walked out of there feeling like an idiot for believing that bullshit would help me find my sister." She turned to Don. "Then you called. You were not vague at all. Never asked for any money. Did not even want to be found. And everything happened exactly as you said."

"That's it, then. Your energy brought about the results you desired. Your will and your determination. God works in mysterious ways. My dumb prank was a distraction. It was your aura that did it."

Siobhan placed her hands on her hips in irritation, looking at him sideways almost. "Reporters are eager for a story, Don. They camp out day and night trying to get a glimpse into the cars going to and from my parents' house. My dad can't go out running without them asking a million questions. They post themselves along his jogging route, trying to get whatever information they can about how Charisma escaped her captors. They even come to my apartment, shoving microphones in my face the instant I open the door. I wanted to tell them so bad about a call I received that could reveal the answer to this mystery."

Don's heart dropped. Not now. He did not need any more attention at this moment. "That would be extremely foolish," he said.

She was watching him with those bright blue eyes that seemed bigger than life. As if she had seen something. Like she'd looked into his soul and he could feel her. He turned away quickly, and it caused a reaction he didn't expect.

"I want to know how you made the couple let my sister go," she demanded.

He was taken aback momentarily but quickly recovered. "What couple are you talking about? Play the message over again. I didn't mention one word about a couple."

"You didn't have to. There was another story in the news. This one was about a couple who was found murdered. Decapitated. They believe it was a drug deal gone bad."

Don said nothing. He was amazed at the things she was putting together, but she was intelligent. Not like that dumbass detective with his wild theories…that seemed to be on point.

She continued, "This couple was murdered on the same night I went to the house to find my sister. I talked to them. They were the couple next door. They were watching the place and made sure we didn't try to go inside."

"Another random thing you are trying to give meaning to," said Don. "It's time you leave." He stood over her as she sat on his bed.

"I'm not going anywhere," said Siobhan. She took off her jacket. Her skin looked soft. He could see the fine hairs on her arms glow in the sunlight. Her T-shirt was tight on her waist and on her chest. Jeans pressed tight against her skin. Her ankles were smooth. Her white canvas shoes were clean. "You are not getting rid of me," she said. "I want to be a part of what you're doing."

"What I am doing?" asked Don.

"Answering prayers."

"I have done nothing."

"Bringing a loved one back home isn't nothing. Providing answers, a sense of finality, dead or alive, is something these families need. I was on that end…of not knowing…and I can tell you there is not a pain in the world like it. But the joy of having my sister back was nothing compared to the ecstasy I felt knowing those two fuckers who took her were dead."

"Enough," said Don. He did not want to do it. Using the eye with someone so close to directly impact what happened to him never turned out as it should. One of its quirks. But it had to be done. He touched it. Images flew by. He thought of ways to get rid of her. Time and time again, it kept coming back to the same thing. "No!" Don screamed. He let go of the eye. It couldn't be right.

She stood up from the bed. She was a few inches shorter than him. Her eyes looked into his. "You were startled when you came back." Her hand reached toward a strand of his hair. She moved it to one side. "The blood rushed to your face."

Don took a deep breath to steady himself. He steeled his body and mind and looked her straight in the eyes. "I don't know what you think you saw in my expression, but you are mistaken."

She inched closer to him. Her lips inches away from his. "I know what that feels like. Once I saw you standing in the doorway, my heart began racing as well. It's the energy between us. You can't deny its magnetic properties. This feeling isn't normal, Don. It's fierce and wild. I could see your pupils dilating. Your face flushed. Your breathing steadily increasing." She moved her head toward his chest as if she were trying to listen to his heartbeat.

Don snorted, shook his head, and backed away from her. He moved to the other side of the room. "You are off your rocker. You need help. But most of all, you need to forget everything you think is happening here."

She walked toward him again, closer and closer. He wanted to keep her at a distance, but she was not going to allow it. She forced him to retreat against the wall. "I know I am right about you, Adonis. You will not deny me this. I want to be a part of this. A part of you."

Adonis thrust himself off the wall and nudged Siobhan with his chest. He kept his body up against hers, looking down at her furiously. "It's about time you leave," he said. "Do I have to throw you out on your ass?"

She stared into his eyes. "Yes," she said. "Take me and throw me out on my ass. Throw me on my ass as hard as you can! Then harder. And harder! Keep throwing me on my ass until I can't take it anymore!"

---

Sara Silver felt as if she were hyperventilating. Breathing so hard in and out she had to sit down to calm herself. Her worst nightmare was those two detectives from Manhattan who had come out to interrogate Adonis. Why from Manhattan?

She gasped.

The night he came home late, was Adonis in Manhattan? They can track cellphones now. They can tell if he was there. She looked around the living room and focused on the chair the detective had sat on. Then to the ottoman, where Adonis had been perched. The detectives had asked him about a woman who died and had two children. Now another woman had shown up at the front door. This woman upstairs in his room, Siobhan, looked like she was in her midtwenties. Was Adonis picking up older women? So much of what was happening she did not understand. What made it more frustrating was Adonis's cryptic assurances that everything was fine.

But how could it be? Adonis had come home with blood on his clothes. The first thing she'd noticed was the hat speckled with droplets. Then he'd pulled the other clothes out of his backpack. Shirt and pants covered in blood. She had taken them outside to the barrel they used for burning leaves in autumn, and she had burned them, the hat included. Adonis said someone was threatening Jasmine, and he had taken care of it. What crime had she helped him cover up?

She put her hands to her mouth to muffle her latest gasp. Her fright about her part in all of this. But the detectives had nothing. They were clearly fishing. Killing people through accidents…was that even possible? How would she explain this to Joe? He would be back any minute. His jovial nature gone. He was dead serious and had every right to be.

*What's that?* she asked herself.

She tried to quiet her thoughts to listen. Sounds that were faint and growing louder. She tried to place them. Familiar but foreign. Then her eyes grew wide with shock and embarrassment. The sounds Sara was hearing were lovemaking sounds. Two people upstairs. Moans and grunts and thrusts and passion all swelled into one definable act. The sounds drowned out her inner thoughts. They got louder and louder until they were the only thing she could hear. The rocking grew to pounding. The moans elevated to screams of passion.

Her sweet boy and that woman. Upstairs in her house. She wanted to scream and pound on his door until they stopped, but by the sound of them, she knew it would be fruitless. They were enthralled in the type of savage passion she had only experienced once in her life. There was no getting in between something like that. Her interruption would barely be acknowledged.

Her son…he was growing…changing.

# CHAPTER 24

Duval was fuming on the ride back to Manhattan. The calming spa music flowing from the car speakers did nothing to ease the knot in his temple. He replayed in his head how quickly the encounter had gone sideways. He ground his teeth at the thought of it. The first solid lead they had in over three weeks, and Carrol had shot it all to hell with his wild theories. Murdering people by accident. *Where the fuck did that come from?* They were working on a murder case in which the perpetrator took a pipe to the head of the victim.

Somehow, they had to get a hold of the backpack. It was their only chance to salvage the case.

"They are going to lawyer up now," said Duval. "If Adonis Silver has the slightest clue we are on to the backpack, he will destroy it. And we will be caught with our dicks in our hands trying to explain why we harassed a child prodigy about the murder of Connor Richardson with no fucking evidence."

"Not really," said Carrol. They were coming up over the Throgs Neck Bridge. A few sailboats were on the East River. Just a couple. "We still have a great chance to get this guy. The people who died mysteriously through accidents were all bad people. Since Adonis

Silver's MO is killing bad people, Connor must have done something bad as well. There's your connection."

Duval felt as if he were going to jump out of his skin. "What connection?" he screamed. "What fucking accident? He beat Connor to death with a pipe! You want to investigate Connor Richardson to see if he deserved to be murdered? What are you thinking?"

As they entered the Bronx, banners appeared advertising candidates running for all sorts of offices. Judges, Senate seats, House seats, district court positions, and then there was the red, white, and blue banner of Barney Richardson for governor.

Duval pressed his fist against his mouth in a thinker's pose. He felt the pressure of his gold wedding band through his lip and up against his gums to help keep him from screaming. It was clear that Carrol had put in the work, and it was the most impressive piece of detective work he had done in years, but where was this leading? Chasing obscure theories about people dying through accidents?

"Excuse me," Duval said mockingly, pretending to be talking to Barney Richardson. "But your son is a scumbag, and finding out what kind of scumbag he really is will help catch his killer…Yes, this is how we investigate murders…Yes…Yes…If you're elected, I do understand I will not have a job in law enforcement. Thank you." He scoffed, turning his head to look out the passenger's side window as they rolled through the Bronx.

Carrol pursed his lips as if to indicate the point had been taken but shifted his eyes as if he knew something Duval did not. "It was a school day," said Carrol. "There was a report filed from a guard in a warehouse not too far from where Adonis Silver lives. You know who the manager of that warehouse was? Connor Richardson. The guard was beat up there by a kid fitting Adonis Silver's description on the same day Connor was murdered."

"What?" said Duval, turning his head to Carrol. "When did you find this out?"

"Wouldn't you like to know, huh?" Carrol said arrogantly, with a little head waggle on top of it. "When I was looking into crimes in the area, this is what popped up. The incident with the guard happened in the early afternoon." He did a shoulder shrug with his head tilted to the side. "If Adonis was home that day or left school early, we could show the guard a picture of him…"

He left it there for Duval's imagination to do the rest. It was enticing. Duval wanted to tell him to turn the car back around and head to the warehouse, but they had already performed a series of missteps on this one.

"Even if he assaulted the guard, how do we connect that to the attack on Connor?" asked Duval. "Adonis tracked him down in the city to kill him? Why?"

"Because Connor did something fucked up to him," said Carrol, turning away from the road to make eye contact.

It brought Duval around to Carrol's way of thinking. Perhaps they were getting nowhere with the investigation because they were thinking in a conventional way. By the numbers. The way Duval operated. He wasn't on board with the accident stuff. That was completely batshit. But the assault had another element they might have been misinterpreting. The phone.

Before the fatal strikes took place, the assailant looked through Connor's phone. It was assumed he was looking for something pertaining to money. Bank account or other personal information with which to siphon cash. The assailant took the phone and was smart enough to remove the SIM card so the phone couldn't be tracked, but why take it?

Revenge or retaliation suddenly made sense. Connor could have a clue as to why he was murdered on his phone. Racy pictures or some other socially damaging information on Adonis or someone he cared about. Whatever was on that phone would link Connor to his killer.

"Let's look into the warehouse," said Duval. "Quietly."

For the second time that morning, the black CTS turned around on its way back toward Long Island. Duval knew Adonis was the man in the video, and after meeting him, he was betting the boy's arrogance would be his downfall. He had seen it too many times. Even when criminals covered all their bases, there was always one thing they did not think of. Something they missed.

Most of the time, the unknown variable was being able to control other people. A feat even the brightest person had to admit was impossible. Unless you committed a crime in a vacuum, there was always someone else who knew something. Even if they didn't know the specific crime, they knew the person was in the area when they should not have been there. They picked up on things like peculiar behavior or attention to detail they would normally be disinterested in. Something different.

Duval could sense it in Sara Silver's voice. *Mom knows what he did.* But he had to piece it together properly. Try to turn the mother against her son in order to unravel the thread. Hopefully, this assault at the furniture warehouse would provide the shock that would cause Mom to slip up the next time they talked to her.

Just before 11:00 a.m., the Cadillac slowed down as it passed Carlo's Furniture Warehouse in Long Island. Duval looked behind him to the corner, off the main street, and followed the concrete path to the warehouse. It was smack dab between a residential area and small businesses. Not a giant warehouse but a decent size. A hub for the main stores in the city. It was advertised quite often on television. Duval had even popped his head into a few of the stores in the past, right after he got married.

The Cadillac coasted down the street a ways until they found a parking spot. Then they walked back to the warehouse. They passed a number of homes and entered the warehouse grounds through the open fence for delivery trucks. Smooth white concrete in big slats was the first thing Duval noticed as he headed down the ramp toward the loading dock. It was clean and orderly.

To the left was the office, with a large glass window and a white door offset from the center. They could see a woman sitting at a desk. Redhead with large glasses. Her hair was tied back. Before entering the office, Duval looked up by the loading dock and along the top of the fence surrounding the warehouse. He saw cameras. A good number of them. Hopefully, they retained the footage.

Carrol walked straight into the office with his girth and cheap brown tie dangling in the wind. He had his jacket open with his hands holding the part where his shield was visible in the side of his belt, although it was partially obstructed by his girth. Duval decided to do the same. Hold his jacket open to display the shield on his waist as they entered the office area.

"Can I help you, officers?" asked the woman behind the desk. She was professional. The placard on the desk said her name was Charlene Camp.

"You absolutely can, sweetie," said Carrol. He leaned over the elevated portion of the receptionist's desk and rested his elbow against the top. Duval shook his head at this. Carrol tried his hand with the ladies quite often. He was a fifty-year-old player who was four times divorced. He was fully aware he had no sex appeal whatsoever, but he didn't care. Carrol behaved as if he had come straight off the cover of a romance novel. "I'm Detective Arnold Carrol, and this is Detective Kevin Duval," he said while directing his thumb nonchalantly.

"Pleasure to meet you," she said. "What do you need?"

"There was a report that a man came in here a few weeks ago

and assaulted a guard," said Duval. "We wanted to get some details on the assailant for another case. Where did the assault take place? Did he come in and rush the guard?"

"He came in posing as some kind of inspector."

"A furniture inspector?" asked Carrol. His eyebrow raised and his forehead wrinkled as he looked at Duval with a certain gullible sarcasm.

"I know it sounds ridiculous," said Charlene. "He said he was from Carriage Sofas. We have many items shipped in from Carriage on a daily basis, so it didn't seem out of the ordinary. He wanted to see our bill and lading on shipments for a specific date. He was looking for a couch that might have been shipped here accidentally."

"Was there a couch shipped here accidentally?" asked Duval.

She hesitated before nodding. Regretfully. Apologetically. "There was. I ended up taking it home with me. It was not on any of the records, and I really liked the couch. I thought no harm, no foul. I came clean to my boss after the incident. I explained everything."

"What was the guy's name?" asked Carrol.

"I don't remember. Or he didn't say."

"Cameras all around," said Duval, waving his finger in a circle. "Did you pick up any images of him?"

"Yes," said Charlene. "Not very good angles, I'm afraid. But he was a young guy, brown hair, athletic build, extremely good-looking."

"And how did he assault the guard?" asked Carrol.

"They had a fight down in the old storage area."

"Where is that?" asked Carrol.

"Inside the warehouse, near the offices inside."

"How did he get in there?" said Duval.

"Again, stupid me. I fell for his tricks and escorted him around the warehouse floor and into the upper offices. When he saw the old storage area below, he asked to check down there. It's too narrow an entrance to fit a couch, so I refused. In any case, it was padlocked, and I told him I did not have the combination. But he went right over to it and somehow got it open. Like he knew what the combination was. When he went down the stairs, I got the guard, Tim."

She nudged her head over to the warehouse entrance door to her left. Outside the office, in line with the large warehouse door that was open, was a hulking figure of a man. Blond, buzz-cut, tanned with a gold chain. The security shirt was like a police uniform except dark blue. Short sleeves showed all of his bulging muscles. His face, however, was slightly scarred; looked like he'd been in a hell of a scrap that was just about healed.

"During the fight, Tim lost balance and slipped," said Charlene. "That's how the guy escaped."

Duval yelled over to Tim, "Is that how it went down, Tim?"

Tim scrunched his face like *Whatever* but didn't answer.

"We would like to see the old storage area where the assailant went," said Carrol. "Is it still open?"

"I put a new lock on there…with a key."

"Who had access to the lock before?" asked Duval.

"I had never seen anyone go down there before. It was always locked, even before I started working here. I was told it was an old storage area and nothing was down there except rats."

"Who told you that?"

"The regional manager, Connor Richardson…He's deceased now. A robbery gone bad when he went out to the store for his wife."

"Tragic," said Carrol.

They decided not to mention to Charlene that they were homicide detectives. They wanted her to assume they were there to investigate the assault. That way, any information given about the assailant would be completely unbiased. If they told her they suspected the same person who committed the assault murdered Connor, they might have problems using her as a witness in the future. A lawyer could easily argue she was biased and her testimony linking Adonis to both crimes only happened after the detectives suggested it.

"How about we check out the space?" said Duval.

Charlene got up from her chair. She was wearing a nice white blouse with a black skirt that ended above the knees. Her black heels were high, accentuating her calf muscles. Her legs were covered in freckles. Carrol followed closely behind, admiring the view. Duval gave them a few steps before he left the office in pursuit. He took his time so he could get a good look at Tim's face. Their eyes met, and Duval stopped.

"It's healing up pretty good," said Duval, waving a finger in a circle around his own face. "Did he hit you with anything? A pipe, perhaps?"

"I fell," said Tim. "No pipe."

"OK, just checking." Duval could feel the rankling anger radiating from Tim. Was it from embarrassment? "How big was your attacker? Was he a strong guy like you?"

Tim cut his eyes. He said it slowly, through gritted teeth. "I slipped and fell."

Not big at all, Duval surmised. "Got it."

He trotted along to catch up with the duo of Carrol and Charlene on their stroll through the warehouse. They walked through several aisles of furniture, paying attention to the caution tape and warnings written on the smooth warehouse floor. People with electric pallet jacks loaded with items rode their machines from one location to the next. The group of three turned at the end of the aisle. There were stairs leading to offices upstairs overlooking the warehouse. Beneath the stairs, in the corner, was a black diamond-plated set of doors on the floor.

"Here we are," said Charlene. She knelt down in her tight black skirt and inserted the key into the padlock. "No one has been down there since that day. What are you looking for, anyway?" She unlocked it and stood with the padlock in hand.

"We have no idea," said Duval. "The assailant went down there, so it's best we find out what he was doing."

Carrol grabbed the heavy steel doors and opened one side, then the next. They looked down and could only see the first couple of concrete stairs; the rest were covered in darkness. Pitch black. Duval reached into his jacket pocket for a flashlight. He turned it on and focused the beam down into the cellar storage area. He could see the stairs of crumbling concrete and stains on the floor below.

"You are the man with the plan," said Carrol. "Light the way, brother."

Duval sneered and took the first step. It was narrow. Only one person could go up or down the stairs at a time. He walked down carefully so as to not let his clean suit jacket touch anything dirty. When he got to the bottom of the stairs, he saw a light switch. He flipped it, and a light came on.

"So much for a part of the warehouse that was closed off," said Carrol, who came down right behind him, kicking crumbling concrete from the stairs across the floor. "Still has electricity."

They looked around the cramped and dampened space, which smelled musty and stale. Old paint and oil stains were visible on the concrete floor. The walls were cinder block, there were cobwebs in the corners of the ceiling, and rats were evidenced by the droppings on the floor. All kinds of huge pipes ran overhead from the north to the south side of the building. There wasn't much headroom. Duval saw a brown wooden door leading to another room. Another padlock was on the latch, but this one was unlocked.

He pulled the door open. There was a light switch in this room as well. He turned on the light, and the room lit up. "Looks like someone has been down here," said Duval. There was a bed against the wall and an old fire extinguisher in the corner. The walls were brick. Old and dirty. Duval felt the grit under his shoes. A chain sat in the corner on the floor, thick and heavy.

"You think the kid was in this room poking around?" asked Duval.

"You can bet your ass he was," said Carrol.

First thing Carrol did was check under the bed. He backed off and kicked the frame hard. A rat scurried out from beneath it, scaring the shit out of Duval.

"How about a proper warning next time?" he said.

"Don't get your panties in a bunch," said Carrol. "I was the one staring into those glowing red eyes down there. He was close enough to kiss me."

Carrol took his leg and thrust the bed down the wall to see what was underneath. A carcass of a small animal and plenty of rat droppings.

"This is disgusting," said Duval. "Are we almost done here?"

"Not quite," said Carrol. "This is just like my days undercover in narcotics. Places like this were notorious for housing heroin addicts getting their fix. They got real creative at hiding things. I mean, who could you trust? Right? After a while, I became good at sniffing out the hiding spots."

Carrol stopped and looked up at the pipes that ran the length of the room. He went over to one and began tapping. These were big, thick black pipes. Either sewage or gas lines; Duval didn't know one from the other.

Carrol tapped on one and went to the joint that held them together. He gave it a twist, and it moved.

"If shit comes flying out of there, I am going to puke," said Duval. "Just letting you know in advance."

Carrol scoffed. "I'd be more afraid of a flurry of rats pouring down into the room if I were you. Get ready."

Duval took a step back, ready to make his way for the door and up the stairs if need be.

His partner gave one swift tug of the pipe, and it came loose. There was nothing. No rats or sewage. Just a slight bit of dust in the air. The pipe was resting on Carrol's shoulder. He looked into one end still held up by a clamp. "Give me your flashlight."

Duval stretched his arm out to give it to him. Carrol shined the light into the open end of the pipe, then reached inside and pulled out a shoebox. Light gray in color with a black lid. He handed the box over to Duval and then hoisted the pipe back into the joint, twisting it so it would stay in place.

Duval shook the box to test the contents. It sounded like objects of some sort. Multiple items. Cards or papers. Then he removed the lid. "Polaroids," he said.

After dusting off his hands, Carrol came over. Together they sorted through the photos. Little girls. Some nude, some fully clothed. Racy. Obscene. Sick. The nude photos were particularly disturbing. Some of the young girls were sleeping, and someone had pulled down their pants and opened their pajamas. Others appeared to be drugged or drunk. They counted thirty-two different kids.

"Is everything OK down there?" asked Charlene. "I'm going to have to get back to the front soon."

Duval looked down at the photo in his hand. Then sorted through several more. "Freckles," he said. "Young girls with freckles."

Carrol nodded. All the young girls had freckles of some sort.

"This is a whole 'nother crime," said Duval. "And another division. This crosses over into our investigation."

"Remember the girl in the car?" asked Carrol. "Adonis Silver has a sister. We passed a middle school on the way here. I bet his sister goes there." Carrol held up a photo of a girl in a school uniform.

"These pictures are old. He was probably trying to recreate these images in this room. I bet that's what Adonis was looking at when he sorted through Connor's phone. It was pictures like this."

## CHAPTER 25

Sex. Who knew it would be so stimulating? The thought of touching himself was repulsive, so he'd never thought to experiment. The female gestures and batting of eyes stirred no feelings inside of him at all. Yet, suddenly, it was as if the primordial side that had long slumbered suddenly had awakened with a vengeance. He could not control it. Nor did he want to. Siobhan had ignited something he had not known was there. Raw and animalistic. The desire to press flesh against flesh. To take your body and use another body for the sheer purpose of pleasure. He knew nothing except unbridled lust as he took her. Nothing else crossed his mind. Not the police, his parents, or what he was doing.

They lay on the bed embracing each other, completely bare. Her black hair draped over his abdomen as her head rested on his chest. He realized then that her single braid had become unraveled as he was pulling it from behind. It wasn't intentional. "It was my first time," said Don, not knowing why he confessed it. He didn't have a history of revealing his vulnerability, nor did he feel the need to be deceptive about such a thing. Still, he had no concept of why he confessed it.

Her soft hand rubbed his chest. "I couldn't tell," she said. "It seemed like you knew exactly what you were doing."

It was semicomforting. "Nature, I guess. It felt completely natural. To the contrary of popular belief, these are things that do not have to be taught. Still, I had no idea I would lose myself in it. It was strange."

She raised her head to look at him. Her blue eyes were so illuminating. He noticed a kind of glitter in her long eyelashes. They sparkled. She took a moment to examine him, and he could not help but take in all of her beauty. "Always in control, aren't you?" she said. "'I cannot always control what goes on outside. But I can always control what goes on inside.' It's a quote from a self-help guru named Wayne Dyer." She laid her head back down on his chest. "It's complete bullshit," she continued. "I believe there is one thing you will never control: the impulses deep within. They don't show themselves. They are revealed to you, and you will often be surprised by what they show you about who you are. Don't ever believe you are in complete control of yourself, Adonis. That is when you are most vulnerable to failure."

She peeled herself away. Her perfect body slid off his, and she stood. She began getting dressed. "I needed that so badly," she proclaimed. She turned to him with a smile. "You have no idea what that means, do you?" Strands of her hair she blew playfully away from her face. "I'll be back for some more, and you better be ready."

He was ready then. He could feel nature taking over at the thought of it. She put on her undergarments and slid into her tight jeans. Her green T-shirt was slipped over her head, and then she put her blue jacket on, slipping one arm inside, then the next. She flipped her hair out and teased it with her fingers. Slipped back on her sneakers and went for the door. "I'm staying at the Viana Hotel and Spa near Old Westbury Gardens. I'll be there until the evening, then I have to head back to Connecticut for a few days. I'll be back for the weekend though."

She gave him one long glance and then slid out the door, closing it behind her. A few seconds later, he could hear Siobhan and his mother talking. The volume increased. It was apparent they were a lot alike. Alpha females. Mom said some choice words from the sound of it, and Siobhan said some strong words of her own. Then the door slammed shut, and his mother immediately began calling for him.

"Adonis Apollo Silver, get down here now!" she screamed.

The dreaded first, middle, and last name call from a mother. An indication she should not be trifled with. Don eased himself to the edge of the bed, where Siobhan had sat moments ago. Her clothes and his clothes had been heaped in a pile right in that spot. He reached down to the floor, shuffling through items until he found his socks. He had slipped a foot inside the warm black cotton when his mother barged into the room.

"What were you two doing in here?" she demanded.

He smiled, but she couldn't see it with his back turned to her.

"Put your clothes on," she said. "Your father pulled into the driveway. He's sitting in the car." She was livid. He could feel her fury radiating on his back. "You are so lucky your father did not come in here when you were with that woman."

Dear old Dad. Sitting in the car wondering how he would barge in and demand the truth. He was quick with a witty response, but when it came to serious matters, he turned into a thinker. Someone who had to gather his thoughts before taking action. He would probably be sitting there for another five minutes.

"How can you be so cavalier?" she screamed at him.

Don pulled up his underwear when his mother appeared in front of him. He put his polo shirt over his head and put his arms through the sleeves. He casually fixed the collar as she was watching.

"Tell me what you did that night," she said, moving her head with his so as not to break eye contact. Desperation contorted every muscle in her face. "Why shouldn't I tell your father about the blood on your shirt if I don't know the truth? Who did you hurt in Manhattan that night? Talk to me."

He exhaled deeply. The pesky detectives had given her one more piece to decipher about that night. She could easily do a search of assaults in Manhattan on the day in question and come up with the answer. But it was more. He was growing tired of hiding. The man he'd attacked was not worth the respect of secrecy. Perhaps it was Siobhan who had changed his mind about his actions. What should be hidden and what should be celebrated. It wasn't that he could not hide it forever; he decided there was no reason to. So he told her.

It was quick and direct, and she sat down in the chair next to his computer looking terror-stricken. Gasping for breath. He continued getting dressed, putting on his pants and shoes. He could see she was not taking it well. Admittingly, he didn't expect her to be so faint of heart. He speculated it was the future she had envisioned for him. Yale, law school, and brighter things to come, all gone by taking another's life. But she did not understand.

"Wha…why?" she asked.

"I told you," Don said plainly. "He was going to hurt Jasmine."

"How?" she screeched in a shivery voice that vibrated the floor. Her hands open in front of her, shaking as she pleaded.

"He had been following her. He was a predator. A pedophile. I saw the pictures of her on his phone. I saw his lair, where he takes the girls. It's not too far from here. In the cellar of a furniture warehouse, close to Jasmine's school. The weekend we went to Connecticut was the weekend he was going to make his move."

They could hear Joe coming inside through the front door. His mother snapped to her feet quickly. It appeared she could not decide what was more startling, Don's revelation or facing her husband under intense questioning. Her head moved to the door and back to Don in a desperate cycle.

"What about these other people the detectives mentioned?" she asked, trying to eke out a few more details before his father reached them.

"They were making stuff up, Mom. Trying to rattle me. Don't worry. They won't be able to touch me."

They could hear the creaking stairs as Joe ascended.

"How can you be so sure?" she asked.

It was time to show her. If anyone could keep his secret, it was his mother. All he had to do was place the eye in her hand, and all would be revealed. She had proven she was on his side, and witnessing the eye's power would surely put her mind at ease. He reached into his pocket. He fumbled around in it. He rummaged through it wildly. He looked down on the floor. He searched under his bed. He crawled along the ground. He tossed the covers on his bed.

"Did you lose something?" asked Joe, standing in the open doorway. "Forget about that. It's time I get some answers around here."

# CHAPTER 26

Pedophile photos. On the surface, some of them seemed harmless: random little girls smiling, wearing dresses or school uniforms. Others were somewhat suggestive, fully clothed while posing sensually and seductively. But then there were the photos that left no doubt. The nudes. The sexually explicit stuff. The owner of the photos had a particular preference. Freckles, a result of an overproduction of melanin, the thing that gives skin its color. Most prevalent when young, they fade as people get older. Duval remembered talking to Connor's wife; she had light freckles across her cheeks and nose. Charlene, the assistant standing at the entrance to the storage level, was covered in freckles. When asked who had hired her, she'd mentioned another name but added it was when she first started working at a store in Brooklyn, and it was Connor who promoted her to her current position and set her up in this office.

Duval had an obligation to initiate another investigation with the Special Crimes Unit. He made the call sometime after noon. Half an hour later, three more officers arrived: O'Connor, Washington, and Patterson. They moved in fast, taking the box of photos and initiating a team to search the room for other evidence. Charlene was the focus of their initial questioning. She looked somewhat overwhelmed. Duval did his best to try and make her feel comfortable, but it was a lot to handle. Eventually, she was reduced to tears. They mentioned nothing to her about who they suspected was the culprit, only it had to be someone who had the combination to that lock. With her insisting she'd never seen anyone ever open that lock, there was no way to connect it to Connor Richardson.

They left the furniture warehouse and made their way back down the sidewalk to the car. A cool breeze swept down the block, blowing grass clippings down the sidewalk. A clump of it came to rest at the base of Duval's shoe as he stood in front of the passenger side door.

"So what now?" asked Carrol. His lips were pursed beneath his mustache as he interlaced his fingers and rested his hands on the top of his stomach.

"We head back to the station and let the captain know what we found," said Duval.

"And our murder investigation?"

Duval prepared himself. He knew Carrol wouldn't like it. "We need to do this first."

"Fuck you," said Carrol.

"Hey!" Duval tossed his hands in the air. "A ton of attention is going to come down on us about this. We are trying to catch the guy who killed the son of a candidate for governor, and things haven't been going too well. There has been rumbling."

"Yeah, about what?" said Carrol, getting defensive.

"We are about a week away from getting pulled off this case in favor of the feds."

"The feds?" asked Carrol, stepping in closer, not believing him.

"Yes," said Duval. He was just as steamed about it as Carrol. "I got a friend in Washington. Said Richardson is making noise about it. They have no jurisdiction because Richardson is one of four candidates running, but with the case leading to pedophilia, it might give them cause to step in."

"All the more reason to snatch the kid up now and drag him into the station for questioning."

"But we need to do this right. That's all I'm saying."

"No, no," said Carrol, waving his finger in the air. "That's not all you've been saying. You took a call from your wife back there."

He left it at that. Duval could only nod in silence. Carrol was hurt and angry. Duval could see it in his face. He must have overheard. "Yeah, I told her your wild-ass theories are stymying this investigation."

"Stymying?" he said snootily with a scoff. "That's putting it nicely. The words you used were 'fucking it up.' We wouldn't even be here if it weren't for my wild-ass theories, OK?"

"Look, I admit. I have no idea how you got us here, but now we are here, what you did back there in the Silver's home set us back. We were there for the backpack. You turned it into some vigilante crime spree. Murder through random accidents? Come on, man!"

"OK, fine," said Carrol, putting a hand on his chest. "I know I am not as clever as you. I am not as keen or as observant, and I am not so good with procedures. But I have to make it up somehow. I want to contribute, not just be some lackey following around in your shoes. You think it's easy being your partner? I heard all about you before I got here. Big man, solving the toughest cases. I was told to sit back and watch and let you do your thing, but you know what, I have something to offer too. So what if my theories are shooting from the hip? Every once in a while, you still hit the target. And this time, I hit the target, so don't you dare try to take that away from me."

Duval rested his body against the car. "I was frustrated. That's why I said it. We were getting nowhere until today. With the news coming down about the feds stepping in, I knew there was no more room for error. I'm sorry."

"Are you?" said Carrol. His eyebrow raised. "Well, you can make it up to me." He quickly shifted his head left, down the block, motioning his chin in that direction. "We can go down to the school, pick up the asshole with his backpack, and then go down to the station to fill in the captain."

His inner senses were telling him no. Bad decision. But Carrol was right. As wild as his ideas were on this case, they seemed to be working. "Let's do it. First I am going to call the captain and let him know what we have. He's going to appreciate the heads-up." Duval swiped open his phone and made the call.

The timing seemed to be perfect. It was just before three in the afternoon. The local high school would be letting out soon. Adonis Silver would be heading to the bus stop to make the trip home. They decided to make a show of it. Arrest him there in front of his classmates. Normally, with a bunch of other people around, arrests could be tricky. Those who had a tendency to run could easily find enough obstacles in the form of people to maneuver away from officers, even take a hostage or two, for the ones that were dangerous. But there was something about Adonis and his arrogance that made them feel confident he would take no such action. He was certain they had nothing on him. Duval couldn't wait to see his face after they placed the cuffs on him and mentioned the furniture warehouse.

The Cadillac cruised past the high school real slow and came to a stop within sight of the front entrance. They were too late to call backup to cover all the entrances, so they were taking a chance he would walk out the front door.

It began slowly. First, a few students exited out the door, followed by a few more. And then a flurry of students poured out of the school from every exit. They paid attention to the front door, trying to keep out of sight from the watchful eyes of students. A Black guy and a White guy sitting in a car with suit jackets most certainly smelled of police no matter what city you lived in. They didn't want word to circle back through the crowd to disrupt their plan.

About five minutes in, Adonis Silver walked right out the front door. He was there with another student. Talking as they walked down the path to the front gates of the school. He was wearing jeans and a polo shirt, the same clothes he had on that morning, and the backpack they so craved was slung over his shoulder in typical fashion. Carrol and Duval prepared to move. Duval could feel the adrenaline coursing through him. Heightening his senses.

"Let's move," he said.

Carrol fired up the engine and put the car in drive. The streets were busy. Many cars were in front of the school containing parents eager to pick up their loved ones for the ride home. No problem for them, though. With a flash of the lights, they would cut through traffic with ease. Carrol took his foot off the brakes and pulled out into the stream of cars coming to the front of the school. They talked it over. As they approached the front, they would light up the car and exit, walk over to Adonis, and make the arrest. They got right behind a blue Ford Explorer and stuck tight to its tail. The approach was slow. A hundred yards, then fifty, then twenty.

Two cars away, Adonis walked to the curb. A black Tesla opened its doors, and Adonis got inside. It was the family car. Carrol remembered it from the morning.

"What the fuck?" said Carrol.

Indeed, this complicated things. It was one thing to arrest a minor on the street, another to make the arrest in front of their parents. And these parents were affluent. Well-off. By the time they arrived at the station, a lawyer would be demanding his release and probably get it. After all, all they had was a video with a strong likeness of tendencies while putting a backpack on his shoulder. The stuff about Connor being a pedophile would also not hold water. Charlene, the woman in charge of that branch, insisted she'd never seen anyone enter the area of the cellar. So that could all be dismissed as speculation or even worse, a tremendous reach by the police. They had to do better. The objective was the backpack, after all. Shoving a bloody pipe inside a cloth pack would certainly leave blood residue. And it was not as simple as washing it in a machine. Blood evidence does not go away easily. Even with the hitting of the pipe on Connor's head, there were bound to be a few hairs stuck to the pipe. How easy is it to wash strands of hair out of the interior of a backpack? Practically impossible. They needed the backpack, and right now the family would get in the way of attaining it.

"Sit tight," said Duval. "Let's follow them."

They allowed the car to pull out into traffic and get a few cars ahead of them before they gave chase. Dense city traffic was their ally. It allowed them to follow undetected. They traveled the Jericho Turnpike onto the Cross-Island Parkway. From there, they switched to the Long Island Expressway going into Manhattan. That was when Duval began to get uncomfortable. He had a feeling where they were going. So much that his face prickled with heat.

"They're going down to the station to talk to the captain about our visit this morning," said Duval.

Carrol tapped his thumbs on the wheel. "I was thinking the same thing. But it might be even better for us. We can nab him right in the station."

Duval wasn't so sure he agreed. A lawyer could be meeting them there. Certain tactics they usually got away with became impossible if a lawyer were present. "We will have to reveal how Adonis Silver became our primary suspect. Remember, we got an anonymous email with a video. We can't even prove the video wasn't doctored. The email was sent from a bogus email account. This stinks."

And if Carrol started talking about his theory of how Adonis had sent letters to assassins in Delaware, or how he'd caused a car to accidentally fall on a human trafficker, the lawyer would have Adonis laughing right out of the station.

They passed Flushing Meadows Park in Queens, home of the Unisphere and the US Open, and went through the Midtown Tunnel. They rode down 42nd Street past Park Avenue, heading west. Duval was preparing himself for what came next when the black Tesla made a left on 7th Avenue and began heading south.

"They couldn't be taking a stab in the dark about what precinct we came from," said Carrol. "Maybe they got our names wrong and some other poor saps are going to get yelled at. I feel sorry for the poor bastards of the Sixth Precinct."

"Quiet," said Duval. "I'm trying to think two steps ahead."

The black Tesla turned right on Christopher Street and pulled into a parking spot across the street from a synagogue near the middle of the block before Bleeker Street. The brown brick building looked much like a typical place of worship. Wide, ash-white concrete stairs leading to a landing. Large wooden doors up front. Stained-glass windows near the top of the building. The Star of David up high above the front entrance. Down the block were some businesses on the ground floor with apartments above. Before the synagogue were brownstone apartments, several in a row. There were trees every twenty feet or so, planted near the curb all the way to the end of the block.

Carrol spun the Cadillac around the corner and slowed down several cars behind the Tesla. He picked an empty parking spot in front of a hydrant and pulled in tight. From there, they had a get a clear view of the Tesla and the synagogue.

"What do you think?" asked Carrol.

"Church service?" said Duval.

"It's not a church," said Carrol. "It's a synagogue."

"OK. Synagogue service?"

"I don't know," said Carrol, shaking his head. "Ya think they got spooked or something? Perhaps going to see the rabbi for some clarity. Some guidance, maybe."

"I'm thinking about what's next. We can't exactly make an arrest in the synagogue parking lot. If we follow them home, we can't make an arrest there either."

"I say we pull them over somewhere around Park Avenue," said Carrol, pursing his lips and nodding. "Snatch his punk ass out of the car and take the backpack. By the time the family calls for a lawyer, we'll have already taken the backpack to the lab for collection."

"Sounds like a plan." The sun was turning orange in the sky, about to set within the hour. "I gather they are inside already." Duval leaned back in the comfort of the black leather seat. "You got first shift."

"Thanks, partner," said Carrol with a grunt.

Duval smiled and closed his eyes. He was thinking about the paperwork he had to do later and if he would be satisfied with a job well done. It all came down to what they found in the backpack. There were many other things on his mind. His wife and daughter. Crab cakes. A baseball game when he was twelve years old. Things got quiet for only a second before sirens erupted. He jumped in his seat, and his eyes focused quickly.

Another police car pulled up to the front of the synagogue before Carrol could tap his shoulder.

"What's going on?" asked Duval, feeling his heart racing after being jolted awake.

"I have no idea."

The sun had almost set. He was out for no more than an hour. They cracked open their doors and exited the Cadillac, holding up their shields high as they crossed the street. They approached a plainclothes officer who turned in surprise with his hand on his revolver.

"Easy now," said Duval, holding his free hand high and open. "We were keeping an eye on a family in there. What's going on?"

The officer was young, wearing short sleeves. Seemed to be in his early twenties. His eyes scanned over their credentials, putting him at ease. "A man snuck inside with a pistol," said the officer. "Tried to shoot up the place."

"Was anyone hurt?" asked Carrol.

"No. It was being streamed. We thought it was one of those sickos transmitting their assaults as they killed people. But this was different. One of the people being held at gunpoint began recording. Caught the attacker off guard. Saved the family's life. Her brother's in particular."

# CHAPTER 27

That bitch! Pretending she was only interested in screwing his brains out and afterward stealing his eye. Now look what had happened. This other psycho had tracked him down and tried to put a bullet in him. The tall, dark stranger appeared before Don, sticking a pistol in his face. Biggest he had ever seen. A revolver. Slugs in the cylinder were as thick as fingers. For an instant, he thought he would be taking his last breath.

Don caught himself fumbling around in his pocket as he stared down the barrel of the hand cannon only to remember he no longer had the eye to fall back on. He tried to muddle his way through, pretending to be confident, but it backfired. He jokingly said something about the dark stranger not being loved by his mother, and that set him off in the worst way. He went dark. Like a transformation. Instantly, he had the fortitude of someone who was ready to kill. He went to pull the trigger, but luckily, Jasmine came out from the back of the synagogue and began screaming. Little Jasmine was so quick on her feet. Her phone was in her hand, and she began live-streaming. This time, little Jasmine had saved Don's life.

"I can't believe my family has to be subjected to such incompetence!" Don's father yelled inside the precinct.

They were in the police station lobby. Kind of like a reception or waiting area. About thirty or more people were in the room. Talking, waiting, complaining, crying. It was cold and bland. Gray walls with white trim. The four of them sat beside each other in hard plastic chairs against the wall. Joe, Sara, Jasmine, and Don.

The officer in uniform at the reception desk called out to Don. He led them farther inside the station, toward the desks where the detectives sat. He was told to wait at a desk. There was only one seat. Don sat down. The rest of the family was instructed to go back to the main area and wait, but his mom was not having it. So they all stood around while Don waited for the detective to take his statement.

All of the desks scattered around the noisy station were brown wooden desks with bulky chairs. Looked like they got their furniture secondhand from principals' offices all around New York City. And every desk had the same round, gray metal trash can at the end of it. There were at least ten officers inside that portion of the precinct with them. His dad had finished screaming at a male officer named Gorky, who had told him the dark stranger had gotten away.

"Is that why the police were there this morning?" asked Jasmine. "They knew someone was after Don?"

Sara and Joe looked at each other in silence. Struggling for the words. "It was an accident they were looking into, Jazzy," said Sara. "Nothing to do with someone coming after Don."

Good lie, but not entirely far from the truth. The tall, dark stranger had been following Don. And he had to be someone special. He had some sort of power of his own. He was able to change the fate of Cynthia Kavanagh at the mall, and even with the eye, Don could not see into his future. Now the eye was gone. Don could feel his heart pounding. The anger growing steadily.

"Why on earth would someone want to kill Don?" said Jasmine, in tears. Her hair, face, and clothing disheveled. Her cheeks red. Her hands and body shaking.

"It was some psycho, Jazzy," said Sara. "Nobody is hunting him. I promise."

She grabbed Jasmine by the head and pulled her close to her bosom. Jazzy was a pet name. It was something their mom used sparingly. It had a tendency to calm Jasmine when she got to the point of hyperventilating. She liked the idea of being Jazzy or cool under pressure. The name seemed to trigger a calming effect.

Not with Dad, though. He seemed more and more on edge. The crowded police station was wearing on his nerves. Too many things happening at once. He was not getting the answers he wanted, which added to his frustration.

A female detective with short hair named Morales returned to the desk and took her seat in front of the computer. She placed a foam cup filled with tea in front of Don, who was sitting at one end with the trash can by his feet. She was Hispanic. Average height and build, wearing a red sweater with a black suit jacket over it. Her pants flared at the bottom and were long enough to cover most of her stylish black leather boots. She offered Don sugar, holding the packet up by her face. Her hands were rough-looking for a woman.

"How are you holding up?" she asked. She genuinely seemed concerned.

"I'm good," said Don.

One eyebrow rose momentarily. "Gun in your face about an hour ago, and you are good now? I guess you're a tough guy. How about everyone else?"

Don made a quick assessment. Dad was flustered. Jasmine, trying to overcome hysteria. Mom was holding Jasmine as if she might disappear if she let go.

"That's what I thought," said Morales. "You seem to be the only one who is good with this."

"Not good with it," said Don. "Just good." He looked up at the clock on the wall and grew anxious. Siobhan had said she was staying at a hotel near where he lived. He doubted she was honest about it. Still, he had to give it a shot. "How long is this going to take?"

"In a hurry to get out of here?" said Morales. She looked around the department with the flurry of officers and other people there, logging complaints, looking hostile. Overall, not a great atmosphere. "I guess you guys want to get home to some peace and quiet."

"Something like that," said Don.

She took a deep breath and shuffled the mouse. Within a second, the screen lit up and Don could see her screensaver. A cat person. Cats frolicking in a field. She typed in her password, which he memorized instantly. Then she took the mouse and after a few more clicks, pulled up a form and turned to Don.

"We will get you out of here just as soon as we can, OK?" she said. "But we need your help to catch this guy, so I have a few questions to ask. Do you know the attacker, or have you seen this man before?"

Don rolled his eyes. Helping her fill out a police report really wasn't going to help one bit, but the sooner he finished, the sooner he could leave. "At the mall," said Don. "Day before yesterday."

Mom let out a gasp, since she had assured Jasmine no one was after her brother. Don had to remember not to be so candid sometimes. Of course, it wasn't a problem. He didn't see the stranger as a threat, more like a curiosity.

"Did you talk to him?" asked Morales. "What was the crux of the conversation?"

"He never said a word, nor did I speak to him. He was just following me."

"Did he seem like he was on something?" Morales had a look of concern. Her eyebrows came together.

He did not answer. Detective Carrol entered the station, distracting his train of thought. He approached an officer seated at a desk near the entrance and started talking. What a fat slob he was. An oaf. His tie was tied too short. His clothes didn't fit properly. He had a shaggy mustache that Don figured he struggled to keep clean after a meal, and he smelled funny. Probably didn't wash for days at a time.

So how the fuck did he connect the dots between all the accidents Don had caused? It took a mastermind to see how it all connected. Hell, Don couldn't have made it all add up if he had been on the other end. Yet this nitwit had managed to do it relatively quickly. This was most disturbing. Don needed to get back at this guy. Expose him for the phony he was. But that would have to wait. Priority number one was getting back what had been stolen from him. Siobhan might have already left for Connecticut.

"Did you hear me?" asked Morales. "Was the guy on something? Drugs or drunk?"

He knew she was trying to help, but right now, she was an annoying distraction. "He was perfectly coherent," said Don.

"No, he wasn't," said Joe. "He was shaking and stuttering. He looked crazed. Like a madman."

The other detective who had visited him that morning entered the station and went to the officer up front. His name was Duval. He was clean and crisp and well dressed. Don liked him. Seemed like a straight-up guy. Knew his boundaries. Abided by the rules.

A thought occurred about their presence. This couldn't be where they worked. This was the Sixth Precinct, Lower Manhattan. Connor lived on the Upper West Side. Surely, there had to be more than a couple of precincts between here and there. Were they following him? Carrol and Duval were in a deep conversation with the officer at the front desk. Back and forth it went until the officer looked in Don's direction.

They were definitely following him.

Now they were plotting something else and enlisting the help of that officer in order to do it. The officer picked up the phone and dialed a number. A few button pushes. Must be internal. Don used his peripheral vision, and all of his senses to get ahead of them. In the far-right corner, a detective sitting at a desk working on his computer picked up the phone. Blond guy with a crew cut in his early forties. Without looking at them directly, Don could see the officer at the front talking while the one in the corner shook his head. What a bunch of clowns. The officer up front hung up the phone.

Duval and Carrol slid quietly out of sight. Waiting in the wings, no doubt. Now if he could only figure out what the plan was. Turn the tables on them.

"Are you sure you two wouldn't like to sit down?" said a voice. The blond detective with the crew cut came up to Sara and Jasmine. "Would you like some coffee?" he asked. "Perhaps the young lady would like a soda or something. My desk is over by the corner there. You could still see everything from over there. And you would be comfortable."

Oldest trick in the book of interrogations. Divide and conquer. Not knowing plays tricks on the mind. Makes it a game of he said, she said. Neither person certain of exactly what was discussed. However, this was not really an interrogation. At least, it wasn't supposed to be. But these two detectives were going to turn it into one. Probably tell Don later that his mother had told them everything. Cute try, but it wouldn't work.

Earlier that day, his dad had grilled his mom about why the detectives came to the house, but she stood firm. Denied everything. Not even a peep about the bloody clothes she burned. Mom was most certainly on his side. Determined to protect her son at all costs.

"We're fine being right here," said Sara. "We want to be close to Don."

"Are you sure?" asked the blond detective. "You can see everything right there." He pointed to the corner of the office. "No trouble at all. Look, if you sit down there and you're not comfortable, you can come right back."

"She doesn't want to go," said Don. "A stranger tried to kill her son. You must understand how a mother would feel at this moment, or do you not care about her feelings? Obviously, you don't!"

Don couldn't tell if the detective was incensed or astounded. He looked to Morales as if asking for help, but she was not privy to the plan, so she appeared to have no opinion one way or the other. He smiled graciously. "If you change your mind…"

"Yeah, yeah," said Don. "We know where your desk is."

He needed to get out of there so he could find Siobhan before she left town. Everything seemed to be slowing down when he needed it to speed up.

"How much longer are we going to be here?" Don asked Morales.

"Adonis," said his mother. "We need to cooperate. What's wrong with you?"

"Sorry," said Don.

"I know it's been a long day," said Morales. "Just a few more questions, and I promise we will get you out of here in no time."

Fat chance. With plan A going up in smoke, Duval and Carrol seemed to be taking the direct approach. They began walking toward Morales's desk. Joe spotted them first and glared at them as they approached. Mom saw them and shook her head as if she could not believe this was happening. Don decided to take them head-on.

Disrupt their train of thought and figure out their motive before they could take action.

"Detectives Arnold Carrol and Kevin Duval," said Don.

Morales was thrown off by this. Suddenly uncomfortable. "You know them?" she asked Don.

"Yes," said Duval. "We met the child prodigy earlier this morning."

"That's right," said Carrol. "Looks like the prodigy son has returned."

"It's prodigal son, you nitwit," said Don. "I'm Jewish. I should know. And I was not returning from anything. You assholes are following me. Why didn't you spot the jerk trying to kill me? Sleeping on the job, I guess."

He could sense no flustering of Carrol's demeanor. His harsh criticism seemed to rattle everyone except Carrol. What the hell was up with this guy?

He looked on unfazed, then raised a finger as if he'd remembered something. "Jewish...isn't that where the expression an eye for an eye came from? I'm no religious scholar, but I do believe I'm right about this. An eye for an eye. I heard someone came in and pointed a gun at that eye right there." He pointed a finger at Don's left eye. "What eye did you take that made him come after yours?"

Don really didn't like this guy. Especially his off-color way of mentioning an eye. Why had he used that term? It was infuriating listening to his witless comparisons come so close to the truth.

"OK," said Morales, "I think it's time we take a break."

She stood up, grabbed her coffee cup, and motioned for the detectives to follow. The three of them walked off in the direction of the coffee machines. There was another snack machine, a microwave, and what looked to be a toaster oven on a table against the wall. Don was certain they were filling her in on why they were there and probably asking for her cooperation. Whether she believed them or not was another story. Morales was pouring sugar packets into her cup while listening. She showed no emotion. Just listened. She was like a rock. However, they seemed overanxious about something. Their body language. Their energy.

"Adonis," said his mother, desperately trying to get his attention.

*Not now, Mom,* he thought. He was concentrating.

"Adonis," she said again.

He'd used the eye so often. Like a crutch. Now it was gone, he was feeling at a disadvantage. Had he forgotten how to read people all on his own? He possessed an unparalleled power of observation. *Think.*

"Don't you hear your mother talking to you, Adonis?" said Joe.

"Hey, Morales," yelled an officer across the room. All eyes turned to him as he appeared to be someone important. A lieutenant maybe. Plainclothes, older. Short, stout, with gray hair. His aura was one of commanding immense respect. "We spotted your suspect in the assault, hiding out in an alley a few blocks from here. We are moving in to make the arrest. I want you down there. Maybe these people can help ID him." The man looked over at Sara and winked. "I'm Lieutenant Grogan. It's almost over. We are going to lock this guy up good and tight."

Another officer jumped up from his desk like he was ready to roll. A crackle of the police radio on someone else's desk barked out the location of the suspect. This was real. They were ready to move. Don grew curious. Was it this easy to take down this guy? Didn't he have a power to protect himself? Morales rushed off. Even Carrol and Duval left to go after the guy. It was all hands on deck for this one.

The officer at the reception desk returned. "It would be great if you hung around a bit to ID the assailant."

Mom shook her head. "No." She was still shaking. "I want to go home. I have to put my daughter to bed." She tightened her grip on Jasmine's body and placed a hand on top of her head. "She has school tomorrow. I want to put this whole day behind me."

"Would you like me to walk you to your vehicle?" asked Lieutenant Grogan.

"No," said Don sharply. "We will be fine."

Lieutenant Grogan dipped his head to the ground apologetically. Like a bow. "It has been a hard day. I understand. Especially hard on you, young man." He placed his hand on Don's shoulder as if trying to comfort him. Don wanted to flick his hand away. He fought every fiber of his being not to.

"Let's get moving," said Joe. Anxious and annoyed. There was a woman with a crying child in her arms sitting at a desk directly across from where Joe stood. The side of her face was swollen and bruised. Her left eye bloodshot. "Is someone going to help this woman?" Joe screamed at the lieutenant. He thrust his hands downward and started walking.

They all walked, except Don.

"Your family is waiting for you," said Lieutenant Grogan.

Don studied him. This was a cool customer. He radiated no feelings of deception, yet all his senses were screaming that this was a trap. How could he escape it? What series of moves would allow him to get away?

Lieutenant Grogan stepped aside and gave Don room to pass, between desks, down the makeshift aisle to the exit at the front of the station. His father had stopped, and so had his mom and Jasmine. They were all waiting for him. He wasn't about to walk into the lieutenant's trap, but with his parents tired and frustrated, it appeared he had no other option.

They exited the station into the cool breeze of the spring evening. They walked to the parking garage next door. Don was leery the entire time. The police were up to something. He could sense it. They got off the elevator on the second floor. All was quiet. Too quiet. Don followed his family across the painted crosswalk to the area where they'd parked their car.

Don stopped in the middle of the walkway. It was about to happen. He wanted to warn them, especially his mother. Tell her to close her eyes and not turn around, but it was too late. Dad pressed the key fob. The car unlocked, and the light came on inside the vehicle.

They came from multiple directions. Don was grabbed from behind and thrown off balance. His chest hit the ground with a thud. He could smell the stench of the dirty concrete, the stickiness from who knew what had been spilled there. His mother screamed. His father was told to stay back. Jasmine was screaming frantically. Tears flowing down her splotched red cheeks. It was a pain he did not want them to go through.

Then his eyes locked in on what really fueled his ire…Detective Arnold Carrol. He was howling and gloating in front of Don's family as if he'd made the game-winning shot. How dare he? He believed this was a sport in which he was victorious? He had no respect for Don's family whatsoever. They didn't deserve to witness the gaudy spectacle of his triumph. They were innocent of all wrongdoing, yet he was rubbing their faces in it. He high-fived another detective as officers peeled Don from the ground and stood him up face-to-face with Carrol. The intense rage cleared his mind. All sound disappeared into a void as Don watched the gross figure of a man before him. It became clear. His callousness was unforgivable.

But why had they waited until now? They'd had him in the precinct. They could have arrested him right there. Ah—he saw Duval walking from the car holding the backpack, wearing blue surgical gloves. They could arrest him, but they could not hold the family.

They suspected his mom knew something, and she would surely get rid of the backpack as soon as they made the move. The arrest had to be made while the car was unlocked so they could retrieve it without issue. Clever.

# CHAPTER 28

On the roof of Lories Bar on Charles Street, the brick wall extended no more than a foot higher than where they stood, so they had to be careful not to get too close to the edge. The two women had a clear view of the second floor of the parking garage, through the openings between floors. The temperature was cool, yet they were warmed by the excitement of an arrest below.

The police had waited until the Silvers were in the middle of the walkway before making their move. Two detectives approached quickly, guns drawn, barrels pointed down slightly as they moved. One came from the east stair entrance of the parking garage, the other from the south. Several officers in uniform followed behind them.

Charisma looked through a pair of binoculars her sister had passed her. She zoomed in on Don's expression, leaden even with the right side of his face pressed against the ground. "Oh God, he is so beautiful," she said to Siobhan. She removed the binoculars from her eyes and twisted her face in turmoil. "So this was my savior. Shouldn't we save him?" she said, turning to her sister.

"No," said Siobhan. "And saying a man is beautiful is strange. Men are called handsome."

Charisma looked through the binoculars once more, using her hands to focus the lenses. "No…he's definitely beautiful."

She handed the binoculars back to Siobhan. The scars on Charisma's wrists were still visible from the weeks she'd spent bound and gagged. She was slowly gaining back her weight, but still thin and wiry. Her wild and untamed curly blonde hair blew across her face with the wind. She looked innocent, but the shackle scars still visible around her pale neck said otherwise. Siobhan took the binoculars and shoved them inside the pocket of her blue windbreaker.

"Do you think he knew this was going to happen?" asked Charisma.

"Not a chance," said Siobhan. She looked down through the opening of the parking garage at Adonis being pulled up from the floor by two officers. His hands were cuffed behind his back. "Earlier, I looked at the future of the detective I saw this morning to try and find out why they were at his home. About an hour ago, I looked again, and their future had changed. That was when I saw what was going to happen to Adonis. He could not have known about this."

"But he stopped before they got to the car…like he knew it was going to happen."

She was troubled by it. "I saw that too. Even without it, he could sense what was about to happen." She moved the long, single braid of her hair from the back of her neck over her left shoulder, where she could caress it. "What a dangerous man!"

"Don't you feel bad for him?" asked Charisma. "I do. He saved my life."

Siobhan loomed over her little sister, glaring down her nose at Charisma. "He didn't want to share his gift," she said tersely. "He wanted to operate in the shadows. Punishing who he saw fit. But they all need to be punished, Charisma. Everyone who has ever gotten away with treating us as objects to be abused. They all need to know the consequences if they step out of line. You've been through that suffering. You know hopelessness and distress. We shouldn't fear going to a party and being roofied or walking through campus alone." She motioned her chin toward Adonis. "He doesn't know what it's like. He's never been the victim of anything. He doesn't know what it feels like to be looked down upon or shamed. He's already a god walking among us. He doesn't need this. It's ours now."

Siobhan spread her fingers out wide, revealing the eye she had been clutching in her palm.

"Take this. You need to learn how to use it," said Siobhan.

Charisma flinched at the sight of it balanced in the middle of her palm. "I'm not ready yet." She reached out and gingerly touched the back of her sister's fingers, pushing them closed.

Siobhan was slightly disappointed. She watched as Adonis's mother argued with the police. She was a fierce one, that Sara Sliver. They were not going to get past her easily.

Siobhan returned her attention to Charisma, still quiet after refusing to touch the eye. "Well, it's incredible," she added. "Knowing what is going to happen and making changes at will is so comforting. Like a magic blanket protecting you from the world."

Charisma wrinkled her nose. "But it's not perfect."

The detectives seemed to be congratulating themselves. She saw a high five and a fist bump after they grabbed the backpack out of the car. "But his mistake won't be ours," said Siobhan.

They watched the father come around the car as officers warned him to keep his distance. He was irate. Furious. The detectives were on the phone. Cruisers pulled around to lock down the exit with flashing lights.

"Now we have the eye, what is next for Adonis Silver?" asked Charisma.

She ran a finger down the contours of her long braid, feeling every knot and bump with the eye still in her palm. "I have no idea," said Siobhan. "We're here because I looked at the future of the detective. The black one." She pointed at him from the rooftop, then sighed, bothered by what she would say next. "I tried to look at Adonis's future, but I had trouble. I can't see anything through his eyes."

## CHAPTER 29

Don sat inside the interrogation room, his hands cuffed in front of him. His elbows were atop a table with a cheap white Formica top that was peeling up in one corner. The room was a pale shade of green with a two-way mirror and a pendant barn light dangling from the middle of the ceiling. He waited patiently, hands folded in front of him, poised and unflinching, for almost two hours. His morning had begun with the detectives' visit, then there was Siobhan, the attempt on his life, and finally his arrest. It was a day full of intense emotions, things he had not felt before.

While in his bedroom, when Don used the eye on Siobhan, all he could see was himself, trapped in the thrall of intense sex. The more he tried to think of a way to avoid it, the more consuming the sex became. He was caught off guard by the infectious nature of fervid passion. He had never felt that before. He was defenseless. His body craved the satisfaction he continued to witness. He had to have her. He wouldn't be able to sleep or eat or think about anything else until he did. It was a humbling experience. A lesson he would not soon forget.

Then when the gun was pointed in his face, when the dark stranger from the mall had tracked him down and aimed to put an end to his life, once again the emotions stirred within, this time fear and uncertainty. Now he awaited his judgment, but this felt more like a pause than an indictment. He had properly prepared for contingencies such as this. Even without the eye, he wasn't worried.

Predicting another's future actions was not about magic; it was an advanced study in observation. Habits, tendencies, and the deepest desires of the soul all collide into one future.

The door clicked open as Detective Duval pushed it wide and entered the room. He ditched the suit jacket, throwing it over the back of the chair. He had a digital recorder in one hand and a notepad and pen in the other. Duval came in alone, but Don could feel eyes on him through the two-way mirror. Duval scraped the legs of the chair across the floor and sat down facing Don. Then he set his pad in front of him and slid the small recorder to the middle of the table.

"Where's Detective Carrol?" asked Don, disappointed. "Chugging down a beer, I guess, for a job well done. It's going to be so satisfying when his harebrained theories blow up in his face."

Duval pressed record on the device. Stated his name, the date and time, and who he was talking to. Very precise and professional. "I would like you to tell us your whereabouts the evening of April 26 at approximately 9:57 p.m."

"What evening was that?" asked Don.

"Don't you remember what you did on that day?"

"Why would I?"

"It was a Monday."

"Again, why would I remember what I did on a Monday nearly a month ago?"

Don had served him a softball, and he could not hit it. Don remembered everything on any given day. If Duval had done his homework on Don, he could've easily tripped him up and gotten it on tape. But most people have trouble remembering what they did the following day, which made it a logical question. Duval knew nothing about who Don really was. Don was insulted. Disappointed.

Duval grunted and fiddled with his tie. "We have you on tape entering a bodega. Confronting, assaulting, and murdering one Connor Richardson."

"You identified me? I saw the footage of the person in the bodega. You couldn't see his face clearly. This is a lame attempt at rattling me. Pathetic, actually."

"Really?" said Duval with a mock smile. "The assailant shoved the murder weapon in a backpack. Same one you own."

"How many people in the city own the same backpack?" asked Don.

"Not important," said Duval. "We found something inside yours."

"I hope you're not going to say porn," said Don. "Police seem to want to blame porn for everything."

Duval slid the notepad across the table along with the pen. "A confession. What you did and why?"

"Where's Detective Carrol?" asked Don, looking toward the big mirror. "I would prefer to have a conversation with him. Ask him a few questions. Like how he became addicted to drugs. I'm guessing it's cocaine."

Duval looked perplexed, then began to laugh. "You certainly are a character. A little too smug for my liking, though."

"I bet Carrol is always rearing to go in the morning, isn't he?" said Don. "Right there first thing. Probably parked outside your house while you are sleeping. You wonder if he gets any sleep, but he can't. The cocaine is there to keep him company."

Don shifted his attention around the room to the cracks and bad patchwork of the ceiling, down the bubbled paint of the walls, then back to Duval. "He comes up with some wild-ass theories, doesn't he? Things that really don't make any sense except to him."

The self-assurance in Duval transformed into bewilderment right before Don's eyes. It was unfortunate but necessary. He needed to be shown who was in charge here.

"The clock is ticking," said Don. "What kind of detective ignores the evidence of a child molester in order to pursue one of New York's brightest students? Just think of how many children can sleep peacefully knowing their nightmares will remain just that. Nightmares. That was because of me. I made them safe. You should be thankful for what I have done. You don't want me as an enemy. Lest your whole life become dismantled."

"What did you say?" asked Duval.

"April 14," said Adonis. "That's the day you should focus on."

"What happened?"

"No, I'm not talking last month. I mean next year, April 14. Something big is going to happen. A turning point in your life. If you don't abandon this obsession with me, that date will ring in your mind as the worst day of your life, and it will be your fault."

Duval made a sound like a dog blowing a half bark. "Let's get back to why I would be thankful for what you've done."

"Not another word," said a woman who swung the door open violently, as if taken by the wind. "I'm your lawyer!"

And she said it more like *loawyer*.

Her oversize, round black glasses were hard to look past. She was wearing silky blue pajamas with sensible shoes. Slightly disheveled as it was after midnight. She reminded Don of a forty-year-old version of Iris Apfel. Better yet, Edna, the fashion designer in *The Incredibles*. Jewish, so she was most likely a friend of the family. Mom always bragged about her hotshot lawyer friend and how she would have been just as good if she'd chosen to continue practicing law. They looked about the same age.

"My goodness, detective, I hope you have a change of shoes," she said with a heavy New York accent. "The stench from the pile of shit you stepped in is making me gag." She talked with her hands. They were going everywhere, dramatizing each word. "If you didn't know who you were sitting across from, let me introduce you. This young man is Adonis Silver, straight-A student, chess club champion, perfect SAT score, accepted to Yale, one of the city's brightest young men, and you are accusing him of what? Murder in Manhattan? He lives on Long Island, for goodness' sake. Tell me what you got, and you better pray it's something that is going to make me reconsider suing this department for harassment and gross negligence. Coming to the Silverses' home in the morning, not for an arrest, not to ask questions, but to spit accusations. No warrant…nothing. And don't think I don't know about the stunt you pulled to get the Silvers to open the car before the arrest. You should be ashamed of yourself."

She paused as if waiting for an answer.

"Ms. Ackerman," said Duval, after turning in his seat. "We have hard evidence."

"I've seen your evidence, detective. A backpack that thousands in the city own seen in an anonymous video sent in the middle of the night of my client having a milkshake at the mall. It shows how desperate and lost you are in this investigation, to believe video footage from the mall security camera of how he puts the backpack on his shoulder. Seriously? But you needed to get that backpack and couldn't get a warrant because no judge would sign off on it, so you had to think of a clever way to get both without going through all the paperwork."

"Wait," said Duval with a finger in the air. "We actually—"

"Don't even try to say you got the blessing from above because they are listening right now. I wouldn't put my foot in it any deeper if I were you. Let's be smart about this. For three weeks your investigation was going nowhere. You were desperate, and you grabbed at any straw you could."

The door opened, and another man leaned in and summoned Duval. He looked like someone higher up on the food chain.

"Excuse me," said Duval. He scraped his chair back and stood up. When the door opened wider, Don could see Detective Carrol. His head was down. He was trying to object to what was being said, but the person talking refused to let him get a word in.

"What's happening?" asked Don.

"It's all about to blow up in their faces, honey. You'll see. We'll have those clowns' badges when this is over. I expect a full apology and nothing less, including monetary compensation for the pain and distress they caused. You have powerful friends, honey. You're a gem of this community. We will not sit back and let this happen without a fight."

Don was patient. The door closed, and all was quiet. Five minutes later, Duval came back into the room. When he did, his head was down; he didn't make eye contact. He walked over to Don and unlocked the cuffs.

"You are free to go," he said. He stood away from Don with his shoulders slouched. "On behalf of the department, we deeply regret this misunderstanding. You have our apologies, Mr. Silver."

"Explain what happened out there," said the lawyer. She stood with her arms folded, waiting for an explanation.

Duval wasn't going to answer. Don could see by his posture.

"It's going to come out one way or another," said the lawyer.

Duval took a breath. "It was a case of mistaken identity, Ms. Ackerman. But we currently have the right person in custody."

"Meaning?" she asked.

"We have the murder weapon. The physical description matches the surveillance video."

"And the backpack?" she asked.

Duval nodded. "The weapon was in the suspect's backpack. Tucked in the back of his closet."

"Where did you find this suspect?" she asked.

"He lives two blocks from where the attack occurred. Connor's wife mentioned this guy was asking one too many questions about how the investigation was going when she went to the supermarket. He was a suspect in another violent crime when he was a teenager, but nothing came of it. When detectives went to his house for questioning, he ran. That's when they found the evidence."

"How long ago was this?" she asked.

"This afternoon. But they found the backpack less than an hour ago."

She smiled. "Detective, I am so glad I crawled out of bed this evening to come down here. This screwup is going to make me a mint."

# CHAPTER 30

It was raining something treacherous. It poured down on Don and the family on their way to the parking garage. They were exhausted. The intense emotional strain was like walking in weighted boots. For Don, it was invigorating.

Because his attack against Connor had been so impulsive, he'd left himself vulnerable to being caught. He'd needed a contingency plan. What was the best way to protect himself from hard evidence? He'd posed the question to the eye while looking into the future of several people. The most shocking response came when he looked into Barney Richardson, Connor's father.

For three days straight, he asked the eye while exploring several actions to initiate the change. Each time, he received the same answer. Send the phone to Barney Richardson. Give him Connor's passcode so he can enter the phone and guide him to the pictures. Especially the pictures taken of Jasmine. Then explain who he is. That's right. Give Barney Richardson the name Adonis Silver. Next, send him the murder weapon so it is in his possession. Then explain to him that if Adonis Silver is ever implicated, this evidence of his son's proclivities will come out.

The instant it did, his chances of becoming governor would be finished. All of his son's crimes would become public knowledge. Everyone would know why he was attacked. The footage would show that when Adonis was talking to him in the bodega, he was warning him to stay away from Jasmine. It would explain where the pipe came from, down in the basement of the warehouse, where other evidence of pedophilia was found. And it would explain why the killer went on a rampage after looking through Connor's phone. It would be ugly. Obscene. People would take sides about taking justice into their own hands.

But no one would be on Barney Richardson's side.

He would lose the election and any credibility he had in the community. He would be shunned and ostracized. The career he'd spent his entire life building would be destroyed before it reached its peak. His only hope for a respectable future was to protect Adonis Silver at all costs. Which he did. Barney Richardson researched who the best possible candidate would be and framed him the instant he was notified Adonis Silver was the suspect. That call must have come in the morning, as Duval had hinted he had received authorization from above. Barney Richardson and the chief of police were good friends. He had to have been told by the chief what was happening.

Don was pleased it all had worked out according to plan. But while in the car, on the drive home, he sensed his parents were not sharing in his triumph. The radio was turned off. The only sounds were the wipers thumping and the white noise of rain falling. Don's father was angry or worried; he couldn't tell the difference. His grip was stiff and white-knuckled, twisting around the steering wheel as if he were revving the accelerator on a motorcycle.

"They arrested someone else for the murder they accused Don of, but that is beside the point," said his father. "They asked you about the whereabouts of Don on that day, and you lied," he said to his wife. "The day Don didn't come home for dinner. I'm tired of being lied to. Ever since that day, I feel like our world has been flipped upside down. You went into a depression. You enacted a strange and extreme punishment on Don. And all the while, I feel like I never got a straight answer. Like you were keeping a secret. Even now. You're keeping something from me. Both of you!"

Jasmine's head was resting on Don's lap as she was sound asleep. Tuckered from the day of stress on her tiny body. Now it was all over, she could finally rest. It was the early morning hours. Sunrise in just over five hours.

"I lied because it would make him look bad," said Sara.

"Seriously? That's all? That's all you have to say to me?"

"Those detectives came in this morning and said all kinds of things trying to entrap Don," she said, pleading her case. "They were so eager to pin it on him that they began accusing him of murdering other people too. They were looking for any reason to arrest him. Telling them he came home late that night would've given them what they needed." From the side, his mother's face was back to the way she'd looked a week ago. Sullen with puffy bags beneath her eyes.

The atmosphere settled a bit; it seemed Joe was absorbing it all.

"Where were you that day?" asked Joe in a voice that implied he would tolerate no more lies.

"What motive would I have to travel to Manhattan on a school night to murder a man in a store?" asked Don.

"Not what I asked," said Joe.

Don looked out the window. The city was a blur through the torrential rainfall. "I was with that woman you met this morning," said Don. "She's my girlfriend."

"Girlfriend?" asked Joe. It was the first time he took his focus off the road to look at Sara. "When did you know about this?" he asked her.

"I found out this morning," she said. "He wouldn't tell me much before that. Which is why I punished him so severely."

"Why would having a girlfriend be such a secret?" Joe asked, his voice grinding rougher at the end.

Sara's jaw muscles flexed tight. Perhaps she was holding back a scream with all the tension. Perhaps she wondered if the lies were ever going to end. Don had dragged her through this hell. Sure, he had come out of it unscathed, but he could see the toll it was taking on her.

"Her age," she said finally. Even under stress, she proved to be his ally once again.

"How old is she?" Joe asked, looking at Don in the rearview mirror.

"Twenty-five, I believe. Maybe twenty-six."

Joe's knuckles were getting their color back as he eased his grip. There was a long silence as he processed the infraction and weighed it against his instincts.

"Is she Jewish at least?" Joe asked. He curled the corner of his lip. An attempt at a smile perhaps. The weight of worry lightened on his shoulders.

"I think it's over between us, Dad. She's not worth tearing this family apart over."

Sara broke down in tears. She covered her face with one hand, trying to be as quiet as possible. "I'm so sorry for keeping this from you, Joe. I thought I could handle it all by myself. I love you so much."

Joe consoled her with a hand on her shoulder. "I love you too. And I understand why you did it now. Don, we are a family and we deserve to know the truth, no matter how ugly or embarrassing. This is a hard lesson on what lies can do to a family. I hope you learn from this. We are always going to do what's best for you."

"Yes, sir," said Don. "My apologies."

Don petted the top of his sister's head. She smiled faintly while sleeping. Would she have been able to have pleasant dreams if he had not taken action? Would his mom and dad have ever been the same if he had not found the eye? Most likely not. He'd saved his family in more ways than one. He'd taken on the pain, that knowledge of suffering so Jasmine and the others wouldn't have to. The proud and happy family would have been torn asunder. Don closed his eyes, knowing that the real villain had paid the price by his hand. And so had the others. No regrets. No remorse.

The real question was, Would he let Siobhan get away with her treachery?

He pondered it for a few seconds before sleep commanded he put his mind to rest. He drifted off peacefully under the motion of the Tesla.

# PART TWO

## CHAPTER 31

William Ridder got out of the car feeling stiff. The cool breeze whipped through his denim jacket. He was in an abandoned gas station, not too far from where he lived. The price per gallon on the old station sign said $1.65 for regular. That was so twenty years ago. He'd just finished a twelve-hour shift at the factory and was looking forward to having the next two days off before the cycle would start again. The fella who dropped him off pulled out onto the road, white smoke floating out of the exhaust. Will followed the red taillights as the car accelerated down the quiet road and out of sight. He scoffed, then buttoned up the top of his denim jacket and trounced through the tan straw grass at the back of the station. It was a shortcut to his apartment building ahead.

The field between the old gas station and the apartment was about the length of a football field. Halfway through was a tiny trailer on cinder blocks. The grumpy old man who owned it paid him no mind. Why would he? He was just walking through as always. The sharp brush and shrubbery poking at his legs set him off.

Why did Jerry always drop him off at the fucking gas station?

It would take him two extra minutes to go to the corner, down the road, turn left, enter the complex, go down a few streets, turn left again, and take him to the front door. He was driving a fucking car. All he was doing was pressing the accelerator and turning the wheel. What was his problem? Some people had it good, and all they did was look down on others that didn't.

Jerry knew Will was in a bad spot. He didn't have a car of his own and couldn't get one. First, his credit was shot. But that was only because he moved all the time. His bills were never delivered to the right address, so he had no clue when they were due. Second, his driver's license was suspended. Last year, some asshole was doing 45 miles per hour in a 55 mile-per-hour zone, and when Will tried to get around her, the driver moved just enough so Will clipped the car, sending it off the road and paralyzing the driver. They said he had to be doing 90, but he wasn't doing anywhere near 90. They just said that because the cop must have known the lady who got paralyzed. The judge must have known her too. She was from the town he was passing through, and he wasn't. That's what they did to outsiders.

Oh, you're not from this town? Then it's your fault.

But what really irked him about the situation was Jerry. Jerry gave him a ride every workday and never took him all the way home. Some people are like that. Once you get down, they want to keep you down. Can't do nothing for nobody. Just step on them on their way through life. No brotherhood, no helping anyone out, just dropping them off on the side of the road when they have a perfectly good car they could have taken you all the way in. Jerry was the kind of person that pissed him off the most. Selfish. Spiteful. Even if Will offered to give him some money for gas, he doubted Jerry would take him to the door. That's why he never offered Jerry any gas money. He knew it wouldn't make a difference.

Will was getting close to his apartment. The gray pit bull chained by the old man's trailer barked at him like always. He would've loved to have a dog like that, but his landlord wouldn't allow it. She was another one who took advantage of people. She had a dog at her place; why couldn't he have one at the apartment? Oh, he had to pay a security deposit if he wanted one. What nonsense. She was looking for any reason to gouge him for more money. Made no sense.

He hit the blacktop of the small complex and climbed the stairs to his apartment. His right hand went into his pocket and pulled out a wad of keys on a ring, twenty-six keys in all the last time he counted. He only needed one. He opened the lock, went inside, and kicked the door shut behind him. It was a one-bedroom place with dark wood-paneled walls, baseboard heat, and a window air-conditioning unit. The floor was a yellow linoleum pattern of random shapes throughout the entire apartment. The kitchen and living areas were all one space. There was a separate bathroom and bedroom in the back. The blinds were drawn all the time. He hated people watching him. Judging him.

Will threw his soiled ball cap on the couch and heard the old, dirty white refrigerator calling him. When he opened the door to grab a bottle of beer, the light illuminated the grit and grime on his fingers. His mother would have told him to wash his hands after getting home. Sorry, Mom, but he paid his own bills now. Besides, she wouldn't speak to him. The last time they spoke was fifteen years ago. She said hateful things like how he refused to take responsibility for his actions. Was always blaming someone else for his transgressions.

Because someone else was always trying to keep him down.

His two sisters had ghosted him as well for the same reason. He never had a chance as the middle baby. All the attention went to the youngest and oldest. Now those same siblings harassed him about getting his shit together. But did they help him out? Nope. He asked for a loan to get a decent couch for the apartment, and what did they say? Nothing, except bring up all the other times he borrowed money.

He moved a lot. He couldn't remember all the other stuff about what he owed to whom.

There was always something at work that caused him to lose his job. Never failed. Someone didn't like him, or they wanted to get someone else they knew in that position, or he was falsely accused of doing something wrong. Just one after the next in rapid-fire succession. Bouw-bouw-bouw. The next thing he knew, he was being called into the office and asked to leave. The nice ones used an excuse like funding and layoffs. The others just came out and said it: You're fired!

He thought about washing his hands in the sink, then used those same grimy fingers to twist the bottle top. The pressure released that sound only a fresh brew makes. He tossed the cap, and it bounced across the kitchen counter with a few tinks. After guzzling half the bottle, he looked around for something to do. He had a television, a small flat screen he'd bought at Walmart. No cable. Wi-Fi and a Firestick a coworker told him was jailbroken. He had no idea what that meant, only that he could watch programs and movies if he was patient enough to put up with the buffering every five minutes.

He sat down on the worn couch with a grunt. The heels of his boots slammed against the wooden table as he took the remote and lit up the darkened room with light from the LCD television. It was going to take a few minutes for his apps to boot up.

As he waited, he heard a stirring coming from his bedroom. It sounded like a mouse. They left traces of their presence around the apartment on occasion. But this was serious. His favorite chocolate caramel clusters, which he'd bought the day before, were in there. They were in a bag on cardboard storage boxes next to his bed that he used for a nightstand. Mice would tear up some chocolate. Didn't matter if it was wrapped in plastic or not. They'd smell the sweet chocolate right through the bag and use their tiny, razor-sharp teeth to go to town.

He stood up. "If there's a mess of wrappers all torn to shreds, I will fucking kill every—"

There was a knock at the door. He checked the time. Nearly nine in the evening. The knocking turned into pounding, like something serious was happening. An emergency of sorts. On the other hand, someone could be trying to rob him. The neighborhood wasn't exactly safe. Then again, it could be the landlord. He hadn't paid rent this month. He was sick and missed a few days of work not long ago. How was he supposed to have the money? There was no paid sick leave at the factory.

The pounding continued to the point he could no longer ignore it. They knew he was home. He crept up to the door slowly and peered through the peephole. The light at the side of the building barely illuminated the man's features. Thick brown beard. Average size. Wearing a red-and-black-checked flannel shirt.

"Yeah?" said Will from behind the door.

"I found this outside the door," said the man. He held up a Polaroid picture. Pressed it up against the peephole so he could no longer see the guy. "I thought these might be yours."

Seemed like a trick to get him to open the door. "Nah, those aren't mine," said Will. "I take pictures on my phone. It probably belongs to one of my neighbors."

He wasn't leaving, and Will couldn't see what he was doing with that picture blocking the peephole. There was a baseball bat left in the corner, just for cases like this. Will maneuvered his hand until the tips of his fingers were on top of it. "Did you try the next apartment over?" he asked.

"They said it was most likely yours," said the man.

Definitely a trick to get him to open the door. He wasn't that stupid. He gripped the bat firmly in his hand. Flexed his forearms and backed away from the door in case the guy decided to kick it down.

"You leave it on the floor there, and I will get it later," said Will.

He prepared himself. If the door flew open, he was far enough away that he would not get hit but close enough that with one step forward, he could split the wig of whoever dared to cross the threshold. He placed the bat up on his shoulder.

"Have a nice day!" said Will.

There was no response. No one coming through the door by force. Nothing at all. Quiet. Peaceful. Will crept back up to the door and peered through the peephole. The guy was gone.

*That was strange*, Will thought. He slipped around the couch to the front window and peeked out the blinds carefully. He caught the stranger at the bottom stair and followed him with his gaze through the complex parking area to a vehicle. It was a brown pickup truck. Big wheels. He had a Nerf bar he stepped up onto to get inside. The engine fired up, and the truck slowly went about its way.

He tried to tame his heartbeat. It was both stressful and strange. Pounding on his door in the middle of the night holding up some picture. Something about it was definitely off, but the threat was gone now. He took the bat and returned it to the corner by the door, then went for his beer. His butt hit the couch cushion only to spring back up again. What the fuck was with that picture anyway?

Will unlocked the door and pulled it open quickly. He looked down. The Polaroid was wedged in the kickplate of the door. Will crouched to get a better look. He squeezed the corner with his thumb and forefinger and carefully plucked it from its spot. He knew this place. Something about it was familiar to him. It triggered a thought about the guy's truck. The license plate. Blue like the sky fading into white. Bright-green sliver at the very bottom. Was that Indiana?

His heart jumped as if it were going to spring right through his chest. He looked down at the picture. Wooded area, nothing special. Nothing really distinguishing it from any other wooded area. A bitternut tree in the middle with yellow buds; the picture must have been taken less than a month ago. Still frost around. Snow on the ground and on the limbs. An American elm tree to the right of it. Vase-like in shape, holding traces of snow on its branches instead of leaves. There were other trees he could see off in the distance. But it was the angle. This particular angle was just like he remembered. As if it had been taken looking through his own eyes.

He'd learned to like camping due to necessity. He had been forced to live in the woods from time to time. People looking for him, no money…that sort of thing. With no television and no phone, he got familiar with trees and the landscape. This was eight years ago when he was living in Indiana for a spell. It was summertime. He'd pitched a tent on some land he wasn't supposed to be on. Nothing official as far as camping. It was private land. A young boy had come up to him while he was sleeping. He said he was ten years old. His name was Joshua.

Will heard the creaking of the floor, like footsteps, not mice. Someone was inside his apartment. The ploy with the picture was a trap. He lunged for the baseball bat and turned around to face his attacker, but he didn't see them. He didn't even see his apartment. He wasn't even upright. He was on his back. He was in the woods at a campsite. Same one as in the picture in Indiana. The little brown-haired boy named Joshua was standing above him. He was wearing a bright-red soccer shirt and shorts. He had shin guards under his knee-high socks as if he had just come back from playing. His little brow scrunched tight with curiosity.

"We have a tent like that one," said Joshua. "Grandpa used to pitch it near the house whenever I wanted to sleep outside."

His heart fell further into the pit of fear and despair. He was reliving the moment. His brain stepped through the timeline perfectly. Moment by moment.

"My grandpa usually never lets me come out this far to play," said Joshua with a childhood lisp. "But he isn't feeling so well, and he's resting." The small clearing where Will had pitched his tent was surrounded by brush. Well hidden, the way he liked it. Joshua's tiny fingers played with leaves on plants next to him. He plucked a bunch off the stem and tossed them one at a time like a dealer in Vegas. Seemed to be his thing to do. Back near the house, Will would often see fresh leaves on the ground. Joshua circled the campsite, plucking off leaves and tossing them.

"Are you out here a lot?" asked Joshua.

Will shook his head. He was afraid. He knew what was coming next. Joshua would look down and around at the spade, the fishing rod, the hammer, and finally the pocket watch Will had taken from the house. He just wanted something to tell time. It was an antique wind-up type, made of brass or copper, not worth much other than sentimental value. Who knows, young Joshua might have been blamed for stealing it or misplacing it. The thing was, he certainly recognized it.

The stern little muscles of his brow tightened when he saw it. He wasn't stupid. He put things together quickly. Will had stolen all of this stuff from the shed. Then came the moment. Their eyes met. Each knowing the other's intentions. Joshua knew Will was a thief, and Will knew he was going home to tell his grandpa. His young legs sprang into action, and Will took off in his direction. He grabbed Joshua's arm before he could get too far.

Before he knew it, his big grown hands were around Joshua's tiny little face. He thought it would quiet the boy down, but he kept fighting. Struggling. He was sorry he had to grab his arm so hard, but he was going to run away and tell his grandpa. He wanted to talk to him first. Explain to him how he was just borrowing the stuff. He needed a way to survive out there. He needed a way to hunt and feed himself. Keep the cold and rain off him. Couldn't he understand? It cost them nothing to let him borrow the tools he needed for survival. But if he ran off and made a big deal out of it…you know how people are. They would chase him away without any regard for how he was going to survive. How he was going to eat and sleep. How he was going to keep the ticks and mosquitoes off him. They were going to take their stuff back and chase him away. Stuff they weren't using anyway.

By the time Will quieted the thoughts going through his head, Joshua wasn't moving anymore.

*Oh my God*, Will thought. *Not again.* It was real. Just as real and vivid as it had been the first time. He felt his heart plummet into his pelvis. His body weakened with grief and despair so thick he could not stand. All of his initial thoughts returned. *Run! No, hide the body first, then run. Wait, clean up the area, remove all traces you were ever here, then hide the body and run.*

*What do I do to hide the body? Bury it. But they'll find it easily. Disturbed soil is easy to spot. Look at this boy. He was loved.* People would go looking for him. Maybe the whole town would search. There would be hundreds of people on foot, with dogs sweeping the entire area. He had to take the boy with him, maybe. Wander into another county and bury him there.

Through the thick fog of panic and confusion came a solution. One designed on the land he occupied. There were swamplands nearby. He'd ventured there once by mistake. Got his feet stuck in the dark, thick concrete-like sludge.

Surely, they would think to venture there. Will imagined them spending days there searching for him. But it was a place where you could disturb the soil and no one would notice. The water above the soil was about a foot deep. He didn't have a shovel. He would have to go steal one from somewhere. But perhaps he would weigh down the body creatively. The water would throw off the dogs to the scent. And if they found him, they might think he drowned.

He carried the boy's body there, found a spot, and put the body down face up. Then he thought of something. There would be no water in the boy's lungs. He'd watched those shows as a kid. They could tell if someone drowned or not by the water in their lungs. He somehow had to put water in there, or else it would be ruled a homicide and they would come after him.

Will placed him in the water of the swamplands. He figured if doing CPR pumped the heart, perhaps the motion would put water into the lungs. So he knelt down in the water next to the body and began chest compressions. Up and down, he heaved the whole of his upper weight onto the boy's chest, trying to suck water into his lungs.

The ground was a sludge of mud, and he felt the body sliding under his weight. But he kept on. Then something unexpected happened. He thought he had heard it before, but this time he felt it. The tiny ribcage of the boy. With no muscle activity to stop it, he was breaking little Joshua's ribcage. He could feel it fall with little to no effort. No resistance. Now he was fucked. They would most certainly know the body had been tampered with.

Will stood with his eyes welling in tears. He was angry with himself and life. He stomped down on the mud beneath his feet and got stuck there. The soil was soft and sticky. He unglued his boot and looked to the sky as if the gods were showing him a solution. He used the same force to step down on Joshua's body. He could feel the body compress under his weight. He stood on Joshua. Walked on him. He kept stepping on the body with all of his weight pressing him into the loose, soppy soil beneath the muddy water. Wedging him in so he wouldn't float up. There would be no trace of loose dirt. No scent for dogs to track. Dense, soppy mud was like a suction cup. He knew it would hold the body. If he plastered it down there good and tight, no one would ever find him.

Exhausted from fear and exertion, Will took a moment to catch his breath. He was a wet and muddy mess. He scampered out of the swamplands, taking the indirect route, careful not to track mud and leave footprints heading back to his campsite. He cleaned up once he got there, changed clothes, and packed up the tent and other items. He removed all evidence that he'd ever been there. He checked the area one last time and took a moment to look in the direction young Joshua was buried, nearly half a mile from where his site was.

Standing in his apartment now, he remembered that angle. That was where the picture was taken. In the direction of the swamplands where the black ash trees grew.

But how would anyone know? How would they know? The crippling feeling he'd had on that fateful day would not leave him. Those emotional barriers he had erected and reinforced during those eight years for protection were somehow torn down. But it was more than that. The feelings were amplified. The fear, the rage, the hatred. It was a swirl of emotions compounded. It wasn't just his pain. And it wouldn't go away. It would not subside. The scene played over again, starting from when his and Joshua's eyes met, and the emotional content was compounded. Multiplied. When he saw it again, his fear and anxiety were twice as bad. Then they doubled again. What was the example his mother used to tell him to try to get him to save?

*If you took a penny and doubled it every day, how much money would you have at the end of the month?*

She'd made him work out the problem when he was twelve because he would toss pennies he found into the lake while asking her for money for various things he wanted. She recognized how wasteful he was with money and everything. He remembered crying in the kitchen, not being able to go outside or play video games until he worked out the problem. Day one, you have two cents. Day four, only eight cents. However, on the tenth day, he would have $10.24. Then came the big jumps. On day twenty, $10,485.76. Day twenty-five, a whopping $335,544.32. And at the end of thirty days, over $10 million. An incredible example of how doubling your money starts small but multiplies quickly as wealth grows.

She explained to him that this is how rich people gain their fortunes. They don't get lucky. It is not about favor falling on their side. Not about being in the right place at the right time. It is about their attitude. How they take what they have and use it to grow their net worth. Doesn't matter how small you start. If you are persistent, you will get there.

But why was he thinking about that? Why, when he was reliving the killing of young Joshua for the fourth time? Oh, yes. The fear, sorrow, and regret quickly growing within him as the events of this tragedy replayed in his mind. If it kept going at this rate, the weight of the effect after the thirtieth time would be well over a billion.

He could not handle it getting that high. The strain on his body would be unbelievable. Unfathomable. Somewhere around the seventieth time, he took a kitchen knife to the side of his neck. Blood spurted out as his heart pumped at an accelerated rate. He felt the life slipping from his body at twenty-one.

He got his wish. Before the emotional weight reached a billion, he was dead.

# CHAPTER 32

Kevin Duval stepped outside his house in Whitestone, New York, that evening with his whole world falling apart. He left an empty house, and as if that weren't hard enough, he looked down the street knowing he would never see Arnold Carrol's black Cadillac parked outside again. No fresh cup of coffee in the cupholder just the way he liked. None of Carrol's rumpled suit jackets draped over the back seat. Just random cars parked on the street, end to end, all the way down the block.

The feeling of loss gripped him. The vacuum of emptiness threatened to swallow him from existence. Arnold Carrol was dead. Killed in Connecticut. Found in the woods after being shot once in the chest. Carrol's only reason for being there was because he was trying to find Duval's missing wife, Rashida, and their eight-year-old daughter, Sherrie. They'd disappeared three days prior after heading to Connecticut to visit Rashida's mother. State police found Rashida's car on the side of the road, about half a mile from a rest stop. They speculated she may have tried to walk back to the rest stop for help but never made it.

This was the lowest low he had ever felt in his life. As if everything had been sucked away from him. As if all the favor God had shown him in his entire existence had then been snatched away immediately as payment due. Repossessing everything. Turning him emotionally bankrupt. Telling him he'd had it too good for too long. And it was true. Duval's entire life had been on an upswing. He had been riding the high of cloud nine. Then this happened.

His thoughts drifted to his historic rise and fall. It took only ten months to be exact. The Connor Richardson murder was solved. An anonymous tip led to the capture of Fanuco Iglesias, an immigration Dreamer who owned a backpack identical to the one identified in the bodega. Was there any mention of how they were on the trail of Adonis Silver? No. Were they a part of the raid that captured Fanuco? No. However, when the chief stood at the podium to issue praise for the arrest, Carrol and Duval were there in the front row, receiving credit for everything. Duval remembered it being a bitter pill to swallow, but he swallowed it, for the good of his career.

But not all was rosy and bright. After the celebration, they'd called Carrol into the captain's office, quietly. When he left the room, he had turned in his papers to retire. Seems like there was some truth to what Adonis had said about him. Carrol had worked undercover narcotics before he got there. Some of those demons while working undercover had followed him to homicide. What did you say to a person who put their lives on the line to get drugs off the street? Fuck you, you know you shouldn't have been doing that shit? No. That's not how the game is played. The streets are too smart. The captain had been covering for him on his piss tests. Now, it seemed the captain's favors were all used up. Carrol was hailed for his exemplary service and landed on his feet as a private investigator.

As Carrol was shelved, Duval's career was on a fast track to the stars. Barney Richardson personally came down to hug Duval and thank him with tears in his eyes for solving his son's murder. He brought a camera crew with him. It was in all the papers. Duval received a medal for his valor and investigative prowess. The works.

Things continued to get better for Duval when Barney Richardson became governor. The department had an opening for a lieutenant. With Duval being a favorite of Governor Richardson, it was easy to see he was a favorite within the department. He went through the rigors of the process and came out on top as a lieutenant. A young, ambitious, decorated Black lieutenant, he was proud of what he had achieved. Within his department, there was no doubt he had earned every bit of his success. Yet, life was there to remind him we are all a moment away from tragedy. One event away from the complete collapse of all we value.

Duval crept down the stairs of his home and walked a few feet to his blue Dodge Charger. The new car he bought to celebrate his promotion. Streetlights still reflected off its polished surface. At the end of the street, he could see the East River and the Whitestone Bridge off in the distance. The borough of the Bronx was on the other side. Homes and apartments lit up like Christmas lights in the background. A subtle breeze came off the water. It had been a chilly spring thus far. He zipped his coat and pushed the key fob to unlock the door. He scrunched down into the black leather and pushed the starter. The engine fired right up, and then he sat. Reflecting. He was headed to speak to the reporter who'd apparently discovered new details about his wife and child's disappearance.

He'd been told to stay out of the investigation. Let others do their jobs. This wasn't in his state, so he had no jurisdiction. But how could they expect him to stay idle? Take days off and wait. He only had to look up at the lamppost a few feet from his car to be reminded of why he couldn't. At least ten flyers were posted there. All of his wife and daughter. This marked the ninth day since they'd disappeared. The forty-eight-hour rule had elapsed four times already. Time was running out.

A sudden breeze flapped the edges of the paper, threatening to rip it from its post. He wasn't going to sit still and do nothing. His heart was being torn asunder from the inside out. Duval put the car in drive and pulled out into traffic. He drove across the bridge and into the Bronx. No need for GPS. He knew this place. Had scoped it out a few days ago. Had fellow officers stationed nearby in case the reporter was setting him up with cameras, looking to capture his painful face on television. The meeting place was Emilia's on Arthur Avenue. An Italian restaurant that reminded him of the dinner scene in *The Godfather* where Michael Corleone shoots Sollozzo and McCluskey in the head. Classy, square tables with white cloths draped over the top. Private setting with great food.

A text from a fellow officer lit up the screen of the cell phone on the passenger's seat. The female reporter he was going to meet had been spotted entering the restaurant. She came in alone, driving a late-model white Civic. That text was followed by another that said she was seated at the table he'd requested. Facing away from the door as he instructed. Great. He would be there in about ten minutes. Plenty of time for his people to do a sweep of the area to make sure there were no cameramen lurking in the shadows.

Maria Martinez was the name of the reporter. Catchy name. Rolled off the tongue. She was tall, over six feet. Midtwenties, Latina, ambitious, long black hair all the way down her back. Used to play volleyball in college. She was recognizable. Easy to spot. Especially since Maria had been in front of the camera, getting national attention as an investigative reporter. A story she broke about a string of suicides had aired a couple days ago. People were taking their lives and leaving behind Polaroid photos.

Police in several states in the Northeast had reported this strange occurrence, which began about three months ago. The first was a case still fresh in everyone's mind. A man named Christian McDonough from New Jersey had pleaded through the media to find his wife, who had gone missing after a morning jog. As weeks passed, he was interviewed by more and more news outlets, breaking down in tears as he begged for her safe return. The nation became sympathetic. There was something about the abduction of the wife from a perfect American couple that captured people's attention.

Entire neighborhoods became active, massive searches, looking into anything that might provide a clue to her whereabouts. Then came the news that Christian had committed suicide. Chewed through a lamp cord connected to an outlet, and electricity did the rest. At first, it was reported as a tragedy. His pain was so deep; he could not live without the love of his life. Then came the bombshell.

There was a Polaroid next to his body. It was a photo of a landfill. An old white refrigerator stood out amid a pile of trash. On a hunch, one of the detectives found the spot in the landfill and discovered the remains of the wife. She had been cut into pieces and placed into seven separate plastic trash bags. The theory was he killed his wife, chopped her into pieces, and took them to work. They were doing remodeling in one of the adjacent buildings. There were several forty-yard dumpsters there for workers to dispose of materials. One of the contractors took pictures of the old break room they were redoing. That was where the refrigerator came from. Christian must have waited a few days, then when the dumpster was emptied, mustered up his tears and gone public about his wife missing after going for a run.

The second part wasn't kept from the public, only the part about the Polaroid. Because oddly enough, a few more suicides had shown up with Polaroid pictures found next to the body. Carrol had been investigating one of them. A woman had hired him after saying she hadn't seen her brother in six months. He was being taken care of in one of those hospice homes. He had always been taken care of to some degree. He suffered from mental illness. He was fifty-five years old, quiet and meek, and his sister would make time to visit him at the home once a month, when her business travels took her to that part of town. The first time she tried to visit, she was told the other patients were very sick. There was something going around, and they could not let her inside. The second month, he was reportedly out with the group at the park. Then her calls were turned away. He was always sleeping or tired or didn't want to speak.

A few months after, Carrol began his investigation. He first looked into the owner of the house, Margaret Rollins. She was an elderly woman, in her midseventies. After digging into her history, he discovered she was an ex-con, a madam, a thief, and a general lowlife. Before he could contact the authorities to take action, Margaret Rollins killed herself. Drowned herself in a tub. There were several Polaroids around the tub. All pictures of her backyard garden. The local police dug up three bodies, all residents who were supposed to be under her care. Her life partner admitted she had killed the ones she thought no one would notice and taken the checks that came in every month for their care.

Carrol was connected to the police network, so he was able to ascertain that this story with the Polaroids was nothing new. There had been twenty-four Polaroid suicides in the last three months in the Northeast. He'd passed the story on to Maria.

Now, Carrol was dead, and Duval's wife and child were missing. Yet the captain wanted him to stay out of the investigation?

Duval squeezed into a tight spot on the side street, then sent a text to his guy spying on the restaurant for cameramen. The response came back in seconds. It was all clear. He straightened up and exited his car. He was down the street from the restaurant. Residential side of the block. There were people walking back and forth, typical busy New York street on a Thursday evening. He put his hands in his pockets and began walking. Beneath the jacket was a blue shirt; below were khakis with comfortable shoes. Casual evening wear.

He turned the corner on his way to the front of the restaurant and spotted the tables outside with umbrellas. A little something more romantic out in the moonlight. Several people were dining there. None of them were interested enough to notice him walking past. He made his way to the host, parked behind her station inside the entrance. A goth girl with oversize black ear piercings looked up from the reservation book.

"I'm meeting someone here," he said. "I know where the table is."

She nodded. He stepped through the small crowd of those waiting to be seated and into the main part of the restaurant. His ears were drowned with the sounds of conversations and dinnerware clanking in the background. He came up behind Maria sitting at the table. She was a gym rat. Toned and fit. She was wearing peach capris with white sneakers. Her lean shoulders were exposed through a white spaghetti-strap blouse. He came around the table and pulled out the chair to sit down. She smiled, welcoming him.

"I'm so glad you agreed to meet, lieutenant," she said. No trace of a Spanish accent.

"Just Kevin," he said. "This is about as informal as it gets."

She was wearing light makeup, but she really didn't need any. Her lips were a natural color with a glossy shine. Bright white teeth. Her hair was parted to one side and came all the way down to her hips.

Two glasses of water sat on the table with a basket of warm bread in the center. Next to it, a small bulb imitating candlelight was flickering, painting her pleasant features in an orange light. She reached for her water and took a sip. Her hands were big yet soft and feminine. "I took the liberty of ordering for us. I hope you don't mind. I figured you wouldn't want too many visits to the table," she added.

"So long as we are not being recorded, I'm OK," he said. His eyes probed the other guests for someone interested in what was going on at their table.

"Lighten up," she said. She reached for the bread and broke off a piece, slathered it with butter, and began eating. "An investigative reporter won't get far by alienating police. I gave you my word, and I'm keeping it."

It made sense to his ears, so he nodded and realized he was stiff and uncomfortable. Eyes naturally gravitate to nervous people. He wanted to look natural. He thought following her lead with the bread was a good start. But her hands had been all over it. They looked clean, but that was beside the point. Duval carefully touched the part he was going to eat and cut a slice off with his knife as if showing her the proper etiquette. He then placed it on the small plate in front of him.

He twirled the butter knife in his hand. "What's the latest word on Carrol's murder?"

"You aren't going to like what I have to say." Her brown eyes glistened in the candlelight, filled with concern. "I'm not going to sugarcoat it." She exhaled a deep breath and looked directly into his eyes. "They are looking at you for his murder."

His grip on the knife handle tightened to the point it shook violently. "Are you kidding?" he snapped. "Is this some kind of horrible joke?"

He could feel the tightness in his chest and neck, as if his veins were going to pop. "What the fuck gives them cause to investigate me?"

"You were there with him…in Connecticut," she said.

Duval's body softened, and he leaned back in his chair. "Yeah, but…" He struggled a bit with his words. "I went with him to the spot where the car was parked. He said they probably took a shortcut through the woods to get to the rest stop. He was calling in someone who knew the area, a retired officer who used to work in town."

"Funny you should say that," said Maria. "They just found his body. He was shot in the leg. He bled out while trying to flee the scene."

Duval's eyes widened. "No. There has to be an explanation. Why aren't they looking for an assailant? This person most likely took my wife and daughter and then killed Carrol and this other person when they got close."

"The cell tower in the area pinged your phone with a call at approximately 10:39 p.m. A hiker found Carrol's body the next morning. Estimated time of death was about eleven that evening. Carrol's cell phone was pinged several times in the same vicinity. His cell phone was not found at the scene. Do you see how this looks?"

"What? What are you talking about? Tell me how this looks."

"It looks like you went out there with Carrol, and when you got close to where you hid your wife and child, you killed him and took his phone. The calls made from Carrol's phone were to your number, but you never picked up the phone. Why?"

"My battery went dead while I was driving back. That's why I couldn't answer."

"If you didn't turn your phone off, it could verify your location at the time of the call."

"I told you, the battery died. I didn't turn it off."

"At 10:39 p.m., your captain called you. You told him you were home, not in Connecticut with Carrol."

"I wasn't supposed to be interfering with the investigation. What else do you expect me to tell him? He asked how I was doing and if I was getting by. Then he asked if he should send someone over to check on me, and I said no, I was all right. That's when I decided to head back and leave the rest to Carrol."

"You were breathing heavily and sounded nervous," said Maria.

"I was breathing hard because we were walking up and down hills, and I was nervous because I was not supposed to be out there," he explained. "How is this all being twisted around on me?"

"Because you are the spouse. Whenever anyone goes missing, the spouse is the first person they suspect. You work homicide. You should know."

"But this is different," said Duval. "We already know who is behind this."

"Adonis Silver," she said, curling the corner of her lip disbelievingly. "Yeah, I heard this all before. The guy you thought was responsible for the murder of Connor Richardson. Then you accused him of causing other mysterious murders around his neighborhood. I heard it all from Carrol. You think he is behind the disappearance of your wife and child, and now he is responsible for the murder of Carrol too. Do you know how crazy that sounds?'

"He told me that on April 16, something would change my life. That was the day my wife and child went missing. He told me last year when we had him in the interrogation room. He said the date April 16. It couldn't be a coincidence!"

"That's what you have to go off? That's it? The Naugatuck Police Department is pissed about the death of their ex-detective."

"Pissed at me?" asked Duval. "I didn't kill him."

"Well, they aren't going to make any progress toward finding your wife and child until they straighten this out."

Duval went from defensive to dejected in one swoop. This was going nowhere. Adding insult to injury. Meanwhile, time was ticking away. The lives of his loved ones were at stake. Frustration began to overwhelm him. At not being able to do anything, especially now they thought he was responsible. Any action he took would only strengthen their suspicions. He placed a hand on his head as his resentment of the Naugatuck Police Department grew more intense.

They were idiots focused on the wrong thing.

"I'm sorry," said Maria, reaching over the table to touch his hand. It was a comforting hand. It was soft and warm.

Duval withdrew uncomfortably. He began looking around the room. A consoling touch could be misinterpreted as affection. Assumptions would be made that he and Maria were having an affair. This meeting could be used against him. What was he thinking?

"I suggest you find a good lawyer," said Maria. "You are going to have to prove your innocence."

"Innocence from what?" said Duval, dumbfounded. "Do they have a body? Is my family dead?"

Maria indicated she did not know. "But they are going to bring you in for questioning."

How dare they even think such a thing? He was Lieutenant Kevin Duval, a highly decorated and respected officer, yet he was being treated like common trash. Like an evil criminal. After all he had done to put the real criminals behind bars, to be suspected of such a thing hurt him to his core.

He zoned out. Disconnected from his surroundings. Plates of food were set in front of him. The server who brought them said some things and left. He did not take notice of her. It was all a blur. He looked down at the lasagna. It was his favorite. He would have enjoyed it, he thought, if he'd had the appetite.

Someone had to do something to straighten all of this out. Someone.

# CHAPTER 33

Jake Coltrane was in his cell. It was a Friday afternoon. He had been informed several hours ago someone had preregistered to visit him that day. He'd met Lieutenant Duval a few times before and was not really thrilled to see him, but what the hell. Jake Coltrane accepted the request because in the seven months he had been detained at the Rikers Island Correctional Facility in New York, Lieutenant Duval was the only person who had come to see him. That and what else did he have to do?

Duval's visits would usually begin with him trying to convince Jake to admit his name was Jake Coltrane. Jake would deny it fervently. His name was Ernesto Flores, he would answer. The identity had been supplied to him by Jericho Black. A billionaire who'd tried to help him disappear when he was being pursued by the Russian mob.

When aliases are given, one really doesn't have a choice in the name. But this name, Ernesto Flores, got him in more trouble than it was worth. In prison, inmates separate themselves into groups for survival. Blacks, Whites, Asians, and Latinos. No one knew exactly where to place Ernesto, so he was an outcast. Knowing not a lick of Spanish kept him from being passed off as Cuban or a Boricua. Blacks were not exactly sure about him since he lacked street cred. So it made Jake a lone wolf of sorts. Completely vulnerable.

Jake stretched out all six feet, seven inches of his frame on the bunk in his cell. His black feet hung off the edge of the mattress. The strong latch sliding through the iron door echoed around the painted cinder block cell as the guard opened the door.

"Flores, it's about that time," said Blackwell, one of the cooler COs on the block. Blackwell was a twenty-two-year veteran at Rikers. He was a large man. Over six feet tall and more than three hundred pounds. His neck and cheeks were a bit puffy. He treated most with respect, not like the other gladiators who roamed the block. "Brass is back to talk to you. What is it he wants you to confess?"

"Conspiracy shit," said Jake. "The usual. They can't figure out who did what, so it's easier to pin crimes on the ones they already have locked up."

"I don't understand why you never ask for a lawyer."

Blackwell was actually probing for information. Trying to find the weakness in Jake's response. The rumor mill said Blackwell controlled the drugs coming into the prison. He was constantly checking to see if he was under investigation. It was probably why Blackwell had protected Jake this entire time. Blackwell was trying to figure out if Jake was an enemy he needed to keep close.

"I can handle this guy," said Jake. "He's harmless."

Jake stood up from his bunk. He must have been on his back for too long because he felt a tad woozy on his feet.

"Whoa there, big guy," said Blackwell. "I expected your muscles to have recovered by now."

"They have," said Jake. "Just getting my legs under me."

Jake had been in a coma for months before being taken to Rikers. He was malnourished and frail. About the worst condition a man could possibly be in before being thrown to the wolves. Jake recalled entering the bullpen when he first arrived, stepping into a pool of blood, and seeing an inmate with blood on his fists sitting on the bench all to himself. His name was LaMichael Scott. On the streets, he was known as Scotty Rock—a six-foot-two, 220-pound psychopath with dreadlocks. His lips drawn in a snarl, he looked like a Rottweiler showing its teeth.

Jake, on the other hand, was weak. His muscles were still recovering from atrophy. There was still tape residue on his arms from the IVs, and he was wearing clothes a couple sizes too small, bought by a kind nurse at the local Goodwill.

It was Jake's luck both he and Scotty were sent to the same house, one that had a record for housing the most violent of the inmates at Rikers. The houses were controlled by gangs, and as an initiation, non–gang members were typically beaten by the swarm. Scotty Rock had people there who dapped him up on arrival, and they all turned in unison to eye down Jake.

It wasn't long before Jake was at the bottom of the pile getting the shit kicked out of him, until Blackwell came to his rescue. He brought in the cavalry with riot gear, pulled the rowdy inmates off Jake, and escorted him to his cell. Ever since the beating Jake took that day, Blackwell kept Jake's cell locked until it was time to take him somewhere. He brought Jake his food as well. Blackwell figured Jake would be out soon because the evidence against him was circumstantial, but it had been seven months and Jake was still there. There was some kind of a delay to the trial date. A stall tactic, or perhaps this was how they treated people with a public lawyer.

Maybe the man he was going to see, Lieutenant Duval, was the reason his case was continually delayed.

"Let's go see the man," said Jake.

Blackwell went to work installing his cuffs. A set around his ankles so he couldn't run, and a set on his wrists attached to another around his waist. When the shackles were secured, Jake walked out of his cell to a group of inmates socializing in the main area of the house. He saw Scotty Rock and received a proper mean-mugging with plenty of teeth. He ignored the alpha dog and followed Blackwell down the hallway through the series of locked gates. The Rikers facility was among the worst detention centers in the nation. On his way to the visitor's area, Jake saw trash, water, and feces in various corners of the prison. He saw broken glass and sewage. Rats and roaches. And social areas in several states of disrepair.

One more gate rattled open, and they entered the visiting area. A large open space that served as a lobby. Private rooms sat on the left side. Guests were waiting to be escorted into the rooms when one was vacated on that side. Guards and prisoners were on the right side. When prompted, the prisoner would be escorted over to the other side and allowed to enter the room containing their loved ones. It was the only time Jake saw any signs of humanity among the incarcerated. The iron-stoned face of "I'm not going to take anyone's shit" was replaced by the thrill of anticipation. It proved most of the brutality was a show for the sake of survival.

Regardless, he hated the shit show.

Blackwell pushed Jake past a group of others to a flurry of grunts and snares. He escorted Jake to room number twelve and opened the door. Inside was a picnic-style table with bench seats attached. The top of the table was layered with white Formica and a Plexiglas barrier down the middle, lengthwise, to keep some space between inmate and guest. The room had white walls and floors and a camera in the upper corner. Lieutenant Duval was already seated on one side of the table. He was well dressed in a blue shirt, black tie, and black pants. He rolled up his sleeves to the forearms and extended a hand to the other side of the table, inviting Jake to sit down. So he did.

"Be good, Flores," said Blackwell. He took his keys and unlocked the shackles around Jake's wrists. "This guy says he trusts you. I will be on the other side of this door, so don't act up."

Jake gave him a thumbs-up, and the door closed.

"Ernesto Flores," said Lieutenant Duval. He stared at Jake while fiddling with papers on the desk in front of him. "Good to see you again."

"I wish I could say the same," said Jake. "But I am still in here with no trial date, no word as to what is going on either."

"Yeah," said Duval. "We've hit a dead end in the investigation. We need to revisit the facts. If everything you say jives, all charges will be dropped. How does that sound?"

"Sounds like another way to fuck with me," said Jake. "Get my hopes up while you play your mind games."

"Not this time," said Duval, stone-faced. "I'm offering you a way out of here."

Jake was skeptical. Typical police tactic: flip questions around and around, get you disoriented and confused, then goad you into a confession. Jake put up his guard but was willing to play along and see which way things were headed. "Fire away!"

Lieutenant Duval flipped over the first page of his notes and began reading to himself. He took his time, preparing his words carefully. When he spoke, his eyes never left the paper. "Did you attack the Silver family at gunpoint in the synagogue?"

"No," said Jake. Same question he had been asked countless times before. *Stick to the script and everything will be fine.* "Just because they attend a synagogue in Manhattan and I happen to live there doesn't mean it was me. I happen to know I am not the first person they identified as the attacker. Didn't they claim it was a man named Jake Coltrane from New Jersey?"

Jake tensed slightly, waiting, as he knew what Duval would say.

"Yeah, well, Jake Coltrane was dead. He died before the attack at the synagogue. He jumped in front of a train and was cut in half a few days prior. There's a record of it. His body was at the morgue in New Jersey, where he lived. He couldn't have done it. About a month later, you turn up as a John Doe at the hospital. A picture passed around the precincts to help identify you ended up pinning you as the person of interest in the attack at the synagogue in Manhattan. So here we are."

"Are you saying all Black people look alike?" asked Jake. "Because that's what I am hearing."

"Don't get cute," said Duval, visibly annoyed. "You saw the photo. He is the spitting image of you, and you know it."

"You can't clearly identify me as the assailant, so why am I still in here?"

Duval didn't answer. He flipped through his papers methodically, searching for his next question. Making Jake sweat ever so slightly.

"Your apartment looks like it was never lived in," said Duval. "I had a peek inside before your landlord served the eviction paperwork. Tell me, what did it look like?"

Jake clicked his teeth as his head bobbed up and down. He wanted to reach over the table and slap Duval for being a smart-ass. Did he think Jake was that stupid? Did he think he could trip him up with a question? "I was in a coma in the hospital, which brought about amnesia. I can't remember. Check with the doctors who treated me. They'll tell you my condition is real."

"None of your neighbors remember you," said Duval. "Why is that?" He looked up from the pages to give Jake time to respond.

"I don't remember them either, due to amnesia," Jake said plainly.

"Can't find any friends of Ernesto Flores either," said Duval.

"Good, 'cause I can't remember their names," said Jake, twiddling his thumbs at the same information they had gone over countless times before.

Duval was much calmer. He shifted through several pages while sliding others across the white Formica-top table. He reshuffled and stacked them, held them upright, and tapped the edges to get them lined up again. All of this was wearing on Jake's nerves. He had to remind himself about composure. The police had all the time in the world. They knew that so long as you were behind bars and they were free, the first to lose their cool would be the person who was waiting for their freedom.

Jake took a breath to ease his tension.

"Your profile online seems fabricated," said Duval.

"Profile?" said Jake. "I have no idea what's online about me."

"Nobody remembers you at the high school you attended."

"I don't remember what high school that was," said Jake.

Duval looked up from his sheet. "In contrast, people remember Jake Coltrane."

"Must have been a popular guy," said Jake. "I guess I wasn't."

If he was using the same approach and same tactics, this was where Duval usually got nasty. He would blurt out several questions in a row, like: Are you really Jake Coltrane? How did you fake your own death so elaborately? Are you working for the government? How did you get your new identity? If you are Jake Coltrane, why did you attack that family? There is not enough proof Ernesto Flores has a solid history, while it seems someone has gone to great lengths to expunge Jake Coltrane's history. Jake's medical records, his dental records, his online history, credit cards, bank account, everything wiped clean. If you had those kinds of connections, why haven't they come for you?

"Strengthens my argument, doesn't it?" said Jake, talking from the dialogue in his mind while Duval was silent. "No one can tell the difference between me and this other guy. Perhaps there is a third person who looks like us? Who is to say? Maybe a fourth or a fifth?

They are cloning motherfuckers. Did you know?"

Duval nodded. Jake wasn't sure if he was agreeing or blowing him off. "It might sound like a mistrial," said Duval. "But since you are still locked away, I would say it's not good enough."

*Why wasn't it good enough?* Jake thought. He threw his hands in the air. This was going nowhere. Same sad dialogue. Same roadblocks. Duval was toying with him once again…or so he thought.

Duval shifted back in his chair. He cracked a nervous smirk, and then it vanished. "I thought we could talk honestly. I was hoping you could confide in me what I have already figured out."

"Which is?" asked Jake.

"Jake Coltrane can come back from the dead."

Jake laughed. Then he laughed even harder. Still, Duval remained stone-faced. He didn't look nervous or unsettled. He was serious.

"You were found naked on the streets of Manhattan," Duval said plainly. "A Russian mobster fell sixty floors and landed on top of you."

"I have no recollection of how I got there. Same story—coma and amnesia."

"Convenient answer," said Duval. "Same excuse for everything."

Duval rubbed his hands together, which caught Jake's attention. His nails. They were typically well taken care of, as if manicured. Not today, though. They were rough and jagged. The edges bleeding slightly. A sign of stress. Was it this case? Couldn't be.

"A street person told police that two people fell from the building," said Duval. "He saw two people hit the ground. One, the Russian, was busted up like you would expect a person to look after falling sixty floors. The other person was you, and you had less than half of those injuries, so it was assumed you were already on the ground when he landed on top of you."

"A *street person*?" asked Jake. He was smiling, trying to make Duval see how crazy he sounded.

"That's why the street person's testimony was never taken seriously. But I am taking it seriously now." Duval tapped on the table. Jake could hear the light thudding of his finger in the quiet room. "Did you know Jake Coltrane's girlfriend was murdered?"

It was like being shot. A surge of pain surged through Jake's body. He was hoping that Duval couldn't see it. The rage and turmoil he tried to suppress. He'd thought time would calm his nerves and revenge would satisfy the rage, but neither was working so far. He turned away momentarily to clear his thoughts. This was a game, and he could not let Duval know that he was winning. "Sorry to hear," said Jake solemnly.

"I showed the neighbors pictures of Jake, asked if they remembered him being aggressive or if the couple argued. I figured if I could demonize Jake Coltrane, I could then weave a tale about how much of a mastermind he was. I could prove Jake Coltrane and Ernesto Flores were one and the same. Jake Coltrane was a vicious monster who killed his girlfriend the instant he figured out she was pregnant with his child. But first, he had to convince everyone he was dead; that way he wouldn't be under suspicion."

Jake swallowed hard. The pain kept getting more intense. He wanted Duval to stop talking. He didn't want to be reminded of what he had lost.

"The neighbors told me a different tale, though," Duval continued. "They told me how much of a gentleman Jake really was. How he used to shovel the sidewalk after snowstorms even though he didn't live there, even shoveled the sidewalk of the old woman next door. But I chose not to believe them. People often hide the monsters they really are. Then, for some other reason, I became curious."

Duval placed both palms on the table flat and stared through the Plexiglas partition. "I reread the report given by the street person. I went back to the neighbors and showed them a picture of the Russian mobster, Alexei Voznesensky, and they said they had seen him before. This Russian came to the house. This Russian was a known monster. He terrorized many. If asked if he would kill a pregnant woman, the response was 'How many?'"

Duval began to change. Not physically, but emotionally. He still had the same no-nonsense look about him, but the vibe he was putting off was one of vulnerability. Almost as if he were confessing… as he had.

"Adonis Silver, the person you tried to kill in that synagogue, told me you could come back from the dead," said Duval. "I thought he was crazy, yet the deeper I probed, the more likely it seemed. But I couldn't wrap my head around it. I was convinced you were a danger to society one way or the other. Before I let you go, I had to know what kind of person you were. Now I know. You are the kind of person who kills monsters. Monsters like Alexei Voznesensky. And monsters like Adonis Silver. He is still out there, you know. Adonis Silver is walking free. So what are you going to do about that?"

# CHAPTER 34

There was no twitch in his voice. No stutter or delay. The only thing that stood out to Jake was a hint of bitterness and acrimony. This was personal. He meant it. There was more going on here than trying to trip Jake up with questioning.

"Are they recording this?" Jake spied the cameras in the top corners of the room angled at the table. "Should I ask for my lawyer?"

"Cameras are off," said Duval. "I requested they be turned off for this interview. I made up some bullshit that I needed to coax you a little and did not want the recordings to be used against me in court. I would edit the bad parts out of my own personal recorder." He pulled it out of his pocket. A small black digital voice recorder that looked more like a cell phone from the nineties. He turned it around so Jake could see he was not recording.

"Why would you ask me to kill the person you are accusing me of trying to kill?" said Jake. "Nothing about that makes sense. Sounds more like some sad attempt at reverse psychology."

"I'm not asking you to do anything," said Duval. "Just listen. I want you to hear how someone gets away with murder." Duval loosened his tie. The air-conditioning kicked in to the sound of brown noise, providing a cooling breeze to the back of Jake's neck. A comfort he could not relish locked within his cell. He closed his eyes and took a moment to soak it all in.

"It started with a murder," said Duval, bringing Jake's attention back to the room. "Connor Richardson had his head smashed in by an assailant. For weeks, we had nothing. Then a tip came in with a video saying this was our guy—Adonis Silver. I didn't think this kid from Long Island was our killer, but my partner was convinced he was responsible for a few more deaths, so we kept digging. His alibi for that evening didn't jibe, plus we had evidence he assaulted someone at the warehouse Connor Richardson managed. He posed as some sort of inspector so he could look around the place."

"You said you had video of the assault that identifies Adonis Silver as the killer?" Jake asked.

"Not really," said Duval. "We couldn't see his face clearly…We went off his mannerisms…Anyway…when we went to the warehouse where he was suspected of assaulting a guard, we ended up finding something unexpected. There was a mattress and some child porn in an old underground portion of the warehouse that was closed off. During the assault of Connor Richardson captured on video, the assailant looked through Connor's phone and saw something that set him off. That's when he went to town on Connor's head."

"So Adonis had a reason for what he did," said Jake, piecing things together quickly. "Connor sexually assaulted someone he knew."

Duval grimaced. "That's where things go blurry. Adonis has a sister, but there was never any evidence she had been assaulted in any way."

"You never questioned the girl?" asked Jake. He'd experienced things like this back when he was in foster homes. It was a delicate issue. Victims did not typically talk about their assaults. It was very hard to gain enough confidence in the victims to confide in a stranger. "She might still need help."

Duval flinched at the assumption. "You think we didn't try?" he said, getting louder. "The family put a restraining order against my partner. We couldn't go near anyone in the family. We asked a counselor at her school to pull the girl aside and talk to her. The best we could do." He stared at Duval sideways for a moment. Duval was obviously thorough. But Jake could never be sure.

"Fair enough," said Jake. "What happened after?"

"We brought Adonis Silver in for questioning. We had a witness who was going to identify him as the person who assaulted the guard. We were going to start there and put pressure on him. Connect him to Connor Richardson. Then the interrogation was stopped short. Another call came in pointing us in the direction of another person for the murder. A man named Fanuco Iglesias. He had the backpack with Connor's DNA inside."

"Inside the backpack?" Jake asked.

"The assault weapon was dropped in the backpack," said Duval. "It was on the video."

"But he didn't do it," said Jake. It was easy to read Duval's mannerisms.

"No. I'm convinced of it now."

"And this guy Fanuco is now rotting in prison," said Jake with a sneer. "How callous of you."

Duval was visibly embarrassed by it. Uncomfortable even. "He was in possession of key evidence…What else were we supposed to do?"

Jake nodded, not because he understood Duval's position. This was more of a judgmental nod because he wanted Duval to know he was forming an opinion and right now it was not favorable.

"The evidence was planted," said Duval.

"By Adonis Silver," said Jake, adding what he assumed to be true.

"No. It was planted by order of the victim's father. Our governor,

Barney Richardson."

Jake smiled and let out a scoff of disbelief. "Top-level conspiracy shit, huh? Seems like you're reaching again. I'm dying to hear how you put these pieces together."

Duval leaned forward and snapped at Jake with exceptional certainty. "The phone...the phone was also dropped into the backpack on the video. The murder weapon was recovered but not the phone. One of Barney Richardson's aides confided with us, off the record, that certain individuals of trust were hired and given the backpack to plant in Fanuco's apartment. You have to ask, Why would he do that?"

"So you are thinking it was to protect himself? Were they a father-and-son pedophile duo? Were there even greater people higher up involved?"

"Don't be so naive," Duval quipped. "Sometimes it's as simple as avoiding embarrassment in order to attain power. Being the father of the pedophile who was killed because he molested the wrong girl would've been devastating to his campaign. He was neck and neck in the polls with the incumbent until his son was murdered and people placed their support behind him. That support would have reversed if the truth was uncovered. I believe Adonis gave him the backpack and told Barney Richardson he would release the contents of the phone if he was ever caught. Barney Richardson agreed to the deal and was elected governor by a wave of sympathetic voters. Especially when it was discovered Fanuco was suspected of murdering his best friend as a teen."

"And Barney Richardson gave you an accommodation for solving his son's murder," said Jake, letting Duval know he was not as naive as he thought. "I read all about you. Not much left to do in here except read."

Duval looked like he wanted to say something right away but held back, likely considering how to phrase his response properly. "I assume you know about my wife and child as well," he said.

"You assumed right. I'm guessing the purpose of this meeting is for you to convince me that Adonis Silver is behind the abduction of your wife and child, and I am the only one who can stop him."

Duval looked down sort of shamefully. "Yeah," he said, raising his head, holding his chin high in a show of pride. "Something like that."

"I'm not going to do it," said Jake. "I see no reason to."

"Is that why you hesitated when you had the chance to kill him in the synagogue? Then why were you stalking him?"

"What?" asked Jake.

"Surprised I know, huh?"

He was. Jake was going through the details in his head but could not place it. How could he have known that?

"The footage of Adonis Silver in a mall in Long Island," said Duval as if reading his mind. "The same footage used to identify him as the killer had something else interesting in the background. You were there, standing by a store, watching him. He noticed you and freaked out. You were stalking him…hunting him. The attack at the synagogue was not some random robbery gone wrong as some would believe. You were after him. So tell me why. Why did you want to kill him?"

There were so many reasons, things Duval could never understand. Probably someday, Jake would explain it to him. But that day was not today. "Are you trying to get me to admit I was the one who tried to kill him?" asked Jake. It was cruel, he knew it was, but Jake had no choice. He was still not convinced he could trust Duval with his secrets.

"Very well," said Duval. "You don't want to tell me why you wanted him dead, then fine." The disappointment swept over his features only momentarily. Duval was normally proficient at hiding his emotions but not today. He wanted this too badly to disguise it. He was desperate. "I thought I could appeal to your sense of pride and respect, but I was wrong. Since you don't want to do this for me, I have to bury you in this prison system because of your crimes. I was giving you one last chance to change my mind. Now, you leave me no other choice."

"Trying to convince me to kill your monster for you was for your benefit," said Jake. "Not mine. You offered me nothing."

The brown noise of the air-conditioning stopped. The air grew thick and stagnant in a hurry.

"You haven't been paying attention, so let me spell it out," said Duval. "Remember when I told you I showed a picture of Alexei Voznesensky to your girlfriend's neighbors? Well, it got me thinking. What was the real connection between you and Alexei Voznesensky? I started doing research into any unsolved cases involving the Russian. It turns out there were two incidences of violence right around the time you went after Adonis Silver. There was gunplay at Alexei's whorehouse in the Bronx. One of the whores inside said a black devil came in and shot up the place with the biggest handgun she had ever seen. The mobsters fled before the police got there, but they left the bodies behind. Three bodies, and all were shot with a .45-70 Government round. Same ammo fired from the BFR single-action handgun registered to Jake Coltrane in New Jersey."

"I'm Ernesto Flores," said Jake, pressing his lips together tightly.

This seemed to piss Duval off something fierce. His face was expressionless, but Jake could feel his seething anger seep throughout the tiny room.

"There was a murder scene about the same time in upstate New York," continued Duval. "Grizzly scene. Body parts everywhere. The victims totaled eight, but there were only seven bodies found in the garage. A woman, the owner of the house, Paul Smith, and five Russian mobsters who worked for Alexei. I said eight victims and only seven bodies because there was another victim. They know from the blood…and the fingers…half of an arm…and a left foot, scattered among all the other body parts at the scene. We think there were more parts because someone tried to clean it up before taking off in one of the cars. But he left a few pieces behind. They were easy to distinguish from everyone else—once the blood was washed off, I mean—because they were the only black body parts in the bunch. DNA in the system shows the samples taken in the Bronx and the residence upstate are from the same person. But that person had not committed any crimes, so there was no positive match to base it against."

Jake could only watch. Wondering where he was going with this.

"You might believe you are safe from DNA evidence because in the state of New York, it is illegal to take DNA from a prisoner unless he is convicted of a crime. But you forget, you were a John Doe in a coma for months. The hospital took your DNA in an effort to identify you. It was never entered into the system because by that time they had a name. I wonder, if I entered the DNA under the name Ernesto Flores, would the crime scenes upstate and in the Bronx come back as a match?"

Jake noticed himself exploring the ridges of his molars with his tongue. He had no clue why he was doing it or for how long. Nervous reaction to what Duval was explaining, he supposed. Duval was certainly a top-notch investigator. No need to play along any further.

"What do you want?" asked Jake.

"I already told you. I want my wife and child found and Adonis Silver taken care of. For good!" Duval stood up and motioned for Blackwell to take Jake back to his cell. The latch released, and the volume of prison chatter increased as the door opened. Blackwell's wide body entered the room, and Duval handed over the papers he had resting on the table. "I want him to have these," he said to Blackwell.

Blackwell took the papers in his huge hands and looked over each page front and back to make sure they contained no hidden drugs or other paraphernalia. He looked satisfied and folded the pages enough to fit them into his pocket. "OK, Ernesto," said Blackwell with a bob of his chin. "Time to head back to your cell."

Jake placed both hands on the table and pushed himself upward. Duval was a tricky character indeed. Jake studied him one last time before making his way to the door. But there was protocol. He stopped short of the threshold and waited for Blackwell to latch the shackles dangling from his waist back onto his wrists. He clicked them on tight and motioned Jake to move. "I haven't decided to help you, but if I do, when would I be expected to get out of here?" asked Jake.

Duval scoffed. "If you are Jake Coltrane, you already know how you can get out of this mess. When you do, I promise to make it easy for you to walk away."

Jake nodded. Blackwell placed a hand on his shoulder, and Jake walked back out into the stuffy waiting area. Blackwell came alongside him and took him to the next checkpoint. Then they walked together, back through the series of gates and checkpoints, buzzing and unlocking and slamming shut again. The farther he got into the prison, the deeper his spirit sunk into the pits of darkness once more.

Jake arrived at his house, the cellblock of eighty-nine inmates. Home sweet home. Prisoners in orange-and-tan jumpsuits were gathered about at the tables, playing cards, checkers, and just bullshitting. Heads turned when he entered. Not many from the house got visitors on a regular basis. Word that a detective had come to see Jake only made it harder on him.

He felt the blood-curdling stare of Scotty Rock, sitting at one of the tables, following him through the common area. Others were giving him the stink eye as well; chants like "Snitch" were whispered. If there was an announcement that Jake had had all charges dropped and was being released, he imagined an accelerant would be poured under his cell door and lit as a going-away present.

Blackwell escorted him all the way to his cell and stood by the door.

"Jake Coltrane?" asked Blackwell, as if something were weighing on his mind. "Why did he call you Jake Coltrane?"

"My doppelganger," said Jake. "The man they are confusing me with."

"All Black people look alike," said Blackwell sarcastically.

When his cell was opened, Jake took a look at who was waiting for him inside. He sighed, knowing it was going to be a long evening. "Lock me up for the night," said Jake.

"No problem, Flores. You'll be tucked in for the evening."

Blackwell removed the shackles from Jake's hands and legs and handed Jake the papers from Duval after he stepped inside. The heavy door slammed shut and locked. The stench from his backed-up toilet grew stronger with the circulation cut off. But nothing compared to the assault he was about to face from his visitor. Jake turned to face him and waited for the barrage of insults to start.

Sly, a parasite inside his body and the source of Jake's ability to revive from the dead, would manifest before his eyes as Katt Williams, playing the role of Money Mike from *Friday After Next*. A pimp. He was wearing all purple today. Velvet-looking slacks with gold trim and a silk shirt, a Cuban link chain crusted with diamonds around his neck, and a gleaming pinky ring. There was a black do-rag on his head. Sly's own personal touch for being incarcerated. Sly sat with his back against the wall on Jake's bed with a glass of bourbon in his hand, shaking his head from disappointment.

"Now that your original plan has gone to shit, are you finally ready to get the fuck out of here?" asked Sly.

# CHAPTER 35

"Oh, be quiet and leave me alone," said Jake. His stomach felt queasy. The exchange between him and Duval had ended with Duval coming out on top. He headed for the toilet, slipped out of his prison trousers, and took a seat on the cold, stainless rim.

Sly was an illusion. Conjured in his mind by Sly the parasite, manipulating his senses and allowing him to appear to Jake as a real person. All of Jake's senses were activated with Sly present, making the distinction between Sly and reality seamless. It was the only reason Jake could somewhat stomach being isolated in his cell every day without going insane. He was never technically alone. However, Sly's personality left something to be desired. He had a way of picking at Jake's nerves. Purposefully aggravating him. Tugging at his strings. Being a nuisance. His most recent appearance was no different.

Jake could hear the ice cube tinkling against the glass of bourbon in Sly's hand as he swirled it. It was a reminder of how bad Jake wanted a drink. Bourbon was his favorite. This was Sly's own brand of torture. Dangling what Jake desired most right before his eyes, knowing the only way Jake could have a drink was if he escaped.

The only alcohol he'd had the misfortune of trying since being incarcerated was Pruno. A bile-tasting concoction made from fruits and fruit juices. It was disgusting, but most who dabbled in Pruno only cared about getting drunk. Jake was a connoisseur. What he would really love was a glass of what Sly was drinking, a Woodford Reserve Double Oaked. He could tell what was in the glass because sometimes Sly would manipulate Jake's olfactory senses to mimic the smell. Other times, it would smell like Colonel E.H. Taylor Small Batch.

"Enough already," said Jake, tired of the harassment.

"Fat fucking chance," said Sly. "Now Duval has your DNA, it has finally brought you to your senses about staying here. I'm ready for fine bitches with tight pussies, not standing guard while horny niggas check out your ass in the shower." Sly shook his head in disgust, then took a sip of his bourbon. "Take a look at those papers Five-O gave you. I'm curious."

Whatever Jake saw, Sly saw. He was so in tune with Jake's senses, it was all but simultaneous. Jake just had to read, and Sly would absorb the material as well. Yet Sly's intellect was separate from Jake's. He had his own mind and thoughts. Jake had nothing but time, and he was sitting on the john. A man's preferred seat for passing the time reading.

Jake placed the pages on his thigh and tried to smooth them out with his hand. The crinkly sound was similar to the one produced by the speed at which he used to work a keyboard. How long had it been since he had access to a computer? He pushed the harsh realities of prison aside and began reading. According to the paper, there was an immunohistochemical study on the expression of the adrenal adrenergic receptor for postmortem analysis. The study revealed immunoreactivity in the human adrenal gland's glomerulosa, fasciculata, reticularis, and medulla zones. The rest sounded like a bunch of scientific jargon.

"I thought this was supposed to be some kind of evidence that supported Adonis taking Duval's wife and child," said Jake.

"No, stupid," said Sly. "This was the research done connecting Adonis to a string of murders. Remember why you didn't pull the trigger in the synagogue? It didn't feel right to you because you were not sure he was a killer."

"These deaths were ruled suicides," said Jake. "Still doesn't prove anything."

"Yeah, but look. They noted where Adonis was located in relation to seven of the suicides. In each case, on each date, he was located less than a mile away. They have gas and hotel records, receipts, and pictures from here to Ohio. When we first met Adonis, I thought his power was that he could wish people dead…like the woman he made fall down the stairs. Now we really know what's going on, don't we?"

The eye of Tartarus. Jake knew its power all too well now. The eye belonged to a demon in hell. The king of demons. Its power was frightening.

"You need to give Duval and his dead partner Carrol credit," said Sly. "They have been tracking Adonis and his kills while you were stuck here in prison. Does that make you feel better now? You now have proof he is a killer."

"Why would I feel better about killing a man?" said Jake. His stomach rumbled. The visit from Duval was upsetting, along with the trash they called prison food.

"Your stupid sense of morality," said Sly. "You'd rather sit there on a prison shitter and be damned to hell for all eternity than do what you need to do to save yourself."

"I tried to save myself before," said Jake. "Remember the cure for the tumor in my head? Look where that got me. Stuck with your smart-ass mouth." The gurgling made its way out of his system. Then he remembered he was low on paper, which made him upset again.

"Killing Adonis is your only way out," said Sly.

No. Not true. If he was wrong, he would only make his situation worse. His soul was sentenced to hell for some reason. Exactly what he'd done to deserve the sentence was unknown. Killing Adonis and taking the eye was something a tortured soul in hell had told him would be the key to escaping. The old man in hell happened to hear Tartarus say it to one of hell's apostles. But how could he trust what was said?

"Fuck!" said Sly. His finger tapped the side of the bourbon glass. "Why didn't you shoot him and find out?"

Jake was careless. He should have checked twice to make sure the family wasn't there. After seeing their shocked faces, he wouldn't have dreamed of shooting Adonis in front of them. That would've made him the monster. Besides, he had never killed anyone at that point. It was vengeance that gave Jake his first kill, and the rest that followed.

Jake threw the rest of the pages in the trash, stood up, and made his way over to the sink to wash his hands. It was a tiny, round, stainless-steel sink with one knob for cold water. A miserable stream of low pressure ran down the drain. He placed his hands beneath it to wet his fingers, adjusting to the temperature.

"Jake," said Sly, "you have to understand this is your way out."

"Way out of what?" he asked, working the soap into his hands. "I owe Duval nothing. He never even told me why he thinks Adonis is responsible for his missing family. Why should I give a fuck about any of it?"

"How about the DNA evidence against you? How about those people suffering at the other end of the eye of Tartarus?"

Jake dried his hands on a towel, small, white, severely worn, without much terry cloth left on it. He checked his face in the small mirror made of polished stainless steel, not glass. It produced a distorted image, but he could make out his features well enough to tell if there was food in his teeth. While he was staring at his blurry visage, his mind drifted to the times he'd died and gone to hell, where he was tortured, usually by drudging up old traumas from his past.

"They say that under hypnosis, people have been touched with ice cubes but told they were being touched with hot coals," said Jake. "The skin would welt and display signs of second-degree burns. When Tartarus looked into my past in hell, the intensity of my pain was magnified. I could feel the weight of the pain whenever he was near. It's just not something I want to face again. Not if I have a choice."

"But you don't have a choice," said Sly. "Once the new DNA evidence is entered into the system, how are you going to explain having all your fingers and toes again? How are you going to keep from becoming a lab experiment?"

A fate worse than hell. Most of his fingers had been cut off by the mobsters just so they could see them grow back. He'd been their own personal freak show. He looked at Sly, staring back at him, pissed off at the world. Jake knew Sly hated being locked up. Some days, he wouldn't speak to Jake at all. That was OK. Sly didn't have the type of personality Jake was comfortable with anyway.

Jake turned around and leaned his butt up against the sink. "I pass. I'll take my chances with the DNA. See what happens next."

Sly flung his drink across the room, disgusted. It ended up disappearing before smashing into the wall, reminding Jake it was an illusion anyway.

Jake put his hand on the cold, painted cinder block wall, feeling the rough edges under his palm. Noting how solid it felt, thinking of the many times he'd died and gone to Hell and how this stint in Rikers was no different. "Everyone in Hell thinks they can escape. It's like a thought put into your soul by God to torture you even further. Make you feel like he made a mistake and will soon realize you don't belong there. But that day never comes."

"So you want to give up?" said Sly. "Tartarus talked about the eye for a reason. It's a physical part of him in this world, with great power. Instead of giving up, you should learn to use that power. The power of sight. You can look into your own past and your own future. Use it to find Duval's wife and kid and save your soul. What do you have to lose?"

Jake let out a sigh of frustration and flopped down onto the bed lengthwise, right through Sly's body and onto his stomach. He scrunched the pillow up under his arms and set his chin on top, staring at the chipped paint on the steel door.

"No," said Jake. "No more talking."

This could possibly destroy the armor he'd erected for protection. Giving way to hope only led to misery. That's how his life had turned out thus far. Something would always go wrong. It had happened when he tried to find a cure for his tumor and again when he thought of a future with his girlfriend. Everything he tried went to shit. Everything. That was why he was sitting in this cell.

"Can't be that simple," said Jake, turning over onto his side.

He closed his eyes. He kept them closed and quickly dozed off to sleep. He was out maybe two hours before his eyes sprang open. It was all his mind was willing to give him. He dreamed he was out in the world, drinking bourbon, eating steaks, wearing his own clothes, seeing the trees and the sun whenever he wanted. Traveling, something he never got a chance to do the way he liked. Living!

But hell was the dark cloud that hovered over the dream.

# CHAPTER 36

Not knowing was perhaps the greatest hell of all. It wasn't like he'd thought about it many times before. Hell was a place for the evil people of the world. Those who showed no remorse. Despicable men who spat in the face of God and refused to humble themselves before him. Those who were ungrateful for what they had been given. He was none of those things. He was respectable and honorable. Decent. Exactly why was God punishing him?

Would the eye show him?

He had to be careful. Show God he was above the sins of ordinary men. That he could repent and he was sorry for his sins.

"Sly? Are you there?" said Jake.

He could hear the other inmates out in the common area outside his cell door. It wasn't time for lights out yet. There was no need to put this off any longer. Sly appeared at the foot of his bed, in a purple gabardine suit with gold trim.

"Do you have enough energy to bring me back?" asked Jake.

Sly snapped his fingers. "Like a fucking magician. My energy reserves could be better, but what can you expect from prison food? I am good enough to revive you, if it means getting out of this shit show. So what's the plan?"

He remembered when he first arrived in the bullpen to a blood-soaked floor. Word was Scotty Rock had beaten another inmate so bad his eyeball came out of his head. It reminded Jake of when he was beaten to death by the two Russians in the Bronx. The tumor he'd carried in his head since he was a child was still active. In conditions of extreme duress, it would disrupt his motor functions, causing his heart to stop.

"The plan is for me to go out into gen-pop and get beaten down by the inmates. This should probably trigger my tumor and end my life."

Sly was visibly upset. "What a bitch move," Sly scoffed. "Those assholes out there are savages. Your body is still in battle mode from when you fought the Russians. You could kill all of them if you wanted to. Are you sure you want to play Jesus and turn the other cheek?"

"All part of my penance, Sly. I have to show God that although I have the power, I can show restraint."

"Pfff," said Sly, eying Jake sideways. "Let's see how that shit goes."

Jake kicked his feet off the bed and placed them on the floor. He thought about putting on his sneakers but changed his mind. Prison comfort wear came in the form of shower sandals. Tan, hard plastic, perfect for lounging. It was what most people wore around the common area. However, when shit was about to go down, the first hint of impending danger was movement in the shadows and the number of inmates wearing sneakers.

Jake wanted to look as vulnerable as possible. So slippers it was. He put his feet in them with his socks still on. They were bound to fly off his feet the instant the fighting began, leaving him sliding around in his socks, but that was OK. His aim was to get killed in a prison scuffle. Show God he was worthy of forgiveness by sacrificing himself.

"Let's go find Scotty Rock," said Jake.

Jake stood up and started stretching. Getting himself warmed up and limber. He didn't really know what he was doing, just what felt good to him. Moving his shoulders and legs, flexing and extending his arms and torso. Twisting his lower back and neck.

"You could just sit here and kill yourself," said Sly. "Take a bite out of your wrists. Should do it."

"My Catholic upbringing forbids it."

Jake finished warming up his muscles and used the bottom of his fist to pound on the cell door. He yelled through the access hole, trying to get the attention of one of the guards. A head popped in front. The new guy. His name was Jacobs.

"What's up?" he asked.

"I want to come out and watch some television," said Jake.

There was a pause. A long one. "Are you sure?" asked Jacobs.

He had only been on the job a few months. His shift usually started somewhere around six in the evening. Most of the truly devious shit that goes on in prison happens after nightfall. That's when all the rage and malice are directed toward other inmates, so guards are mindful to stay out of the way until sunrise. For Jake to come out at this time was most surely a recipe for trouble. One Jacobs was not prepared to get in the middle of.

"Blackwell is not here," said Jacobs, reminding Jake one last time that he was on his own.

"Open it up," said Jake. "I'm tired of being locked in here. I need some space."

There was still a good chance Jacobs could tell him to fuck off, especially if he was looking for a peaceful evening. But Jacobs caved in to the demand. With a clunk of the latch giving way and a rattle of the door opening, Jake stepped out of his cell. First thing he did was look back into his small cell, knowing it was the last time he would see it. He was also looking for Sly, who was gone from sight. He would often disappear, especially when Jake made a decision he didn't agree with.

Jake turned back toward the common room and stared into several faces with wide eyes and open mouths throughout the cellblock. Prisoners usually congregated by race: White, Black, and Hispanic. Whites had their areas, Hispanics had theirs, and the Blacks were in their usual locations. Despite the race barriers, everyone knew what was going on in regard to Jake. The protected prisoner had come out of his cell. Whispers began to grow louder. Inmates dashed in and out of their cells, most likely to trade their shower shoes for sneakers. One inmate, with cornrows, stood fixated, making sure he was seeing it right with his own eyes. Another light-skinned brother with tattoos on his neck took off in the direction of the TV room. No doubt to tell Scotty Rock what was going on.

Jake saw it as a blessing. Things would happen fast. The faster the better. Jake walked out to the middle of the cellblock and stretched his limbs as if he were tired. It was a ploy to look completely ignorant and relaxed. Then they wouldn't hesitate. He stood near a couple of tables with several Hispanic inmates playing cards. They stopped to look at him as if to say, *Don't you dare take a seat here. Keep it moving. Take the trouble heading your way somewhere else.* Jake read all of that with a simple stare. He respected and honored their request.

Down the main block, a few paces away, was the television room. He decided to head there. Whispers followed him. He felt the adrenaline rising. Bloodlust was growing thicker, trying to suffocate him. But he was prepared. This was his means of redemption. His sacrifice to God for killing the Russians.

He arrived at the television room. A space of about four hundred square feet with bench seats and a television hanging high near the ceiling. About thirteen inmates were there. Scotty Rock was in the corner surrounded by three others, plus the kid with the tattoos on his neck who took off to notify him. Jake purposely took a seat at the other end, farthest away from Scotty, and focused on the television. A horror movie was on. An older one. A guy was running after a girl with an axe through the woods, and inmates were cackling about how stupid she was. Jake pretended to get lost in the show while feeling the thick coat of tension building in the air. He had help that gave him super senses. Sly.

Guards began to disappear. Slow like. Subtle. Scotty's people came in and out of the room. Slow like. Subtle. Everyone who reentered was wearing sneakers. No shower shoes like Jake was wearing. No one came to whisper a warning to him. All too afraid of Scotty Rock to speak up. Besides, there was the code of no snitching, which extended beyond the police. The word had circulated, and everyone who was not going to be involved slowly disappeared. Had other things to do. Places to be.

"I count six," said Sly, reappearing before Jake. "They are serious about fucking you up. They have been waiting a long time for this. They won't go easy on you."

Jake was counting on it.

An inmate a few benches behind spoke loudly. "Looky here. It's Flo-luva!"

Jake didn't turn around. Flo-luva was a pet name for Flores.

"Flo-luva's out of his cage tonight!" said the inmate. "Lucky me."

The voice sounded like the inmate who would often bang on his cell door and blow kisses, talking about what Jake was missing being locked up inside his cell. Falling under a guard's protection came with an effeminate stigma. And so they treated him accordingly. Like a bitch.

"Damn, I'm going to sleep good tonight! I don't think you will sleep so good, though," he said to Jake, laughing. "You might be experiencing a little discomfort. Did you eat yet?"

"Somebody is going to be swallowing babies tonight!" someone from the back yelled.

Sly stepped around in front of Jake so he could see him. He looked pissed. "Fucking gross," said Sly. "Are you sure you want to let them get away with this kind of ridicule? Don't play Jesus with these motherfuckers." Sly looked over Jake's head at the inmate behind him. "This guy wants to fuck you! Literally! Don't tell me you want to succumb to an ass fucking just to prove you can be pious?"

Jake sat still while feeling the eyes upon him. He could sense that Scotty Rock was directing the provocation. Waiting for the right time. The crack about him not sleeping so good was meant to send his mind rolling downhill into a river of fear. Get his blood pressure flaring and his heart racing so fast it would burst. But he was unaware of Sly. Sly was tapped into his endocrine system, pushing buttons to control the chemical impulses released throughout his body. Jake wasn't afraid; he was eager to get this thing started.

He stood up and made his way to the exit, further provoking a response. When he got close, an inmate stepped in front of the entrance, preventing him from leaving. He was a muscle-bound guy. Bald and ugly as sin. He had his sleeves rolled up higher than normal to show off his biceps.

"Yo, I need to talk to you about something, Flo-luva," he said. Jake recognized the voice as the guy who wanted to rape him. Just seeing his face caused Jake to flinch. "This hard-on ain't going away by itself." He grabbed his crotch and started rubbing it, causing his bulge to swell. "Why don't you kneel down and talk to it? Make it go away."

Things got quiet. Almost to a dead silence. This muscle-bound freak was serious, and he didn't care who was watching. His fat lips were flapping as he was missing most of his teeth. He tensed his face like he was getting off on Jake's fear.

Sly appeared behind the muscleman. "Are you sure this is the guy you want to turn your virgin asshole over to?"

"Get the fuck on your knees, bitch!" he shouted, with his lips flaring.

Jake heard sneakers squeaking across the floor as people began to stand and move. They were going to make sure Jake got raped. They intended to hold him down and humiliate him. Send him back to his cell crying and bleeding as they laughed. He could feel the malice in the air. They were enjoying this. It was fun for them. Doing this to other people was their means of entertainment.

Was this what it meant to be humbled before God?

The disgusting muscle-bound inmate lunged to seize Jake with those thick arms. As he got closer, something inside Jake snapped. Something primal. This was fight or flight. Piousness disappeared in the face of a cross-eyed inmate looking to butt fuck him. Jake sidestepped the attempt and grabbed the inmate behind the head. Quick and in one fluid motion. He brought the inmate's head down upon the knee he was thrusting upward. Jake felt something in the guy's face break upon impact, nose or eye socket. One of the two. But Jake wasn't done. He pivoted back in front of him and delivered a kick to the groin that lifted him off his feet about six inches. Jake's Patakis shot off his feet and into the hallway, hitting the wall with a smack. The muscleman dropped in a heap on the floor. A thud, devoid of all consciousness.

"That's what I'm talking about!" Sly screamed. "Nuts all in your guts, nniyigga!" Sly nudged his head toward the others. "Time to fuck the rest of these niggas up!"

The speed with which Jake moved caught them off guard. For a fraction of a second, they froze. Barely perceptible. However, Jake caught it. So did Sly. "Their adrenaline spiked, Jake," said Sly. "They know they gotta kill you now."

Jake opened his arms wide and screamed like a madman, "Bring it on!" Summoning every fiber in his being to prepare for war.

They came at him with a renewed sense of urgency. He'd fought a group of people in hell once before. Nothing new to him. But back then, they took turns attacking. One, then another, and another. This was nothing like that. They all came at him at once, looking to subdue him. Giving him no space to pick them off.

His first punch landed on the chin of one of the bigger inmates. His head snapped backward, and he was out instantly. But he kept falling forward from the momentum. Dropping at Jake's knees as he delivered an elbow to the face of the next person who came into range. Then the clutter of bodies at Jake's feet tripped up his balance. Gave him no room to maneuver. With the muscle-bound guy on the floor behind him and the two fresh ones in front, he felt pinned.

*How do they do that in the movies, anyway?* Jake thought. *Each guy that gets knocked unconscious will get in the way. How do you not trip over them?*

Jake struck the third with a backhand fist to the neck. He fell atop the growing pile, and that was it. The rest of the charging bunch was able to subdue him. One of his arms was captured. Then another snuck in from behind and grabbed him around the midsection.

Jake was about to start swinging wildly, but he saw Scotty Rock coming into range. Targeting Scotty's big head, big chin, big nose became Jake's only concern in the foray. His dead black eyes drew closer, and Jake no longer cared about the punches being thrown in his direction. All he saw was Scotty. With his free hand, Jake lunged forward. His socks slid on the tiled floor and he began falling, but before he lost balance, he managed to get a hold of the top of Scotty's orange jumpsuit. With a massive heave, he pulled Scotty close to him. As he did, the first shank caught him under the ribcage on his left side.

*How dare he?* thought Jake.

He spotted the sharpened red plastic shank in Scotty's hand and couldn't believe it.

The nerve of this guy, going for the kill with a shank.

It fueled Jake's rage to another level. Carnal. Berserker. Jake pulled Scotty closer to him, pinning his arm with the shank against Jake's body to where Scotty could not remove it. So Scotty began to twist it. Jake summoned all his strength to move the other arm, being held down by the wild-haired inmate. Jake brought the inmate around with his arm, flinging him across the room, so he could get a hand around Scotty's neck.

The weight of tossing a human being knocked Jake off-balance, and he tumbled to the ground, but Jake had the source of his ire in his possession. Jake wrestled and squirmed like a snake, coiling his legs and arms around Scotty's body. Scotty twisted the shank and pushed deeper until the butt of his hand was up against Jake's ribcage, but Jake never faltered. His grip around Scotty's neck remained like a vice. And Jake slowly began increasing pressure. He was face-to-face with Scotty. Scotty could not utter a word.

"You know, they say you are born into this world alone," said Jake, whispering into Scotty's ear as the others kicked and punched in flurries. "But they're wrong about dying alone. You can die together and arrive at the same place. I've done it before. Rode an asshole sixty floors to his death. I am prepared to die once again, but tonight I am taking your ass to Hell with me."

Jake spoke to Sly in his mind: *The minute this guy dies, I want you to stop my heart and the impulses to my brain. I want to die at the same exact moment. I want to see this asshole in Hell with me.*

"Will do," said Sly.

Spectators were howling like wild animals. Crazed inmates cheering on the fight. This was gladiatorial combat at its finest. Other inmates with shanks joined the fray, and Jake felt them penetrating his back as they stabbed with a flurry of parries. But Jake never flinched. Sly took care of that. There was enough adrenaline flowing through Jake that he could've picked up a bus if he needed to. The pain of puncture wounds had been reduced to love taps.

"OK, buddy," said Sly. "He's almost gone. Time to let you get some rest too."

Jake squeezed as hard as he could. He felt the vertebrae in Scotty's neck give way. The crunching was followed by the lifelessness that a body falls into. The tension fell to mush in his arms. It would take a few more moments for his brain to die. He was counting on Sly to synchronize it perfectly. When Jake felt the heat coming for his own body, he braced himself. Hell was just around the corner.

## CHAPTER 37

Jake opened his eyes to a bright light overhead. The stinging heat hot enough to melt flesh was gone. The screams and smells of Hell were no longer in the air. A frightful sense of anxiety settled into a welcomed feeling of relief. He smiled. He was glad to be back. But where was he? A thin white sheet was covering him up to his chest. He lay on his back on a hard surface. Stainless steel from what he could see peering over his shoulder. The look of the office was familiar to him. His memory kicked in. It was the examining room at the coroner's office in Newark, New Jersey.

Someone he had not seen in close to a year walked into the room with a cheerful squeal. She came up and placed a hand on his chest.

"Welcome back," said Dr. Carrie Blake. Locks from her curly black hair dangled above him. Carrie was the first to see new body parts grow back on his body. Scared the crap out of her…the first time.

"Hey," said Jake. He felt warm and tingly inside. She was still as cute as ever. Light-brown skin, curly black hair, petite, long eyelashes, stylish black-rimmed glasses perked cutely on her little nose. She frowned at him and slapped his chest.

"Still getting yourself murdered, I see," said Carrie. Her hands went to her hips. "This isn't a body shop where you can park your carcass until the engine gets fixed. How many times has it been?"

"This is the third time I have revived to see your beautiful face standing over me," said Jake. "I was murdered three other times… maybe four. Died from my tumor twice. The other times I died, I was actually trying to kill other people, so I don't think that counts as murder. Anyway, great to see you again." He looked around the walls of the examination room for a calendar or a clock. "How long have I been out?"

"Almost a week since your official death certificate."

Sly hadn't said it would take long. Maybe he had his reasons for taking his time. Jake put a hand on his face and felt scraggly patches of hair. Growth was about a week's worth. Then it occurred to him: he shouldn't be there. "I was incarcerated in New York City," he said. "How did I get to the coroner's office in New Jersey?"

She rolled her eyes. "Lieutenant Duval had you transferred here," she said with a kind of ire. "He's been a thorn in my side for about three weeks now. He told me this was his way of making it easier on you."

He understood. "Send him my thanks," said Jake. "But not really."

Jake sat upright, and the white sheet slid down to his waist. He swiveled his head left and right, taking in as much of the room as possible. Nothing new stood out. It was just as he remembered it when he was last there more than a year ago. Stainless steel examination tables to his right, the storage doors where they kept the bodies to his left, Petri dishes and other storage containers behind him. It brought back memories, mostly of him in need of help. He owed Carrie big time. She'd bailed him out in his time of need. She was a true friend. But questions about Duval kept flooding his thoughts. Carrie was standing near him at the table. His nose wrinkled in confusion.

"How did Duval know to bring me here?" asked Jake. "To you. In New Jersey."

Carrie froze like a wife being caught with a new credit card. "He was the one who came here to identify your body after the synagogue incident," she said slowly. "He's a smart guy. He figured it out."

That didn't jive. "He couldn't have figured it out, Carrie."

Her wide-eyed glare continued. "What do you mean?"

"When I came back to life the first time, in front of you, you had just picked up pieces of my body from the train tracks. And your first response was someone was playing a prank on you. Your partner jumped from a moving car and had to be coaxed into coming back to work two weeks later. People don't believe this sort of thing, Carrie."

She quickly began examining Jake as if she were his personal physician. Ignoring the point he was trying to make. Her fingers probed around his neck, checking the lymph nodes.

"Never mind," said Jake. "I don't know why I'm harassing you about why I was brought here. He had my DNA evidence from several crime scenes. The only explanation was I could come back from the dead."

She blinked with astonishment several times before saying, "Your DNA matched? Hard to believe."

"They had my fingers and a foot from the crime scene in New Haven."

"Why are you leaving body parts behind?"

"I didn't forget to grab them on my way out the door. They were torturing me…cutting off…you get it. Duval said when I was in the hospital, they took my DNA to try to identify me since I was incapacitated. DNA from New Haven and the place in the Bronx was already in the system. All that was left was to match the hospital DNA to the other two, and my ass would be cooked."

"But in order to cure your tumor, Sly tinkers with your DNA

slightly," said Carrie. "Look, you can't even grow hair on top of your head anymore. At best, the DNA would come back as being a close relative. Like a brother or something. It would have only reinforced your argument that someone else is out there who looks like you."

"So he was bluffing?"

"Had to be."

"Motherfucker," said Jake.

She continued her examination of his body, moving her hand from his wrist up to his shoulder. Her hands were soft and glided across his skin like a massage therapist's. She felt along the side of his abdomen and moved to his back, searching for the puncture wounds that killed him. Everything was smooth. No cuts, no scabs, nor any sign of any damage whatsoever. His body was as good as new.

"Amazing," said Carrie. She motioned to a chair inside the door. "I bought you some clothes. Seems you didn't have any decent clothes when you were arrested. Nothing that would fit you, anyway. Were you going for the homeless look?"

Long story. He didn't feel like going into it.

"These clothes should fit fine," she said. "I had to find a specialty store. Big and Tall."

"I appreciate you," said Jake. He slid his legs off the table and hopped down onto the floor, pressing the sheet against his privates. His bare feet slapped against the cold, slick tiles as he got his footing.

"Before you get dressed, ask her if you can get some of that fine booty," said Sly. He appeared to Jake wearing a shiny black silk bathrobe and slippers, lying on his side on one of the examination tables. He held a cognac glass in one hand and a tobacco pipe in the other. "Rubbing felt good."

"She wasn't rubbing. She was examining," said Jake. He gave Sly the once over, concentrating on the baby-blue ascot around his neck. "Are you supposed to be Hugh Hefner now?"

"Hugh was a playboy. With me stuck inside you, I am just a jerk-off boy."

"Piss off," he said. Then Jake remembered he had a bone to pick. "Did you know the DNA wouldn't match?"

"Oops!" said Sly playfully, with a smile. "Must have slipped my mind."

"You didn't say anything because you wanted out of prison, you little…" said Jake, jaw clenched.

Carrie looked to the examination table, where Jake was focused. "Are you talking to Sly again?" she asked, as she knew all about his troublesome parasite. He'd explained to her how he had tried to find a cure for his tumor and was given the parasite as a means of solving his problems. The tumor was still there because Sly had the power to recreate from his DNA footprint, not cure anything. Since the tumor was encoded in his DNA, Carrie suggested Sly alter it slowly in order to find the right sequence to get rid of the tumor for good. Her recommendation got Sly on the right path, but out of billions of sequences of code, the search for what caused the tumor still eluded him.

"Tell Sly I said hi." She waved cheerfully.

"It's not like he's on the other end of the phone," said Jake. "He heard you."

"I know. I feel like he is my friend too," said Carrie, glancing toward Sly at the examination table. "I remember you saying he talks to you because he doesn't want to feel alone, so when you were on the table and I was in the room alone, I would talk to him. We had quite a conversation. I would tell him all about what was going on in my life and what I was feeling at the time. I thought of it as therapeutic for both of us."

"What?" said Jake.

"Did he say anything about me?" she asked, smiling. "What does he think of our conversations?"

Jake laughed and shook his head. "Let me fill you in on what you can't hear." He pointed sharply in Sly's direction. "The first thing that came out of his mouth was to ask you for some booty. Says you got him all hot and bothered. Just so you know what kind of parasite you're schmoozing with while I'm dead."

"Seriously?" said Carrie. However, she did not seem as appalled as Jake thought she would be. She put a hand to her chin in thought. "I mean, I haven't had any in a while. Lord knows I could use some. I'm a pathologist who works odd hours. Not really conducive to meeting people." She was kind of speaking to no one in particular, airing her thoughts. Then she turned to Jake. "But I am afraid I have to decline because of your anatomy."

"Oh. See that, Sly?" Jake screamed in his direction. "She likes women. Women!"

"I'm not a lesbian," she said quickly. "I'm talking about you, Jake. More specifically…that!" She pointed down between his legs at the sheet plastered against his manhood. "I'm a petite girl. I think I'm a bit too small for you. Frankly, I have no clue how your girlfriend survived it."

"Excuse me?" said Jake.

"Come now, Jake," said Carrie. "You must have heard this before."

"Awwww, damn!" Sly screamed, tossing his head back. "Now your big dick is getting in the way. Can't I get a fucking break around here?"

"What are you talking about?" said Jake uncomfortably. "Women like it big. They say so all the time."

"No. No!" she said emphatically. "Not that big. I think you would frighten porn stars with that one."

"How about this?" Sly jumped on top of the steel examining table and opened his arms wide like a gymnast after sticking a landing.

"I am just the right size, baby." Sly first exposed himself to Carrie, then swiveled toward Jake.

"Dear God," said Jake. "Put it away. You're embarrassing yourself."

"You look like you've been sucking on a lemon or something," laughed Carrie. "What did he do? What did he say?"

He wasn't going to answer. Slightly perturbed by the talk about his manhood, Jake dropped the sheet between his legs and made his way over to the bag of clothes sitting on the chair.

"Thanks for denying me punani once again," said Sly, dropping down to sit with his legs crossed. "I am still technically a virgin, asshole." He crossed his arms to pout. "I thought being locked up in prison for nearly a year would get you horny enough to finally get some, but nooooo! You're not even trying. Not even thinking about pussy." He threw his glass of cognac at a wall and then disappeared before it made contact.

Sex. It had been more than a year. Perhaps the horrors of Hell had thrown his mind out of whack. His sexual impulses were barely noticeable. Nonexistent, even. They say a young man thinks about sex once every six minutes. Jake couldn't recall the last time his mind wandered into sexual fantasies or the desire to satisfy his urges.

He opened the bag and dug through the clothes Carrie had bought him. He liked what he saw. Apparently, she'd picked out clothing with his tastes in mind. Too well, even. He was surprised she paid much attention to his tastes in the short time he knew her. She must have also taken measurements to get the size right. Shopping for a fit, six-foot-seven male was not easy. Coroners measured body parts all the time, or maybe she liked shopping for others. Either way, he was thankful.

It started with a nice pair of boxer briefs. They fit snug around the waistband but great around the thighs and butt. Then there was the navy-blue crewneck, long-sleeve shirt. The arm length was just right. The stretch jeans were soft and comfortable, perfect fit. The length came right down below the ankles. Thin black socks for those with feet larger than size thirteen, and a nice pair of blue shoes with no heel.

Jake stood up after putting on his shoes. Moved around a little to check for pinching. It was perfect.

Meanwhile, Carrie was prepping a body. A male who looked to be in his early fifties was on the table. White as a ghost. The light shining down on his skin was almost reflecting off it. She was spraying him down with water from head to toe. The drainage system at the end of the table funneled the water down and out of sight.

Jake took a stroll around the office, trying to clear his head. He passed by the cold stainless-steel doors that held the dead for examination. Past the microscopes and various glass tubes. Past the gas burners and what looked to him like a space-age microwave oven.

His mind was swirling. He was worried, mostly about his own sanity.

"You are going to try and kill Adonis Silver again, aren't you?" asked Carrie.

It was nothing new. He'd left Carrie to kill Adonis last year and come back during the torrential rainstorm ashamed he had pointed the gun at the entire family in a house of God.

"Duval is convinced he is a bad guy," said Carrie.

"Duval thinks he is responsible for his wife and kid being missing. Says Adonis is punishing him for continuing to pursue the case against him."

"And what do you think?" she asked.

Great question. He wasn't sure what to think of Adonis. Sure, Sly was convinced he was dangerous. Tartarus, the most frightening creature in Hell, didn't want Adonis to have his eye. But what would be the angle when Jake had the eye? Sure, he could use it to see into his past and future and possibly atone for any sin that caused him to go to Hell, but what then? What about that?

"I met Adonis, you know," said Carrie. She sighed and tied her hair back in a scrunchy, from her wrist to her hair in one fluid motion. Then she straightened out her glasses, seemingly having trouble finding the right words. "He came here to view the body. Both he and Duval."

"And?" Jake asked.

"He was frightening in a way. Spooky. His level of intuition was otherworldly. He knew you could come back from the dead and I was helping you."

*The power of the eye,* Jake thought. He didn't want to tell her. It would make her fearful. "Do you mind if I use your phone?" asked Jake. "I need to call someone for a ride."

She nodded and pointed down the hall. "Phone is in my office, three doors down on the right. My assistant isn't here right now. He went to grab us something to eat. You and I are the only ones in the building."

Jake thanked her and gave her a hug for being there for him. She felt stiff and tense. She patted him on the back and pulled away abruptly, as if she were upset about something. "I need to get prepared for this exam," she said.

Carrie stepped into the doorway and stopped. She didn't turn around. "When I began medical school, I had high hopes," she said. Jake couldn't help but notice her mannerisms while looking at the back of her white lab coat, sensing the reason she was not turning around was because she was too emotional. "Saving lives was my ultimate goal. During my residency, I saw death firsthand. Call me a coward, Jake. I deserve that. But the reason I chose to be a pathologist was I couldn't handle the emergency room. Working so hard to save someone's life and failing made me depressed. I decided I couldn't do it. My heart couldn't take watching a life slip away when it was my job to save it. But I had dedicated my life to this. I couldn't throw it away. I couldn't quit now. So I decided to work the opposite end. Discover the causes of death in order to prevent them."

Her shoulders dipped slightly. Then she took a deep breath, arching her back to gain strength. "I don't know how to feel about someone being murdered for being dangerous. Part of me thinks it's justice. An eye for an eye. The other half of me says it's wrong. I don't want you to think I condone this, Jake. I don't. It's that somehow, when it comes to Adonis, there is something about him that concerns me. Like a voice warning me this guy is not to be toyed with."

She turned to face him. Her eyes glistening with concern. "Be careful, Jake. He's the type of person who might figure out how to put you down for good. It would be a shame to know once again that death is permanent. I've enjoyed this little game we've been playing. Watching someone actually get up from my table."

Carrie stepped out into the hallway and out of sight.

## CHAPTER 38

He went to the back door, pushed the lever bar running the width of the door, and immediately felt the rush of cool air. To Jake, it felt ultra refreshing. He had been locked in a hospital and then a prison for almost a year, followed by a steamy trip to Hell. He wanted his skin to be speckled with goose bumps. He wanted the fine hairs of his body to stand so tight that when he rubbed his arms, it felt like porcupine quills. It stimulated the tops of his ears with a prickly, numbing sensation.

"You just had to call Jericho Black, didn't you?" said Sly. He stood next to Jake wearing a white mink and a fuzzy white fedora. His mutton chops were back, his hair curled, and he was flicking a toothpick in the corner of his mouth. He looked cool. Everything a pimp was supposed to be.

Jake turned to the night sky full of stars. "Who else is going to help us out of this mess? I got no money, no car, and damn it, Ernesto Flores is now dead as well."

"Fuck! Jericho Black is ten times more dangerous than Adonis Silver. You know that, right?" Sly barked. He took the toothpick from the corner of his mouth and flicked it to the ground. "I guess I have to keep saving your ass if we are going to survive this."

Jake walked the concrete path to the security gate with Sly beside him. He pushed the button to release the electromagnet used to keep it locked. He walked out into the parking lot all the way to the front of the building. There he paused to take in the nostalgia. It was a lot like he remembered it. On the corner of the street was the gas station. The pumps were lit up, and one of the workers, in a gray hoodie, was pumping gas into a green Suburban.

The office building across the street was dark. Only two cars in the parking lot. The dumpster near the alley was full of trash; several bottles and papers had spilled out onto the blacktop. He slid up his sleeves to get fresh air on his forearms while thinking about how good it felt to be free. Not trapped in prison or hell. No inmates looking to beat the shit out of him, and no demons chasing him for the same reason. No one screaming for help in the darkness of their cell in the middle of the night. No one screaming for help after being trapped in a pit that slowly digested them in Hell. This was quiet. Nearly two in the morning, and there was nothing but the cars on the road and random people stopping for snacks.

Just then, a car rumbled around the corner and slowed as it approached the coroner's building. Beautiful blue color with a shine as slick as liquid. The large trident at the front told him it was a Maserati. Jericho must've sent it. He was a billionaire, after all.

It drifted into the parking lot and stopped next to Jake with the passenger's door beside him. The tinted window slowly rolled down, and Jake saw a slim, fair-skinned female with a bright smile waving at him. It took a couple of seconds to register. Probably because he had not seen her with makeup on. Her pale-blue eyes and strawberry-blonde hair triggered his memory. It was Arina. A Russian woman he'd met in the altercation in the Bronx about a year ago.

"Hey!" He was a bit surprised to see her. She looked great in a thin leather jacket, red sweater, and tight jeans with heels. But he was confused. "Did Jericho send you?"

"Of course," she said with a Russian accent. "Think a beautiful girl is going to pull up in a fancy car because she thinks you're cute?"

"A man can dream," said Jake. "How do you know Jericho Black?"

She nodded as if she'd just remembered. "You missed all of that, didn't you?"

"Yeah, you tend to miss a lot when you are locked up."

He took a moment to circle around the car and check out its features. It was sharp. The license plate read POLE LIFE, so it wasn't Jericho's. There was a blue-and-white Maserati logo on the hood. Black wheels with yellow trim and yellow brake calipers with *Maserati* written in bold script. The yellow stitched trident on the headrest of the black leather seats gave it extra flair.

"Nice car," said Jake, circling back to the passenger's side.

"Do you know it?" said Arina. Her Russian accent was not as strong as he remembered it. "It is a Maserati Ghibli F Tributo Special Edition. It pays tribute to the first woman to compete in a Formula 1 race, the fearless Maria Terese de Filippis. There were only a hundred of these made. Very rare." She pushed a button to the click of the doors unlocking. "Hop inside. We have plenty to catch up on. Besides, you are letting all the heat out."

He lowered his head farther and spotted someone sitting behind Arina. Black leggings. Female. He opened the passenger's door, but before even attempting to sit, he found the button to move the seat all the way back to the stops. After scrunching down into the cool leather seat, there was still barely enough room for his knees. He turned around to introduce himself to the person in the back.

"Hi, Jake," said the woman. The face, with bangs coming down to the top of black-framed glasses, he recognized right away. It was the hacker who'd caught him snooping around Jericho Black's schedule, Cardigan Paige. She was wearing her Catholic high school uniform even though it was early Saturday morning. White blouse, blue pleated skirt, black leggings. She had the most radiant tanned skin, with sparkly pink nail polish on her fingers. A laptop lay on the seat next to her, closed. He would expect nothing less from a professional hacker.

"Awful late for you to be out, don't you think?" said Jake. "I guess you're seventeen now, right?"

Her face was flushed red, and she nodded emphatically. "Great to see you again, Jake."

"Oh jeez," said Arina. "Try not to pass out from excitement back there. She talks about you all the time. Jake this and Jake that!" Arina shook her head. "Babysitting duties. This one's mother asked me to keep an eye on her daughter while she's working at night. Cardigan can't keep off the dating sites. She goes crazy for older men."

"Dating sites?" asked Jake. "What do you need with dating sites?"

"She can pretend to be older there," said Arina, rolling her eyes.

"But I tell them how old I really am before I meet them," Cardigan interjected.

Jake felt very uncomfortable around a touchy subject. "Uh... let's get out of here."

Arina put the car in gear, spun out of the parking lot, and headed down the street. She turned hard at the next corner. The wheels hugged the road with a slight chirp. "Are you hungry? I know you are. You eat like a Tasmanian devil. There is a place in the city open all night. We can sit and talk there. My treat."

The Maserati roared through the streets of Newark as Arina dipped in and out of traffic like a woman possessed. She drove far too fast for Jake's liking. It reminded him of their escape from the Bronx under a hail of bullets. Back then, it was her first time driving. Now it seemed she'd adopted that experience as normal.

After navigating the Lincoln Tunnel, she turned left in Manhattan to head north on 10th Avenue. They rode through Hell's Kitchen and turned right on West 58th Street.

The Flame Diner was on West 58th and 9th Avenue. Blue fluorescent lettering with *Flame* in bright red. A brick restaurant on the corner with big windows by the dining area. They parked down one of the side streets and walked to the diner entrance. Three in the morning in Manhattan, and the place was half full. At the opposite end, Jake could see the staff working diligently in the kitchen. Glasses and plates clanked along with silverware as tables were cleaned and dishes were being prepared. Jake, Arina, and Cardigan were escorted to a booth along the wall. Jake sat on one end, while the two women slid into the opposite side. The menu placard was on the table, laminated. Jake began looking over the many options.

"Since I can't have any pussy…" said Sly. The fourth member of the group appeared to Jake only. Sly sat beside Jake still wearing the white mink coat and white fuzzy fedora. "You might as well feed me with good food," he continued. "All I've had was nasty hospital food, then prison rations. Order the good shit, brah." He rubbed his hands together in anticipation of the meal. "We get real bacon again. Thank God you did not turn to Islam while in prison. Plus, you managed not to get butt fucked, which would have been traumatizing for me. Imagine that big, ugly, smelly nigga with his hands wrapped around your hips pounding away. Yuck! I'm glad you kicked his nut sack into his stomach. Are you going to ignore me, nigga?"

Jake took a peek at his guests. Cardigan had one hand on the menu and another on her phone, taking turns glancing at each. Arina was focused solely on the menu. He couldn't respond to Sly there. He would look crazy if he did it out in public. Jake speaking with his thoughts would not work either. That asshole Sly wouldn't answer.

"Can I get you guys started with drinks?" asked the server. She swooped in quick, catching Jake off guard. A Middle Eastern woman a few years older than Cardigan. She smiled patiently. "If you are ready to order, I can take that now as well."

Arina plopped the laminated menu down on the table. "Eggs benedict and coffee," she said.

Cardigan mulled it over a few seconds, twisting her glossy lips. "The French toast and a Sprite."

Next up was Jake. Arina placed her elbows on the table and rested her chin in her palms as if eager to watch the show. "Three stacks of blueberry pancakes, four Western omelets, extra hash browns, extra sausage, and extra bacon with a tall glass of chocolate milk," said Jake.

Arina smiled, while Cardigan's jaw dropped slightly.

The server was busy writing. Blinking and furrowing her brow as the order kept growing.

"Is this to go?" she asked sheepishly.

"Nope," said Jake.

"He'll be able to finish it," said Arina. "Trust me." She giggled.

The server scurried off to place the order, heading into the busy kitchen.

He took a moment to watch Arina as she looked through the sugar packets in a small cup at the edge of the table. She certainly looked good. Much healthier emotionally and physically than when they'd first met. And how could he hold the first meeting against her? She was in Alexei's house for escorts serving her time as a stripper, wondering if her sister was OK after being taken away by his order. The healthy hue of her cheeks coming up to her almond-shaped eyes was that of a person who was living the dream. "Fill me in on what you have been doing for Jericho?" said Jake after she noticed him looking.

"I don't recall saying I worked for Jericho," she replied snootily.

Her delicate little neck cutely bobbed her head from side to side. "I work for myself."

"Really?" he said, distracted by the distinct smell of a well-sautéed steak and eggs delivered to the table behind him. His stomach rumbled. "How did you get that car?"

"Bought it. I am a spin pole instructor," she said proudly. "I have a studio in Manhattan. Also, I have sites on multiple platforms with millions of followers."

"Ahem," said Cardigan, never looking up from her phone.

Arina twisted her lip. "This one here helped set it up." She pointed a thumb at Cardigan. "She is the one who gets the followers, the thousands of views on my videos, and likes on all my stuff. Cardigan is my precious Lisichka."

"Why do you call me that?" asked Cardigan.

"It means 'little fox.' It's a pet name for people who do things like you do."

"Pole instructor?" Jake asked. "You mean the moves you learned while stripping?"

"Hey!" Her finger pointed straight at him. "I don't have to take my clothes off anymore," she snapped. Her eyelashes fluttered playfully. "Besides, I was an artist when working at those clubs. I didn't prance around trying to look cute, barely able to stand in six-inch platforms while begging for tips. I was like a graceful butterfly, fluttering in the breeze. My pole tricks were the very best."

"She is really good," said Cardigan. "Graceful and sexy. People love her."

A moaning sound echoed his consternation. "I just didn't know you could make a living off that stuff," said Jake. "All I'm saying."

"Misogynist pig," said Arina.

"I didn't know you knew such big words."

Cardigan raised both eyebrows high, knowing Jake had screwed up.

"Ladies scolding the assholes like you online taught me," she said, with a little neck wiggle. Arina placed an elbow on the table and rested her chin in her palm, as if to signal she'd made her point.

"Fine! How much money are we talking?" asked Jake.

"Six figures," said Cardigan, talking while working her thumbs on the smartphone. "Who knows, the year isn't up yet."

"Six figures for teaching people how to work a pole?" Jake squealed. "You've got to be kidding."

"Watch yourself, mister," Arina warned. "Pole is an art form. People see it as a means of expression. It's not just for strippers anymore."

"Son of a bitch!" said Jake. "I used to tell young kids that being an influencer is not a career!"

"Because you think like a grandpa," said Arina, showing her sassiness. "You are only pissed because you are broke."

"Ain't that the truth," said Jake.

The waitress came with the drinks. Sprite for Cardigan, coffee for Arina, and a tall glass of ice-cold chocolate milk for Jake. He guzzled it all in one gulp.

"Damn, that was good," said Sly. Then he got quiet. He stared at Cardigan, who was sitting innocently, playing with her phone. "Tell this girl to stop it, Jake!"

Jake didn't want to speak out loud. *Stop what?* he thought.

She sipped her Sprite through a straw, then focused her gaze on Jake. "I am so glad they let you out of prison."

"They didn't let him out, Lisichka," said Arina. "He escaped."

Her black-rimmed glasses slid down her nose ever so slightly as she appeared to gasp but stopped short. She pushed them back up with her index finger. "I see," said Cardigan.

"Lisichka," said Arina. "Give him his phone. Jericho said he will go apeshit when he gets it. I am curious as to what ape shit looks like."

## CHAPTER 39

Cardigan reached to the side of her skirt and slipped a hand beneath. Apparently, she was not wearing black leggings under her Catholic school skirt. They were thigh-high black stockings. The phone was tucked into the elastic portion at the thigh, the same way female spies hid their guns, garter belt style. She pulled her hand up and presented it to him across the table. He stared at the phone mysteriously before taking it. Surely, this couldn't be his personal phone.

"Jericho said he took it from you before you went into hiding to protect yourself," said Arina. "He's returning it."

"Tell her to cut it out!" said Sly, getting louder. His arms were crossed, and he had the most snide and disgusted look on his face.

"Aren't you going to check out your phone?" asked Cardigan.

"Oh…yes," he said, reaching over to take the phone from her hand. Jake clicked the button on the side, and his screen came to life. There was no passcode or fingerprint enabler active. He didn't know if it was the same phone or if Jericho had replaced it with a new one. It had been updated. But more importantly, it had his software program. The one that could track anyone at any time.

Then his heart began to race. One thing that would prove it was his phone was the pictures he had taken. In particular the ones of his girlfriend Catalina, the one killed by the Russian mobster Alexei. In prison, pictures were the only thing that kept most inmates sane. However, he'd been denied that. No one had called or written to him. Every person he knew thought Jake Coltrane was dead.

Jake found the images icon and pressed the screen. He saw Catalina and froze. Her bronze skin, flowing black hair, and beautiful smile, captured digitally, were even better than he remembered. He was getting emotional.

"I miss my sister too," said Arina. Her voice turned somber. "Unfortunately, there are very few pictures of her I can find. You are fortunate to have those as memories." She took a sip of coffee, blinking several times.

Jake continued to scroll through the images of Catalina until he came across a few unexpected pictures. He slowly looked up at Cardigan, who sat there like a rock, no expression whatsoever. There were pictures of her on his phone. Most were Cardigan in her schoolgirl uniform. Selfies. Duck mouth and all.

"Is everything OK?" asked Cardigan. Her face was completely neutral. No expression whatsoever.

"She's acting so damn nonchalant about it," screamed Sly. "We ain't trying to go back to prison messing with your young ass!"

Jake reached out to touch Sly on the arm to calm him down. But there was no arm to touch. Cardigan watched his motion, feeling around for the air.

"Are you OK?" she asked.

"Just fine." Jake clicked the button on the side, putting the phone to sleep. "Thanks for bringing me my phone," he said to Cardigan.

"That girl wants to jump your bones," said Sly. "But she don't know jack squat. I want the one over there."

Sly pointed his finger at a table in the middle of the restaurant.

Two women were sitting there. Looked like they had just come from a club. Party clothes. The woman Jake could see clearly had her hair tied in a bun. Dark-skinned, long eyelashes, pretty, thick, and tall.

"That's a butt clapper right there," said Sly. "And she is putting off those sexual healing vibes, brotha man. Time to ditch these two, nigga. I bet she's a swallower."

She looked over at Jake as she was putting a strawberry in her mouth. She froze while keeping her eyes fixed on him. Her soft lips pressed up against the fruit before she sucked it into her mouth.

"Wake up, little children," said Sly. "It's time for you to swim your way to your new home! Jake, get your ass up and walk over there right now."

Jake turned away and returned his attention to the women at his table. "Did Jericho give you anything else?" he asked Arina. "Money, perhaps?"

"Oh, fuck you, you bitch-ass nigga," said Sly. He jumped up on the table and threw a fit like a child, trying to kick the drinks off the table. His foot passed right through everything. Then he got on his back and kicked at the wall. "I want some pussy!" he screamed before calming down. He remained on the table, between Jake and the girls.

Arina passed her arm through Sly and handed Jake a credit card. Black like the one Jericho had given him previously.

"Bitch…ass…nigga!" Sly screamed while throwing a tantrum. He exhausted himself, then vanished as he hated trying to talk to Jake when Jake neglected him.

With one less distraction, Jake focused on his new credit card. "Thanks," he said to Arina. Jake flexed the card between his fingers and read the name. "Bert Ols-zew-ski…"

"It is pronounced *O'shevsky*," said Arina. "Like the Russian name Olshevsky. Except this is the Polish version. Cute, huh?" She wrinkled her nose.

"But it's spelled with a *z* and a *w*," said Cardigan, looking into both palms of her hand. "How do you get this *sh* and *vec* sound with that? You saw how Jake pronounced it."

"He better learn to say it right, or else people will know right away this is not really his name," said Arina with a chuckle.

"Or I could pronounce it any fucking way I want because that seems to be the thing now," Jake snapped. "Danielle is now Da-Neal. Blazay? No, it's Blaze. A-A Ron?" The girls began to chuckle. "Old-Jew-ski is how you pronounce my new last name. It comes from my ancestors. A bunch of old Jews who loved to ski. And my first name isn't Bert. It's Be-rot!"

Arina's chuckle was fast like a dolphin chattering. "Be-rot Old-Jew-ski!"

Their laughter was a much-needed lift to his somber spirits. Then the food came. As the first plate was placed on the table, Sly reappeared and rubbed his hands together in anticipation. Ten plates' worth. Eight for Jake. Two for the girls. Cardigan stopped several times in disbelief to watch Jake shovel enough food for a week into his body in one sitting. Drinks as well. He downed his fifth glass of chocolate milk before she cut into her last slice of French toast. Jake leaned back in the booth with eight empty plates in front of him.

He took in a deep breath and sighed. Sly, loving the intake of food energy, had Jake's endorphins on overdrive. It was a food high like none other. Sly the parasite showed his thanks after a year of shitty jail food by increasing Jake's dopamine receptor activation in the postsynaptic neuron, producing a state of euphoria. Jake felt the smile from ear to ear. He used a finger to touch his cheek. Even that felt good.

"So what's the plan, Jake?" asked Arina. "You're free. Have a new credit card and identity. What are you going to do now?"

"Ah...I wish I could tell you. But I can't," he said.

"Spit it out," said Arina.

He didn't know if he should say anything about his power around Cardigan. Arina had witnessed him coming back from the dead several times firsthand. Telling her his plan to escape hell would not be shocking. Cardigan, however, would think he was crazy. Then there was the other thing. What Duval wanted him to do.

"I need to find out what happened to a friend's wife and child," said Jake. "They've gone missing."

"What friend?"

"Duval."

"Wait," said Cardigan. "The police officer whose wife and child have been missing for weeks? And then his ex-partner gets killed looking for her? No way! This is a famous case."

"Let's do it," said Arina. There was no hesitation in her response. Determination was etched in every wrinkle of her cute little nose.

Jake was more than a little apprehensive. The situation demanded he investigate their disappearance alone. He started talking fast. He needed to tamp down this enthusiasm. "You have your new life now, Arina," he said. "You have a great future and a nice car. Jericho… he's got you legal and everything. He's taking care of you. The both of you. You don't want to mess that up. End up in jail like I did. And you, young lady…you've been in trouble with the feds before. And your mom has Arina watching you? You don't need this kind of trouble. Nope. Uh-uh. This is dangerous. Dangerous stuff."

Arina blinked twice. "Are you out of your fucking mind, Jake?" she said. "This sounds like exactly what you did for me. When you came in and rescued me and helped me find my sister. I owe you, not Jericho." She then said some Russian curse words. Didn't matter that Jake couldn't understand them. In any language, you know when you are being cursed out when you hear it.

"*Mudak!*" screamed Arina.

Jake coiled his head back. "Mudak…I know that one. Definitely a curse word."

Arina pounded her fist on the table once to get his attention. Then spoke slowly. Her strong Russian accent had returned, like the first time he met her. "I am doing this, Jake Coltrane." She paused, glaring at him. Fingers sprawled out flat on the table. "I remember sitting in that apartment with the escorts and strippers crying for three hours straight, wondering what happened to my sister. She was taken from me and given to this monster in the apartment upstairs." She addressed the last part to Cardigan, probably because she had not heard the story before. "I wanted to kill myself, but I was afraid to do it because my sister would suffer even more if I did. Then you came." She returned her focus to Jake, with a sense of conviction. "Most people pray for someone to save them, but help rarely comes. You came, and you conquered. I wish to do this for someone else."

Jake felt a pang of guilt. He had actually been there to avenge the death of his girlfriend, but a bastard like Alexei Voznesensky left multiple bodies in his wake. Hell's apostles thanked Jake for the precious offering of a vile soul when he delivered Alexei to Hell. It was the only trip into Hell in which he had not been tortured. When he thought about it, arriving in Hell with Scotty Rock hadn't been too bad either. No Tartarus torture sessions.

How could he not take her seriously? She may have looked like a lightweight, with her slim figure, but Jake knew deep down she was a tough one. But then there was Cardigan, still engulfed in whatever was happening on her phone. Jake sent a nod in Cardigan's direction.

"Worried about her?" Arina asked. "You know what she does. She's a hacker working for Jericho Black, handling all of his cyber dirty work. No, she's not innocent. She just dresses like an innocent schoolgirl. Sort of."

"I can't be responsible for her," said Jake. "She's a minor. We take her home and come daylight, we…"

"I don't think so," said Cardigan, lowering her phone, boring a hole through Jake with her gaze. "Lisichka comes with. It's the weekend, and Mom will have me locked in the apartment making me help her put shelving in her closet. This sounds much more exciting. We both come as a package, Jake."

"Then the answer is no," said Jake. He felt every fiber of his being rejecting this. "Have a spa day, ladies. My treat. I will see you when I get back. The guy I'm hunting might be the one responsible for those suicides with the pictures."

Her entire face lit up. "The Polaroid Suicides?" asked Cardigan. "Oh, I'm definitely going now!"

"Jake, you expect us to get our fucking nails done while you find missing people and solve the Polaroid Suicides?" asked Arina. "No way. Besides, you need a driver." She tossed over two hundred dollars onto the table and ushered Cardigan out of the booth.

Cardigan slid out, followed by Arina, and they both stood over Jake, who refused to move.

"I don't care, Cardigan," said Jake. "You're not going."

Cardigan knelt beside him and placed a hand on his knee. "You want to try me? Fine. I will take an Uber to New Jersey, hide out in a hotel room, and issue my own Amber Alert. I will name names, Old-Jew-ski, and describe your accomplice in that pretty little blue Maserati." She looked to Arina to show she was serious. "Only a hundred of them were made, so it won't be too difficult to spot. An escaped convict and an immigrant kidnapper taking an innocent little White girl from private school. You'll be all over the news—again."

Arina nodded. "I told you she wasn't innocent," she said. "Good work, Lisichka. Jake, let's get going."

## CHAPTER 40

When Jake, Arina, and Cardigan left the diner, it was just before five in the morning. Arina was out in front, followed by Cardigan, with Jake and Sly in the rear. The days were slowly getting longer. The sun was not out yet, but the dark-blue sky was a shade lighter than it was hours ago. He could faintly see the sky behind the backdrop of skyscrapers in downtown Manhattan. It was picturesque.

Arina was strutting out front in her leather jacket, skintight jeans, and red suede boots. Graceful, especially while walking. He could see where her followers came from. Women would kill to learn to walk like that, in or out of heels. Cardigan was behind her, head buried in her phone, wearing her schoolgirl outfit with no jacket, seemingly immune to the cold. They rounded the corner and headed down the street to where they'd parked the car.

The blue Maserati sat among a stream of bland cars and stood out as if a spotlight were on it. Arina was swaggering confidently up front while Jake was visibly nervous. These two women were younger than he was. Arina by about five years, and Cardigan was half his age. They had their whole lives ahead of them. It would torture him if any harm came their way. Somewhere down the line, he had to ditch them, especially when Sly sensed danger. It was another of his otherworldly traits. Sly could sense the intentions of those around him. He could also sense how strong they were. He said it was a trait lost to humans during evolution. Arrogance at the development of the human mind deemed those skills unnecessary, so they vanished.

Sly took the theory of evolution one step further. He said humans became far more vicious than any other creature on the planet, so they didn't need to sense the strength of others. The human mind had developed a *do unto others before they do it to you* means of survival. An example of Sly's theory was realized when Jake watched a nature show with tigers about to fight over territory. Both of them roaring and sizing each other up, yet the fight never even got started. The older tiger simply conceded and vacated her territory. It was an example of the strength Sly spoke about. The older tiger sensed the strength of the younger and knew a fight would be fruitless.

However, man in his viciousness developed a trait known as revenge, which led to creating all sorts of things in order to even the odds. Weapons, poison, sabotage…who needs warnings of danger when deception and malice are humanity's greatest weapons?

"Must be nice being a ballplayer," said a voice from the shadows. "Get all the money and all the girls."

A man was sitting on the stairs out front of his brownstone, smoking weed. It was strong. The Maserati was on the other side of the street from where he was sitting. He must have been eyeing it for some time, wondering who owned the car.

Arina stopped by the trunk of the car and waited for Jake to catch up.

"Ballplayer?" asked Arina.

"Yeah, I get that all the time. Being a six-foot-seven Black man, I must play basketball. Especially if I am getting into a nice car like this. Typical stereotype stuff. It annoys the hell out of me."

"I think it annoys you because you can't play basketball," said Arina.

"No!" said Jake. "It annoys me because not all Black people like basketball. But that's the stigma. You see a Jew and think he is a lawyer or a doctor. An Asian student is assumed to be great at math. The first thought about Black people is they are from the hood and might rob you. Except if he has money; then he has to be an athlete. I'm so sick of it."

"I see," she said. Arina peered over Jake's shoulder. "That is a Black man on the stairs who said it to you."

"Yeah, so?" said Jake.

Cardigan stood nearby without giving the exchange a second thought.

"You know what perplexes me?" said Sly. He appeared standing next to Jake in his typical pimp attire, working a toothpick between his teeth. Jake was mindful not to respond or acknowledge him this time.

"Nobody," said Sly. "No rich motherfucker, no playboy, nobody gets more pussy than a professional basketball player. Football, baseball, hockey…they can't compare to the pussy these motherfuckers get. It's something about being tall and balling that gets bitches crazy wet. They come out of the woodwork for these motherfuckers. Exotic bitches. Bitches with all kinds of eye color and skin tone combinations like you would never imagine. You see this NBA player in the magazine, and I know you saw them, Jake. These fine bitches make a nigga say, 'Damn, did they make that bitch in a lab or something? Where the fuck did you find her?' But your dumb ass wants nothing to do with it. You can't even pretend to be a ballplayer to get some pussy because"—Sly mockingly put up air quotations—"it's insulting!"

Arina popped the trunk, and they all huddled around it. "Look, I have something for you," she said to Jake. There was a black leather jacket inside. A long one. "I kept this as a souvenir. Something to remind me of you. I had it cleaned and the bullet holes repaired."

"Bullet holes?" said Cardigan. "You were hit?"

"Don't worry about it," said Jake, shrugging it off. "Arina... thank you."

Jake held it by the shoulders and lifted it out of the car. The black leather made him nostalgic. It belonged to his father. There were several possessions his father had put into his will before taking his life. Things he wanted Jake and his sister to have when they came of age. This was kept in storage and paid for by his dad's friend Chuck. As Jake learned from his time in Hell, Chuck's role in his father's life was a little more complicated. They were more than just friends.

Despite that, Jake cherished the jacket. His father was tall like Jake and actually used to play basketball professionally. It was a short stint and he was only a bench player, but he was good enough to make it.

Jake folded the jacket under his arm proudly.

Underneath his jacket, on the floor of the trunk, was another item belonging to him.

"Jesus!" said Cardigan. "Look at the size of that thing!"

The BFR. Magnum Research's ten-inch barrel juggernaut of a handgun, the biggest and most powerful ever made. It shot .45-70 rifle rounds developed for the Springfield Model 1873. Silver with black rubber grips inside his shoulder holster.

"I kept both of these on a mantle," said Arina.

"Mantle?" said Cardigan. "It was in a closet all to itself. Like a fucking shrine. Creepy."

"It was my special place," Arina growled. "The jacket and gun. My plan was when I died, these two things would be buried with me. I planned to tell stories to my grandchildren of the black demon who showed no mercy to my enemies and carried me to freedom. A great story, yes?"

Jake reached down and touched the black rubber grip. It spawned memories of the first time he had to use it. He also got a little choked up hearing what it meant to her. He absolutely could not put her in harm's way now. How could he deny her telling her story to her future grandchildren?

"Thanks," said Jake. "But having a gun in New York City could get you years in jail. You shouldn't have taken the chance to bring it."

"The criminals all have them," said Arina. "That's why I got my own." She reached behind her, under her jean jacket to the small of her back, and pulled out a small pistol. Silver automatic. Looked like a .380 caliber.

"Nice piece!" said the man from his stairs.

"What the hell are you doing?" said Jake, appalled she was waving it around proudly.

"Don't worry. Jericho got me a license to tote this puppy around. He looks out for me."

"How did he do that?" said Jake. "Only off-duty cops have a license to carry around in the city."

"I don't know." She shrugged. "It's Jericho Black. He can do anything. Look at all he has done for you."

"Well, put that thing away. Let's get the hell out of here."

They got inside the car. Jake in the passenger's seat, Cardigan in the back. They typed the GPS coordinates into the navigation system, and they were off. A half hour later, the sun was beginning to peek over the horizon. The light-blue sky with traces of orange was a sight he had no idea he had missed. Sunrise. There was music playing on the radio. There were no clanking or whirring sounds of armored gates and steel doors. No cacophony of screaming inmates, no rancid smells. Only sweet sounds and sweeter fragrances in the company of two women who thought highly of him. He'd never felt so alive. He drifted off to sleep despite knowing he might have to kill someone on this day, before sunset.

# CHAPTER 41

Jake cracked one eye open, then the other. Arina was focused on driving, almost straining to concentrate. He felt bad for being selfish. How long had she been awake? Landmarks alongside the highway sped by. Cardigan was typing away on her laptop. Her well-tanned skin soaked up the sunlight as her nose was buried in the monitor. Sly was in the back seat next to Cardigan. This time wearing a fuzzy white fedora, a white mink jacket, no shirt, gold chains around his neck, white pants, white shoes, and designer sunglasses. He said nothing. No snide remarks. No comments about having sex or how stupid Jake was. He was quiet. Reserved. It wasn't like him. If he showed himself to Jake, it was typically because he had something to say. He didn't appear only to be seen. Something was bothering him, making him uneasy. It was like he was keeping watch over things. Guarding them.

They passed the town of Bridgeport, Connecticut. The colorful navigation system noted they were approximately half an hour from Yale University, putting them there ten minutes before seven in the morning on Saturday. He expected students to be out and about enjoying their first of two days off after a long week. The mood should be light and relaxed. He expected coffee shops to be full and plenty of lounging around the campus. Causing a stir at this hour would be inappropriate. Besides, he had no plan.

"I need a shower," said Jake. "I got off the slab at the morgue and never got a chance to freshen up. Find a hotel around here. My treat." He patted his pants pocket with the black card. This would give him time to come up with something, and also time to ditch his little entourage.

Arina pushed the touchscreen and asked Siri to find hotels nearby. A list popped up.

"What did you mean by 'getting off the slab at the morgue'?" asked Cardigan.

Arina and Jake exchanged glances. "Just like he said," Arina answered with a devilish grin.

Cardigan pointed to a choice on the menu. "Delamar Hotel in Southport. Go to that one."

Arina selected it with a touch. A trace outlining the route turned blue. "Back in the other direction," said Arina.

"We're not in a rush, are we?" said Jake. "It's the butt-crack-of-dawn early. And you two haven't had any rest. After a good nap, we will be ready and fresh to tackle the mission at hand."

"I've already booked a couple of rooms," said Cardigan. "We're set."

"When did you do that?" asked Jake.

Arina sighed as if he should not have asked. "This is what she does, Jake. Just roll with it."

Jake turned around to see her buried in her computer once more. Her eyes reading what was on the screen. The soft glow of the monitor reflecting off her tanned skin. Sly was sitting next to her, all pimped out but not saying a word. Oh well. He shrugged it off and leaned back in his seat, trying to relax his body and his mind.

"You wanted to say something," said Sly.

Jake's eyes sprang open. It seemed resting would come later. "What makes you say that?" asked Jake.

"Say what?" said Cardigan, typing away on her laptop.

"Sorry, I wasn't talking to you," said Jake.

"Then who were you talking to?" asked Cardigan, shifting her attention upward from the monitor. "Were you talking to Arina?"

"No. Not her either." He turned to look at the scenery speeding by on the highway. "Don't worry about it."

"He is talking to his demon," said Arina, changing lanes in preparation for the exit. "He does that a lot. He has conversations with him. Asks the demon for help. That sort of thing."

"Not a demon," said Sly. "And don't call me a fucking parasite, Jake."

"He's a fucking parasite," said Jake. "Floating through my body disrupting my peace. However, he is quite useful."

"Useful? Nigga, you wouldn't be here if it weren't for me." Sly crossed his arms, then reached forward and plucked Jake on the back of the head—Jake held back an "Ow." Then Sly looked out the window as if pondering something. "I get the feeling he knows we are coming."

"I think you are wrong," said Jake. "He has the eye, but I got the drop on him before. My guess is the eye didn't work on me. Remember when I confronted him? He asked, 'Why can't I see you?' I always thought it was an odd thing to say. After thinking about it, the only thing that makes sense is the eye doesn't work on everyone."

"I'm not convinced he had the eye when you approached him in the synagogue," said Sly.

Jake rubbed his temple. "Are you shitting me?"

"I wish I were," Sly continued. "The power I sensed from him was different. Still dangerous and calculating, but about half of what it was at the mall. I believe he was evolving, which means that little handicap of not seeing you may have been overcome by now."

"Is everything OK?" asked Cardigan.

Jake tried to play it cool. He turned back around to face the windshield. "Everything is fine."

He didn't want to worry them. The only reason he felt empowered to go after Adonis was he believed Adonis would not see him coming. There were so many other things he wanted to ask Sly, but in a crowded car, he struggled for the right words. "Why can't you talk to me inside my head?" Jake screamed.

"Must be frustrating living with a demon…I mean, parasite," said Cardigan. "You looked back here like he was in the car."

"He's right there in the back seat," said Jake.

She looked over at the empty seat. "What does he look like?"

"Like Katt Williams," said Jake. "The comedian."

She twisted her bottom lip in thought. "Never heard of him. Is he as funny as Kevin Hart?"

"My Black ass!" screamed Sly, becoming unglued. "Ever heard of that? Beeatch!"

She went back to her phone, using her thumbs at an accelerated speed, then stopped suddenly. "I'm curious why he would he appear to you as someone else?" asked Cardigan. Her glasses were sitting at an off angle, in a cute and innocent kind of way. "And why don't you talk to him in your mind?"

"There!" said Jake, startling everyone in the car. "Same fucking thing I've been saying. Talk to me in my mind, Sly. Well, let me tell you his reason for not doing it that way, Cardigan. He thinks if he speaks to me in my mind, I won't be able to distinguish my thoughts from his. But I really think he is trying to be cool or something. He dresses like a pimp and then talks shit about my style. Has me rambling on now just thinking about it. The bottom line is he'd rather have everyone else think I am crazy for talking to myself."

"Are you done monologuing, you capri-wearing bitch?" said Sly. "Let meeee give her the proper explanation, and don't add any words to what I fucking have to say. Got it?"

Jake turned to Cardigan with a deep breath, trying to calm himself. "He wants me to repeat his words to you," said a composed Jake.

For some strange reason, she glanced over at the empty seat as if she could see Sly, raising an eyebrow quizzically. Eerily, Sly slid closer as if he could speak to her directly. "When I first tried to contact Jake in the hotel room after I was introduced to his body, he would not answer."

"What do you mean I wouldn't answer?" said Jake.

"Was that his explanation?" asked Cardigan, scrunching her nose. "I don't get it."

"No, wait, hold on a minute. Let me talk to Sly for a sec. When was the first time you spoke to me?"

"In the hotel room. Then in the elevator. Then when we got outside, and I started getting hungry."

"Nope. I don't remember. What did you say?" asked Jake.

"I was telling you, 'Those hot dogs at the stand smell good, but we need a whole lot more to eat; let's find some real food because a snack isn't going to cut it.'"

Jake scratched the skin on his head. "No…I remember wanting the hot dogs but changing my mind."

"You do realize you are proving my point, jackass," said Sly.

"You wanted to eat the hot dogs?" asked Cardigan. "It's getting difficult for me to follow along."

"Explain it to the girl, you dumbass!" said Sly.

Jake turned back around to face the road. Defeated. Dejected. Confused and beaten, all at the same time. He thought those were his thoughts. Could he even think for himself anymore? It was as if his mind were collapsing.

"So the gist is he tried the direct route first," said Cardigan. "I get it now. He has to appear as someone else so you don't get confused. If you physically see someone talking as the words come to you, then you know it's him."

Jake put a thumb in the air. He no longer felt like talking.

"Thank you, sweetheart," said Sly. "Maybe later I can be put into someone smarter who can tell the difference." Sly paused for dramatic effect. "After you figure out how to save your soul from going to Hell."

Jake's heart began racing. He tried to calm himself, but he couldn't. "So I really don't have any thoughts of my own anymore," he said to no one in particular. "None I can hide."

"I can't read thoughts," said Sly. "I just know you. I know that's what you were thinking. Once you figure out how to save yourself from Hell, then you want to go to Jericho and have him remove me from your body. Since deep down you believe the main reason you go to Hell is because he put me inside you to begin with. I get it, motherfucker. Trust me. Your dream was to raise a family with Catalina. Now she is dead and you know there is an afterlife, you figure, What's the fucking point? Well, let me tell you, I have no desire to be anywhere I am not wanted. If you want me gone, then I want out too. Maybe I can be inserted into one of these two. I ain't going back to no fucking Petri dish, that's for sure. You find me a willing host, and we can part ways. After you ensure you're going to Heaven. Deal?"

Jake rested his head on the window beside him. He knew it was a fucked-up way to think about it, especially after all Sly had done for him. But it was true. That was how he felt. He didn't care to live for three hundred or more years. He wanted a woman to love and to raise a family. Now he knew what life was truly about, dying young didn't seem as terrifying as he'd first thought. His aim now was to avoid an eternity in Hell. And yes, deep down he blamed Sly.

# CHAPTER 42

The Delamar Hotel was high-end. It had a sort of old-world New England luxury feel to it. It was classy and sophisticated, which surprised him a bit. After coming from a prison cell, this was what he needed. The décor possessed the perfect balance of embellishment and modern opulence, yet it was pleasantly refined. This was his style.

Cardigan had reserved the Pequot Suite for herself and Arina. She opened the door to a ten-chair dining table, hardwood floors, and over two thousand square feet of space. It featured a full gourmet kitchen and a Waterworks air tub with a separate shower.

"I would invite you to stay, but the third bedroom only has a pull-out sofa," said Cardigan. "You're much better than that."

"Kind of snide coming from a seventeen-year-old," said Jake. "Don't forget who is paying for this."

"It wasn't paid for with the black card or Jericho's other funds," she said. "This is my money. Crypto." She smiled proudly and handed him a key card. "Perks of being a first-rate hacker. Your suite is across the hall."

He took the key card but decided to go check out how Arina was doing. Her room was on the opposite end of the suite. He went past the dining area and through the open door, where he heard rustling. Arina was going through some of the drawers, checking inside them. Her room was as big as Cardigan's, except it had two queen beds. The bathroom was as luxurious, minus the jet tub. He could tell Arina was tired as she strolled past. Her typical strut with red heels lacked the usual snap about the hips.

"You look tired," he said.

"It's been a whole day now since I slept."

"I thought it was something like that."

There was nothing left to say. It felt uncomfortable. Time for him to leave. When he walked past her, she looked as if she wanted to say something but decided not to. Her long eyelashes dropped down. Her cheeks slightly flushed. "I wish you a great few hours of rest," she said. Her Russian accent changed depending on her mood; this time it was soft and cute.

"Thank you," he said.

Jake waved bye with a single drop of his fingers and made his way out of their suite. He went down the red-carpeted hallway to his own suite. It didn't disappoint. It was half the size of the others but had a living and dining room area. The single bedroom had a king-size bed. The bathroom had a shower and a claw-foot tub off to the side. Not a full kitchen but a kitchenette. Overall, there was nothing to complain about. His first room outside of prison was magnificent.

His primary focus was taking a shower. A nice, private shower without having to watch his back, his front, and both sides. He stripped down as he walked, leaving a trail of clothes until he reached the bathroom. He stepped inside the shower before turning on the water. With the knob all the way to the left, Jake was hit with a burst of ice-cold water straight to his chest. He'd gotten used to cold showers in prison. He didn't so much as flinch. Slowly, the water got hotter and hotter until it was scalding. Once again not bothering him much. He used to hate hot showers, but after his many trips to Hell, he'd become more tolerant of heat. He let it blast away at the short hairs on the back of his neck.

He stretched his fingers to the far wall and pushed the little squirt bottle dispenser with shampoo or soap. With all the steam, he couldn't read it and didn't care. It made lather. He hit his entire body with it. Rubbed it all over once, then twice. He shut the water down and walked out of the bathroom without drying, letting the water droplets on his skin cool his body with time. Oh, how he needed that. He plopped his wet ass on the couch and turned on the television. Some news broadcast was playing. He tried to change the channel, but the remote didn't seem to work. He fumbled with it a bit, then gave up. Crummy news was what it would have to be.

Then Sly came into view. He was sitting on the chair adjacent to Jake. He, too, looked like he had taken a shower. Except he was dressed in a fluffy white robe with a towel over his permed hair, wrapped up the way women do. He was holding a small mirror while using his finger to brush his thin mustache straight. Then he tossed the mirror and rested his head on the back of the chair, with his arms collapsed on the side.

"So you know I blame you for me going to Hell," said Jake.

"Wasn't hard to figure out," said Sly. His eyes were closed, and it looked like he was relaxing at a spa. "It's an ugly assumption, and I prefer not to talk about it."

It felt weird. He wanted to explain himself. Tell Sly he didn't think Sly was a bad person…parasite…whatever. But this was the only thing that made sense because *he* wasn't a bad person. Jake was suffering the trials of Hell for reasons that did not make sense. Therefore, he had to blame Sly. There was no other answer. But it would make things between them more difficult than they already were. His mind was swirling. Like it didn't want to calm down. Yet, how much of Jake's thoughts could Sly read, anyway? Perhaps he should change the subject. Get his mind focused on something else. Talk about the other things swirling around in those thoughts of his. Perhaps pry into Sly's own personal thoughts. Maybe that would ease the tension between the two of them.

An uncomfortable silence stretched between them. Jake wanted to say something. Deflect the tension. "Why haven't you made any sexual remarks about Arina?" he said.

Why did he start with that? Perhaps it was because Jake had felt the sexual tension between them when they were alone in her room. Silent vibrations in the air. Jake fully expected Sly to interrupt with banter about him finally getting some, yet he remained silent. "Is Arina not your type?" asked Jake.

"Of course she is my type," said Sly. "She is my type because she is a woman and you are a heterosexual. The feelings of attraction come from you. I want to siphon those experiences from you. Firsthand, not in dreams or you jerking off. It's one of my only requests of you. Keep pissing me off with no sex, and I am going to retaliate eventually. One of my other conditions before I leave your body." Sly turned to Jake to let him know he was serious. "You will do this for me!"

Jake showed his palms in a calming motion to say he would, eventually.

"I won't press you on Arina," said Sly.

"Why?"

"Because she has feelings for you, Jake. They both do. For different reasons. I prefer Dr. Carrie Blake or some stranger who isn't emotionally attached."

Strange coming from an insensitive parasite like Sly, who was coarse, brash, self-centered, and a prick in general. This sounded more like a human. Like someone who cared.

"The young one continues to send out these deep sexual impulses," said Sly. "Instead of jumping at the opportunity, I told you to tell her to cut it out."

*Yes*, he thought. In the restaurant. He was wondering why Sly had a problem with her.

"She believes you share a connection through coding and you two are perfect for each other. I think it is because she sees you as being on her level of skill. That excites her…along with your age, I'm afraid."

Suddenly, sliced cucumbers appeared on Sly's eyes. He held his hand out, palm side down, when a tiny Asian woman appeared in white. She began working over the cuticles on his left hand.

Sly continued, "Arina, on the other hand, loves you because you saved her and avenged her sister's death. But she is also deeply scarred. Her time as a sex worker changed her. Distorted her ability to love properly. Her sister fell in love, and it cost her sister her life. Deep down, she still remembers. What would falling in love with you be like? She might be in love with the danger of it all. The adrenaline rush of being around you. I can't tell."

Sly elevated his feet, and another woman appeared there, massaging the soles.

"But most importantly, I know you, Jake. If you hurt one of them, you will be the one to suffer. You are not some playboy who doesn't give a shit about the women he screws. Remember, I am tuned into your feelings, not just for sex but everything else. When you worry, I worry. When you feel pain, I feel pain. Not just physically but emotionally. The physical pain can be turned off. The signals disrupted and rewired. The emotional pain cannot be so easily dealt with."

"Damn," said Jake. "Every so often, you surprise me. You actually have a heart."

"Not a heart. It's all about survival." The woman disappeared, along with the cucumbers, and Sly raised his head off the back of the couch. "I personally don't give a fuck about them or you. I want my time inside of you to be pleasurable, and I can't enjoy myself with you stressing over everything."

Jake was pissed. He almost exploded up out of the chair. "You're a piece of shit…Do you know that?"

"You are delusional, Jake. Don't think your reason to do anything is better than mine. Deep down, we are all selfish. That is what survival is about. It's programmed into life, Jake. You can call it noble or moral if you want. You're only fooling yourself. Each and every part of life is wired for one thing only: the best way to survive."

"You know, Sly, I couldn't disagree more. You're talking about not caring for someone because you might get hurt. Worthless way to live."

"It's exactly what you did, avoiding Catalina when your tumor had reached the critical stage."

Jake fought for a response, but he could say little. It was exactly what he had done. He didn't want Catalina to carry around the burden of his death. Now he knew that was a mistake. "Two people expressing their passion for each other is worth risking the pain," said Jake. "I may have not known in the past, but I see the light now. I shouldn't have been the one who decided how much a person can handle."

"How much can you handle?" said Sly. "You're like a pussy-whipped bitch whenever you have sex with someone you like. Do you really want to fall in love again? You can come back to life. She can't. Can you live with that? You can't fool me, Jake. You haven't even thought about sex after Catalina's death."

"Screw you, Sly."

Jake grabbed the remote and put the television on mute. The added noise was annoying him more than Sly was. Political jibber-jabber with talk, talk, and more talk. Discussing how fucked-up their opponents were while overlooking their own missteps. Opposing legislation, no matter how good it was, just because their opponent proposed it. It was as if the state of the world wanted to join in on his problems. The state of the fucked-up world piling onto his fucked-up situation.

"Stop dillydallying," said Sly. "You need to get on the phone, activate your program, and go after Adonis right now."

Jake sneered. "Don't order me around. I'm tired of you. Time for you to disappear."

"Put your fucking clothes on and let's go. The girls should be sound asleep by now. It'll give you a few hours head start before they find you. Hopefully, the deal will be done by then. You get Adonis, take the eye, dispose of him however you need to, and then return to them. You can fuck them both and be a happy little threesome afterward."

"Fuck you, Sly."

He was furious, but it motivated him more than anything. The quicker he finished the job, the faster he could be rid of Sly. Jake sprang to his feet, huffing and snarling as he tracked down his pants on the floor. He took his phone out of the pocket and performed a search for Adonis Silver, using a variety of social media platforms.

Thank God for teenage hormones. It made his job easy. He was able to locate a number of photos of Adonis Silver. Whether he knew it or not, girls were taking pictures of Adonis in the background and tagging him in them. Jake used one of the more recent photos, one with his face clearly visible, and loaded it into his search program. Within seconds, he had a hit. Adonis was spotted at a bus stop around campus. The blue line at Prospect Street. He had a hot beverage in hand. About fifteen minutes ago.

The beauty of the program he'd created was its ability to adapt and anticipate. It automatically jumped to the camera on the bus and tagged him as one of the passengers seated near the middle, left side, visible to oncoming traffic. Now it was operating in real time. Jake locked the program for tracking, which anticipated the projected stops due to the schedule and subsequent arrival times. If there were any cameras at the various bus stops along that route, they would start to record him and provide updates for any possible destinations.

With that taken care of, Jake decided to get dressed. He went back to the bathroom, finished toweling off, then put on his clothes.

"Let's go," said Sly, appearing before him fully dressed, in bright-green pants, a black turtleneck, and a black flat cap leaning to the side.

Jake was slipping on his shoes, taking umbrage with anything Sly had to say, until he remembered something. "I don't have my gun. It's in the car."

"Skip it. It will just slow us down anyway. You are going to have to get dirty with this one, Jake. Up close and personal."

"Are you saying that because you want to punish me and see me get roughed up a bit?"

"Hell na, mafucker! I don't want to hear your bitch ass crying about how he kicked your ass down the street. I'm saying it because you will be able to do it."

Jake scoffed in frustration. "You said in the car you believe he is ready for me."

"Yeah, I know what I said. Calm the fuck down. I got mixed up for a second with all your anxiety screwing with my signals and shit, OK! It's like this. I believe your program is what fucks up the eye."

He had a hard time trying to grasp the meaning. "Elaborate."

"Your program looks at all kinds of images—thousands of them, giving you multiple angles. It accesses so much information that when you look at all the images, it makes it appear as if you are looking through someone else's eyes. It must confuse the eye of Tartarus somehow."

"That's what you are going with?"

"Do you have a better explanation, asshole?" Sly snapped. "Sneak up on him, and I'll wait to sense his intentions. If the typical Adonis danger signals go off, we pause and regroup. If not, we smash his head in before he knows what hit him."

Sly disappeared, and Jake mumbled under his breath, going for the door. He pushed down on the handle, slipped out, making sure it didn't slam shut, then made his way down the hallway to the staircase. The red-carpeted stairs were quiet. The arch of his shoes balanced on each stair nose as he traversed. When he reached the bottom, his phone vibrated with an update.

Adonis was entering an office building. A doctor's office.

# CHAPTER 43

The cool breeze and saltwater smell of the air in Cape Cod was something new for Jake. He walked around the parked cars to the edge of the sea wall and saw a lighthouse off in the distance. Waves gently crashed against the rocks beneath it. Seagulls squawked above. He was a city boy and rarely got the urge to venture out from electric lights and concrete. This felt nice. Peaceful.

His thoughts returned to Adonis, and the stitch of fear in his gut returned as well. For his plan to work, Jake had to catch Adonis completely off guard. That would mean letting Adonis come to him. Many things could go wrong with the plan. Success relied upon minimizing those options. Like a funnel guiding grains of sand into a bottle, he needed Adonis to fall in under his own volition.

Jake went to the pin of Adonis's location and typed in possible exit points. He selected a route back to the bus terminal. Just like GPS apps, his program mapped out several possible routes on foot. One of the routes was back through the same path Adonis had taken to get here. The next route it provided was a little shorter. It took Adonis through a nearby park. It was an interesting choice, so Jake clicked on it, selected street view, and went 3D so he would be seemingly walking through the route.

He pressed the arrows down the path, taking a good look at the scenery. He could see the path provided few areas of cover. Plenty of people present that day. It was a poor choice, and there was no guarantee Adonis would take that way back. Both routes were poor choices.

Point blank: his best chance was inside the building.

There were many cameras inside. According to Sly, this would help further confuse the eye of Tartarus. Through his program, he was able to access the cameras to get an idea of the layout. The third floor, the location of the doctor's office, had three other offices. The renovation signs he saw outside the building pertained to two of those offices on the third floor. The one other business, an insurance company, was closed on Saturdays.

Jake took a break from his phone to survey his surroundings near the pier. He saw fishermen and sailboats out on the ocean. The water sparkled with the tide. There was a park bench nearby. He decided to sit down facing the ocean and watch for a while. This was the part of life worth preserving. Parts he didn't get to see while being locked up. He had a better appreciation of it now. He wanted his journey to be one of peace and enjoy moments like this. But that would have to wait until after this job. When he'd solved the mystery of why he was sentenced to hell and fixed it. Then he could relax, knowing his next life would be just as peaceful.

Jake worked his magic on the phone once again. He viewed footage from two other cameras on that floor to make sure the layout was correct. There were no physical guards. The renovation of the office space had resulted in only an opaque sheet of plastic over the door. It was located between the doctor's office and the elevator. It was perfect.

Getting up from the bench, Jake breathed in the saltwater air before heading to the bus stop. It was on schedule. He rode it into New Haven, where he transferred to the blue line. Then he walked a bit. Maybe a mile or so to catch the bus to get to where Adonis was located. The pin location stayed put, which meant he was still inside the doctor's office.

The office building was made of brick and mortar, standalone with windows going up three floors. Suites separated the businesses. Jake stood outside and counted the cameras he could see. There were enough to confuse the eye, if that was indeed how it worked. Plus, he had time to set up his attack. Adonis was still in the waiting room. Jake took the stairs in case Adonis decided to leave early. He got to the top and checked the phone. Adonis hadn't moved. He swung the door open wide to check the floor.

"I feel that motherfucker." Sly appeared for the first time since leaving the hotel. "He's here for sure. Same creepy feeling. Like shit can pop off at any time."

To his right was the doctor's office. The door was solid, so no one could see him outside of it. But he could hear people. Jake looked over to his left all the way down to the end, where the hallway turned left toward the elevators. The office suites had some space between them. Blue-and-tan striped wallpaper lined the hallways a good thirty feet or more from office door to door. At the very corner, before the hallway turned left, was the office under construction.

Jake walked on the shiny, dark-brown tiles all the way to that office. The plastic was open at the bottom. He used a hand to raise it slightly to get a peek inside. The floors were torn down to the concrete. Metal studs had been erected, sectioning off the spaces, but there wasn't much else besides loose wiring. Only a steel table near the window, with various tools and hardware on top. He scanned the ceiling in the construction area for cameras, then out in the hallway. The camera at the end faced the elevators. It was close enough. This would be the place Jake would attack from.

Jake went back out into the hallway and peered around the corner to take a better look at the elevators. Then he turned around and looked down the hallway, past the staircase all the way to the doctor's office. No sign of anyone else wandering around. Jake slipped inside the construction space and waited.

Seemed like forever. Sly looked nervous. Pacing back and forth with his arms folded. It was becoming annoying. The advanced senses Sly possessed were warning him of danger. But in Jake's mind, what was the worst that could happen? He'd die and go to Hell once more? Been there, done that, several times. Being stuck in Hell for all eternity was far more of a threat than an eighteen-year-old kid. The time for caution was over. He was going to jump into this headfirst. The means of saving his eternal soul was in the building. He was going to take the risk whether Sly was there for him or not.

The vibration on Jake's phone finally provided the image he had been waiting for. Adonis left the office and was headed down the hallway in his direction. Timing was of the essence. The camera was focused on the doctors' entrance but not down the hallway. In order to intercept Adonis at the right point, he had to pace this out just right. When Jake walked the hallway, he timed his steps. One one-thousand…two one-thousand…It took nine seconds to get from the stairwell to the corner office. The distance seemed about the same from the stairwell to the doctor's office in the other direction. Eighteen seconds total for Adonis to be at the doorway, walking at a reasonable pace.

Adonis was out of the eye of the camera, and Jake began counting silently. When he reached ten, he would attack. Jake approached the plastic sheet covering the entrance. It was opaque, hard to see through. He was getting nervous. Palms sweating. Seconds ticked off. He looked for the shadow image of Adonis through the plastic. It wasn't there. Was his timing off, or was he so nervous it only seemed that way? No. Something was wrong.

"He's gone," said Sly.

"What do you mean gone?"

Sly stuttered. "He disappeared."

Jake stepped out into the hallway bold and strong. Ready to tackle Adonis and pull him back into his makeshift lair. But there was no one there. The hallway was empty. The doorway to the stairwell was closing slowly.

"He took the fucking stairs," he said to Sly.

"No…he's gone," Sly reiterated. "Disappeared."

"What do you mean 'disappeared'?" whispered Jake. He moved toward the stairs and stopped short of the door. "Pull yourself together," he said, frustrated.

Sly ran beside Jake. "I don't sense his presence anymore. I don't like this!"

"What the fuck are you saying?" Jake whispered, a few feet from the stairwell.

"I sense nothing from him. The senses I have that warn me against him are completely gone. It's as if he shut off his aura."

*Shut off his aura—what is that supposed to mean?*

Convinced Sly was losing it, Jake shook his head and pushed the stairwell door open. They were on the top floor so there were no stairs leading upward, only down. He could see the first landing below. It was clear. Cautiously, he stepped inside. His eyes were trained down the middle opening. He was hoping to catch a glimpse of Adonis traversing downward in a spiral.

Sly screamed, but it was too late.

Jake was struck with something sharp in the side of his neck. A pinch. It burned something fierce. He grabbed his neck and spun around to see Adonis standing before him. There was a syringe in his hand. The plunger had been pushed. It was empty. Jake tried to reach out and grab Adonis, but he lost all control of his motor functions. His vision blurred. Arms and legs refused to work according to his commands.

"What the…"

*Son of a bitch can see me now.*

Jake's world went black, if only for a second.

Then he heard Sly screaming at him to wake up.

# CHAPTER 44

Jake opened his eyes. The wake-up did not include a trip to hell, so he hadn't died. Just knocked unconscious, but now he was strapped down to a table. Against his back, it felt like cold steel, similar to the ones at the morgue. Thick white plastic tie straps were cinched against his wrists and ankles. The table appeared to have holes drilled through to facilitate the straps. A few more were around his thighs and biceps. The straps were especially thick around his neck, as if two or more had been used. He tested his restraints a few times. They were sturdy. After looking around a bit, he could see he was in the room he had hidden inside in order to ambush Adonis. It brought out a nervous chuckle. He had planned to use this room to attack Adonis, but Adonis had planned to use this space for him.

"Family practice," said Jake. "Had a venereal disease you were hoping to clear up?"

Adonis was sitting on top of a red roll-around toolbox against the wall. "Nope! Sex really isn't my thing after being screwed over the first time," said Adonis. "I'm only here for you. I picked this place out because it was special."

He was the picturesque image of perfection. Perfect hair, face, body, clothes. His yellow-collared shirt was crisp and perfectly rolled up to the forearms. His jeans, snug. White tennis shoes without so much as a smudge. He hopped down off the toolbox and walked up to the table.

"I found out from your social media history that *Dexter* was your favorite television show, just like mine," said Adonis. "Dexter used to secure his victims to the table with many layers of plastic wrap. Plastic ties on a steel table are my version."

"Fuck you for ruining my favorite show," said Jake.

Adonis smiled. It was weird. In all the images Jake had seen of Adonis, he had never been smiling. It looked warm and inviting, yet foreign.

"I've waited so long for this day," said Adonis.

How could his keen senses have failed him? Where was Sly? Jake spotted him on the other side of the table. Walking fast, hands to his lips, visibly worried. "Sorry, Jake," he kept repeating. "I am still trying to figure out how he did it. He shut off all impulses driven by emotion. It made him impossible to track."

"Your eyes are following something over there," said Adonis. "Something you can see." He turned his head in the direction of Jake's gaze.

Jake's heart shivered as Adonis stopped right where Sly was standing.

"Wha…" said Sly. "What is he…" Sly moved left. Adonis followed. Then right. Adonis followed again. "Tell him to cut that shit out!" Sly screamed.

Adonis turned his head to Jake as if he could hear Sly as well. "I want one. Tell me all about it."

"About what?" said Jake. "Just kill me and get it over with."

Sly ran over to the table, getting closer to the conversation. Adonis was on one side. Sly on the other.

"Come on," said Adonis. "Jake Coltrane was a frail kid. Weak and demure." He took his manicured finger and tapped on Jake's forehead. "There was a tumor in your head that interfered with certain motor functions responsible for strength and coordination. You received a diagnosis last year that within the year, all motor functions would cease and you would die. Wanting to go out on your own terms, you jumped in front of a train to take your own life. You were severed in two. Then you came back to life. New body and all."

Duval had told him Jake's medical history had been expunged. He'd assumed it was Jericho Black who did it. No. It couldn't have been Adonis, after he had compiled it all. Jake refused to believe it. He stared at the ceiling and clamped his jaws shut so tight he felt the pressure building on his molars.

"Didn't jump in front of the train, huh?" said Adonis. "Were you pushed?"

Jake felt the knot in his brow as he turned to Adonis, astounded.

"Was it a man who pushed you?" asked Adonis.

Jake said nothing but felt the pressure on his molars softening as his jaw began dropping slowly.

"Not a man," said Adonis. "A demon, then. Wow, this is great stuff."

"How the fuck is he doing this, Jake?" asked Sly, the pitch in his voice elevated. "How are you not saying anything but he is answering the fucking questions correctly?"

"I don't…" said Jake before realizing his mistake.

Adonis looked like a cat that had spotted something moving in a dark corner. His pupils dilated fully. His fast-twitch muscles waiting for the impulse to strike. "You were not talking to me, were you?" said Adonis. "You are talking to it as if it is standing on the other side of the table." His hand was on Jake's forearm, and Jake could feel him squeeze gently with excitement. "This would make sense if it was tuned into your body functions. Speaking in your mind would be all too confusing. That's why you have to speak out loud. Seeing it makes it easier for your mind to communicate." Adonis looked around the room, talking to no one in particular. "Language is the main way we humans communicate with each other. I take it he makes himself look like a man to make it easier on you?" He returned his attention to Jake, looking even more fascinated than before. "So what does he look like?"

"What the fuck, Jake?" said Sly, huffing slightly faster. "This is motherfucking creep show shit. Who is this motherfucker?"

"He was talking to you just now," said Adonis. "What did he say?"

"Fuck!" Jake screamed, closing his eyes so tight it hurt.

*Play the politician*, Jake thought. *Never admit guilt. Deny and deflect. Be like a child. Playground rules. Rubber and glue. Whatever you say bounces off me and sticks to you.* "I have no idea what you are talking about, asshole," said Jake. "Talking to myself? I'm talking to you! Do you talk to yourself? Is that your problem?"

"Humph," said Adonis. "I gave you more credit, Jake Coltrane."

Adonis went back to the toolbox to retrieve a heavy-duty black rubber apron. He placed his head inside and tied the straps at the back. "If you haven't figured it out yet, I don't need you to say anything in order to get my answers," he said. There were rubber boots at the side of the box. He replaced his tennis shoes with the boots. "Think of it as a lie detector test," he continued. "The accuracy of the test lies in the person administering it, not in the equipment. If questions are asked properly, all you have to do afterward is monitor the physical responses."

The last thing Adonis put on was a pair of black latex gloves. He snapped them on tight and returned to Jake holding a battery-powered reciprocating saw. "I don't need sensors to measure heart rate, blood pressure, and skin conductivity. I am very perceptive when it comes to physical responses. Phrase the questions right, and you can't hide the truth."

Adonis placed the reciprocating saw down on the table next to Jake. He felt the cold plastic of the handle on his thigh.

"How does this thing inside you work?" asked Adonis. "Was it administered orally, or is it injected directly into the bloodstream? Yes and not sure. It is something in the blood? Yes! So it's like taking a vitamin. See, now we are getting somewhere."

"Jake, shut your eyes!" said Sly. "That's how he is doing it. Don't let him see."

Jake shut them tight, like a kid playing hide-and-seek when they don't understand the principle of hiding.

"Come now, Jake," said Adonis. "Do you really think that is going to stop me?" He sighed. "Is it part of your DNA, or is it independent of you? Independent. Got it!"

"Damn it, Jake," Sly screamed. "You're peeking or something. He's still guessing right!"

"Chemical or biological?" asked Adonis. "Not chemical, but you are not sure about biological. OK. Plant life? Bacteria? Parasite? Oh…that's it. A parasite!"

"Fuck you, I ain't no goddamn parasite!" said Sly, screaming across the table at Adonis. "Jake, you're a lousy poker player."

Sly pulled back his sleeves, exposing his wiry forearms. "OK, pretty motherfucker. Let's see what you do with this response." He wriggled his head and waited. Shit-eating grin on his face.

"This parasite…" said Adonis. He pulled his head back ever so slightly, confused. "Wait. Something changed."

"I released endorphins to get this nigga high," Sly chirped.

Jake felt warm and tingly inside. The pressure of Adonis's questions faded. The tension of being trapped eased. He felt no worries or concerns. Everything was fantastic.

"You're not responding the same," said Adonis. "People typically don't have such precise control over their bodies. Shut down responses like that. It's more like you are high or something."

"Asshole still figured shit out," said Sly, standing on the other side of the table. "But that's OK. I'm driving the ship now, motherfucker. You won't be able to influence me!"

"Parasite, can you hear me?" said Adonis. "I know you are intelligent, and you don't want me to know about you."

Adonis picked up the reciprocating saw. "I thought it might ultimately come to this little guy." He checked the blade with his finger. It looked especially rough. Big teeth for rip cuts. "Since you can grow back body parts and you're not fused into Jake's DNA, I can just hack off pieces until I can isolate you, little guy. Yes! I am speaking directly to you, little parasite, since you are the one who made Jake unreceptive to my questions." Adonis moved the blade over Jake's thigh. "Not threatened, huh?"

"I didn't say shit!" said Sly from the other side of the table. "You're putting words into my mouth." A disheveled Sly made the zipper move across his lips.

"You can most likely move throughout his body freely," said Adonis. "My best option is to cut Jake into as many pieces as I can. Keep them separated and monitor."

"Ha!" said Sly. "Got you now, bitch! Jake, we can wait him out." Sly flipped his hand in the air as if it were simple. "He won't be able to guess which piece I'm in if I do nothing. Eventually, someone will find us. It's better this way. Your dumb ass can't give him any clues either if you're cut in chunks." Sly leaned across the table toward Adonis. "Go ahead, smart guy. Cut away!"

Adonis was focused on Jake. "I get the feeling Jake is indifferent about being cut into pieces and you being taken away from him," said Adonis. He looked at Sly. "Are you a nuisance?"

"No!" said Sly quickly. "And how the fuck do you know where I'm standing?"

"Have it your way," said Adonis. He raised the reciprocating saw and moved it away from Jake's thigh and over to his neck. "You are probably wondering how I will guess which piece you are in," he said to Sly. His eyes moved left to right like a crazy person's. "Simple! It's the part that doesn't decompose."

Jake began laughing. He was so high he cared about nothing. He wasn't fearful of going to Hell. He wasn't afraid of the pain. He found the whole exchange humorous because Adonis was getting the best of the smug prick that was Sly.

"Is that true?" Jake giggled. "The part you are in won't decompose?" Sly looked troubled. Jake laughed even harder. "Ha ha haaaaa…he's smarter than you, motherfucker."

"Right," said Adonis, glaring across the table at Sly. "I am smarter. I will cut down the pieces until I have it small enough where I can eat you. Then you are mine."

"Wait, eat me?" said Jake, abruptly stopping his laughter. "Cannibal bitch motherfucker!" he said, laughing again. "Won't work." He began howling, hysterical. "He can grow me back fast. Full size in under a minute," Jake howled. "I will bust right through your body like that guy in the movie!" He could hardly catch his breath. His voice was distorted as he coughed and sniggered. "Wasn't that from *The Matrix*? He jumped in the dude's mouth and busted right back out. What was his name?" Jake guffawed so hard he could hardly breathe. "What was his name?" he chortled. "His naaaame?"

Adonis looked uncomfortable for the first time. "Don't you think that's enough?" he said to Sly, looking directly across the table.

Sly pouted. "Fine," he said with a sneer. "And stop talking to me as if you can see me! It's creeping me out!" Sly waved his hand like a magician for dramatic effect, and Jake stopped laughing. There was a moment of silence before Jake's face tightened once more. It was sadness. It gripped his entire being.

"I feel so bad now," said Jake, through tears. "What did you do to me?" he shrieked at Sly.

"Shut up, you whiny son of a bitch!" shouted Sly. "Not so funny now, is it?"

"You didn't have to turn it off so hard," whined Jake. "Make it stop!"

"It's withdrawal symptoms. Man up!"

The hammer being pulled back on a revolver had a distinct sound. This one in particular latched with such a tone one that anyone would be fearful of how forcefully it struck the pin. Adonis heard it and froze because he had heard it before. Last year, that sound had echoed through the synagogue.

"Put down the fucking saw," said Arina in a strong Russian accent.

Through eyes blurred by tears, Jake could see Arina standing behind Adonis. The BFR was held up with both of her arms. The ten-inch barrel seemed to extend forever in her small hands. Her legs were spread apart wide, prepared for the kick. Her finger on the side of the trigger. The tip of the barrel was pointed center mast, maximizing her chances of hitting him. Nothing was obstructing her vision with her strawberry-blonde hair tied in a ponytail. There was a slight sheen on her pale forehead, but she showed no sign of nerves. She was steady. Alert.

"You have friends?" asked Adonis, his back still toward the threat. "With your new power, I find that awfully careless of you." He moved the saw blade away from Jake's neck and placed it on the table next to his head.

"Did he hurt you?" asked Arina.

"No," said Jake, trying to keep from whimpering. "Fucking Sly did this to me." After a few sniffles, he felt he could finally speak without bursting into hysterics. "How did you find me?"

Cardigan crept inside the room, carefully maneuvering down the side of the wall. She held up her phone. His program was on it, tracking his location. "The front camera had you entering the building about seven hours ago," said Cardigan. "We waited outside for hours for you to come out. Then at nightfall, we decided to break in and check the place out. Just in case you were in trouble."

*Nightfall?* "What time is it?" asked Jake.

"Just after seven in the evening," said Cardigan.

He had entered the building in the morning. Had he been out all this time?

"Which is why no one came into the office space with you laughing like a jackass," said Sly. "It's Saturday. The building has been closed for about an hour."

"Ladies," said Adonis as Cardigan came into his line of vision, walking around the table by Jake's feet. She pointed the silver .380 automatic in Adonis's direction.

With a gun pointed at Adonis's back and one at his left side, Jake should have been relieved he was being saved. But these were different circumstances. Adonis now had the ability to make people commit suicide. The thought of seeing both of them turn those pistols on themselves brought out the fear of God in him. This must have been part of Adonis's plan. Pulling the girls in closer by pretending they had snuck up on him. Then using one of them as an example to get what he wanted.

Adonis turned his head to examine Cardigan. He looked down at the weapon, then her school uniform, and scoffed.

"This is bad," said Sly. "His bloodlust spiked."

"Run!" screamed Jake. "Get the fuck out of here!" He tried to lift his head and felt the thick straps against his neck compress his windpipe. He pulled on his arms, cutting his skin against the plastic on his wrists. He flexed his thighs and feet, ripping at his flesh in order to free himself. "No!" Jake screamed. "Don't you dare!"

Adonis turned around quickly to size up Arina. The barrel of the huge pistol was less than two feet away from his chest. She was locked in a staring contest with him. Both of them waiting for the other to flinch.

Adonis held up his hand to show her it was empty, then moved slowly to place that hand in the pocket of his apron. Arina watched him carefully, wary of this being some sort of trick to distract her, but to Jake, it was too late. An incredible sense of rage swept over him, fueling something deep within. Adonis was not going to have his way tonight.

He heaved, against all limits of pain, and used the battle enhancements made to his body to pop the plastic straps off his left wrist, then his right. He retracted his legs, popping the restraints on them as well. Then he reached up to grab the double ties around his neck. He strained to get his fingers between the ties and his neck. Blood pouring from his wrists made them slippery. He fought to get enough force to pull them apart while maintaining his grip. The other limbs were freed in less than a second; the one around his neck was being stubborn.

"Wait," said Sly. "Something changed."

Adonis pulled his hand out of the apron pocket and held up a pair of diagonal cutters for Arina to see. He moved slowly, reaching for the ties around Jake's neck and snipping them free.

Jake sprang to his feet. Loose flesh hung from his wrists and ankles. He tried to grab Adonis by the shirt but had trouble due to the number of tendons he'd snapped in his wrist while breaking free. He barely had the strength to hold on to the rubber apron.

"Don't you dare try anything, you son of a bitch," screamed Jake.

"I won't," said Adonis. "It's over. The blue-eyed one would have most certainly killed me. There was no doubt about it."

Jake could see that as well. Her eyes had an air of emptiness to them, as if her mind had already discarded a future with Adonis in it. She wouldn't hesitate to end him. But was that all there was to it?

Was it really that easy? Sly was once adamant there was no chance of defeating Adonis and Jake would be a fool for even trying. He shook those thoughts from his mind. This wasn't the time to think about it.

"Give me the eye!" Jake screamed.

Jake's fist was up against Adonis's chest. He could feel the tension in his muscles. Adonis offered no resistance. No tautness. He turned away from Jake and stared straight down the barrel of the BFR. "Do you think any of you would still be alive if I had the eye on me?" he said coyly.

# CHAPTER 45

He was lying. This was a trick of some sort. A stall tactic to set up his next move. The only reason Adonis had not brought about the suicide powers of the eye previously was because he needed to question Jake. Immortality was a dream of mankind. Now he knew Jake's secrets. He knew about Sly; therefore he did not need Arina or Cardigan. Jake had to separate him from the eye as soon as possible. Time was running out.

"Check his pockets," said Jake. They had to be quick. They could not get caught staring at the eye, or they were toast. Arina began to lower her gun and took a step forward. "Wait!" said Jake sharply. It was loud and frantic. Elevating the level of tension in the air. "Cardigan, you check him," he said, much softer.

"Check him for what? Did you say an eye?" The gun was unsteady in Cardigan's hand. "Like, a real eye?"

"Yes," said Adonis. "A real eyeball."

"You know the eye can make people kill themselves out of pure fear," said Sly. "If you want her to blow her own brains out after seeing it, go right ahead."

"Shut up, Sly," screamed Jake. "She's going to be OK."

"What? What did you say?" Cardigan asked.

"Never mind, just check him…but if you find it, don't look at it."

She shook her head emphatically. "You check him, Jake," she said, waving the gun. "You're right there."

"My hands aren't quite working yet, if you haven't noticed!" Jake screamed.

The tendons in his wrist were practically shredded. He could barely grip the rubber apron Adonis was wearing. He held Adonis close as best he could, knowing if he really wanted to, Adonis could break free. The pistol Arina had pointed at his temple was the only thing keeping him from making any sudden moves. "Sly, stop the bleeding and fix these injuries now."

"You know I can't heal you as fast when you are alive, asshole," said Sly.

One of the drawbacks of his gift. Sly was not a healer. He was more like a cloner. If an arm was severed, he could grow it back lickety-split. Reattaching tendons and repairing skin and muscle took a bit more time. If Adonis fought back, they were done for.

"Now, Cardigan," Jake barked.

She crept toward them at first, slowly increasing speed as she got closer. Cardigan held the pistol loosely with one hand and stopped about an arm's length away. With her free hand, she reached out and under the rubber apron, to the nearest pocket, and slipped her pink gel nails inside. She cringed, sinking her hand deeper, wriggling her fingers to slip them down to the bottom. She came out empty and slipped her hand into the closest rear pants pocket. Two more times, and she withdrew with her face contorted from disgust.

"Empty," she said. "No eyeballs or anything else." Cardigan quickly backed away to the far end of the examination table, training the gun on Adonis as best she could. "Now what?"

"I knew this would happen," said Adonis. "The eye sees the future. I prepared for it."

"What does he mean?" asked Arina. "What future is he talking about?"

"Da…" said Jake, feeling sick and frustrated. He knew about the eye looking into the past and he knew looking into the eye triggered an ungodly response that made you want to kill yourself, but he'd had no idea it could see into the future. It must have been how he knew Jake was coming for him. Now they had captured him, could this be a trap as well?

"I can't see you with the eye," said Adonis, as if reading Jake's thoughts. But then Jake remembered. Adonis had said this before, when they first met. He looked troubled by it, as if it were strange. Perhaps he was telling the truth.

Arina's gaze was steady, straight down the long barrel of the BFR, straight into Adonis's temple. "We came here to find this woman and child he kidnapped. Remember? Your friend's family." Arina stepped closer, putting the barrel of the BFR less than an inch from Adonis's ear. "Where are they?"

"Rashida and Sherrie Duval," said Adonis. "Lovely people. I would never dream of hurting them."

"Something isn't right, Jake," said Sly. "I can't tell if he is lying or not. It's like he knows something we don't. It's not making sense."

"But he said he could not see me before," said Jake. "The eye can't see what I am going to do next."

"He set this trap for you, dumbass," said Sly. "He might not be able to see your future, but he can see theirs."

His plan was derived from Arina or Cardigan's future, which explained why he was so calm, even with Arina threatening to kill him.

"Where are they?" Arina demanded.

"You won't find them without me, that is for certain," said Adonis. "The question is, do you have the stomach to do what I was willing to do to your friend?" He motioned to the table and the electric saw, making Jake's stomach cringe at the lengths he was willing to go to. He wasn't normal. Like someone who lacked empathy and knew others who had it were beneath him.

But Arina put the gun right up against his head. The barrel pressed into his skin. "Try me," she said. "Jake can come back from the dead, but you, you will be gone forever."

"All of this talk about coming back from the dead and finding eyeballs is insane," said Cardigan. "Are you listening to yourselves?" Her tanned face was still contorted with disbelief behind her black-rimmed glasses. "You've all gone batty."

After the thud of Arina's pistol being placed on the table, Cardigan marched to the door and swatted back the plastic sheet covering the entrance. She vanished into the hallway. Jake felt terrible, like a hole had been ripped through his chest. He couldn't blame her for feeling frustrated and angry. Who in their right mind would believe such things, unless they witnessed it firsthand? Arina had been there to witness Jake return to life multiple times. Her mind was forever ingrained with a new reality of what was possible. For Cardigan, it must have felt like a joke everyone was in on except for her.

Now she was out of the room, he had one less person to worry about. The eye seeing into the future was something Jake had not anticipated. He had to formulate a new plan, but the question remained: How much of what he decided to do from here on out had already been seen by the eye? Jake had to get Arina and Cardigan away from him for their own good…and his.

"Take me to the detective's family," said Jake. This was Arina's main concern. With the family found, she would leave and take Cardigan with her.

"The eye and the family are in the same place," said Adonis, shocking Jake once more as he hadn't believed Adonis was behind the kidnapping.

Jake wanted to ask a few more questions. Get a feel for what Adonis was thinking. But screw that. Adonis had other powers. An unnatural sense of deduction. Getting into Adonis's mind meant he would have a pathway into Jake's, and that was a terrifying thought. *Work it out on your own*, Jake decided.

He motioned for Arina to lower the pistol slowly. She pulled the pistol away from Adonis's temple and looked down at Jake's wrists. "How are your hands?" she asked.

He wiggled his digits. They were fully healed. He looked around for Sly, but Sly was gone. Sly worked his magic best when Jake couldn't see him. It was about time. He released Adonis and backed away, taking the BFR from Arina's hand and securing the rubber grip firmly in his palm. It gave him a sense of comfort. Now he could protect his friends.

"Let's go," he said.

Arina secured her pistol from the table and tucked it inside her jean jacket pocket and out of sight. Down three flights of steps the three of them went. Adonis out in front, Arina and Jake following behind armed and ready. They went out the back of the building and into the parking lot. The lot was fenced, but the gate was open. Streetlights lit the surface, displaying neat white lines painted on the blacktop for parking spaces. A few cars were scattered around the lot.

The night air cooled Jake's neck as he looked around. He saw Cardigan resting against Arina's car. Her arms were crossed. She was fighting off the cool breeze by hugging herself. Angry or frustrated, he couldn't tell the difference.

"You expect us all to fit in that thing?" asked Adonis. "I'll be cramped in the back. Besides, the two of you have the pistols. Wouldn't it be better if one of you was sitting next to me instead of up front? I have a better idea. How about we take two vehicles?

Mine is right over there."

Adonis pointed to an old Ford Bronco. Looked to be from the nineties. Jake recognized it from the O. J. chase. This one was brown in color.

"But you took the bus here—" Jake stopped. Remembering not to let Adonis in on his thoughts. How much could he see, and how much was he guessing? Too hard to tell. But it did appear he knew enough to bring his vehicle along and park it out back.

"I suggest you ride with me, Jake," said Adonis. "The girls can follow behind. Duval's family isn't too far from here. Less than an hour's ride."

*This might be his first mistake*, Jake thought. He was trying to think of a way to be separated from the girls, and Adonis was the one to offer it. "Sounds good," he said.

"I don't trust him," Arina said sternly.

"Neither do I," said Jake. "If he can see into the future, then everything we do may be predetermined."

He said it more for Adonis than Arina. Make him think Jake hadn't figured out the secret as of yet.

"You need your jacket," she said. "Can't be walking around with that thing in your hand." She trotted off in the direction of her car, went into the trunk, and returned with the leather jacket and shoulder holster for the BFR.

"Nice-looking car," said Adonis. He walked around the side to get a good look at it. He approached Cardigan, resting against the door.

"Back away from my car, you creep," said Arina.

Cardigan shot Adonis the finger.

"If anything happens to that family, I will kill you," Arina said to Adonis. "I'm sure the future says I will."

Adonis waved bye. "Be sure not to get lost."

"No way I'm going to lose you driving that thing."

Jake put on the holster and the leather coat. He kept hold of the BFR until he was certain the girls would be safe. He used his free hand to squeeze Arina gently by the arm, thanking her for coming to his rescue. "Talk to Cardigan for me, will you?" he asked her.

Cardigan looked as if she still hadn't forgiven them for keeping her in the dark. Her attitude was as cold as the breeze in the night air. She opened the door and sat in the passenger's seat. Shut the door and looked straight ahead. No playing on her phone or the laptop.

"She's the one who insisted on coming," said Arina. "But she is also strong and smart. She'll come around."

Arina got into her Maserati. Meanwhile, Jake followed Adonis to the Bronco, walking behind him in step all the way, cautiously looking over his shoulder. For what he did not know. The dark-brown Bronco was in good shape for a thirty-year-old car. No rust spots or dents, no discoloration in the paint, nor any noticeable replacement parts. He opened up the passenger's door and stepped up on the Nerf bar and inside. The interior was surprisingly clean for an older car too. Smelled clean, even. Not chemical clean like used cars of this age usually smelled. This was a neutral kind of clean smell.

Don got in next to Jake and turned the key. The rumble of the engine sent tremors through the whole cab. He put it in gear—standard—released the clutch, powered a smooth U-turn, and coasted out into the street. The shifting was smooth too. Jake had ridden in cars with people shifting gears before only to be jostled around in the seat. This was like someone driving an automatic. Arina's headlights were right behind him. Stuck up close to his backside.

Adonis drove through several streets, turning where he needed to, until he got to the highway. He entered the interstate and headed south. Meanwhile, Jake watched him closely. Examining every move while looking around the cab in case the eye was close by.

"Just curious," said Adonis. "Why do you want the eye, anyway?

You have been hunting me for almost a year now. The ability to regenerate limbs and return from the dead should be more than enough power."

Jake really didn't feel like explaining his situation, but talking might put Adonis at ease. Give Jake a chance to figure out the angle. "Hell is real, and I am destined to return there whenever I die. I want to know why. During one of my trips to Hell, an old man overheard the owner of that eye, Tartarus. He was talking to some of Hell's apostles when he said the eye was the key to my salvation."

"Tartarus, the king of Hell, you say?"

"Right," said Jake, steadily observing all of Adonis's movements.

"Doesn't make much sense now, does it? Tartarus is part of Greek mythology. Tartarus is both a being and a place. Christianity is one of the many religions in which hell is described as a place for the wicked to be tortured along with fallen titans. But it doesn't date back far enough to be original. Only to about 300 BC."

"Meaning…"

"This being isn't old enough to be the original Hell…if indeed he is Tartarus."

*It's just a name,* Jake thought. *One is as good as the other.* Who cared how old it was? "You seem to know a lot about Hell."

"I know history, that's all."

"I thought the Jews did not believe in Hell."

"An overused joke at this point," said Adonis with a scoff. "We do believe in such things. Just not the same Hell as the Christians do. When wickedness needs to be punished, we take care of it ourselves."

"An eye for an eye. Kind of poetic, don't you think? You use the eye of Tartarus to kill. But were all those you've handed justice to killers? An eye for an eye means justice must fit the crime."

"You mean the woman at the mall? The one who broke her neck falling down the stairs."

"The one I witnessed firsthand. Let's start there."

"Cynthia Kavanagh killed her family. Her husband and children. Sent them barreling to the bottom of the lake in a car after rendering them incapacitated. She was cunning. Planned every detail out and executed it to perfection. She would have been caught in the following month if she hadn't remembered her husband's cell phone was at the shop. She dropped his phone in some water so it would need to be repaired. That's why when police went to track his whereabouts using his phone, they found nothing. The reason she dropped his phone in water was she used it to set up a meeting to obtain Rohypnol, the drug she used on her family. So when she turned her phone over to the police, they found nothing suspicious.

"However, if she had forgotten to pick up her husband's phone at the mall, the repair shop would have called the owner of the phone, not her. Her mother-in-law owned the phone. She would have thought it nostalgic and would have picked up the phone from the shop to contact all her son's friends. When she got to the most recent number, the conversation would have been suspicious enough for her to turn the information over to police. The pressure on the dealer would have led to Cynthia's plot unraveling, and they would have found the bodies and prosecuted her. But because she retrieved the phone that day, she never would have been caught. That is why I intervened. She deserved to die."

"Then you made her kill herself," said Jake. "The poetic interpretation of an eye for an eye."

"I did not make her kill herself. She died by her own fears and foolishness."

"No. That's not how it works," said Jake. "Being someone who has stood at the opposite end of the eye's vision, I can tell you. As the eye looks at you, the emotions are so dark and so intense you believe the only way to make it stop is to kill yourself. I felt it every time I was in Hell when Tartarus looked at me. I wanted to kill myself, but I was already dead. That is what Hell is. Which is why I don't care about the name Tartarus not being old enough. The torture is real."

"Is that why you jumped in front of the train?"

"I didn't jump," he said sternly. "I was pushed." Jake was tired of explaining it. Everyone believed he had jumped. "Plus, I said the torture was when I was in Hell. I was already dead when I felt it."

"I never directed the eye at anyone," said Adonis. "I did it another way, by looking into the future."

"But you changed the future," said Jake. "Which means the future isn't set. How do you know the future you changed is going to work out the way you want it to?"

"I experimented. There is only one way to change the future. It is to know what choice you would have made before. See, people often think a reaction to a situation will be different depending on what they choose. That's actually backward. You will naturally make the same decision every time. One might say the unconscious mind makes the decision for you. Nevertheless, if you know what is going to happen, you give your unconscious mind a choice it would have never thought of, therefore changing the outcome. The more information you have about your future, the more unpredictable you become to the eye. Which is why I can't see you."

"What?" asked Jake. "What does any of what you said have to do with me?"

"Deep down, unconsciously, you know what your future is."

Jake felt his face screw into an incredulous, perplexing, contorted mess. "What the fuck are you talking about?"

He thought his eyes were lying to him after glancing in the side mirror. The headlights with the shape and intensity of the Maserati were not behind them. The highway was filled with traffic. Cars darted through lanes in a hurry, while others kept at a reasonable pace.

"Looking for your friends?" asked Adonis. "They had some car trouble about ten minutes back. We were in such a pleasant conversation I forgot to mention it."

Jake was infuriated. "Stop, you're going back."

"Sorry, Jake Coltrane, this is where we part ways."

"I said turn around!" He pulled the BFR from the holster and pointed it at Adonis.

"If you shoot me here on the highway, you will not get far." Adonis pointed to a camera aimed at the road, used to monitor highway traffic. "This road is full of cameras."

"Stop bullshitting. Turn this fucking car around and find them!"

Adonis frowned as if to signal Jake was not getting the point. "I lied to you earlier when I said I could still see into the future of those around you…or I should say I misled you. I really don't have the eye any longer. It was stolen from me by a woman. Her name is Siobhan Starlette. Just before she stole it, I couldn't figure out why I could no longer see her future. I was so frustrated that I looked into the future of the first person I could think of to see if the eye was still working. That person was Detective Arnold Carrol. He had pissed me off so much that I couldn't get him out of my mind. I looked forward as much as I could, and I saw how his life ended. That's when I switched to his partner, Kevin Duval.

"Duval is going to die tonight, at the end of a silver .380 automatic pistol. You know the one. I couldn't see who was at the end of it and did not know who it belonged to until today. You should hurry if you want to save him. Your friend, the pale blue-eyed one, seemed very capable of taking a life. I could see it in her eyes. She is a lot like you now. I wonder what Duval could have done to his family to piss Arina off so much she would blow his brains all over the wall tonight?"

Adonis pulled to the side of the highway. He unlocked the doors.

"I'm sure shooting me won't help your friend out of this situation. I would hurry if I were you. Toodles."

He jiggled his fingers individually, waving bye. Jake frantically jumped out of the vehicle, and Adonis sped away. With the conversation still fresh in his mind, he knew he could change this future. All he had to do was call Arina and tell her what she was going to do. Jake reached down for his phone, and his whole world seemed to stop. He didn't have it on him. Adonis must have taken it before tying him down. With all the excitement afterward, he never thought to check for it.

Jake rushed out into traffic, trying to stop someone to use their phone. Vehicles swerved and sped around him, honking horns, and some drivers gave him the finger as they passed, but no one stopped.

He ran up the hill and hopped over the small fence onto the sidewalk of the road running parallel to the highway. He rushed out toward an oncoming car, and the driver slammed on their brakes. Once they were stopped, he ran up to the driver's side. "I need to use your cell phone—please!" he said. He must have looked like a crazed madman behind the rolled-up window. But the old man behind the wheel caved and gave him the phone.

It was then he realized he didn't have Arina's number, nor did he have Cardigan's memorized. "Shit," he murmured. The only person he could get in touch with was Duval.

# CHAPTER 46

The screw was in the right rear tire, buried deep enough to cause a small leak and not deflate it quickly. Arina flashed her lights after seeing the warning light, but Adonis kept driving. The car began wobbling on the deflated wheel. It became hard to control. The only option was to pull over. Cardigan called Jake's number, texted him, called again, but got nothing. Soon they were out of sight, lost in the waves of traffic on the highway. Luckily, someone pulled up behind them to lend a hand. Thirty-five minutes later, the tire was changed.

If Adonis was behind the kidnapping, he would probably take Jake to the location of the missing wife and child first. Then subdue him again, cut him open, and steal the parasite that kept Jake alive. Arina was convinced of it. She pleaded with Cardigan to come out of her funk and help. So she did. Her findings led them deep into the woods.

It was dark. The two of them tussled with the branches and thorny obstructions in their path. Dark limbs reached out to try to touch them, like spindly fingers looking to scratch and taste a bit of their skin and blood as they walked by. At least, that's how it felt. They heard all manner of creatures chittering and trilling, some off in the distance, some within arm's length. But there were two of them, and they were armed, which gave them some comfort.

Cardigan had to admit she was not built for this sort of thing. The boredom of being trapped helping her mother was her only motivation. She was only seventeen, damn it. Still a virgin, wanting to marry someone rich and powerful. Wanting to be pampered while exploring the world. It was then, reliving the dreams of her mind, she realized this was far from it and surrendering to the chores of her mother may not have been a bad thing after all.

An hour and a half had passed since they were separated from Jake. Jake's tracking program put his last sighting off the highway fifteen miles from where they'd stopped. Then there was nothing. No sightings whatsoever. To find him, Cardigan had to think. Duval's partner Carrol had been shot near where they were. He was found in the woods. He must have been onto something. He got too close, and Adonis killed him.

She began with an internet search about the story of a hiker who came across the body of ex-detective Arnold Carrol in these very woods. He'd been shot once. The confusing aspect was the gun by his side with the empty clip. Sixteen rounds were fired. Nine-millimeter brass casings were scattered around his body like tossed pistachio shells. All of the shells found were from Carrol's gun.

Investigators had no idea who or what he was shooting at since the rounds went in all directions. They figured he went delusional in his final moments due to the loss of oxygen to the brain, causing him to see things. Then they discovered another body. A man was mistakenly hit with a round from Carrol's gun. He was a pillar of the community. A retired detective of the town. He was found nearly a mile and a half away from the scene. A gunshot wound to the leg that pierced the artery. It appeared he was crawling to get help when he finally succumbed to the injury.

That pissed off the locals something fierce. It was a small town used to their share of people traveling from the city, bringing their baggage and stinking up the place. It had been a pit stop for drug runners during the late nineties. They went to great lengths to keep the filth from infiltrating the town, but they kept finding their way there. Now this ex-detective from the city had emptied his clip in their woods and killed one of their own.

After that discovery, the local police began investigating Duval. His pleas were ignored, like something important told to someone in the front row of a metal concert. They looked and nodded, and that was about as far as it went.

As a long shot, Cardigan executed the program to find Arnold Carrol. She got what she was hoping for. Jake's program used a sequence that checked all cameras active in public and private spaces if they had internet capabilities. Most camera manufacturers created their systems to be controlled by computers. Just hack the computer, and you had access to the video. Jake's supercomputer systematically gained access to random computer networks, combing through billions of possibilities in order to siphon the requested digital information.

However, the real beauty was the means by which it gained access to phones, searching for images through each and every library. That took a bit longer to do. Days or even weeks, depending on the security settings. But Cardigan knew ways around the massive amounts of data. She limited the search to phones in the area, and within minutes, she got a hit. The phone was owned by someone no more than three hundred yards from where they were searching.

Three images taken on the phone had Carrol's likeness. They were all taken in the woods. The camera was below Carrol's head. Much lower. As if taken from the ground at a distance. Probably around thirty to fifty feet away, according to the magnification. The strangest part of it all was that one of the images contained no GPS information. Very few people realized camera phones stamped GPS information on the image at the time it was taken. This was primarily how Jake's program could even track a person's past movements.

Why was a local sneaking behind Carrol taking pictures of him? He must have been crawling around on the ground to avoid being seen.

Cardigan snapped tiny dead tree limbs on the ground with her weight as she kept walking. They were not too far from the location in the first picture. Carefully sweeping the beams of the flashlights they'd purchased at the local Walmart back and forth. No other light could be seen, not even the moonlight; it was covered by the clouds. They kept the flashlights low. Sweeping back and forth. Reflecting off leaves and brush. Swallowed by the shadows whenever they shined the light overhead.

They came to the place where the last photograph was taken. She spun around 360 degrees to get a bearing on the direction of the photograph. It was hard to pick out the landmarks with just flashlights. It didn't look like the place, but GPS said this was the location, so they moved on. The location in the second picture was about twenty yards away. They navigated through the brush and leaves to find that one. Again, it was hard to pick out landmarks from the picture. From the direction, she estimated the third picture was taken east of that location. The one without the GPS stamp was actually the first picture taken. They headed in that direction, slowly, paying attention to the ground.

Cardigan swept her light past a group of pine trees. One of the trees was dead. The needles below it were thick and long. Brown and spindly. It was broken off near the top. Lonely and abandoned of life. But the majority of the trunk was still there.

"This must be it," said Cardigan. "Concentrate on the area near the dead tree."

Arina nodded and shined her flashlight downward across the ground as she paced carefully. Her red heels sinking into the soft ground, covered with layers of long brown pine needles. She was the first to spot the rope on the ground, partially covered by the dead needles. It looked as if it had been discarded by a hiker or something. It was over an inch thick, dirty, and braided. Arina bent down with her buttocks resting against the back of her heels. She used her soft and delicate fingers to slide the rope out from underneath the needles.

Arina pulled upward on the rope. It swept to one side, uncovering more of it from the dense needles. She kept pulling until the rope went taught. Twenty feet of it. They followed it to the far end where it sank back into the ground. On the floor of the forest was a wooden door. About two feet wide by two feet long.

"Damn, you are smart, Lisichka," said Arina.

It was the picture. The person taking it had to be either crawling around on his belly or hidden in a hole somewhere. They anchored themselves, one behind the other, and pulled on the rope, trying to lift the door from the forest floor.

No luck. The door wouldn't budge. At first, Cardigan wondered if it was locked from below, but she prayed it wasn't. She looked around hard, shining the flashlight against an adjacent tree.

"Look," said Cardigan. "Rope strands around the trunk."

It made sense why the rope was so long and thick. The adjacent tree had been used as a pulley. They tucked the flashlights away and got into position. Arina threw the end of the rope around the tree and placed a heel on the trunk for leverage. Cardigan was behind her. One hand over the next, they pulled and walked their hands over the top. They heard the stretching of rope and the creaking of wood until the edge of the door lifted off the surface. They continued to pull until the door teetered on its hinge and came to rest against the dead tree trunk.

"Damn it," said Arina. "I think I cracked a nail." She sucked on her index finger and shook it a few times, trying to subdue the pain.

"If that is all you suffered, feel fortunate."

Cardigan wrapped the end of the rope around the tree trunk for good measure, and together they crept up to the gaping hole and shined their flashlights down inside. At first, she was thinking this was some sort of hunting trap. A small hole dug out to trap prey or even hide beneath it to attack from the ground as in some sort of Special Forces movie. But after getting it open, she realized it was something far more ominous. This was an engineered tunnel. The light bulb came on. She remembered why the ex-detective was so revered in that town. He'd put an end to the drug runners. She remembered watching a documentary about how elaborate tunnels were used to smuggle drugs into the country and had even been used to break El Chapo out of prison. A prison video showed the Mexican drug lord squatting behind a partition to use the toilet, never to emerge again. When guards finally entered the cell to investigate, they found a gaping hole where the toilet used to be, connected to a tunnel large enough to ride an off-road vehicle through. This was just as large. There was a ladder going down to the surface beneath. It looked to be about eight or ten feet down until it hit what looked like a solid ground of dirt. The walls were reinforced with wooden planks staggered to make stairs for climbing in and out of the tunnel.

"I'm not sure I want to go down there," said Cardigan.

She was motivated before, possibly a little naive, but now she'd come face-to-face with the dark unknown, the cracks in her armor were beginning to show. Her nerves would not be tamed. Her knees wobbled at the thought of going any farther. She wasn't built for this kind of thing. She knew it. But Arina was different. She got down on her belly on the dirt and leaves, with her stylish leggings and blouse, and slid legs first into the hole, stopping at the waist to feel for the makeshift stairs.

"Shine the flashlight down into the hole and tell me if I am close to reaching the stairs," said Arina.

Cardigan was reluctant. It was mainly her fear talking, but the fear was there for a reason. "This seems like something bigger than Adonis. I say we wait. We can call the local police and have them check it out."

"And if Jake is down there getting cut up, Adonis might be gone by the time they get here. Besides, I'm thinking about the family that was taken."

The moment Arina looked up from the ground, Cardigan knew there would be no turning back. She recalled the things Arina had told her about her ordeal. Being captured and smuggled from Russia, serving the whims of the bastard Alexei Voznesensky, sleeping in piss and filth, beaten and shamed. Forced to work in the sex trade. Arina understood how easy it was to snatch someone, not just in theory; she had lived it. There was a ten-year-old girl who was also missing. Traffickers in sex had no age limit, no morals, no conscience.

Cardigan was going to have to suck it up. She shined the flashlight into the hole and guided Arina's feet to the ledge. She crawled down into the tunnel and lit the way for Cardigan, who went down on her stomach like Arina did and backed her way across the slippery forest floor feet first. Her legs dangled at the waist while she searched for footing. With Arina's guidance, the tip of her toe felt the solid wood structure on the walls, and she placed pressure, increasing it slowly to feel it was sturdy enough for her full weight. Then she traversed downward and onto the soft dirt floor of the tunnel.

Instantly, her heart began racing. She shined the light against the walls of the tunnel, reinforced with large wooden beams at various spots. It was murky and dank. The sound muted. She wasn't claustrophobic, but somehow the walls felt as if they were going to collapse and swallow her. When it came to hacking, she was known as one of the best. Most people believed hacking into other systems was about knowing the ins and outs of computers, but it wasn't. That was less than half of what made a great hacker. Hacking was really about knowing people. How they thought and what actions they would take if put into a particular situation. Who designed the system, what language they were using and why, and more importantly, what the protections were. She put those same skills to use to get them below ground, inside that tunnel.

But from this point on, the action would be live. Hacking was anonymous; no one knew who you were. If they got close to finding out, you could sever the connection. You were protected by the internet. Like a shield. But this was up close and personal. No hiding behind a monitor. This was the dark web of reality. Fear was tightening its grip.

On the flip side, Arina was amazing. The silver pistol was in her right hand. Her left held the flashlight the way police officers do, with the lighted end at the back of her hand. Her crossed wrists helped stabilize the light and the barrel of the gun, both aimed out in front of her. Where the light pointed, so did the barrel of the gun. She swept it across the darkened space as they walked deeper into the tunnel.

"There is a turn up ahead," said Arina.

Cardigan saw it. It went over to the right. The beam of light from her flashlight only went so far before it was swallowed by the darkness. She guessed she could see about twenty-five feet ahead, then it went black, like gazing into space. They began walking. Slowly but surely. She kept looking over at Arina, who looked steady as a rock, and wondered what made her so strong. Why was she so willing to put her life on the line for a stranger? Was it her rough life in Russia or something in her DNA?

This tunnel had clearly had a great deal of time and money invested into it. A structure like this had to be protected. The thought of what lay ahead had Cardigan shaking in her shoes. Her legs wobbly. Her heart fluttering. It was shadowy, stank, musty, cold, and eerie. She kept feeling little sprinkles of dust or moisture fall on the back of her neck. Tiny speckles of something causing her to cringe. Her impulse was to stop and swipe at whatever it was she felt. The dust was everywhere. She could see it falling down gently. Floating particles. Tiny. Floating through the beams of light like stars in the night.

Then there was the first sign of trouble. Bags. Old trash and other items of food. Some potato chips. Old bottles of water. Strewn in the corners of some of the dirt walls.

"We are getting close," said Arina.

There was no telling how long the trash had been down there. Trash hangs around forever. But it was a sign that heightened Cardigan's sense of awareness. She wondered if Arina felt the same. The answer was delivered when she heard the hammer of Arina's pistol click back. She was taking this seriously. Very few words passed between them. Fear drove them, or maybe natural instincts. Perhaps there was nothing to say. Their focus was on finding the girls, and deep down, Cardigan could feel in her bones they were close.

It felt like something was waiting for them. Something unseen in the darkness. But Arina marched toward it. Waving her pistol left and right with the flashlight. When she turned left, the light illuminated another intersecting tunnel. This was a whole network of tunnels.

A switch sounded as lights as bright as the sun shined upon them. People began screaming. Cardigan went to the ground instantly, but not Arina. She was yelling something in Russian. Aggressive. Angry. With loose dirt and grit on her cheeks, Cardigan pleaded for Arina to comply.

Shadows of bodies moved in. Five—no, eight of them, holding rifles, creeping in slowly with barrels pointed at Arina. Cardigan began crying. She did not want to see her friend killed. This was bigger than them. They had tried to be brave, but these men were out of their league. Their only chance at getting out of this was to surrender and hope someone would find them in time. Arina didn't appear to embrace those sentiments. She was not going down without a fight. Not until a pistol was pressed against the back of her skull.

Arina dropped her silver pistol into the dirt, and the rest of the men moved in like a swarm.

# CHAPTER 47

They were ushered at gunpoint past the lights. Cardigan's eyes adjusted to the darkness once more, and she saw what they were protecting. Drugs. She was certain that's what it was. It confirmed her suspicions about what they had stumbled onto. As she delved deep into the dark web, people had attempted to recruit her into the intricate network of criminal activity. Coordinated by people who knew how to organize and conceal. The drug trade was part of that network. Structured in ways the ordinary citizen would never imagine.

These tunnels were used to transport drugs from one spot to the house they were under, with another tunnel leading out to the middle of the woods. It was a short walk from the entrance they'd found to the resting area off the highway, about a quarter of a mile walk. That was their exit route. Cardigan could hear dogs upstairs in the house barking from their kennels. She imagined when these drug dealers left the tunnels, they took the dogs as cover. Nothing suspicious about someone coming from behind the bushes with a dog at a rest stop. From there, they could get into a vehicle and drive off as if everything was normal.

Gray plastic-covered bricks of something stacked four feet high were against the far wall of the tunnel. Above was the entrance leading to a house. She couldn't see where the other tunnel ended, but she imagined it was a warehouse of sorts. The far end of the tunnel had lights with wires strung down the wall like oversize Christmas lights. Cameras were down there as well, monitoring the traffic back and forth. They were working diligently. Taking the bricks down to who knew where. Seemed like they were evacuating…tying up all the loose ends.

Arina and Cardigan were bound. Tied up good with duct tape and left sitting on the floor, knees to their chest, with wrists taped around their ankles. The one guy who kept walking around with a sense of importance, the boss, was whispering to one of the other guys in the crew. The boss was short with dark hair, a scruffy beard, and tattoos covering one arm and up to the side of his neck. Despite that, he didn't give her the impression of being ruthless, yet the other men treated him with the respect demanded by a stone-cold killer.

"Don't worry," said Arina. "We will get out of this. Stay positive. Some believe abandoning all hope and accepting you are already gone is the way to cope. But I say no…I saw it with my sister. She stayed smiling, always positive, defiant, fiery. That is the way to be. Spit in the face of your aggressors. Make them know you are full of life, always."

Her optimism had the opposite effect. Arina's sister had ultimately been killed. Cardigan felt sick and numb all at once. She counted eight people armed to the teeth with fully automatic weapons. Rifles, handguns, you name it. She even saw a hand grenade on one of the men. They were not playing around.

"What happened to the woman and her daughter?" asked Arina. "They were lost in the woods here three weeks ago."

The scruffy-faced boss came over and squatted in front of them. He used a finger to play in the dirt while speaking. Looking down at the images he traced, he asked, "Are they friends of yours?" He spoke with a New England accent.

"You could say that," said Arina.

"You are not police or any other agent of the law," he said. "What were you doing walking through my tunnels packing heat?"

"You killed the first guy looking for them. I wasn't stupid."

"He was a cop…Both of them were. Retired or not, cops have cop friends. We couldn't have them bringing heat down on the area. Not when we were so close to being out of here."

He made eye contact with Cardigan. No expression she could identify, but he was putting off a vibe. One of regret. "Your friend is upstairs in the house. The kid's there too. You can see them after we are finished here."

That didn't sound right. It didn't sound at all like the energy he was putting off. She tried her hardest to show defiance in the face of danger like Arina had said, but at the moment, Cardigan struggled to imagine a future in which any of them survived. They had seen and heard too much. Slowly, the stash of drugs stacked inside the tunnel began disappearing. It wouldn't be long before they were all gone. She figured they had until then to make their peace.

---

Jake was taking a huge risk contacting Duval, one he hoped would pay off in saving his life. Actually, he was more concerned about Arina's life. Coming from where she had, she did not deserve to be locked up for the rest of her life, and Duval did not deserve to be dead. He wanted them both to have long, productive lives. Since he could not locate Arina, sticking by Duval was his best bet to save them both.

His plan started with calling the department and insisting he needed to get in touch with Lieutenant Duval. "Tell him it's Ernesto Coltrane," he said. Duval would surely figure that one out. He then gave the department the old man's number and waited.

The old man was cool. A widowed, retired Italian pizza shop owner originally from Brooklyn. He lived nearby and didn't have much else to do most evenings. He had stepped out to grab some cat food and dip right back before Jake ran out into the road. His evenings were usually spent watching twenty-four-hour news channels. He said he had no idea why he watched so much news. He had absolutely zero interest in the news when he was young, and now it was all he thought about, what was going on in the world.

Jake told him to hold on to his hat because this one was a doozy. He told him he had called Lieutenant Duval about his missing wife and child. It immediately sparked a reaction. The man had heard about that case. Time was of no importance, so he parked his car in an open spot against the curb. He didn't have to wait long. About ten minutes later, Duval called the old man's phone.

"What are you doing?" said Jake.

"I'm home…trying to digest this whole business about you being alive…and how my life has been flipped upside down. There are jerks and assholes who got my number calling me, texting me, fucking with me. Now internal affairs is telling me someone is poking around into the Connor Richardson case, saying they believe Fanuco Iglesias was set up to take the fall."

"You already know he was innocent," said Jake. "You told me."

"Do you think the governor is going down for this?" he snapped. "I'm being screwed every which way…What do you want?"

Jake was on a mission to save his life. Unfortunately, telling him might end Arina's life. In the state Duval was in, he would surely shoot first and ask questions later. Jake had no idea where Arina was. She could have been heading back to the city for all he knew.

If he kept Duval close…"I need you to come out to Connecticut." He thought of something that would get Duval out of the house and on the road. "You need to show me where your partner was killed. I believe I'm really close to finding them. I am here, in Connecticut, already. I need you to walk me through it."

There was a bunch of moaning and hemming and hawing to boot. Eventually, he agreed. Jake gave him instructions on where to pick him up. The phone clicked dead, and Jake was satisfied he had done the right thing. Duval didn't seem like the bad guy in all of this. So for Arina to shoot him, she had to have some bad intel.

While they were waiting, the old man shared the current reporting from about an hour ago. Duval was now a suspect due to recently uncovered evidence. They never said how he was involved, just that the police had their suspicions. Thinking back to Arina, in order for her to become angry enough to kill him, something bad had to have happened to Duval's wife and child. Something horrible. Jake would keep it under his hat for now. The last thing he wanted was for Duval to lose it.

It would take Duval about an hour to get there. Meanwhile, the old man and Jake sat in the car chatting. It wasn't long before Jake noticed the old man eyeing his full-length leather coat and the BFR hidden on his side.

"Are you a cop?" asked the old man.

"No," said Jake. "More like a fixer." Jake thought that would make the old man comfortable. "From here on out, things are going to get edgy. You should go home, feed your cat, and watch some more TV. There might be breaking news on this case. Sit tight."

He poked his lips out with a gentle nod as if he understood. "I ran a pizzeria in the Bronx in the early eighties with members of the Genovese family visiting from time to time," he said in his soft, aged voice. "I'm very familiar with fixers."

"Thanks for all your help," said Jake as he got out of the car. The old man nodded. He left Jake on the side of the road and pulled out into traffic to head home.

Jake commanded a few stares as cars passed by, the occupants wondering what a tall Black man was doing standing on the side of the road at this time of the evening. But no one gave him any trouble.

An hour later, a blue Dodge Charger pulled up to the curb. Jake heard the door unlock. He opened it, got inside, and put on the seat belt.

Duval looked like shit. Worn down and run over by the many tales circulating about his integrity. "So it's like that, huh?" said Duval, eyeballing Jake in the long, black leather jacket. Same one from the synagogue video. Duval pulled one side of the jacket open, exposing the massive BFR pistol. "This is all so incredibly hard to believe. How many times have you murdered someone and then pretended to be dead so you could get away with it?"

"It's not like that," said Jake.

"Am I next on your list?"

"Is there a reason you should be?"

"No," said Duval, turning toward the windshield. "You said you wanted me to show you where my partner was killed."

"Right," said Jake. *There is a reason you are under suspicion*, he wanted to say, but he couldn't. Jake sought to clear all doubt out of his own mind first before deciding to protect him. "Let's get going, then."

Jake peeked over his shoulder after seeing some movement in the back seat. It was Sly. "I figured it was time for your wingman to make an appearance," said Sly. Fuzzy white fedora, white mink jacket, no shirt, black slacks, white-and-black shoes. He was wearing those designer sunglasses, the ones with barely any tint to them. He was sitting nonchalantly. Cool as ever. "This motherfucker is nervous,

Jake. His heart's fluttering like a hummingbird over there. I can't tell if it is because of you or because of the situation. I'll keep you posted."

Jake nodded. Getting Duval to process the explanation of an intelligent parasite inside Jake's body was the last thing his feeble mind could handle. Duval pulled out into traffic and down the road to the highway. Surprisingly, they were not far from the site. Twenty minutes by car, which was probably why the reports of the disappearance had stood out to the old man.

Duval hit the blinkers as if he were exiting the highway to pull onto another but stopped halfway down the off-ramp and pulled over to the side. It looked like an ordinary wooded area abutting the interstate. A grassy area on the side dropped off steeply about fifteen feet or so. At the bottom were drainage rocks, the big, jagged kind. The rocks ran about five feet wide. Then on the other side was grass and brush. Then the trees. They both got out of the car and stood shoulder to shoulder, looking into the wooded area past the drainage rocks.

"This is where Rashida's car was found," said Duval. "A friend of Carrol's was going to meet us here, when I got the call and went back to New York."

"All three of you drove?" asked Jake.

"No…Carrol rode with me."

"And you left him here?"

"I know how it looks. Carrol said a friend of his who lived nearby was going to give him a ride back to the city."

Jake began testing the footing where he stood. The decline wasn't as sharp up top. It was gradual for a good five feet before it went nearly vertical. "Why blame Adonis for this?" he asked.

"He knows how to trick people into having accidents that end up killing them," said Duval. "We found out how Adonis killed the woman at the mall. We interviewed one of the custodians there, and he said Adonis came every day, feeding the pigeons at the exit. Put them on a schedule like clockwork. Then, when he walked outside with Cynthia, the pigeons got excited and began to fly over to him. Like a magician using the sleight of hand, he pushed her and made it look like she lost her balance due to the pigeons. We have him in the area of at least two other accidents we suspect were homicides. We know how he does it."

"So what do you think happened here?" asked Jake.

"The car had damage on the side. The rear passenger-side door was hit. He sideswiped them. When my wife got out of the car to look at it, he must have pushed her down there. He must have done the same to my little girl. There was no sign of a struggle. Rashida is a fighter. She's no joke. He wouldn't have been able to take her without a real fight on his hands. He had to incapacitate her by pushing her down onto the rocks."

"What about the bodies?" asked Jake.

"He came and took them. That's how he lured me and Carrol to this spot. He planned to kill us here, but I got a call from the station and had to leave."

"A bit of a stretch, don't you think?" said Jake.

"You know what he's capable of," Duval snapped.

Indeed, he did. Didn't make it any less of a stretch, though. Jake examined the surroundings. Although they had been standing there for several minutes, there hadn't been another car coming down the off-ramp. "Is this not a popular exit?" asked Jake.

"It used to be," said Duval. He pointed off in the distance to the circling interstate connections to the left. "They built around this. Only people going into town use this exit. Not a big population. No reason to exit unless you live here."

"Was the sheriff's car left here?" Jake asked. "Why would it take them a couple of days to find the body of former local law enforcement if his car was left on the side of the road?"

"He parked at the rest stop," said Duval. "It's on the other side of these trees. You can't see it from here."

Jake needed a better picture from the view below. "Let's climb down and do some exploring."

Duval reluctantly began the decline. His legs were wobbly. His arms and hands barely had the strength to brace him on the hill and slide. Jake found himself grabbing the collar of his jacket several times to keep from tumbling into the rocks below. At the bottom, the large rocks were arranged where it was awkward to traverse. They were slimy and slippery, and it was easy to lose balance.

He looked upward at how steep a climb it was going to be to get back up. How would Adonis have moved the bodies if they did fall to their deaths? His style was more hands-free. "Let's go in deeper. Check out the area where your partner was shot."

Duval raised his eyebrows but trotted ahead into the woods. Immediately, Jake thought it was a bad idea. They couldn't see a thing. They used the light from Duval's phone to keep from running into thorny bushes. A woman wouldn't venture down this way, would she? Over to his right, Jake could see lights. "Let's head this way."

There seemed to be a path through the trees. A walkway where people didn't have to worry about limbs and brush. It went up gradually, then around a bend, and they found themselves at the rest stop. It was right off the intersecting interstate they had exited. They walked toward the brightly lit parking lot until they hit solid pavement. The large brick structure had signs leading the way to the restrooms and food.

Jake looked to the right, and his eyes widened in shock. Arina's blue Maserati was parked by its lonesome, near the trucks and campers.

## CHAPTER 48

He let out a nervous laugh. The kind of nutty, inappropriate laugh that made him look like a psycho to anyone not privileged to know what was going on inside his head. Duval eyed him strangely, as he should. Jake wasn't about to explain it. No need to stir up a frenzy inside his breakable emotional state. Jake bottled up the hysteria all for himself, letting another laugh slip before he could put the lid on. To think, he would be the one to lead Duval to his death.

Growing anxiety about each choice made it impossible to decide. "We need to head back to the car," said Jake, looking back at the path they had taken.

"Through that shit?" said Duval. "No way. I'd rather walk around."

Cars were steadily pulling into the rest area from the left. Trees blocked him from seeing any farther. They were standing right by the main building, where the food and bathrooms were located. If Arina was inside, he did want her to see them. He thought about his program and looked for the cameras located up on the poles. If they were trying to find him, Cardigan would get a ping on his location any minute.

"How long of a walk if we go that way?" asked Jake.

"Less than a mile. We did it before. We wondered if Rashida and Sherrie came this way to get help and were then abducted. The camera footage came up empty. They never walked this far." Duval motioned upward at the camera pointed down at them from behind. *Great.*

"Then we walked out to the road," Duval continued. "There is a path right off the interstate you can walk around safely, all the way back to the car. That's how I knew where the rest area was from the other side."

"Let's get going, then," said Jake.

They began walking to the left, where Arina was parked. The car caught Duval's attention. His gaze stayed on it as they walked past. Was he looking because it was an attractive vehicle, or was fate warning him somehow?

They traveled past the truck area where the big rigs and campers were parked, all the way to the edge of the lot and beyond. Away from the bright lights of the rest stop, they were once again engulfed by the darkness of night. Duval led the way. They scraped past the tree line to the point where the two interstates intersected. The roads went in big swirls like the turns of a roller coaster, from one interstate to the next, enough to make Jake dizzy. Roads went above and below, looping around them. The hills they walked upon would take them up to level ground. That's where the car was parked. But they could also head down the hill farther, to another road. Jake had seen this type of lonely road before. The forgotten road, which used to be the main road many years ago, before the construction of the interstates. It led to a town that was bypassed. Businesses that saw better days in the past now barely holding on.

"Let's head under here," said Jake.

Duval gave him a bit of attitude, but Jake didn't care. People often disappear in towns that have been forgotten. At least, that's what he was thinking. His mind went from saving Duval to finding his wife and child like he wanted. They took baby steps down the steep decline with the majority of the pressure applied to their toes, weight back on their heels, head behind their knees to keep them from tipping over. They arrived at the bottom without so much as a slip of the foot. The road was as Jake thought. Two lanes led to a stop sign at an intersection with traffic lights beyond, off in the distance, blinking yellow due to the hour of night.

They walked to the stop sign. The curb was cracked in several places with weeds sprouting through. They crossed the street, and Jake looked behind him at the parallel sidewalk. He could see the big sign leading traffic onto the choice of interstates. One of those on-ramps would lead them back to the car, but he wasn't interested in heading back yet.

After a few more steps, he could see a house across the street to the left. It was a private residence with a huge three-car garage. But that was not what struck him. His first thought was this was an auto repair shop. The three garage doors dominated the square building with the entrance door on the side. It had two levels. The upper level had regular windows and looked more like a residence than the lower part. Perhaps when this was the only road that passed through, this was the repair shop and after the interstate was built, they turned it into residential housing.

Jake took a long look around to get his bearings. He could hear the cars on the interstate up ahead, but which road were they on exactly? After looking above the home, he had his answer. Duval and Carrol had pulled their car off to the side of the road and gone into the woods on the adjacent side. But if they had crossed the road and looked down, they would have seen this house or, more importantly, what appeared to be a repair garage.

This was where a woman would go for help with her car.

Jake detected movement and the orange glow of a lit cigarette. He focused in on that point until he could make out a person. It was a man. He saw them before Jake saw him. That much was obvious. He quickly put out the cigarette and went inside. Nothing weird, he guessed. Two Black men walking into town and staring down the lone person outside at this hour was something that would send most people back inside the house to bolt up the doors and windows. But the gnawing at the back of his neck said otherwise.

Jake crossed the street. Duval followed. They walked down the long driveway to the home. The closer they got, the more Jake could see. Heavy equipment in the backyard. Dump trucks and front-end loaders. Then he saw a flatbed. The sign on the lawn said this was an equipment rental place. A big fence around the property protected the equipment. Jake wanted to talk to them. He knocked on the door.

The front light came on above the door. Bright. He heard the locks unlatching, and the door cracked open enough for a head to peep through. He had brown hair and fair skin, clean-shaven, wearing a white T-shirt. That was about as much as Jake could see. His hands were hidden, but since Sly didn't warn him about any danger, there was nothing to worry about.

"What do you want?" said the man. His voice was gritty. Hard.

"We are investigators looking into the disappearance of a woman and child," said Jake. "It happened almost three weeks ago, not too far from here."

"Yeah, police came by asking already. They didn't come by here."

"And you didn't hear anything from that night?" said Jake. "Neighbors didn't see anything?"

"I figure they went the other way, toward the rest stop. That's where everyone else goes when their car breaks down."

"I noticed you have a flatbed truck back on the side," said Jake.

"It's used to deliver heavy equipment," said the man.

"A woman might confuse that with a tow truck...if she needed a tow."

"Maybe," he said, narrowing his eyes as if he didn't like the suggestion.

Just then, someone else came around to peek at who was at the door. Another man, looked like he worked out. Rough-looking like the men Jake had seen every day in prison. He stood back about ten feet from the door. He was saying, *Enough, and you best be on your way before you get hurt.* He never even moved his lips, but that's what Jake heard.

"I appreciate your time," said Jake. "Duval...do you have a business card or something?"

Duval came forward into the light and extended his hand with the card. The man at the door looked at it. He read it.

"His blood pressure spiked," said Sly. Jake looked over to Sly, now standing to his right. He was wearing the same fuzzy white fedora and white mink jacket with no shirt. Sly dipped in and out from time to time, so much that Jake never paid much attention to when he disappeared. But when he appeared with a warning, it always meant trouble. "Something on that card he doesn't like, hoss. You know how they be shootin' niggas through doors nowadays."

Jake pushed Duval's hand holding the card down to his side. "We will not take up your time a moment longer," he said. "Thanks for the help."

"Don't mention it," said the man.

Jake and Duval turned around and walked back down the long gravel path to the road. This time, Sly was walking with them.

"You ain't gon' like what I have to say, nigga," said Sly.

"Spit it out," said Jake.

"Spit what out?" said Duval.

"Arina is inside that house," said Sly.

Jake stiffened. "No. It can't be."

"Can't be what?" said Duval. "I haven't said anything. What the fuck is wrong with you?"

Jake stopped at the end of the driveway. "Are you sure it's Arina?"

"Positive," said Sly.

"No, I'm not sure it's Arina," said Duval. "Who the fuck is Arina?"

"What are we looking at, Sly?"

"We got a bunch of niggas in there. I believe somewhere about eight."

"What about…" Jake stopped. He had to be careful about what he was asking. Sly could sense the essence of people. He knew Arina and Cardigan. He could sense the bloodlust of the others. But could he sense the missing family members of Duval? "You know what I am referring to," said Jake.

"I can't tell you," said Sly. "They could be two of the other eight I sense in the building…or around the building, actually. In any case, that leaves six niggas. How many bullets do you have?"

"Just the five in the chamber."

"God damn, why don't you have nine like every other nigga pulling the trigger?" screamed Sly. "A Glock or maybe even a MAC-10. You need to change your arsenal if you are going to keep taking on multiple niggas at one time. Fucking around with a single-action revolver."

Jake glanced over at Duval, who had given up trying to decipher what Jake was talking about. He looked at Jake like a weirdo, which he could accept considering the circumstances. They continued walking back in the direction they'd come from. Through the underpass, up the hill, all the way to Duval's car.

Jake said nothing. He was frustrated, angry, and a bit confused. He was trying to keep Arina as far away from Duval as he could. In the end, he had led Duval straight to her. He remembered what

Adonis had said: people will always make the same decisions unless they know precisely what they are going to do. Arina was able to figure out where Jake was going because of the clues left behind. If Arina was led here and Jake was led to the same spot, then this must be where Duval's family was being held.

"Are you satisfied?" asked Duval. "This is where it all happened, yet there are no leads here. Adonis must have taken them somewhere."

Any more delays would be a waste of time. "You can leave now," said Jake. "I am going to head back to the house, sneak around back, take a peek in there."

"I know people don't always like the police," said Duval, correctly determining the man didn't like his business card because he was a homicide detective. "But that's not enough of a reason to head back there."

"Yes, it is," said Jake. "And I can take a few rounds if I need to. You can't."

Duval was stymied. He seemed to be thinking carefully about what he was going to say to Jake. And when he was ready, he led with one word. "Books…Inmates, the smart ones, tape up soft-cover books around their midsection before a fight, limiting the depth of the shank wounds. I thought that was how you did it. You would bleed some, as the knife got through a portion of the pages, but nothing would be fatal. Then you would call your contacts, and they would pay some people off, and somehow, you would be pronounced dead.

"Then your people would bring in a replica body. A fake one. Something that would fool the common person who looked at the face and such, but not enough to fool a coroner. But when I looked at your body, it was real. You have these marks on your back. Identifying marks. Tattoos of some sort. The interesting thing is they have these pictures of them from when you checked into Rikers, and they were on the body when I came to inspect it. You were dead. Really dead.

"I wanted to confirm the marks with the coroner's office in New Jersey where I inspected the body with Adonis for identification. I looked over those notes, and amazingly, those marks were there on your back, except of the seven marks, five were filled in from the pictures of your body in the morgue. Now six are filled in. Is that the number of times you can come back to life?"

"Long story," said Jake. "One I don't have time for right now. I just need you to leave. If anything turns up, I will be sure to call you."

"Is that where my family is being held?" Duval asked, fear strangling each word.

"I will call if anything turns up! You are in enough trouble already. You don't need this on your hands."

Jake watched Duval as he sat down in the driver's seat and looked straight out through the windshield. Still no cars on the off-ramp. Jake took this time to check his gun. He slipped it out of the holster. He counted all five shots and rejoiced that Arina had found the proper rounds to load in his gun. He then turned around and walked down the off-ramp once more. Crossing the street on his way to the house.

His feet hit the gravel driveway, and that is where he stood. All six foot seven of him. Black leather, full-length coat flapping in the breeze. He wanted to give them notice. Wanted them to see him before he approached. Wanted to give them a chance, to see what type of people they were. Were they the type to call the cops because they were innocent and Arina just happened to be inside, or were they really guilty of something?

"They see you," said Sly, appearing beside Jake once more. "This time I can feel the bloodlust. If you walk up again, they will be shooting a nigga through the front door."

"It's decided, then," said Jake. "We know what kind of men these are."

"The niggas inside are ready to go buck wild,"

Jake let out an annoyed sigh. "Why are you so racist? I saw two White guys in there, and all you keep talking about is how the Black people inside are going to go buck wild. How can you even tell who is Black without seeing them?"

"Excuse me, nigga, but my niggerism is all-encompassing. White niggas, Black niggas, Latino niggas, Asian niggas—all you motherfuckers are niggas. So when I say nigga, don't get your panties in a bunch…niyiggaaaa!" Sly finished his tirade by brushing fluff off the white mink with his fingers and readjusting his hat to the proper tilt.

Jake shook his head. "Fuck it. Let's go!"

# CHAPTER 49

His body began to overheat, as if lava were coursing through his veins. It must have been Sly. He gassed Jake up whenever needed to confront the danger at hand. This time was no different. He was walking down the gravel path to what he knew was going to lead to bloodshed. In the past, he would have shied away from such confrontations. Was it because he knew he could not die? No, that wasn't it. When he died, his soul was transported straight to Hell, and that was far worse than any pain he had experienced on Earth. Perhaps it was his recent stint on Rikers Island. Something about putting assholes in their place that motivated him. And if they had taken Arina and Cardigan, they were surely assholes.

"I'm stepping you up a notch because the situation has changed," said Sly. "Cardigan is panicking. Young, dumb, silly girl who insisted on coming along is now scared shitless. Try to limit the emotional damage on her, Jake."

Jake banged on the door with the back of his fist. "Hey! I know my two friends are in there. Two women. Must have gotten here about an hour ago. How about you let them go?"

Jake listened at the door. He heard someone moving inside.

Pushing things and jostling other items around the floor.

"I sent the police detective away," said Jake. "He doesn't need to know about this. All I want are my two friends…and if you have his wife and child, I suggest you give them to me as well."

Nothing. No sounds of movement. No response to his request.

"Last warning!" said Jake, cocking back the hammer.

The porch light was still on. The small glass at the top of the door revealed it was pitch-black inside. Jake stepped back and, like a two-step dance, raised his foot and thrust his heel into the door as hard as he could. The door flew open with a crash. Splinters of wood flew through the house as the frame gave way. He was at a disadvantage because the light outside the house would illuminate him brightly, while he would not be able to see where they were hiding inside. But they didn't know about Sly.

"Give me a second," said Sly. "Behind the couch. He's getting ready to shoot. I'll send the coordinates."

It was like GPS straight to the brain. Jake pointed. He squeezed off a round from the BFR. Flames shot out of the barrel bright enough to flash the room. The kick was fierce. A reminder of how powerful the gun and the rounds were. The recoil bent his arm back at the elbow all the way until the barrel was pointed at the ceiling. If it had not been for Sly's enhancements, firing the pistol with one hand would have been impossible. Whoever was hiding behind the couch never had a chance. The round zipped through fabric and cotton before tearing through flesh. Jake heard the thud of his head hitting the tiled floor.

"Shit," said Sly. "Prepare to take on some gunfire."

Sly must have done something else, improved his night vision or something, because suddenly the room came into view. It wasn't like some kind of super ability where he could see things he could not see before; it felt more like being in the dark for a long period of time. This was the waiting room of the business. The walls were lined with wood paneling. The couch he'd fired through was on his left with magazines on a coffee table in front of it. Then over to the right was a wall with a mounted television. Straight ahead was a counter where they waited on guests.

This part of Sly's enhancements was what Jake valued the most. The adrenaline rush. It made threats appear to be moving in slow motion. Jake spotted the head coming over the top of the counter. It was the stringy-haired guy who was smoking earlier. He was bringing his weapon up to fire. Good choice. Sawed-off shotgun. Great for shooting in the dark in tight spaces.

The barrel came up on over, but Jake never gave him the time to fire. Flames erupted from the barrel of the BFR. The top of the guy's head came clean off, everything above the bridge of the nose. The shotgun flew upward from the momentum and back against the far wall. Blood spray was almost instantaneous. The sound of the shotgun hitting the ground rang out first, followed by the thud of the body.

Then it got quiet.

"Where's the rest of them, Sly?" asked Jake. His heart was racing. Air came whistling through his nostrils. A warm streak flashed down his spine. As if he could feel where these souls were heading. He wasn't in much of a mood to join them. In hell, even seconds felt like weeks.

"I feel people off to the side," said Sly. "The next room over."

That would be the garage to the right. There was a doorway behind the service counter. Perfect place for an ambush. "Is it clear?" he asked Sly.

"Sort of," he said.

"What's that supposed to mean?"

"Three niggas—uh, excuse me—motherfuckers on the other side.

Hunkered down and waiting. Only one of them is itching to blow your head off. The other two are more scared than anything else."

"Could the other two be Duval's family?"

"Possibly."

It would make sense they were held by a single assailant. It would mean Jake hit the jackpot.

"Where are my girls, Arina and Cardigan?"

"That's the strange thing," said Sly. He pursed his lips. "It appears they are in the basement, but not quite under the house, if you know what I mean."

"No. I don't know what you mean."

"Like...in the dirt out back."

Buried?

Jake lifted the end of the counter and walked behind it, stepping over the man with only half his skull. He reached down to pick up the sawed-off double-barrel shotgun in his left hand and never broke stride. The service door leading to the garage was straight ahead of him. Dingy, brown, stained door that didn't even align properly with the frame. He pushed it open with his toe and stepped out into the brightly lit space. It was one big open garage with three doors at the front and three at the back. There was a scissor lift and a small bobcat on top of a flatbed. Around it were drab, green-colored bricks of something. Drugs came to mind. They were loading them, packing them into hidden spaces on the Bobcat, except the operation had stopped.

He wasn't sure if he heard the first shot fired or if he felt it. He was still operating in slow motion. Even more so due to his rage. He saw the one person firing what looked like a nine-millimeter semiautomatic handgun. Then he saw the other two people nearby. They were pointing weapons but had yet to pull the trigger. That made it easy for Jake. Duval's family was not there, so there was no need to hold back any longer. Whether the other two shot at him or not, it made no difference. They had used their heavy equipment to bury his friends alive.

*The kids, the dog…everybody dying.*

He walked toward the shooter and raised the shotgun, pointing it like an extension of his arm. The shooter had a chance to hide behind the flatbed but chose not to. He was probably thinking one of his bullets was sure to drop Jake before he got close enough with the shotgun to pull the trigger.

He guessed wrong. Shot number one from the double barrel tore into the shooter's arm, knocking the gun from his hand. Jake stepped right up to him without hesitation, tucked the barrel under his chin, and fired. He tossed the shotgun to the ground and headed to location number two, on his right.

This guy was hiding behind the stack of drugs but jumped into the open, thinking he had a chance to take Jake out. He had a small machine gun. MAC-10 probably. Jake didn't wait around to learn what thirty rounds in half a second felt like. He raised the BFR and took him center mast. It was like he had hit the guy with a sledgehammer. He flew backward about seven feet and skidded across the smooth concrete floor.

Third guy was already running. He recognized a monster when he saw one. He ran frantically to a hole at the far end of the building. It appeared he wanted to dive down into the hole to escape, but his brain must have calculated he didn't have enough time. So he spun around quickly, ready to shoot, as Jake took him out. Again center mast, sending him flying past the hole.

"Nigga, please," said Sly. "Will you calm down for a moment?"

He suddenly recalled that Sly had been trying to talk to him the entire time. He had tuned him out.

"Motherfucker, I was trying to tell you they are not buried alive.

Its not that sort of peril they are in."

Jake looked down into the square hole cut out of the concrete. Down below, a ladder led into a tunnel of sorts.

"They must be down there," said Sly. "In that fucking tunnel."

Jake went to look around the garage and felt a sharp pain in his side. Instinctively, his free hand went to feel the area of pain, and his hand became wet with blood. He looked at it, startled. "I'm hit?" he asked.

"Hell yeah, you got touched, nigga," said Sly. "You can revive, not have bullets pass through unharmed like a fucking ghost. You stood out in the open shooting at niggas that was shooting back at you. The fuck you think was going to happen?"

Jake winced once more. The pain became sharper as he moved around. "Pump up the adrenaline. And stop the bleeding. I'm going in."

# CHAPTER 50

Five minutes after Jake left him, Duval was still staring out through the front windshield of his car. If Jake did anything that came back to him, he would be in deep shit. It was one thing to go after Adonis Silver and another entirely to target some creeps in a rental business. He thought he knew who Jake was. Thought he'd vetted him properly. But he could have made a mistake. Jake was talking to himself. Never a good sign. He remembered pointing out the cameras overhead while they stood in the rest area parking lot. Duval was with him in that shot. If Jake was caught, that part would be hard to explain.

Duval was starting the engine to take the chill out of the air when he got a call. It was Captain Reynolds, the third time he had called. Duval thought it was best to answer this time. Captain Reynolds would often make wellness checks on Duval, to see how he was holding up. If he ignored the first, the second meant it was important, but three was an emergency.

"Hey, Cap," said Duval through the car system.

"Kevin, I wanted you to hear it from me first."

Two things wrong, right off the bat. First was addressing him as Kevin. *Lieutenant* was professional. *Kevin* was personal. The second, whenever a cop said, "I wanted you to hear it from me first," whatever followed was not going to be good news. Was he being fired? Nope. There was a union rep and procedures and a host of other laws and red tape that said that would not be the case here. He could accept almost any disciplinary action at the time. Even a suspension without pay. The only thing he was not prepared for was…

"They found them, Kevin. I'm sorry."

His breathing accelerated. The time between each breath steadily increasing. It gained in force and volume until he found himself dizzy. Then came the hole. The emptiness. The innocuous flame of life that had been ripped from his body. Snatched away, violently, without any regard for the pieces of him torn away with it. He tried to hold it off as best he could. Push it away and pray it was a mistake.

"Where are you?" said Captain Reynolds. "I'm outside your place. I figured you could use a friend right now. I'll wait for you."

Duval cleared his throat before speaking. It felt heavy and painful. "I'm heading over to Rashida's mother's place. I was going to check on her."

"Please don't tell me you are passing through Naugatuck," said Reynold. "I beg you to stay away from there."

The green sign at the bottom of the off-ramp that pointed to the left indicated Naugatuck was three miles that way. "That's where they were found, wasn't it?" He felt like screaming but waited. Meanwhile, his mind swirled and tossed around a thousand possible scenarios in a matter of seconds. "How did they die?"

"It was an accident."

His lips pressed together tightly. The dense night outside the car managed to get even darker. An accident—why was he not surprised? That was how Adonis Silver operated. Make it look like a random series of events that led to one's demise while he orchestrated the entire thing from the shadows. He wouldn't get away with it this time. There was a bullet with his name on it.

"Give me the details, please," said Duval.

Captain Reynold's reluctance was filled with dead airtime. Duval wasn't about to prod him. Just wait him out. "They pulled off on the shoulder after clipping the guardrail at the exit," said Captain Reynolds.

Duval looked around the wooded area next to where she'd stopped and behind him. Plenty of guardrails to hit coming off the highway. "Go ahead," he said.

"Rashida wanted to take a look at the damage, scared you might freak out if it was too bad. Sherrie was sitting in the back near where the car was hit. She was excited and tried to look at it from the window. Rashida told her not to roll it down. The door might have been crumpled and that would only make it worse, probably would have broken the glass if she tried. Sherrie wasn't supposed to get out of the car. She was excited, that's all."

His facial muscles tensed as he thought ahead of the captain's story.

"She opened the door too fast, stepped out a bit too far. Rashida saw a car coming and jumped out to grab her. Both of them were hit."

Duval clenched his jaws tight. "Then what did he do?"

"The…the driver of the pickup truck was on his way home. He was scared because he hit them pretty good. He'd had a drink earlier at his friend's place…a beer. If they died, the story of them running out into the road would be his version of the story. He wanted them to live so they could tell the police it wasn't his fault. So he put them in the pickup truck and drove them to the hospital. It took him ten minutes, less than the time it would've taken for any ambulance to get there."

So many things were wrong. Too many for Duval to count. The main thing being that you don't move someone who has been in an accident. Broken bones, internal injuries…You don't know how much worse you will make it. It wasn't a surprise when the captain said…

"Sherrie was the first to pass."

It still stung, just hearing it. The burn in his chest as his upset stomach fought to expel its contents. Rage driven by the despicable, senseless actions of one Adonis Silver.

"She died halfway to the hospital," said Reynolds. "The driver was talking to Rashida, trying to keep her engaged, but by the time they pulled into the parking lot, she, too, had passed."

"So they were in the hospital all this time?" asked Duval. "The morgue? Unidentified? How could anyone fuck it up this bad?"

"He never took them inside," said Reynolds quickly. "The driver panicked. He sat in the hospital parking lot for more than an hour, not knowing what to do. After which he drove home. John Kipchak is his name. A sixty-nine-year-old man who just retired. He was in shock. He went home, pulled into the garage, went into his living room, and tried to muster up the courage to do the right thing."

"It's been three weeks," said Duval, fuming. "What did he do with the bodies?"

"They were still in his pickup," said Reynolds.

"The bodies were decomposed then…badly."

"Unrecognizable."

"How do they know it was them?" asked Duval, letting a glimmer of hope spark.

"They worked all day to identify them. The classic way. Dental records."

Duval threw his head to the side and kicked the floor in frustration. He had held out hope all this time, knowing the odds were not in his favor. He had gone to countless families to deliver the gruesome news that their loved ones would never return home. There were always questions; that's why they had to be sure before approaching the family. Yet, he'd fallen into the same trap and allowed his mind to grasp the concept of them mistaking their identity. From the other side, he could only imagine what it was like. Now he was living it.

He had been denied seeing their lifeless bodies just as he remembered them. They were decomposed beyond recognition. He could not touch them to see if they were real, or hold their hands, or cry at their side. He'd been deprived of a final goodbye. What a vicious and demonic creature to orchestrate this. Adonis Silver truly had no soul. He cried a bit. Letting it all out. Then his mind turned to vengeance.

"Adonis Silver caused the accident that made them pull over to the side of the road!" he declared.

"No," said Captain Reynolds, dumbfounded. "There's no way to check. How would you prove that, anyway? John Kipchak is in custody. He's the one who hit them. They've been taking his statement all day."

"When are you going to arrest Adonis Silver for causing it?" said Duval.

"Are you listening to me?" said Captain Reynolds. "This has absolutely nothing to do with him."

"He called out the dates, Captain!" said Duval, getting loud. As a reminder of the one thing that could not be explained away. "He said on April 16, my world would fall apart if I didn't leave him be!"

"It's the wrong date," said Reynolds softly.

"No…" How could the captain say that? It was a moment in his life he would never forget. Adonis had threatened him, just as he had been caught red-handed. "I remember specifically," Duval emphasized. "It was a day after Tax Day. Tax Day is April 15."

"I looked at the recorded evidence of the interview," said Reynolds in a calm and even tone. "Right after I got the news about your family. Adonis said April 14. That's the day *before* Tax Day. You remembered it wrong."

"No, it's…" *The fourteenth*, he thought. That was the day he'd decided to send Rashida and Sherrie away to her mother's in preparation for something Adonis might try. He knew Adonis was back in New York that weekend. Carrol had been tracking him. He sent them away so they wouldn't be involved in anything Adonis was planning. He didn't want them to get hurt out of fear that Adonis would target them. "Rashida sent me a message saying they were stopping by a friend's place before visiting her mother on the fourteenth," said Duval. "She called me."

"Yes, Kipchak said she called her husband after they got in the car as she was still conscious. She wanted to tell you they were on their way to the hospital, but you didn't answer. John Kipchak sent you that message about going to stop at a friend's place in Connecticut. Then he sent another message saying they were now headed over to her mother's the next day. The first message was sent from the hospital parking lot; the second was sent about an hour away, which was why the routes didn't make any sense. John Kipchak was trying to throw us off, and he knew enough to not turn on the phone while he was home."

Duval remembered the phone call that evening, on the fourteenth. He didn't answer because he was busy with Carrol. He was going to call her a few hours later. Then she sent the text about visiting a friend. He thought that was what she wanted to talk about, so he never called back. He just replied, "Have fun!"

"Mr. Kipchak confessed to everything, Kevin," Reynolds continued. "The most egregious part of all this was how they tried to make you the main suspect. For that boneheaded blunder, I am truly sorry. It was all in-house in that county. The guy lived about three miles from where the car was found."

He wanted to be upset. He wanted to be angry at the world for turning on him, at himself for thinking he was no different from the filth he put behind bars, but for some reason, he couldn't. His mind, once jumbled with rage, opened up, releasing all that fury in a puff of breath. The threat Adonis had laid upon him twisted his thoughts, making him see and assume things that were not real. Those assumptions went to work like demons. Forming false narratives that took on a life of their own. This is what hate does to a man. It runs with scenarios, playing the worst possible outcomes based on the things it despises the most. Real only within the confines of one's mind.

Now, with hatred for Adonis gone, he found himself back in the interrogation room. He listened to what Adonis said to him, through the clarity of his mind.

"If you don't abandon this obsession with me, that date will ring in your mind as the worst day of your life, and it will be your fault," he said.

The fourteenth was when he'd sent his family away to prepare for what he perceived as a threat from Adonis. He did not answer the phone call after the accident because he was busy plotting against Adonis. He'd spent a year trying to figure out a way to counter the attack and take Adonis down. He even went to the one person Adonis feared the most and…released a monster who was lying dormant.

"Are you still there?" said Reynolds. "Tell me where you are. I'll come get you."

Duval rushed from the car and crossed the road over to the guardrail on the other side. He looked through the trees to the building below that Jake had targeted. Things were about to go from devastating to catastrophic, and it was all his fault.

No more death on his account. He couldn't take one more death.

# CHAPTER 51

Jake stood in the garage looking down into the hole. According to Sly, there were three people down there besides Arina and Cardigan. He thought to call out to them by name and tell them it was OK, he was coming to get them, but it might backfire. They might use the girls as hostages. He wanted those below to believe this was something else, like a police raid or enemies looking to steal their stash. But how was he going to get down there without being torn to pieces with gunfire? Even if he jumped in, he was at a disadvantage.

He decided to try and talk his way through.

"Hey," Jake screamed down into the tunnel. "I'm coming down there. Don't anybody shoot. If you do, I'll kill the fuck out of you. My head is coming through to check. Don't shoot, motherfuckers."

"What the fuck are you doing, Jake?" asked Sly.

"Let me handle this one," Jake answered.

He got on his knees and pressed both hands firmly on one side of the hole in the floor. Straight down, about eight to ten feet below, was the dirt floor in this brightly lit space. The ladder was permanently mounted to the wall. He leaned down, twisting his head to get as much view of the area as he could, and used his arms to slowly lower his head down inside the tunnel.

"My head is coming through now, motherfuckers. Don't shoot."

He inched his head down slowly. The moist, musty smell of the tunnel hit his nostrils. He kept lowering his head downward, looking upside down at the layout below. He could see lights strung up along the walls and bright work lights on stands. He could see the pile of drugs. Then he saw Arina and Cardigan. They were tied up on the ground not too far away from the drugs. Two men stood beside them, one on each side. They were pointing their weapons toward the opening.

Movement to his right caught his eye. Someone was tucked against the wall adjacent to the ladder. He was closer than the others. He had the perfect angle. Before Jake could warn him not to shoot, he felt a little pop to his head as if someone touched him for a brief second. Followed by the intense heat of Hell.

---

The tape around Cardigan's face pinched and tore at her flesh as she tried to scream. Duct tape had been plastered against her cheeks and lips for about an hour. Arina had received the same treatment. It was mainly to shut up Arina, who kept warning the main boss of the operation that someone would be coming for them. If he did not let them go immediately, he would regret it. If he hurt them in any way, he would pay dearly. When he asked exactly how many, Arina told him one man and his imaginary demon. She said the demon gave him power like you would never believe. The demon would bring him back from the dead just to kill them. That's when the tape came out. Secretly, Cardigan was hoping she would shut her mouth. Praying if they sat still and cooperated, the men would walk away and leave them there…alive.

But then word was passed down to the men inside the tunnel that someone was out front, a tall Black man in leather. They prepared themselves, stopping the shipping operation and taking up weapons. A flicker of hope entered her mind as she heard the gunshots from above. A brighter flame erupted when Jake yelled down into the hole. Then the boss put a bullet in the side of Jake's head as he peeked inside, and it was over, just like that.

Jake fell down into the tunnel in a heap, landing directly on his head, breaking his neck by the sound of it. Then they started unloading. The sound of rapid gunfire was deafening. The machine gun clips were emptied in a matter of seconds. She watched the bullets tear through Jake's motionless body. Knocking bits and pieces of him off. His coat jostled with each shot. Then came the kill shot, as if he wasn't dead already. Perhaps the boss was pissed about all Arina had said about Jake. He walked over to Jake's already disfigured head and shot him once more for good measure.

Cardigan screamed through the tape until her stomach ached. Her face got hot and prickly. The smell of gunpowder was making her gag; the thick smoke of gunfire made it a struggle to breathe. The phlegm oozing out her nose compounded the problem. At one point, she felt she was going to throw up, but realized that would be a mess with her mouth taped shut.

The boss with the tattoos on his neck turned his attention to them. He stepped across the dirt floor with fire in his eyes. Cardigan thought it was over for them. She wanted to close her eyes but could not take her gaze off him. Her life was about to end.

"Is this the guy coming to save you?" screamed the boss, pointing the gun at Arina.

Her mouth was taped, too, but she wasn't crying. She didn't even look worried.

"Look at you...speechless!" said the boss. He pressed the barrel of his pistol into her skull. Then she realized it was Arina's pistol he was holding. "Look at the irony of it," he said. "I used your pistol to kill the motherfucker you said had the demon with him." He pushed her head with the barrel of her gun, pressing it into her skill so hard she could see the ring on Arina's head from the barrel after he moved it. "Fucking crazy bitch. He ain't got no crazy demon powers. Fucking foreigners always have some stupid myth they believe. He's just a man!"

The boss had turned around in time. "Hey!" he screamed. "What the fuck are you doing?"

One of the men with the machine guns had a grenade in his hand. He looked like he was about to toss it up through the hole to the floor above.

"Destroying the evidence left up top," said the thug. "You said when the time comes to bounce, we will blow up the garage."

"What the fuck is wrong with you? I didn't say throw it from down here. If your aim is off, it's going to bounce back down here," said the boss. "Give me that."

He took the grenade from the guy's hand, making sure the pin was still intact. "Get ready to move. You climb up the ladder, and I will hand it to you. Fuck everything else. Then we escape through the tunnels to the woods. Take the cash and regroup."

"What about those two?" said the thug closest to them.

"The only reason we didn't shoot them before was I didn't want the dead bodies distracting you two from loading," said the boss.

A hand snatched the grenade from his grasp, and he backed away as if he had seen a ghost. That's what Cardigan thought she was seeing as well. A ghost.

"How many times did I get shot?" said Jake.

The shock to her heart was like nothing she had ever felt before. Jake was sitting upright, his legs spread wide, toes pointing to the ceiling. Everyone stood still. Motionless. Speechless. They couldn't move. She couldn't move. The only person who appeared to take this in stride was Arina. Somehow, through the gray duct tape around Arina's mouth, Cardigan could tell she was smiling the biggest, most devilish grin.

"Damn, that many?" said Jake, talking to himself, it appeared.

The imaginary demon. She knew that's what they were all thinking. They were frozen. Unable to even breathe. Jake's face was fully healed. Sure, there were speckles of blood still on his skin, maybe even bits of brain on his forehead. But it looked as if it were someone else's blood and guts on him.

Just seconds before, his face and body had been riddled with holes. She remembered the gory, carnal mess that was his face. It looked like Hollywood makeup from a scary movie. Half of his cheek was missing, along with most of his teeth. The teeth were still on the ground next to him. However, when he spoke, his mouth and all of his teeth were right where they were supposed to be.

Jake was having a conversation with himself.

"The bullets that are not through and through, what did you do with them?" asked Jake. "I'll shit them out later? What the fuck do you mean? I could get lead poisoning…What…Then why do they say 'pump you full of lead' if there is no lead in them…No, it's not funny, son of a bitch! How the fuck am I going to flush the toilet with bullets in my shit?"

The boss got up the nerve to raise his gun, and Jake quickly raised the grenade in his hand, showing it off to everyone. "Not so fast, mister." He looked to his left. "Him?" Jake swung his left arm around, holding the massive hand cannon, and pointed it at one of the men. "How about you cut these girls loose? That wasn't a request."

The thug came over to her first. Cardigan winced as he ripped the tape from her mouth. He knelt down and cut the tape from her hands and wrists. Then he walked over to Arina, who was waiting like a snake, coiled and ready to strike. When the tape was ripped from her mouth her laughter flowed instantaneously.

"You thought I was crazy, huh?" she said. "Crazy Russian woman…I heard you say that." A slew of Russian words followed. She berated them in her native language as he cut her loose. Whatever she was saying was filled with her rage at being tied up and made fun of. She spat at their feet and walked around them, circling them like prey.

"Are you all right?" Jake asked, looking at Cardigan. He stood upright.

It was then Cardigan noticed all three men still had weapons in their hands. They had already reloaded previously, yet they didn't even have the inkling to point and shoot. She doubted they were even aware they were still holding them. They were in shock and afraid. Arina yelling at them in Russian was adding to that fear.

What was the demon going to do now?

"I don't feel like killing anyone else today," said Jake. "The girls are OK, so get the fuck out of here, and we will call it square."

They wondered if it was safe to move. All machismo was gone. Their balls were clipped. Testosterone drained from their bodies. At least, that's what Cardigan thought. Jake made a motion to them, waving them along after holstering his weapon. They crept along at first, then gained speed, making their way down the depths of the tunnel to safety.

"How the hell did you two find this place, anyway?" said Jake. "I knew it was a bad idea letting you two come along."

Before she could even grasp what was happening, Cardigan was hugging Jake. Gripping him tight. Trying to squeeze every ounce of air from him. Her ear pressed against his stomach. Her hands feeling his back, touching every part she could reach without losing contact. She didn't want this to end. It was the most wonderful feeling she had ever felt.

Out of the corner of her eye, with her head pressed against Jake's stomach and her emotions running high, she could see the boss toss something on the ground, before they vanished into the darkness of the unlit tunnel. Was it another grenade? No. She might not be able to see as well without her glasses, but that was up close. At a distance, she could see fine. It was the wrong color to be a grenade. She was about to mention it to Jake but then thought again about what it might be. It came to her. A reminder of a terrible day.

It was Arina's pistol.

## CHAPTER 52

"Get off of him already," said Arina. "Save some for me."

Cardigan finally let go. She backed away, and Jake could see the blood on the side of her face transferred from his shirt. A bloody-faced teen in a school uniform was not a good look for her. Neither were his clothes. He had time to examine the multiple holes in his coat, shirt, and pants. The holes were small but visible. His skin wet and sticky with the fabric of his shirt pressed tight against it. He was a tattered, bloody mess.

Cardigan looked up at him with her brown eyes still shimmering. "Hey, what happened to your glasses?" he asked.

"They broke them," said Arina. "They were assholes to us." She came in from the side and hugged him under his arm. Arina was not as disheveled as Cardigan. Her hair was tossed a little, and there were slight bits of tape residue around her mouth; still, she was taking it better emotionally than Cardigan.

"Were the girls up there?" asked Arina. "These jerks probably took them like they took us."

"No," said Jake. "This was everyone Sly sensed. No one else here… alive, at least. With all this heavy equipment around, it's possible if they were taken, they were killed and buried out back."

Arina hung her head. It was possible, knowing they were seconds away from killing Arina and Cardigan. "Where's Adonis?" asked Arina.

"I don't know, and I don't care," said Jake. "This has been a long day for me." He took a moment to look around the tunnel's dirt walls and the lighting snaked along the top of the walls. The stacks of drugs and what appeared to be money were off in the corner. This was a high-dollar operation. He must have spooked them pretty good for them to leave it without a fight. However, greed breeds recklessness. They would undoubtedly be back. "Let's get out of here. I'm ready to go home," said Jake.

"What about the eye you've been chasing after?" asked Arina.

"Suddenly, I don't care again," said Jake. "In the last few hours, all I could think about was you two. Especially you, Arina. I wanted to make sure you were safe."

He didn't want to go into any more detail. Explaining it to her now would only confuse her. Duval was on his way home, and so long as Arina was by his side, she would not get the chance to shoot him. At least not today. Maybe Duval was not the person Jake thought he was. That was the only answer. That, or it was a mistake somehow. Arina was put into a position where she thought he deserved to die. But those thoughts were long gone.

"I'm starving," said Jake.

"Ah yes, you seem to want to eat like a pig after fighting." Arina chuckled. "OK. We will get you something to eat."

Jake made his way to the ladder heading back into the garage, but Arina stopped him. "The car is this way," she said. "At the far end of the tunnel." She was pointing to where the bad guys made their escape.

It made sense. He climbed back down, waited for Cardigan, who was retrieving the portion of her glasses still intact from the ground, and followed Arina down the tunnel toward the darkened end where the string of lights ended. On the way, he admired their resourcefulness. On their own, they were able to find the house where Duval's family was most likely taken. The drug angle made it even more plausible. They must have stumbled onto the drug ring and become casualties. Sad story, really. One he had to break to Duval. He didn't know how he would tell him. Just that he should get a team to look there in the yard. Start with search dogs, perhaps. They might lead him right to where they were buried.

The girls stopped walking. "I can't see a thing," said Cardigan.

"It's OK," said Jake. "I can see just fine." Sly's enhancements at it again. It was pitch-black, yet he could make out where the walls were and where the tunnel turned. He took each of them by the hand, and they continued to walk down the tunnel.

"We would be able to use the light from our phones, if they hadn't been taken," said Cardigan.

"They took everything," said Arina. "They even took my pistol."

*Good riddance,* Jake thought. It made it even harder for Adonis's vision of the future to pass.

"He didn't leave the tunnel with it," said Cardigan. "He tossed it in the corner right where it begins to go dark."

Jake's heart dropped.

"I'm going back to get it," said Arina. She slipped her hand free faster than Jake could squeeze it.

"Leave it," said Jake.

But it was too late. She was trotting back in the darkness, toward the light.

"I'm going back to help her find it," said Cardigan. "I saw exactly where it was thrown."

She slipped away as well, on her way to the lit-up end.

He stood there for a moment, not knowing what to say. He was sticky, bloody, and hungry. He thought about going back to the same hotel room. He was looking forward to a nice shower and a fresh set of clothes. *Damn.* He remembered he didn't have any clothes other than what was on his back, and it was too late for any of the stores to be open. He would have to walk around in a fluffy hotel robe all day tomorrow, he supposed. He would send Cardigan and Arina out to get him something to wear. Maybe send just Cardigan. He didn't know why, but suddenly he was feeling a little something for Arina. Perhaps it was the threat of losing her to jail or something worse. No doubt, Jericho would ship her back to Russia if the heat was looking for her for killing a cop. He wasn't sure how he felt about not seeing her again. Then again, maybe Sly's pestering about not having sex in over a year was finally getting to him.

*Why not?* he thought.

"Jake?" said Arina. She was too far away for him to see her, around the first corner of the tunnel. "You need to come over here."

He sensed her tone. There was trouble. He stepped across the dirt floor quickly and turned the corner. Both Arina and Cardigan had their hands raised. Someone had beaten Arina to her gun.

It was Duval. He was holding it toward them. They met eyes, and a flood of emotions overcame Jake. This was how it would happen. This was the moment. Duval was going to die after being shot by Arina. How she'd get the gun at this point was anyone's guess. He would have to play along, and when the time came to move fast, he would do so. Taking the bullet for Duval if he had to.

"Why you?" said Duval. "Why do you get to come back from the dead when no one else can?"

"We all need to calm down," said Jake. "We've all been through a lot. Let's talk this out before anyone gets hurt."

Duval was flabbergasted. His face scrunched as if he had a mouthful of sour lemons. "We've been through a lot? Who here has been through more than me, huh?" he screamed. His pitch getting higher and higher. "My wife and my daughter are dead!"

"You don't know for sure," said Jake. "Not until they do a search of the property."

"What the fuck are you talking about?" said Duval. His hands shook as he pointed the pistol at Arina, then Cardigan. "They were found this morning. I was just told after they identified the bodies. Some drunk hit them and hid the bodies in his garage." He broke down in tears, wailing even. "Adonis said it would be my fault, and it was."

"Wait a minute," said Jake. He was cautious, stepping closer slowly. He crept along until he was even with the girls, then he worked his way closer to Duval. "Adonis can see the future. That's how he is doing it. But he told me something. An important detail. He said a person really doesn't have free will like they believe. He said when put in a particular situation, a person will always choose the same actions. He said the only way to prevent it is if the person knows exactly what is going to happen. It is only then that the person can change his or her future."

Duval trained the gun on Arina. "I know pointing the gun at you is fruitless. But I can take away other things from you that will hurt you just as bad."

"Don't," said Jake. "I'm going to tell you your future. Afterward, you can take that knowledge and change it however you want. We can make it better for you. You will have your whole life ahead of you to heal. Make amends to whoever you need to. Make the world better."

"I'm listening." Duval cocked the hammer back. "Don't even think about getting between this bullet and your friend. I will kill her for sure if you try to make a move. Let's hear what you have to say. What could possibly make me feel better about this situation?"

Jake stopped walking. He was about ten feet away from Duval.

The gun was pointed to Jake's right. His sights were on Arina. This made it difficult for Jake to tell him. What if he didn't like the answer? Would he kill Arina from spite, simply because she was supposed to kill him tonight?

"Tell me!" Duval screamed.

Jake took a deep breath. "You were supposed to be killed tonight. Arina was supposed to shoot you."

Duval blinked several times, and Jake prepared to move in on him. But then Duval smiled. "That does make me feel better. In fact, I am going to change the future right now."

Jake stepped in front of Arina. He thought he was quick enough, and he would have been if the aim had been to save Arina, but Duval had something else in mind. Another target. He pointed the gun at his head and pulled the trigger. He fell to the ground quickly and hard.

Jake could feel his lower lip trembling as Cardigan gasped. Arina began crying.

Jake felt lost staring at Duval's lifeless body. He was ashamed. He had done everything he could to save Arina, never taking into account it was Duval who needed the saving. Clever words from a clever beast. Adonis had said he'd looked into Duval's future and seen Arina's gun as it fired. He'd left out the part about Arina not being the one pulling the trigger.

Adonis was a heartless asshole indeed.

"Change of plans," said Jake as Cardigan came forward to take his hand. "Do you have a copy of my tracking app on your computer?"

She nodded.

"Good. I'm going to need it to kill Adonis Silver after all."

# CHAPTER 53

At 2:13 a.m., Don pulled his Bronco up to the front gate of a warehouse in Mechanicsburg, Pennsylvania. On the other side of the fence was a line of semis and trailers that seemed to go on forever. To his right was the main building. It was as long as a city block with loading docks on one side that ran the length of the building. He had no idea what they were storing and loading and didn't care. The text he had sent to Siobhan came back with a reply about meeting her there. She told him to text her again when he arrived, but he sat in the warmth of the running Bronco, going over the plan in his head. Preparing himself for the fated reunion. The first time he was going to meet Siobhan since she stole the eye from him.

There was a reason he'd waited until today. Testing the limits of the eye once more.

It began almost a year ago, when Detectives Duval and Carrol came to his house, accusing him of murdering Connor Richardson with a pipe. That day, Carrol explained how he had pieced together Don's ingenious plot to kill others after he got a taste for killing Connor. He named three local deaths, all of which Don was responsible for, which on the surface was impressive. In reality, he was a conspiracy nut. A crackpot known for wild theories. Everyone knows even a clock that doesn't work is right twice a day.

Don was going to brush Carrol's deductive reasoning off as a fluke, but he had to be sure. He asked the eye to see the future through Carrol's eyes, and what he saw was a decade of future success, beginning with the arrest for the murder of Connor Richardson. In fact, all of the murders Don disguised as accidents catapulted Carrol to success. He was hailed as some crime-fighting savant. He became flooded with cold cases. Television appearances and biographies were in his future. All for stopping what would later be called the most dangerous mind in criminal history…Adonis Silver.

No. It couldn't be. He stood dumbfounded in his living room, with his parents arguing in the background, after the pair of detectives left. This dullard was the one who would take him down? It made no sense. There had to be someone helping him. Some outside force influencing his weak mind. The eye was something supernatural; who was to say Carrol hadn't stumbled across another item that had helped him solve this? There was the man at the mall whose future could not be seen, so it was possible Carrol was getting assistance somehow.

Don shifted the vent in the Bronco to blow air on his chest. He looked out the rearview mirror, then at each side mirror. No one around, no one approaching. The parking lot had a couple of cars sitting in random spots. Probably the security people inside. It didn't feel like anyone was working inside the warehouse. It was Sunday morning, after all. The warehouse might have been closed.

Was this where he would die? It wasn't like he hadn't seen his dead body several times through the eyes of others. The last time he saw himself get killed was through the eyes of Duval. Whenever he would think of going after Carrol and killing him through traps, Duval would retaliate by killing him directly. The strangest part about going after Carrol and then trying to stop Duval was he could not change Duval's path no matter what he tried. It didn't matter. He couldn't stop Duval from killing him.

But then the future changed. Carrol was no longer a hero. He would be murdered. Duval would die as well. The only drawback was Duval's family would also perish. At first, he was thankful for the switch, however the eye would not just gift him a solution without him working out the details. Something else must have triggered it. Something significant. It all made sense when he discovered he was no longer in possession of the eye. The change must have been triggered by Siobhan being the next owner.

During his arrest, Don was faced with a moral dilemma. Would he allow innocents to die to get what he wanted? *No*, he thought. He was about to change it back. Let that clown Carrol have his future as the savior, with Don the serial killer going to jail. But when Carrol and Duval tastelessly high-fived each other as his face was pressed down on the piss-soaked concrete, all remorse left Don's body. If those two had no respect, humiliating him in front of his family, then he would have no misgiving for theirs.

Now his only threat was Siobhan. His biggest threat yet. He had prepared himself for a year. His advantage was that he knew she could not see into his future. She needed to look into the future of other people who knew him to be seen. That's why he was surprised she had picked this warehouse so late at night. There was no one else around to lay eyes on him. Was this a sign of her trust or her confidence? She was killing people in a way he didn't think was possible. Making them commit suicide with the most brutal means available.

Don shut off the engine to the Bronco and exited. He zipped up his windbreaker and closed the car door. He sent his text to her, then waited. She replied back in seconds. The main gate to the loading docks was unlocked. All he had to do was push it open.

Don placed his hands in his pockets and walked up to the front gate. It was a tall, chain-link gate with three strips of barbed wire at the top, nothing fancy about it. When opened, the two halves provided enough space for a semi and its load to coast straight through. The two halves were locked at the center with what appeared to be an electromagnet. Don got close and was reaching his hand for the gate when he heard a click. The gate gently left its locked state and drifted open a few inches.

It said a lot. Not only was she in control of the situation, but there were cameras on him and she had help. Possibly a team of people. Don now had his answer to his previous question. She was confident in dealing with him because where the eye could not see him directly, she had other eyes filling in the blanks. Now the only question was, How many?

Don pulled at the right side of the gate, and it swung open. After stepping inside, he closed the gate behind him. The magnet reengaged and locked the gate shut with a clang. The vibration of the chain link made a sound like loose change rattling. He took a look at his Bronco on the other side of the fence and wondered if he would be able to drive out of there. After a year of being separated, he refused to leave without the eye, so that made it a fifty-fifty chance.

The phone buzzed in his pocket, and he read the message. *Walk up to the main building and enter through the first access door on the corner.* He looked for it and saw it was on the nearest corner of the building, about three hundred feet away. Wind whipped at his legs as he walked toward the building. He peeked upward, trying to locate all the cameras. They were the black domes pointed downward, articulating 360 degrees behind the lenses, he imagined. No doubt they were trained on him now. He played along, trying to hide his wandering eyes, taking in all he could about the layout of the warehouse.

He reached the corner of the aluminum building. It was a light tan color with a dark-brown door. The handle was stainless with a thumb latch. He pressed it down and pulled it open. Warm air hit him as the difference in temperature and the wind howling created resistance. He pulled hard enough to slip his body inside and stepped onto the smooth concrete floor. The door slammed shut behind him, echoing through the warehouse.

It was lit up. He saw cardboard boxes of all sizes stacked and grouped together. Solid frame shelving made into aisles that went up to the ceiling. It reminded him of walking through the storage areas at IKEA, only ten times the size. Neat and orderly. Plenty of room between aisles. Boxes of inventoried items identified by a numbering system. It was relatively quiet.

Don heard footsteps approaching. He waited by the door, somehow knowing it would not be Siobhan. Too easy. She would feel him out first. Explore his true intentions. From the space to his right, a man came into view. He looked to be somewhere around his late fifties, early sixties. In good shape. Clean-cut. Speckles of gray on his beard. He was dressed in khakis, with a long-sleeve dress shirt. Crisp and pressed. Certainly not a security guard. He stopped in front of Don with an expression of slight irritation and motioned for Don to raise his arms for a pat down.

Don complied while sizing up Siobhan's middle-aged protector. They were of similar build, but he was slightly taller. His hands and hair were well groomed. He probably had his own personal athletic trainer, barber, and manicurist. That's the impression Don got, just by the way he carried himself.

He pulled three items out of Don's pockets: Don's car keys, with a penlight attached, his phone, and a cosmetic case. He opened the small round case shaped like an oyster shell and looked strangely at the mirror inside. He made a face, looking at Don as if he were a freak, then shoved the items back into Don's pockets. He worked his way down Don's legs and straightened after patting him down all the way to the ankles. Then he began walking backward, keeping his eye on Don the entire way. He didn't give Don an invitation to follow, so he didn't.

"Why now after all this time?" said a voice. Female. Not Siobhan.

It was coming from one of the aisles in the center of the building. The man who patted Don down was heading that way, then he turned down the center aisle, still walking backward. That was Don's cue, perhaps. He began walking across the front of the aisles toward the center. He could see it was wider than the other aisles. Well lit. Few places to hide. He turned down the center aisle of the massive warehouse to see a slim blonde in a long-sleeve pullover and jeans standing in the center. Her blonde locks were parted in the middle, partially draped over her eyes; she was trying to conceal her identity. The man who patted Don down was a good distance away from her to Don's right. His hands were folded at the waist. In the ready position. He raised his hand for Don to stop.

Don was still a good two hundred feet away from her. Yet, even with the change in hair color, she was familiar to him. It was Charisma Starlette, Siobhan's little sister. That made two people helping her so far.

"You must be strong-willed," said Don. "Just as strong as your sister. There are not many instances where a victim becomes the hunter. I'm wondering if she forced you into this." Don began looking around the warehouse for where Siobhan could be hiding.

"You never answered my question," said Charisma. "Why now?"

"We were fuck buddies," said Don. "We shared a wild romp I will never forget. She was so tight and slippery. I realized she fucked me so she could steal the eye, which makes her a whore. I tried to forget about her, but all I could think about was her tight ass bouncing up and down."

He hated to talk that way. It was vile and disrespectful. But he needed to gauge the relationship of this other man. Was he with Siobhan or Charisma? Was it sexual? Were there feelings attached, or was this strictly business? He studied the man's reaction carefully just as he had studied Jake. He determined it to be business; however, there was something personal about it as well. He wanted to defend Charisma with every ounce of his being.

"I don't believe you," said Charisma. "To wield the eye like you did makes you an extreme intellectual. You sounded like a weak-minded kid. A slave to his penis."

*Touché*, thought Don. Siobhan was smart enough to track him down at his house, and now he could see Charisma was no slouch either. The two of them together with the eye might be a match for him. Don's heart began to race. This was so exciting. After sitting dormant for almost a year, waiting to see if the change in the future was real, he had finally connected with what thrilled him the most. A challenge related to life and death.

"Who's the help?" asked Don, flipping a thumb at the man.

"Why don't you guess?" she said.

Don looked at the bodyguard closely, his posture, head position, and demeanor. "The Polaroid Suicides. He's the father of one of the victims you got vengeance for. You convinced him you needed his help, probably because Siobhan saw he had a large private space we could use for this reunion. After proving you were the hand of vengeance, he pledged his loyalty to you. He is someone important. Not just a manager; he probably owns this place. It's the only conclusion—a business this size having no physical security at this hour; only the owner could send everyone home."

He stood there, trying not to show any emotion, all the while being ignorant that he had already affirmed Don's presumptions.

"You are everything my sister said you were, Don," said Charisma.

"And where is Siobhan?" he asked, looking around the space. "I would love to look into her bright-blue eyes once more."

Don noticed something out of the corner of his eye while looking for Siobhan's hiding place. Charisma's reaction at the mention of looking into Siobhan's eyes. Her body language. It was off. Stiff. Apprehensive. He didn't know what it meant except there was more to this story. He needed to probe.

"Making people commit suicide," said Don, changing the subject. "Neat trick. I would think Siobhan could do better."

"It must be too simple for your taste," said Charisma.

"Right again. I did it by looking into the future of others and discovered that with a single action, you could set an entire chain of events into motion. A poke here, a prod there. Miniscule, seemingly inconsequential adjustments that changed the entire outcome weeks, even years, away. It's how I guided your sister to find you, and how I provided justice for your captors with one simple phone call."

"Like the butterfly effect," she said. "But I wouldn't look down on my method so quickly. I use the weight of the other person's evil to crush them. It's like Karma. Letting the judgment of the universe rain down in a force equal to their own misdeeds."

*She spoke in first person.*

She alone was master of the eye. Siobhan was out of the picture. Charisma put her hands in her pockets. She was about to make her move. Don got ready for action. She could only see his future through the eyes of the man standing nearby. But his fate was already set, and it was too late to warn him.

"You really are a clever one," said Charisma. "What an ingenious plan."

She parted her hair, revealing her face clearly for the first time. Don was shocked. One eye was blue; the other was amber. It wasn't a contact lens. She had replaced one of her eyes with the eye of Tartarus.

# CHAPTER 54

"The lights!" screamed Charisma.

Don pulled his hands from his jacket pockets. In one hand, he held the flashlight from his keychain. The other hand held the cosmetic case. His advantage was he could change what she saw faster than she could relay that information to anyone else. Don pointed the mirror of the cosmetic case at both of them and shined the flashlight into it. The reason the bodyguard had looked at him strangely after patting him down was because of the mirror. Don had placed a high-powered lens over the ordinary mirror. Anyone looking into it would not be able to make out much at all. However, when the penlight was shined into it, it cast a beam as bright as a beacon.

Charisma and her helper were both temporarily blinded. The man reached behind him, drawing a weapon from the back of his belt. Don deduced that was the reason he walked backward, never showing his back to Don. Anticipating this, Don was already moving toward the shelves as the gun cleared. He fired at Don in rapid succession, but Don was in the next aisle before the first gunshot rang. He moved down and through aisles to avoid the gunfire as it popped off behind him, using the contents of the storage warehouse as cover.

His movements may have seemed frantic, but Don was not running indiscriminately. He had a destination. With his keen sense of observation, he had spotted a series of circuit breaker panels for the building. The one he was after was a huge gray panel about as big as a door with *Floor Lights* in big, black letters stenciled above it.

The eye of Tartarus tapped off optics to mirror what people saw. If he took that sight away, Charisma would also be blind. His immediate worry was being shot in the back before he could kill the lights. He ducked through aisles and ran, zigzagging his way through cover. About ten feet away, his heart began to patter with glee. With all the running and shooting, the man could not hear Charisma's instructions about his final destination. Otherwise, he would have held fast in the aisle he was in and waited for Don with a clear shot at the circuit breaker panel.

But he followed Don's last zig and was out of position. Don ducked through another aisle and arrived at the panel. He opened the cover, reached up high, and pulled down on the massive circuit breaker at the top.

The sound of the giant switch disengaging echoed throughout the warehouse. They were cast into darkness. All was quiet for an instant. The gunman should have stopped right where he was for fear of running into something; Charisma couldn't provide assistance because she was as blind as he was. Don calculated where he should be standing. He got low and worked his way over the aisle. Then he placed his mirror on one of the boxes facing the man's direction. After crawling away a few feet, he shined the penlight into the mirror.

He got the desired effect. Startled, the man fired several rounds in the direction of the mirror. Don dropped the flashlight and made it sound like he was hit, bringing the warehouse into complete darkness once more. Footsteps pattered across the floor as the man moved toward his intended target. Don was in a crouched position, waiting.

Listening. When he got close enough, Don leaped at him. He got behind the man rather quickly and twisted his head so violently that he was sure the only reason the man's head was still attached was because of the muscles in his neck.

Since the room was pitch black, there was no way for Charisma to see what happened. The gunman saw nothing, and so the eye showed her blackness. She should have no idea whether he was dead or alive. Now Don had the advantage. His photographic memory and sense of time and distance made navigating through the aisles a piece of cake. He'd seen enough of it when he entered and while he was running. He knew the layout and all the obstacles. They were there in his mind, picture-perfect, as clear as if the lights were on.

A good distance away from him, he could see Charisma shining the light from her phone, or was it Siobhan's phone? She couldn't have given real-time instructions to Don through Siobhan's phone if Siobhan wasn't there. Yet, her sensitivity when he mentioned her sister was apparent. The answer came to him as bright as a clear blue sky. He was going to use it and get the eye back into his hands.

He was hiding behind boxes as she approached. She was walking down the aisle, searching for the recently deceased owner of the warehouse on her way to the circuit breaker panel. He was not going to be there when she arrived. His death should rattle her enough for him to put plan B in place.

Don made his way toward Charisma a few aisles down, using the cover of boxes when necessary. He passed her and walked all the way to the opposite end of the warehouse. He got low, on one knee, and tried to gauge her reaction. She reached the owner's lifeless body. The light shook in her hand. Don wondered if it was then she realized she was overmatched.

He didn't want to take the life of someone he saved. That would be a waste.

"Pull the eye of Tartarus from your head and place it by the body," said Don. "Then walk away, and all is forgiven. I have no reason to come after you."

She shined the phone light in the direction of his voice. He ducked behind one of the large boxes at the end of the aisle just to be safe. "Forget it," she screamed. "I owe it to my sister! This is my power now, not yours!"

Don could see the light from the phone shine high on the circuit breaker panel. The main breaker was in a place she could barely reach at her size. Plus, it was big and stiff and she was thin and wiry. It would take some effort for her to flip it back on. He needed the darkness of cover to approach her from a different angle. He needed time.

"I remember I probed the violent past of one of my teachers," yelled Don. "He was twenty feet away in the cafeteria when I did it. I saw how his father abused him. Then he screamed out in pain as I witnessed his father striking him. I thought it was a strange coincidence, but I took it as something to learn. Now I know different. I always kept the eye in my pocket."

Don was easing his way toward her as he spoke, being careful not to get caught in direct sight of the eye. Otherwise, with the way she wielded it, he was toast.

Don continued his verbal assault. "Now I know if the eye is looking at that person, while those memories are being drummed up, the feeling is far more intense and leads to that person killing themselves. Isn't that right, Charisma? Oh yes, you must have been experimenting with it. Then you held it up where your sister could see…and you must have been curious. I know I would have been."

She was holding the light up at the switch, her other hand struggling to push it upward. Her thin hands and fingers shook under the strain. He moved closer, getting into position.

"You saw the suffering Siobhan went through while looking for you," Don continued. "It must have been terrifying from her perspective. I know how hard she searched, what pains she went through to try and find you, how exhausting it was. Having to relive the anxiety intensified must have been too much for Siobhan to bear."

Charisma fumbled with the light. He could hear her whimpering, partly from her struggle to flip the switch and partly from his words hitting home.

"She killed herself right in front of you, didn't she?" said Don. "Took her own life with the kind of swift precision that scarred you even further. That's why you went on a rampage of justice, isn't it? For Siobhan. But you wanted to show her you suffered as well. You needed to sacrifice something for her. Prove your undying loyalty. For making such a fatal mistake, you needed to be reminded of it every time you looked in the mirror. That's why you took your own eye and put the demon eye in its place."

"Shut up, damn it!" she finally screamed. "You are a monster!" She turned away from the circuit breaker panel. The phone light twisted this way and that as she let out her rage. "Shut your mouth! Now I know why she was so afraid of you," she cried. "Siobhan could never figure out how you killed without being there. Nothing she tried worked the way you did it. That's why she gave the eye to me, to see if I could figure it out. But it ended up costing her her life. And you are to blame."

"Everybody wants to blame me for everything," said Don, moving into position.

He was close. She was startled, by the way she moved the phone light. Don could see it pass over and around him as he was hidden behind one of the many boxes. He was careful not to say anything else. He didn't want her moving from that position.

He was close enough to strike, but he had to get past the eye's last defense. It was the ultimate defense. He needed the lights on for this, or it wouldn't work. The eye protected its user whenever threatened. Both times, when his life was in danger while facing Connor Richardson and again with the security guard at the furniture place, the eye had shown him how to move, practically stopping time until it calculated the proper solution. Of course, time was not stopped; the inputs were so fast it only appeared that way. The level of information passed to the brain in microseconds was unfathomable.

Don calculated this phenomenon as something the human brain would not be able to sustain. He had practiced getting past this obstacle for almost a year. He felt now he was ready.

Charisma returned the phone light back to the panel to concentrate on the main circuit breaker. He could hear her grunting. She knew that once the light was back on, Don would be defenseless. Charisma let out one final cry, and Don heard the latch of the breaker. He jumped out at her as the lights came back on. Moving as fast as he could. Her back was to him. She could not see him. If she had experimented with the eye, she would also know this defense and would not be worried about an attack from behind.

Don was quickly within striking distance, with every intention of smashing her skull into the metal circuit breaker panel, but then he changed his mind. He decided to kick her in the small of her back, simultaneously grabbing her chin and pulling backward until her head was severed from her spine, but he didn't. Then he decided to grab her by the throat and choke her to death but changed his mind.

This was his plan. His test. The eye would warn her of his intentions and provide a solution, which she would have to work out in her mind to counter. But before she could calculate it, Don would choose a different method of attack. The eye would show her what Don was going to do next, and she would have to figure out the counter to that as well. The main detail was that Don had to think of his attack with every expectation of executing it. He had to mean it, bloodlust and all, then decide on another method. Another movement. A different attack.

The system employed was not designed to fool the eye but the mind to which the information was delivered. He had prepared himself to go on like this for as long as it took. He'd trained his mind for hours at a time, never losing focus. If he did, he was dead. The goal was to trap Charisma in her own thoughts. Drive her mad. Imprison her in a loop of misdirection. Confuse her to the point he would simply pluck the eye from her grasp.

The one potential downfall was this could take hours. Don had to steady himself and focus. This led to him being vulnerable in the real world to outside attacks while he battled inside his mind. He had no clue how long he had already been there. It felt like he had performed a thousand different methods to kill her.

The click of the pistol and its barrel pressed against his temple was the first sign he was in trouble. He was so engulfed in what he was doing that he had no clue someone had snuck up on him. But the sound of the hammer was all it took to bring him back to the present. He shifted his eye over to Jake Coltrane, standing in a dried, bloody mess of tattered clothes. Holding the gun in one hand and the eye of Tartarus in the other.

## CHAPTER 55

The two of them were standing there, one behind the other, in front of the large circuit breaker panel. The body of a man lay not too far away from where they stood. Dead. His head twisted around to face his back. Jake crept up on Adonis, wondering why neither he nor the girl was moving. As long as they stayed where they were, this was going to be easy. As he got closer and looked into Adonis's eyes, he could see Adonis was somewhere else. In a deep trance of some sort.

It was freaky, but not as freaky as the woman he was standing behind. She was also in some sort of a trance, shaking. Making sounds without moving her mouth. The corners of her lips dried white with gunk. One of her eyes was blue, and the other he had seen up close while in Hell. The eye of Tartarus. Jake went to probe her cheek with his finger, to see if she would respond; in turn, the amber eye popped right out from her socket. He caught it before it hit the ground. That's when he raised the pistol to Adonis's head. Game over.

"What piss-poor timing," said Adonis, coming to the present.

"Depends on how you look at it," said Jake. "Couldn't be any more perfect."

Adonis looked down at the eye in Jake's hand. Alarm bells went off with Sly.

"Shoot that nigga," said Sly. He was in his Black Panther getup once more. Beret to the side and all. "He turned that girl's brain into a vegetable, and he's going to do the same with you."

Jake pushed the barrel harder into Adonis's temple. "You're not scrambling my brain like you did to this girl. So don't even try it. Sly is in here, too, remember?"

Adonis raised his hands chest high. "Fine," he said through gritted teeth.

Jake took a few moments to examine the girl. She mumbled something incoherent and then giggled. It was clear she was no longer in control of her faculties. The Polaroid Suicide master had been rendered innocuous.

"Hurry up and use it," said Adonis. "Get your answer to why you are destined for Hell and then leave the eye there on the ground. You don't need it. You have your superpower."

"I say you kill this motherfucker," said Sly. He stood beside Jake, looking Adonis up and down. "Can't leave someone this dangerous free to do what he wants. You'd be doing the world a favor."

The blonde girl giggled as she stared off into the distance. She used her teeth to pick at the flaking skin on her dried lips. At one time, she may have been considered the most powerful person on the planet, yet Adonis had defeated her without laying a hand on her. Jake didn't need Sly's warning to recognize how impressive that was.

"Agreed," said Jake. "I can't let you live."

He got as far as flexing his finger before Adonis said, "Wait!"

Jake paused.

"Before you kill me, at least give me the satisfaction of knowing why you were destined for Hell," said Adonis. "I'm curious."

Jake pulled the tip of the revolver from Adonis's temple. "Why?"

"Because I would also like to know if I am destined for Hell."

Sly scoffed. "Of course you are, motherfucker."

"What does that matter to you now?" said Jake.

"Because the first life I took was a lowlife scum who was going to rape and kill my little sister," said Adonis. His statement was packed with emotion. "The eye showed me what would happen to my sister just by holding it in my hand, and I decided to do something about it. Afterward, I killed another who was a human trafficker who kept women and then boiled them for stew when he was tired of them. Another woman killed her family. A fourth was responsible for genocide in his own country and escaped prosecution by obtaining a new identity in the US. All of them would have gotten away with murder if I had not intervened. Is it fair to be punished to Hell for killing these people?"

"This motherfucker is powerful," said Sly. "Devious and despicable, with or without the eye. You can't allow him to live one second longer. I don't know what else to say."

"God knows what those people I killed did," said Adonis forcefully. "Why was God's plan to let them get away with it?"

"But they were not going to get away with it," said Jake. "Hell is real, and that's where they are."

"Are you so sure?" asked Adonis.

Jake had personally delivered two souls to Hell. He was sure about them. But what about the others? What about the ones Adonis mentioned?

"You were sentenced to Hell before you took any lives," said Adonis. "Are the rules as clear as you believe? Is it set up that everyone goes to Hell regardless of how they live? If that's the case, then why bend over backward to be a decent human being? Why forgive others? Why give a shit about morality? It didn't help you any."

"He's fucking with you, Jake," said Sly. "I'm telling you, he is fucking with you. He's in your head. Shoot him."

"What about the racist, murdering, misogynous, degenerate, child-molesting phonies who go to church every Sunday?" Adonis continued. "Are you positive all of them are in Hell?"

This went right along the lines of a host of things Jake was feeling at the time. There were rules and laws that were impossible to follow. Thousands of different religions each claiming they had the answer to salvation. So many different sects all believing in being pure, telling you how the other religions were false and damning. It was so confusing. Why was there no clarity? It begged the question, What did God really want from us?

Jake became aware of the eye in the palm of his hand.

"Just think of what you want to see," said Adonis.

Jake took a few steps back, away from Adonis. "Take a seat. Cross your legs and sit on your hands."

"What are you doing, Jake?" asked Sly. "Don't fall for it."

"Come on, Sly." He felt his face twisting in consternation. "I have to do this."

Adonis did as instructed. He sat, crossed his legs, and placed his hands beneath him. Jake moved the eye to the tips of his fingers. He asked, *Why was I in hell?* A flurry of images from his past went by. The murder of his mother at the hands of his father. His father killing himself over his homosexuality. His romp through foster homes. Being ridiculed because of his height and his illness. Countless badgering and attacks. Wanting to strike back at his aggressors but not having the courage or ability to do so. The death of his sister. And finally, his precious love Catalina being slain. It left him pained more than anything else.

He snapped back into the present feeling the tension in his face. Adonis watched with a finger across his lips, fixated on Jake's grimace.

"Sometimes you have to go back far enough to get an answer," said Adonis. "Try going back as far as you can."

He didn't want to do it. It was too painful. Perhaps he needed a little break, or a test. He thought about looking into Adonis's past. That might be helpful. Give him a little insight into how to properly use the eye. He remembered not to show the eye to Adonis while he was doing it. With Adonis's past he would probably kill himself within a second. Not that Adonis didn't deserve it, he wanted to learn from him first.

Jake clasped the eye tight in his palm and asked about Adonis, but it wasn't working. Jake saw nothing. It was blank like the black screen at the end of a movie. So he thought even deeper, farther into the past. Suddenly, images began to flash by, too fast to make out. He asked the eye to slow down and start again. Jake was looking through the eyes of someone in a war. Actively fighting. Reloading his rifle with grimy fingers. He was inside a room but looking through a broken window to a neighborhood of abandoned brick buildings, half standing, some with whole sides missing. There were those smashed to rubble and others fully intact. The road was strewn with rubble, mostly bricks and wood. He turned and looked up a narrow stairwell with several steps missing. He charged ahead.

He got to the top and turned quickly, firing at the first thing he saw move. He put a bullet right through the torso of a child the enemy had used as a shield. The enemy smiled at him with grimy teeth and attempted to shoot, when the reflex of the child's dying body dislodged the gun from his hand. Startled, the enemy went to regain what he had lost, but it wasn't the gun. A bullet was put through his chest as he reached for it. Jake followed as the person he was looking through walked up slowly and put another bullet through the enemy's head.

It seemed puzzling as the vision scanned the room for what exactly what the enemy soldier was looking for. Then it all made sense. The eye was picked up from the floor. He saw someone pop out from another room and shoot him. Then the view returned as if time was rewound. After which it seemed like it happened again, but this time the soldier holding the eye shot first, right through the center of the enemy's forehead. He must have then called out to his fellow soldiers because they all came running up the broken stairs to join him. The SS insignia on the dead enemy's arm was all Jake needed to understand the time period. He reached down and touched the dead boy on the shoulder with tears drops staining the dusty wooden floor.

His first encounter of its power.

Jake got the impression he didn't want to use the eye for some reason. Possibly because of how he came into possession of it. So he kept it to himself. All the while the eye showed him flashes of danger. Should he go left or right, duck or jump, hide or simply stand out in the open among gunfire, he was completely safe. Protected. But he quickly learned that he couldn't save everyone. That was not in the eye's design.

Naturally, he made it through the war unscathed. He tried to build a life, however there was one problem. The eye would not let the travesties that occurred during the war go without resolution. He was driven insane by the images of the horrible war crimes perpetrated through the eyes of those who performed them. His own living hell. This was his people who suffered. He saw the conditions of the camps, the abuse and the mass exterminations. Jake understood how that could change a man. Forge his future to a path of vengeance. And that's what he did.

He worked as a salesman and travelled throughout South America. Nicaragua, Venezuela, Brazil, Uruguay, Columbia, but most of all in Argentina. He took his time, using the eye to track down each and every one of the war criminals that escaped capture. He wasn't the only one hunting them, but he was the best. He was methodical, in his hunt and his kills. From what Jake could see, he was at it for about three decades. There were so many Jake lost count. And he grew to be as brutal as the Nazis were in the extinguishing of lives. Not just physical, he took everything. Orchestrated a complete destruction of the lives they built. He stripped them of their possessions and livelihood. Broke apart their families. And gave them hope for the rebuilding of their future, just before taking their lives.

It was a wonder how he retained his humanity enough to start a family. It was like he was another person around them. Completely loving and caring. As if what he did on the road was his therapy. The last image Jake was shown was the eye being placed into a black jewelry box and tucked behind a bunch of old newspapers. The dirty young hand that once fumbled to load the rifle was now old and wrinkled, with joints swollen from arthritis. Then it went black again.

Jake shoved the eye into his pocket to give himself a moment.

"That took a bit," said Don. "Did you find out why?"

Jake shook his head sheepishly.

"Did you try looking into my past?" asked Don.

Right. He was abnormally perceptive.

"You shouldn't be able to see my past or future," said Don. "It's a waste of time trying."

Yet, he must not have ever tried to look back far enough, into the past of the previous owners now deceased. It didn't take Jake long to determine one of the children bouncing on his knee was young Adonis. This was a past Jake felt he had no right divulging. He remained tight lipped.

"How about giving your future a shot?" said Don.

Jake placed a hand in his pocket to touch the eye once again. This time he thought about what the future held. Why was he destined for hell? The images that flew by showed Jake in hell, but they weren't clear. Sometimes there were up to three different things happening at once, which broke off into twelve. He tried to concentrate on one but quickly lost the sense of where he was exactly. He took his hand off the eye. Dizzy.

"I got nothing," said Jake.

More giggles from the girl. She didn't move from her spot. She shook and stared, one eye turned toward Jake but not really seeing him.

"I wouldn't recommend it," said Adonis.

Jake didn't bother wondering how Adonis knew what he was thinking. They were long past that. However, when Jake was looking through the eye at the future, it felt like he was trying to see across multiple dimensions. They were there, at different ranges, and it was hard to focus. It gave him the impression there were too many different inputs hitting his optic nerves. Like trying to look through a telescope with both eyes open. Close an eye, and everything became clear and in focus.

"You are going to ruin it!" said Adonis. He stood quickly with a panicked expression.

"Sit the fuck back down," said Jake with the gun trained on his chest.

"Jake, your heart is racing," said Sly. "Are you thinking of doing something stupid? Your body says you're about to do something stupid!"

"I need to know the answer," said Jake. After seeing the sacrifices of the past owners, Adonis's patriarch, and the girl, he decided it was time for an extreme sacrifice of his own.

Jake took a deep breath and shoved his hand into his eye. He winced and screamed. "Sly, help me out here!" But it seemed Sly was refusing. The pain became unbearable. He was about to abandon this insanity when he looked at the blonde once more. If she had the courage, then so would he. Jake's fingers trembled as he strug gled to get them into and behind his right eyeball. He cried and screamed and pushed. He thought of the suffering he had faced in Hell, where he might spend a thousand years of demons pulling out this very eye and shoving it back in again. A few more seconds was nothing compared to that. He finally worked his index finger between his eye socket, and with one hard pull, he endured the pain and slung his eye across the floor.

"You imbecile!" said Adonis.

"I am not going to dull the pain for you, Jake," said Sly. "This is a bad idea, Jake. Very bad."

Blood trickled down his cheek. All of his senses were still active. He reached his bloody fingers into his pocket to retrieve the eye of Tartarus. With a trembling hand, he raised it to his right eye socket and shoved the eye in place. His breath was labored. His chest quivering. He thought, *Show me why I am destined for Hell.*

There was nothing. Then Jake felt sick. Really sick.

"Sly?" he said.

There was no answer. He felt different, an odd yet familiar feeling. Jake felt a pressure in his chest like someone was standing on it. He lurched forward, dropping the BFR in the process. He was so weak he could barely stand. His knees buckled and crashed down onto the floor. He knelt there, trying to recover.

Jake looked over at Adonis, who was standing once again. He thought Adonis was going for his gun. He tried to stretch his arm out to retrieve it. He gave the command, but his arm barely moved. Adonis walked up to Jake and leaned over, never looking at the pistol. He was more interested in Jake.

"I told you not to do it," said Adonis. "Remember when I told you I was after your parasite? I said I knew how to find it. I told you the part that doesn't decompose will be where the parasite is."

Jake's lip began to tremble. *No…but…*He looked at the blonde, who was off in her own world, completely unaware of the troubles he now faced.

"She must have not had enough energy to revive it," said Adonis. "The parasite inside the eye needs a shock of energy after being deprived for so long. Like paddles on a defibrillator. However, your parasite is strong enough to revive a body. Your parasite is probably being ambushed right now. He's fighting for his life. Forgive me for not sticking around to see who wins. But the eye is most likely gone forever. Good luck."

Adonis walked away, heading back toward the exit. It was the third time Jake had sought him out with the intention of killing him and the third time Adonis was leaving Jake in distress as a result of it.

"Sly!" Jake screamed. There was no answer, and he wondered if there would ever be. It was his fault Sly was under attack. He had to help.

But then he got his answer. It wasn't Sly's voice speaking. It was the voice of Tartarus, in his head, just like when Sly spoke to him.

"The instant I saw you, I knew my time in Hell was about over," he said.

Jake mustered every last bit of strength in his body. He raised his hand, trembling, summoning his muscles to obey his command. He stuck his finger into the bloody socket, managed to wrestle the slippery sphere between his fingers. Jake flung the eye from his head, sending it rolling across the smooth concrete floor. His arm dropped to his side, and his body toppled. His shoulder hit the ground, followed by his head. He could only watch with one eye because he barely had the strength to breathe.

The eye rolled and stopped. Was Tartarus a part of him now?

"Sly," Jake called out, weak and winded. There was no answer. Only a loud pop.

The eye popped like popcorn on one end. Something was hang

ing off the back of it. Then it started growing. Nerves sprang out and formed a brain. The brain grew another eye, and then the rest began to fill itself in. The bones of the skull began to form. Then the spine. The heat coming off the transformation was intense.

This was a creature from Hell, Tartarus. In Hell, Tartarus was over eight feet tall. Slim with a void for a body. Jake cringed at the thought of his wide smile bringing Hell upon anyone who would look at him. How could he be so stupid? No wonder he was destined for Hell. He was responsible for releasing a demon into the world.

Jake closed his eyes and began crying. The heat from the transformation glowed and felt like a space heater at close range. He could hear the gristle stretching and the popping of bones snapping into place, skin forming, and fluids circulating. It took five minutes before Jake could hear the demon's first breath. Another minute before the heat began subsiding.

What was going to happen next? Was Sly still alive? Did it matter?

A hand touched Jake's shoulder. It stayed there, waiting.

Jake slowly cracked open his eye to see a man standing before him, bent over with a hand on his shoulder, smiling. His body was stocky. Thick fingers and large forearms. Solid thighs and wide calves. He looked to be a little over five feet tall. He had thin lips and a large nose, and his teeth were crooked. He had shoulder-length, light-brown hair, tanned skin. His eyes were amber in color. He stepped away from Jake after seeing he was OK and went right to the man with his head twisted around.

"What a waste," he said.

Jake lumbered to his knees. The blood dripping from his eye socket was cooling and drying. The pain from it diminished to a constant ache. Jake looked around as if he had missed something. The demon might be hiding in the shadows, ready to unleash Armageddon.

"Tartarus?" Jake asked, examining the man with the crooked nose.

"In the flesh," he answered. He knelt down and flipped the dead body onto its back, then started unbuttoning his shirt. He fumbled with it a bit, as if it were foreign to him, but quickly caught on. He stripped the body of the shirt and slipped his arms inside. The fit was a little tight around the arms and long at the sleeves, but it would work. He started fastening the buttons from the bottom up.

"You're a man," said Jake.

"Not what you expected, is it?" His voice sounded ordinary, nothing like the monster he had sounded like in Hell. After the last button was fastened, he took a deep breath. "I suppose you're still confused."

He turned to Jake, walking back to him with just an oversized shirt on his body. "Your entire quest since gaining immortality was trying to figure out why you were in Hell without ever considering it may have been for a higher purpose. You're not a prisoner of Hell. You're a psychopomp."

## CHAPTER 56

What the hell is a psychopomp, you might ask? Great question. You might be familiar with the Viking's Valkyries, who escort the souls of fallen Vikings to Valhalla. Perhaps even the Greek deity Hermes, who moved through worlds on winged sandals and led souls to the River Styx. Maybe you've heard of Charon, the ferryman of Hades, who escorted the souls of those given funeral rites across the river that separated the living world from the dead. These are the psychopomps. Those who can travel freely through the world of the living and the dead in order to escort souls to their final destinations in the afterlife. The psychopomps don't need any guidance. They are willing and able to make it on their own, free to do as they wish. It's the other souls that need ferrying.

Every culture has them. Egyptians call him Anubis. For Hindus, it's Yama. Greeks call him Hecate. Morana is Slavic, and for Aztecs, it's Xolotl. Their roles might be foreign to you since these cultures are long gone, but you should be familiar with the current form of psychopomp known as the Grim Reaper.

In order to become a psychopomp, a person has to endure a sort of *catabasis*. In this process, a mortal is granted the ability to return to his body after death by paying an exceptional fee. Many who feel their mortal lives were going to be cut short are given the option of becoming a psychopomp. Few are chosen. And once someone passes the requirements to become a psychopomp, the longest-serving psychopomp is returned to a normal life to live out his term and die.

My role as a psychopomp was determined the instant I sought vengeance for my girlfriend. I was now serving as a reaper for Hell's Apostles.

I know what you're thinking: Why did I need to kill when everyone dies anyway? The unforgiven never escape Hell no matter when they go. The answer is because souls are like fruit. How you live your life determines how sweet or sour your soul might be. I know you are thinking good souls are sweet, but it is the opposite. The more wicked the person, the sweeter the soul gets. Precious, succulent flavors and aromas come from those who stand no chance of getting into Heaven.

We all know fruit doesn't remain sweet forever. If it stays on the vine too long, it over-ripens, falls to the earth, and rots. This is what happens to evil souls that live to a ripe old age. The sweetness goes away, and they rot. The enforcers of Hell, Hell's Apostles, get really pissed when they're delivered rotted souls. They want sinners when they are at their sweetest. That's where I came in. I picked them when they were ripe and sweet. Cut them down with my BFR, sent them to the Apostles. For that, whenever I was in Hell, I was given a pass.

When I delivered Alexi Voznesensky to Hell, the apostles went into a frenzy, tearing him to shreds. Conversely, they ignored me completely. I noticed this again when I took Scotty Rock to Hell with me and so on. If I did my job as the reaper, they would leave me unharmed while in Hell. Otherwise, they got angry. They tortured me for the lack of delivering tasty souls. I guess it was their way of keeping me motivated. Aruru especially. She was a seven-foot-tall transvestite who lived in a giant Barbie playhouse and wanted to ram me up the ass with a broken glass-covered phallus. She said I was her type. She liked screamers.

As for Tartarus, he was another interesting creature. He was a human who paid the price of catabasis and over time worked his way to becoming the king of Hell. He was the most senior psychopomp, and my parasite reviving his meant his time of serving Hell was complete.

I remember asking him, when he was trying on clothes in the warehouse to make himself decent, "I thought everyone in Hell was being punished?"

He rolled his eyes as if he had been asked that question a thousand times. "Is the warden of a jail a prisoner? Are the guards serving a sentence? No. Hell's Apostles, the ferrymen, the reapers, and the kings, are in charge of the punishments. We are not prisoners. We are the enforcers. Each with our own unique roles."

"Aruru is one of the good guys?" I had to ask. "She sure seems like someone who belongs there."

"Aruru is the sweetest old lady you will ever meet," said Tartarus. "She bargained for her life to protect her grandson many moons ago and paid the price to become a psychopomp as one of Hell's Apostles. She lives in a small village in Italy. Keeps to herself."

"I would love to meet her," I said.

"Don't," he said quickly. "We don't mingle in this world. It's dangerous. Nothing good comes from psychopomps intermingling. The smart ones disguise themselves behind demonic forms while in Hell. Human souls can't do that, which is why it's easy to pick them out. You are going to have to learn a demonic form for use in Hell. If the new king allows it."

It was so much to swallow at one time. I could turn into a demon form in Hell? Awesome. I thought of all kinds of twisted creatures I could become. If I were allowed. "Who serves as king now?" I asked.

"Wall," said Tartarus.

Ah. The jaundice-colored demon who flies. He seemed like a good choice.

You would think it would take a great deal of time for me to fully absorb all this. I mean, I was frantic. Literally about to sweat blood because I thought I was the catalyst for unleashing Hell on Earth. However, due to my many trips to Hell and back, this was kind of a sobering moment.

Tartarus was still stealing clothes from the deceased male's body. He removed the shoes, pants, and socks from the cadaver. He sat on the ground fumbling with the socks first. "These are weird," he said after slipping a foot inside. He wiggled his toes around. "I don't like how they feel. My toes feel trapped. I was wearing sandals when my body lost its ability to regenerate." He fumbled with the pants, flipping them around backward and forward. "Then there are these things. A simple cloth would be much easier."

I had more questions like, What were the rules? Certainly, I could not be expected to go around shooting people at will, hoping I made the right choice as to where that soul belonged. It seemed like such a great responsibility. I asked him, "How am I supposed to know what lives to take?"

"You've listened to your gut so far, haven't you?" he said. "That's precisely why you were chosen."

"No," I said. "I mostly listen with Sly's help."

"Bingo," said Tartarus. He started on a pant leg while sitting on the floor, bending his knee awkwardly.

"I'm still nervous about it," I said. "I don't always listen to Sly. He's obnoxious."

"You're meticulous and thoughtful," said Tartarus. "Even when you were told killing Adonis Silver would save you from hell, you still hesitated and wondered if he deserved to die. Sly was screaming at you to kill him as well, but in each case, you did not. That's because Adonis was influenced by the eye. Somehow, you could see through that."

"What do you mean?"

Tartarus looked over at the girl, who was playing with her fingers now. Moving them in a rhythmic sequence as if they were an instrument. "Notice how everyone who used its power was out for vengeance? With the eye, it would make sense to get rich, control the world, have everyone bow and serve you. Yet each person who possessed it ended up killing people who have wronged. This is the influence of the eye."

"Yeah, but…" I didn't feel special. Didn't feel like there was any purpose to my choices.

"You have empathy," Tartarus explained. "You're not a killing machine. This job is for special souls, not madmen. Look at the weapon you chose. A single-action revolver because you don't like the idea of spraying rounds indiscriminately. You are the perfect reaper."

My mind suddenly flipped from Hell to the real world. I was on Earth in human form. I couldn't go around killing people who were guilty of murder and get away with it. "What about the law?" I asked. "I spent a year in jail for attempted murder. What's going to happen to me if they catch me killing someone?"

"Ah, yes. Things were much simpler back in the times when they used to just hang people," said Tartarus. "You would be hanged, lie around in Hell for a while, and then return with no one any the wiser. In these times, you must get a bit more creative. Choose your moments. You know how to do it already." He waved his hand as if that were small potatoes. "But you have to do your job," he warned with a finger. "Piss off Hell's Apostles by not killing, and it will be you who gets tortured. Don't think you can hang out, stay alive, and escape their wrath. The Apostles will send someone to kill you. Then when you get to hell…oh boy!" He shook his head, indicating I didn't want to know.

It got me thinking. "When I was in Hell, you didn't treat me like a psychopomp. You treated me like I belonged there. You tortured me."

"Oh please," said Tartarus, wrinkling his crooked nose. "Did you really suffer my wrath? Come now, you wouldn't have been able to return coherent if you had." Tartarus looked at the girl, still wandering aimlessly, mumbling and laughing. "You would have revived only to kill yourself again and again," he explained. "And the other Apostles, they were providing you a sample of their skills."

"Sample," said Jake, dumbfounded.

"You were allowed to escape every trap before it got too bad," Tartarus explained. "Each Apostle you encountered wanted to show you how they torture souls that have sinned."

"What kind of bullshit is that?" I said. I was angry.

Tartarus wagged a finger. "Didn't I help you when you needed to avenge your girlfriend's death in the real world? Didn't I lend you my power?"

I could say nothing.

"Oh, you thought you outsmarted me and tricked me into using my power in the real world, didn't you? How arrogant of you."

I knelt, thoroughly scolded, while Tartarus sat on his naked butt and worked the pant legs up his thighs. They were tight on his thick body and long enough to cover his whole foot. He jumbled the excess at the ankles, then stood up. The clothes looked like a crooked mess on him.

"How do I look?" he asked, holding his hands wide.

"Like shit," I said.

"Right." He pursed his lips, looking at my ragged, blood-soaked, bullet-ripped clothes. "I'm going to see Nukial. He'll get me straight."

"Who?" I asked.

"You know him as Jericho Black," he said with a smile. "Don't try to figure out who he is right now. That might be too much for you to handle."

I agreed. I wasn't in the mood for any more shocks to my system. I might die of shock before Sly restored himself. I decided it was best to be helpful. "Do you know where Jericho is and how to get there?" I asked.

Tartarus pointed a finger at his amber eye. "Of course I do."

"Wait," I said. "About your power. Sly would always warn me about how powerful Adonis was when he had the eye. How did it work?"

"God knows everything. All you have done and all you are going to do. I was given a parasite from the angel Camael, which means *he who sees God*." Tartarus looked around the warehouse at nothing in particular, to emphasize everything God sees. "God has no shape or form. It's impossible to explain, other than, if you can see God, you can then see what he sees."

"Why do people kill themselves when the eyes are on them?" I asked.

"It's a natural reaction." Tartarus raised his eyebrows as if it were simple and elementary. "You can't escape the truth of what you've done when God is looking right at you."

Tartarus waved, then left the building, and shortly after, two angels came to my rescue, Arina and Cardigan. They carried with them bags of food bought at the all-night diner after dropping me off to face Adonis. Thank their blessed souls for knowing how best to help me. I couldn't stop smiling watching them unbox steak and pancakes to shove into my mouth as I was too tired to raise my arms.

Arina noticed the young blonde woman with one eye wandering close to the circuit breaker panel. She was clearly out of her mind. "What happened to her?" she asked.

I didn't know, really. Best guess was Adonis had done something to her to make her lose her mind. I regained my strength after several boxes of food, enough to stand and walk out of the warehouse. We took the young blonde with us, got her the help she needed the next morning, then made our way back to New York City. I told them all about my encounter with Tartarus and what he told me about my role in Hell. They were pretty freaked out about it, and I didn't blame them.

As the months passed, I went to visit Charisma Starlette at the mental facility from time to time. Hoping one day she could share her story about the Polaroid Suicides. I felt it would help me be a better reaper. For now, that story was sealed away within the confines of her mind.

Another year passed. I was in the windy city of Chicago for the winter. I had heard that in his second year at Yale, Adonis changed his major to medicine. I didn't know if it was truly to help people or if he was trying to find another way to steal my parasite. Sly was still convinced I should kill him. I was willing to wait and see. Maybe he would surprise us. Cardigan was a senior in high school, getting ready to go off to college. She was already getting recruited by major software firms. She deserved it. She was a gifted woman. We talked code from time to time, bouncing ideas off each other.

Arina was still an influencer. She traveled to exotic locations teaching the basics of spin pole. How to look elegant and sensual and confident. Her students came in all shapes and sizes, and she encouraged that. It was about building self-esteem. She was like a guru in that regard. She really had a gift for it, and that's why they loved her. We hung out whenever we were both in town, and occasionally she drove me where I needed to be.

My favorite pathologist, Dr. Carrie Blake, was still doing her thing in New Jersey. I popped in from time to time still, sometimes walking in, sometimes on the slab. As Tartarus indicated, sometimes I couldn't get away clean and had to end my own life to keep investigators from looking for me. Life as a psychopomp is grueling and unforgiving.

One night, I was standing outside in downtown Chicago not too far from a club, keeping an eye on a silver Range Rover parked on the street. The street had a sour smell like in most cities. I was concealing myself in a store entrance so I could not be seen by people walking down the block until they were right up on me. The store had been closed for hours. I had been tracking a case for about a month, and I finally had enough to be sure I had the right guy. He had taken three girls so far. Brunettes, twenty-one to twenty-five years of age, slim, with brown eyes. Killed them and assaulted them afterward. Necrophilia. Police were doing their best and getting nowhere, but I had my highly illegal tracking program, and I had Sly.

"Put the earbuds in and give me some Nas," said Sly.

I did as he requested and played his favorite song, "Thief's Theme." The Incredible Bongo Band's intro to "In-A-Gadda-Da-Vida" played through the buds. Sly was standing next to me with this over-the-top mink hat, looking like a Russian oligarch going to a fashion show. His matching mink coat and mink shoes were too much for me to comment on. It was cold. Wind was howling.

Sly rapped along with the lyrics. A sheepkin coat was mentioned.

"Is this why you insisted I buy this coat?" I asked as the music pumped through the buds. It was keeping me warm, I had to admit.

"Hell yeah. Can't have you walking around in damn full-length leather all the time looking like a creepy flasher. It's time to teach you some style. Next, I gotta get you out of those ankle-squeezing pants you wear."

"Quiet," I said as I looked down the block. "Here he comes."

This guy was the classic charmer. Good-looking, fit, dressed nice, had money. Brown hair, tanned skin, really took care of himself.

Watching him through the app, I could see he had no problems picking up women. He had a girl with him. She didn't seem inebriated. Walked straight, was making solid eye contact, leaning into him. She was feeling it. Brunette, slim, exactly his type.

"Let's get this nigga," said Sly.

"Wait," I said. "I need to make sure the girl is going to take off and not try and help him. I need to time this right."

"You said the moment that nigga—"

"Right there, you are wrong," I said to Sly. "I don't use the N-word! It's derogatory and weighted with emotional malevolence. It has weaved itself into the fabric of our communities as something harmless, so long as we say it. But it was born out of bondage and will continue to hold us down so long as we are ignorant to the fact it shackles us every time we use it."

"Lick my balls, nigga. Your dumb ass trying to spit knowledge. Shut the fuck up!"

"I'm glad no one else can hear your foul mouth." They got closer to the car. "In any case, I want to avoid a confrontation on the street."

The couple arrived at the Range Rover. Like a gentleman, he started the car electronically and opened the door for her. She was wearing a skirt. Her legs were toned and long. She eased inside, and he closed the door and began to walk around to the driver's side. That's when I made my move. I stepped out from the store entrance I was using for cover and made my way over to the car. I opened the back door before he had a chance to lock it and pushed the barrel of the BFR up against his ear while sitting down.

"This doesn't concern you, sweetheart," I said, closing the door. "You can get out of the car and scream for help." He reached for his phone, but I reminded him that was a bad idea with a gentle tap of the barrel against his head. "This guy had plans to strangle you and fuck your dead corpse," I told the young woman. "Those murders of late? It's him. You should thank your lucky stars I am on the case. I suggest you walk back to the club and call yourself an Uber."

I could tell she didn't know what to think, but she got out of the car without a fuss. The door closed, and I gave him instructions: "Drive."

We went around the city, and he began saying it was not him and I had the wrong guy. I was trying to find a secluded spot to finish the job, but he got stupid and started driving erratically. He said he would take us both out if I insisted on holding him hostage. He sped toward the water purification plant on East Ohio Street.

*Perfect*, I thought. I pulled the trigger and blew a hole through his chest from the back of the seat. The car continued straight, elevated after skipping over the guardrail, and headed straight for the water.

As we crashed and water started rising in the car, I thought about escaping but then remembered something I'd heard whispers of the last time I was there. Rumor had it that one of the psychopomp reapers had been causing a disturbance. Wall was considering putting out a hit on him or her. The decision to take one out might cause a greater revolt, a sort of Psychopomp Revolution. In any case, things were about to get interesting.

## ABOUT THE AUTHOR

Jeremy Fulmore left his hometown of New York City to join the US Navy, where he worked in aviation electronics for four years and many more after being discharged. He then continued his career in testing and evaluation of ground electronic systems.

Today, Fulmore lives by the water in southern Maryland, where he enjoys cigars, whiskey, golf, and spending time with his two children and three grandchildren. You can contact him by email at jfulmorewriter@yahoo.com.

Printed in Dunstable, United Kingdom